PRAISE FOR
DAEMON OF THE DARK WOOD

"No doubt, this novel is a 'creature-feature' page-turner in the finest tradition, but as with all of Chandler's writing, read a little deeper and you find an austere, knowing treatise on the human condition. Chandler's examination of character is outstanding as well; the widow Leatherwood and hillside wanderer Edgar are both particularly well-drawn. You not only get into their heads, but Chandler makes you wear their skins and feel their heartache, loneliness and sheer dread and terror."
— Walt Hicks, *Hellbound Times*

"*Daemon of the Dark Wood* starts off with the comfortable feel of an 80's horror novel. You have the rural setting, well-drawn characters, and an ancient evil coming forth. It starts off at a leisurely pace, and gradually builds to a frenzy. Chandler offers up wild situations and images that bring to mind Bentley Little. Or maybe even Edward Lee."
— Mark Sieber, *Horror Drive-In*

"Prepare to have your world rocked! Randy Chandler delivers the goods once again with *Daemon of the Dark Wood*. Horror fans need this!"
— David T. Wilbanks, co-author of the *Dead Earth* books

"The legend of Widow's Ridge should be entirely believable to anyone familiar with American folklore and folk music, as those stories and songs are replete with betrayal, death, murder, grief—most all of the negative aspects of human life, in fact. *Daemon of the Dark Wood* will please any reader who relishes a well-written tale of ancient knowledge and hidden dangers, and those who fight to keep the human realm free of unbridled evil."
— J.G. Stinson, *ForeWord* Magazine

RANDY CHANDLER

OF THE DARK WOOD

WWW.COMETPRESS.US

A Comet Press Book

First Comet Press Trade Paperback Edition
February 2012

ISBN 13: 978-1-936964-46-8

Visit Comet Press on the web at: www.cometpress.us

About the Author

Randy Chandler is the author of *Bad Juju*, *Hellz Bellz*, and co-author of *Duet for the Devil*. He is also the author of the novellas *Dead Juju* and *Howler*. Randy is a frequent contributor to Comet Press anthologies. He lives north of Atlanta.

*For the Stimson girls
and the women they became*

CHAPTER ONE

THE LAST THING HER LOVER said to her was "Watch out for the deer," but those words of warning vanished in the lingering afterglow of their lovemaking, and by the time she turned onto the road to Widow's Ridge, Judy Lynn Bowen's thoughts were on their upcoming wedding. In three weeks she would become Mrs. Joshua Lee Jordan, and her life would change from the roots up.

"Judy Lynn Jordan," she said aloud, and not for the first time. The name was a perfect fit for her, and she took it as a sign that their marriage would be nothing short of conjugal bliss.

The evening shadows deepened to dusk, and Judy Lynn switched on her headlights. The winding blacktop took her up the forested mountain, her home in Widow's Ridge a welcoming destination at the end of a busy day. With one hand on the wheel, she dug her pack of Virginia Slims out of her purse, shook one out and placed it between her lips. She punched in the dash lighter and waited for it to pop out with its coils hot enough to fire her cigarette. She inhaled deeply, savoring the rich smoke and wondering if she could keep her promise to Josh that she would quit smoking whenever they decided it was time to make a baby. She exhaled, confident that she could kick the habit when the time came.

The creature came out of the dark trees and bounded into the hazy shafts of her headlights. Before her foot reached the brake pedal, the deer slammed into the front end of her car and a smothering blackness hit her full in the face, smashing her cigarette, momentarily disorienting her. The air bag was already deflated before she realized it had deployed from the steering wheel, and the car lurched to a stop in a shallow roadside ditch on the left side of the road.

The engine died. She stared in dazed wonder at the blood-tinted spiderwebbed fissures in the windshield and at the single beam of the remaining headlight that illuminated the ditch and the trees beyond the shoulder of the road. She touched her fingers to her face, relieved to find no blood of her own. *I'm all right. Just a little twist of pain in my neck.*

The deer. Where was the poor creature? After the impact with the front-end, it must have bounced off the windshield and fallen to the road. It became imperative to find the deer and see how badly it was hurt. Judy Lynn opened the car door and tried to get out, but something held her fast.

The seatbelt, stupid.

She pushed the release button and the seatbelt retracted, grudgingly letting her go. She stepped carefully from the car and into the ditch. She moved quickly around the rear of the car to the road, her eyes searching the dusk for the injured animal.

"Oh God," she said when her eyes found the dark shape stretched out in the center of the road. She took a step toward it, then halted when she remembered the flashlight in the Honda's glove box; she spun on her heels and went back for the Mag-Lite. Leaning across the front seat, she thought to turn off the remaining headlight and turn on the hazard lights.

She congratulated herself for such clarity of thought so soon after the shock of collision, and then steeled herself for an assessment of the deer's injuries, dreading what she would probably be forced to do. She took a deep breath, clicked on the flashlight and walked quickly toward the four-legged casualty in the middle of the two-lane blacktop.

The doe was alive but grievously injured. The bone of the right foreleg protruded obscenely through blood-matted fur, and blood bubbled from the snout and leaked from the corner of its mouth. The doe's brown eyes were big with fear, or so they appeared to Judy Lynn when she shined the flashlight at them. The animal tried to lift its head from the road, then convulsed, hind legs thrashing as if trying to run to the safety of the surrounding woods. "God, I'm so sorry," she said, sobbing. The animal convulsed again, harder this time. Judy Lynn wished she had a gun so she could end the doe's suffering. *A tire iron. I could hit it in the head with a tire iron and put it out of its misery.* Without giving herself time for second thoughts, she hurried back to the Honda, popped the trunk and dug out the tire iron. With the flashlight in one hand and the tire iron in the other, she stood over the dying deer and told herself she *had* to do it. She had to put an end to the creature's suffering.

It was the only humane option she had.

She set the flashlight down on the road with its beam aimed at the doe's head, then gripped the cool iron in both hands. "I'm sorry," she whispered, raising the instrument of cold mercy high over her right shoulder.

She was still frozen in that position when the headlights from an approaching vehicle bathed her backside in harsh light, her long shadow stretching out in front of her like some creature of nightmare. As the pickup rumbled to a stop behind her, she lowered the tire iron and turned toward the truck.

"Damn, Judy Lynn," said the driver, "you aim to change a flat on that critter?"

"Billy Ray?"

Billy Ray Threadgill jumped out of his mud-spattered pickup and squatted beside the fallen deer. "She's a goner. You okay?"

"You got a gun in your truck?" she asked him.

A smile twisted up the corners of his droopy blond mustache. "Does a possum shit in the woods? Hell yes, I got a gun."

"Get it," she said, staring into the animal's eyes. "Hurry."

He went to his pickup and came back with a pistol dangling from his hand. "*Vaya con dios*, Bambi," he said, then raised the gun and shot the doe in the head. The animal twitched once, then was still.

Judy Lynn sighed heavily with relief—and regret. Billy Ray stuck the pistol in the waist of his jeans, grabbed the hind legs of the deer and dragged it to the rear of his Ford F-150. "Help me get her into the truck," he said. "Lotta good meat on this here roadkill."

She didn't want to touch the dead creature, but neither did she want to leave it to rot on the roadside, so she bent to the task, and a minute later the doe was in the bed of the truck, and Billy Ray was wiping his bloody hands on his faded jeans. "I'll bring you some of the meat after I get her dressed."

"No thanks," she said with a shudder.

He turned his attention to her damaged Civic. Using her flashlight, he examined the front end of the vehicle. "Damn lucky you ain't hurt bad," he told her. "Little car like this going up against a deer . . ." He shook his head. "Ain't drivable. Come on, I'll take you to Grubb's and he can send his wrecker."

"I'll use my cell phone," she said. "It'll be quicker."

"Want me to take you home?" His face was bronzed from his

construction work under the Georgia sun, and in the flashing red haze of the Honda's hazard lights his smile became a sinister leer.

"No. I should stay with my car."

Billy Ray shrugged. "Suit yourself. Ain't like nobody's gonna steal it."

"Thanks for your help, Billy Ray."

"Any time, darlin'." He climbed into his pickup, gunned the engine and drove off, waggling his fingers in farewell.

Judy Lynn sat behind the wheel of the Civic and used her cell phone to call Grubb's Service Station in Dogwood. Jerry Grubb answered and said he'd send his son out with the wrecker. She thanked him, hit the END button, lit a much needed cigarette, and settled deeper into the bucket seat to wait for the wrecker. She turned on the car radio for company but turned it off when all she could find amid the shrill static was a radio preacher ranting about the End Times of the New Millennium.

She would've called Josh to tell him what happened—that in spite of his warning she had hit a deer—but she knew he was having his customary pre-prayer meeting supper with his folks and that Reverend Jordan always took the phone off the hook before the family sat down for the blessing and a big meal of greasy vegetables and overcooked meat. She smoked her cigarette and listened to the steady chorus of insects, embellished by the occasional cry of a night bird and the *hoo-hoo-hoo* of an owl.

She didn't like being alone on this road at night, stuck in a ditch and cut off from civilization. Unnerved, she opened her phone and stared at the little illuminated window. She considered calling her mother to tell her what had happened, but then she remembered that this was her mother's bridge night at Sally Jensen's and she didn't know Sally's number. *The police*, she remembered. She should call the police to report the accident for insurance purposes. Without an accident report on file, the insurance company probably wouldn't pay.

All at once the cicadas stopped singing and the woods went completely silent. Judy Lynn stiffened in her seat, tingling with a sense of intense foreboding at the sudden change in the evening's ambience. Her ears popped as if there had been a fluctuation in atmospheric pressure. Saliva surged around her tongue with a metallic taste of inexplicable fear.

Something came crashing through the underbrush to her left.

Something big.

Before she could move to roll up the window and lock the door, the eerie silence of the woods shattered, broken by a terrible screeching that seemed to go on forever. It was unlike any sound she had ever heard, and she suddenly had the crazy idea that it was neither animal nor human in origin.

Judy Lynn began to tremble. She lost control of her bladder, and warm urine pooled in her panties and leaked onto the car seat. The cell phone slipped from her hand. The darkness deepened.

The screeching finally subsided, and the terror it had engendered within her became something altogether different. Overcome with absolute awe, she removed herself from the wrecked vehicle and walked fearlessly into the woods to meet the one who had called to her.

* * *

Arcadia County Deputy Sheriff Rob Rourke was hunkered over a pile of paperwork when the phone rang with an old-timey jangle. Ida Mae Harris was still in the bathroom, so Rourke got up, strode to the dispatcher's desk and snatched up the receiver. "Sheriff's office, Rourke."

"Hey, Rob, how you doing?"

He recognized Jerry Grubb's smoky voice. "Just fine, Jerry. What can I do for you?"

"Did Judy Lynn Bowen call y'all about that deer she hit up on Widow's Ridge Road?"

"No, she didn't. She okay?"

"She was all right when I talked to her. Just shook up a little. I sent my boy up with the wrecker after she called, but when Jack got there, she was gone. Her car was half in a ditch but there weren't hide nor hair of the girl. Didn't see no deer neither. Just a puddle of blood in the road."

"She probably got a ride with somebody before Jack got there. And the deer's probably dead or dying somewhere in the woods."

"Maybe. But why would she leave her pocketbook and cell phone in the car?"

After a thoughtful pause, Rourke said, "I'll look into it. Exactly where was this?"

"Jack said it was about a mile and a half up the mountain from Jackson's General Store."

"Where's her car now?"

"We got it here. Front end's all tore up and the windshield's cracked. Them little Honda's buckle like tin cans when they hit something solid. I wouldn't have no little foreign car myself."

Rourke ran a hand over his close-cropped hair and said, "Here's what I want you to do, Jerry. Put the car in your bay and lock it down. Don't touch anything any more than you have to. Is her purse still in the car?"

"Yep. I was fixin' to put it in my safe."

"No, leave it where it is. And don't say anything to anybody else about this. We don't know that she's missing and I don't want to start tongues wagging."

As he dropped the phone in its cradle, Ida Mae returned from the bathroom down the hall. She cut a fine figure in her tailored khaki uniform—especially for a woman in her mid-forties. "I miss anything?" she asked.

He told her about the call, then asked her to phone Miss Bowen's home in Widow's Ridge and to try her parents' home if there was no answer. While she worked the phone, Rourke poured himself a mug of aging coffee and went back to his desk to mull over the possible whereabouts of Judy Lynn Bowen.

A few minutes later, Ida Mae informed him that there was no answer at Judy Lynn's home and that Mrs. Bowen had just returned from a friend's house and hadn't seen her daughter since yesterday. "I didn't let on that anything was wrong," Ida explained. "I just told her I needed to talk to Judy Lynn about the wedding. She's marrying Josh Jordan, you know."

Rourke nodded. He tossed down his pen, stood and grabbed his hat from a hook on the pine-paneled wall. "I'm gonna take a ride up the mountain," he said. "I'll keep you posted."

His boot heels tapped a snappy rhythm on the hardwood floor and echoed in the empty hallway as he headed toward the rear door leading outside to the designated parking area for sheriff's department cruisers. Boots were not officially part of the uniform, but Sheriff Gladstone always sported cowboy boots, and most of his deputies were happy to follow his example. The boots went with the western-style white hats. Good-guy hats.

The sheriff's office was housed on the first floor of the courthouse building, one door down from the office of the District Attorney. The county jail was located just off Dogwood's town square, on Confederate Avenue. Because Arcadia was the smallest county in North Georgia, its law enforcement arm was short rather than long; in fact, it was the smallest sheriff's department in the entire state. And that suited Rob Rourke just fine. There was less bureaucratic aggravation in a smaller governmental organization.

He left the air-conditioned interior of the old courthouse, and the fresh air of the fine June night washed over him like a soothing balm. To his way of thinking, artificially conditioned air was one of many modern conveniences he had rather do without. His own modest home was cooled by an attic fan because a fan didn't suck the moisture from the air and leave him feeling mummified the way central air-conditioning did.

Rourke took his hat off as he slid behind the wheel of Unit 3 and set it on the passenger seat. He checked the gas gauge, cranked up and pulled out of the parking lot. He drove across town, by-passed Dogwood Community College and turned onto Widow's Ridge Road. The cruiser smelled faintly of cheap aftershave, stale tobacco smoke and greasy fast food. He fingered the buttons on the driver's door armrest and let all the windows down, the welcome rush of night air blowing away the lingering scents—the territorial markings—of his fellow deputies.

Two miles up the mountain past Jackson's General Store he found the apparent site of the accident, marked by shards of broken headlamp glass and a shining glaze of blood smeared on the blacktop. He parked on the shoulder of the road, turned on the cruiser's rack of flashing blue lights and radioed his location to Ida, which she acknowledged in the nasal monotone she affected for her radio broadcasts.

He explored the area with his flashlight and pieced together what had likely happened. After the collision between animal and machine, the deer had been dragged to the side of the road, leaving a smeared trail of blood. There the trail ended, suggesting that the deer had been removed—probably thrown into the back of a pickup truck. It was, of course, remotely possible that the blood on the road was *human* blood and that Judy Lynn's bleeding body had been loaded into a pickup, but Rourke had no reason to seriously consider *that* grim scenario.

After inspecting the area around the disturbed earth where the vehicle had obviously plowed into the ditch, Rourke returned to his cruiser, switched off the flashing blues and drove back to Dogwood.

It was quarter past ten when he arrived at Grubb's Service Station. He found Jerry Grubb finishing up a paint job on an old Mustang in the body shop behind his gas station.

"Thanks for waiting for me, Jerry," he said.

"Hell, I'd as soon be here working as falling asleep in front of the TV. You find her?" Grubb pulled a handkerchief from the back pocket of his bib overalls and wiped sweat from his receding hairline.

"Not yet. I want to take a look at her car."

Grubb jerked his thumb toward the front building. "It's in bay number two. I'll have to unlock it for you."

Rourke followed Grubb to the bay housing Judy Lynn Bowen's damaged Honda Civic. Grubb unlocked a large padlock and rolled up the door with a metallic clatter, then he turned on the overhead light. "There she is. The pocketbook's on the front seat. I didn't touch it."

Grubb went back to work on the Mustang, and Rourke began his examination of the vehicle. He put on a pair of latex gloves and opened the driver's door. The car's interior smelled of recent cigarette smoke and perfume, but it was another smell that troubled him—the unmistakable odor of urine. He bent down and sniffed the seat, then touched his bare wrist to the seat's cloth upholstery and felt dampness there. Had the accident scared the piss out of her? Could a woman as young as Judy Lynn have a bladder-control problem?

He picked up the leather purse, set it on the hood and took a cursory inventory of its contents. Her wallet contained several credit cards and sixty-eight dollars in cash, ruling out any possibility of robbery. There was a small assortment of women's makeup; a half-empty pack of cigarettes (Virginia Slims) and disposable lighter; a little stack of clipped coupons, bound with a paperclip; a ballpoint pen from Dogwood Savings & Trust; an opened roll of breath mints, wintergreen flavored; an oval packet of birth-control pills.

After replacing the contents in the purse, he checked the glove box and found nothing unexpected. The cell phone was on the passenger-side floorboard. He didn't touch it. He looked in the trunk and noted that the tire iron was out of its vinyl sheath. He left it where it was and softly shut the trunk.

Grubb entered the bay, a cigarette dangling from his lips. "Find anything, Rob?"

"Nothing to indicate anything more than a typical vehicle-deer collision," Rourke replied, lapsing into the language he would use when he wrote up his report.

Except the urine on the seat and the persistent scent of fear.

* * *

It was almost midnight when Dr. Trey Knott pulled up in front of Ridgewood Psychiatric Institute. Flashes of lightning in the western sky and the subsequent rumbling of thunder prompted Knott to put up the top on his convertible Jaguar before going inside to deal with the emergency admission. Thirty minutes earlier he had been slipping quietly into bed so as not to wake Susan, settling in for what he hoped would be a restful night of sleep when the bedroom phone cut loose with its irritating electronic warble. He picked up before the second trill, but he felt his wife stir beside him and knew she was waking from a shallow sleep. Her hand moved beneath the sheet and found his bare hip as the faraway voice of the charge nurse whispered in his ear. Carrie Sanders, the night-shift RN who was better at assessing patients than most of the physicians on staff, briefed him on the new female admission and suggested that he see her immediately rather than wait until morning for his initial visit. "I'll be right there," he said, just above a whisper. He kissed Susan good-night, dressed, and drove to the hospital in Goat Head Hollow, three miles south of Dogwood.

To an unschooled eye, Ridgewood's "Big House" is usually mistaken for an old antebellum plantation house, renovated to accommodate mental patients; in truth, it was built in 1919 from the blueprint of a renowned mental hospital in Vienna. Dr. Browner had visited the Viennese facility in 1910 and had been so impressed with it and its director—the illustrious *Herr Doktor* Bruno Kesselring—that he vowed to erect a replica of the hospital back home in Georgia. By the early '20s Ridgewood Psychiatric Institute was known as one of the finest private mental hospitals in the Southeast. Dr. Browner died the same year the stock market crashed, but the Browner family managed to hold on to it despite great financial difficulty, and the facility never shut its doors through the ten decades of its existence. In 1965 the Browner family built another hospital in Vinewood, Georgia, but the Graves County facility had always had trouble attracting good psychiatrists and administrators and never achieved the prestige of Ridgewood.

Knott went up the brick walkway, mounted the concrete steps, passed between the central white columns of the portico and used his key to unlock the front door. Haloed by fine mist, the ornate light fixture above the glass doors created a pool of murky, yellow light, and the nine cane rocking chairs arrayed in linear formation across the wide porch seemed to be floating in the nebulous pool. A rising wind set some of the rockers in ghostly motion as Knott entered the building. The receptionist's alcove was darkened and deserted at this late hour, as was the well-appointed sitting room on the opposite side of the vestibule. He paused at the foot of the wide stairway and glanced down the shadowy corridors to his left and right—the north and south wings whose rooms had been converted to offices for social workers, physicians, and administrative personnel. While not completely dark, the corridors were just gloomy enough to

send an unexpected chill up his back as the vivid memory of his child-
hood fear of darkness came fleetingly to the fore.

He climbed the carpeted steps, wondering why, after all these
years, his old fear of the dark had reached out from the past to yank his
memory chain.

Midway to the second floor, the wide stairway gave onto a landing
beneath a high stained-glass window and branched left and right at
180-degree angles, the two narrower stairs leading to the second-floor
landing and to twin doors which opened in front of the nursing station.
The doors were locked electronically from the inside but could be opened
freely from the stairway side; the patients could not get out unless one
of the nursing staff disengaged the lock with a push of a button or a
turn of a key. With a hand on the banister, Knott swung to his right
and climbed the narrow stairs to the second-floor landing. He glanced
through the small Plexiglas window in the door and saw Carrie Sanders
writing in a chart. He opened the door and went inside.

"Oh, hi, Dr. Knott," Carrie said in her whispery night-shift voice as
she looked up from her charting. "Sorry to call you out so late, but I felt
you would want to see Miss Rampling tonight."

He waved off her apology. "I'm the doc on-call. Comes with the territory. I trust your judgment."

"Right." She smiled, her perfect teeth flashing brightly from the
smooth ebony of her face.

Knott half-sat on the long desktop built into the nursing-station wall
and leaned his back against the shelf of numbered slots filled with the
medical charts of the current admissions. He folded his arms across his
chest in a gesture at definite odds with those proponents of body-language
correctness who maintained that such a posture denoted defensiveness and
even hostility. Knott thought it was all psycho-hokum; for him it was a
comfortable habit and nothing more. "What can you tell me about her?"

"Sharyn Rampling, a forty-two-year-old unmarried Caucasian,
professor of English literature at the community college. She's been an
outpatient of Dr. Crandle's for five years." Carrie paused to consult her
admission notes. "Diagnosed as bipolar and hospitalized once in 2004
when she stopped taking her lithium and went into a full-blown manic
phase. She responded well to treatment. Dr. Crandle got her stabilized
on her medication and she was discharged after two weeks. She says she's
been taking her lithium religiously since then.

"She presented tonight in an agitated state. A state of near-panic,

I'd have to say. She said she had to be admitted because this was the only place she had ever felt completely safe and protected. Patient stated, 'I desperately need to be safe right now.' When I asked her what she needed to be protected from, she said she would only discuss that with Dr. Crandle. I explained that Dr. Crandle is on vacation and that you're covering for him. I don't know if she will share her big dark secret with you or not."

Knott nodded. "Does she seem manic to you?"

"No. She seems like something scared the bejesus out of her. If she's delusional, she's keeping her delusions to herself."

"Go ahead and do the routine blood work and a lithium level. You have her old chart?"

"Just brought it up from Medical Records." She handed him a manila folder containing the records of Rampling's previous hospitalization.

"Thanks. I'll look this over while you draw her blood."

Ten minutes later, Knott rapped on the door of room 207 to announce his entrance. "Miss Rampling, I'm Dr. Knott. Dr. Crandle asked me to see his patients while he's on vacation."

She rose from a seated position on the edge of the bed. Sharyn Rampling was a tall, attractive woman who looked a little younger than her stated age. The stark whiteness of her oval face was framed by the dark bangs and tresses of her shoulder-length hair. Her dark eyes shone wetly, as if she had been recently crying. She clasped her trembling hands in front of her, interlacing her fingers, and rested them beneath her abundant breasts. Each finger bore a gemstone ring. "I've seen you on campus," she said. "You taught Abnormal Psych."

"Yes, I did, last year. As a guest lecturer." He sat in the wing chair in the corner of the private room, crossed his legs and rested the unopened chart on his knee.

She turned her profile to him and appeared to be studying the uninteresting painting on the beige wall. "I don't know if I should confide in you, Doctor. I'm sure you know your job, but I don't know that I can just start in cold and trust you with my . . . my problem."

"Nurse Sanders told me you said you came here to be protected."

She turned to face him directly. "Yes, I did say that. But now that I'm here, I don't feel any safer."

"What is it that's threatening your safety?"

"I . . . I can't say. I mean, I don't *know* what it is. I just know it . . . something . . . wants something."

"Wants something from you?" he asked as gently as he could.

She unclasped her hands and slid her bejeweled fingers into the front pockets of her tight jeans, the sparkling rings resting just above the seamed slits and creating the illusion that the pockets were embroidered with gemstones. "I know it sounds at least a little delusional," she said in a husky voice, "but that's what I believe. Whatever it is, it *wants* something from me. I can feel it pulling at me."

"Wants you in what sense?" Knott deliberately shifted the focus onto the patient as the desired object. He hoped he wasn't being too abruptly obvious with his tactic.

Her eyes narrowed and she puffed herself up in the manner of a cat trying to make itself look more formidable when threatened. "You're asking me if it wants me *sexually*? Just come right out and say what you mean, Doc. We're adults, are we not? Does this . . . this *thing* want to *fuck* me? To defile me in every way imaginable and then in ways you could never *even* imagine? To sully my soul?! Make me do things that would *damn* me *forever?!*" Her shoulders slumped with the release of some of her pent-up emotion. Her voice softened. "I don't know. I don't know what it wants. I don't . . ."

A volley of thunder shook the building and blowing rain pelted the windowpanes. A tear rolled down Sharyn Rampling's cheek. She moved to the window and parted the curtains. "All I *do* know is that it's out there, waiting. Probably watching."

"And you know this, how?" Knott scribbled a note in the chart: *Pt. histrionic with a flair for melodrama.* But she was a teacher of literature, so it was possible that her melodramatics might be, in part, a function of her educational vocation. He penned a question mark after the notation.

She turned away from the window, letting the curtain fall over the dark glass. "I know it because it *touched* me."

A hollow laugh escaped her lips. "That's funny, isn't it, Doc? I say it touched me, and you're thinking, 'Yeah, she's *touched* all right. Touched in the head.'"

"That's not at all what I'm thinking," he said.

"Shrinks are all alike. You never really *say* anything. You just run through your list of premeditated responses and use the ones most likely to hit the patient's hot buttons. I know how the game is played. I'm not a novice."

"This isn't a game. Games are played for amusement, for fun, or for profit. You're clearly not having fun. Something has pushed you right up to the edge of panic and I'm trying to find out what that something is. Now, tell me how it touched you."

Her face seemed to relax a little. The patient had challenged the therapist and the therapist had risen to the challenge without getting angry or sidetracked. "There was this *sound*. A terrible shrieking sound, sort of like the cry of a wildcat, but I've heard wildcats and that's not what it was. More like a fox, maybe. No, it was like nothing I'd ever heard before—a wildcat's cry notwithstanding. I was sitting at home in my study, reading Yeats, and this screeching comes out of nowhere. It was outside the house, but it got louder and louder, almost as if it were somehow inside and outside at the same time. One long, continuous cry that seemed to . . . *penetrate* me. It was as if I were being *violated* by the sound. I was terrified, so frightened I couldn't move. Then everything fell out of focus and . . ." She shook her head. "My memory is fuzzy on this part, but when the shrieking finally stopped, I was shaking all over in terror and I discovered I had actually *wet my pants.*"

She gave him a pointed look, waiting for a reaction. When she didn't get one, she added, "I mean, my God, I'm only forty-two. I'm hardly old enough to start wearing Depends."

"Have you been taking your lithium as prescribed?"

"Oh yes. My lab results will prove it. I'm not going manic, Dr. Knott. I'm not delusional, I'm *scared.*"

He nodded. "We may need to adjust your dosage. Although they are rare, incontinence, ringing in the ears and blackouts are possible side effects of lithium. Since you've been taking it for several years, I don't think that is what's going on here. It's more likely that you are in the early stages of lithium toxicity." He opened her chart to the Physician's Orders section and began writing as he continued to talk. "You've been taking three-hundred milligrams three times a day. I'm going to with-hold your lithium until I see the lab results tomorrow, then we'll know how to proceed. How have you been sleeping?"

She shrugged. "Okay, I guess. I've always been a light sleeper. I doubt I'll sleep tonight, though. Not with that—whatever the hell it is—out there."

"You're perfectly safe here, Miss Rampling. If there *is* something 'out there,' I'm sure it's no threat to you. What you probably heard was a couple of cats going at it. Or something just as innocent. I'm prescribing a mild sleep medication. In the morning the internist will give you a physical exam, and I'll see you again tomorrow afternoon."

Knott closed the chart and stood to leave.

"I want you to be right about all this," she said, crossing her arms beneath her breasts. "I hope it's just a simple matter of adjusting my medication. But you want to know what I *really* believe? I believe something's happening here that's beyond the realm of medical science. If that sounds delusional, I'm sorry. That's what I believe. You're familiar with the concept of synchronicity? That seemingly random events occurring within a given timeframe form a pattern that isn't at all random?"

"Yes, I am. I considered myself a Jungian when I first started my practice."

"Well, I always thought the point of synchronicity is that there's some underlying Godlike intelligence that pulls cosmic strings to create those patterns. Like Fate."

"Or the collective unconscious."

"And that those patterns might provide hints of things to come. Well, when I heard that God-awful shrieking, I was reading Yeats' famous lines: 'And what rough beast, its hour come round at last, slouches toward Bethlehem to be born?' How's that for synchronicity?"

Knott smiled. "One of the curses of a strong intellect is an overabundance of imagination."

"Did Jung say that?" She cocked the brow over her left eye.

"No, I did." He allowed a small smile.

"Oh." She rubbed her arm as though she were cold. "Those lines of verse keep running through my head like a song you can't stop humming. But in my twisted version, the beast is slouching toward *Dogwood* to be born."

* * *

Knott envied his colleague, Steve Crandle. Sharyn Rampling was the type of patient a good psychiatrist hopes for but seldom encounters. Witty, well-educated and, above all, challenging. And it didn't hurt that she was alluringly attractive. The bulk of Knott's patients were middle-aged deadly-dull depressives and poorly educated schizophrenics whose treatment consisted primarily of medication maintenance, and only a very few of them were amenable to true psychotherapy. Sharyn Rampling was the exceptional patient, and Knott wished, for selfish reasons, that he could engage her in ongoing psychoanalysis. A patient of her caliber was wasted on a doctor like Crandle, whose psychoanalytic technique consisted of engaging the patient in aimless chit-chat or babbling on about his collection of antique cars, while scribbling scripts for medication. Knott consoled himself with the fact that he would have nearly two weeks to work with Miss Rampling before Dr. Crandle returned from his European vacation.

On his way back to the nursing station, he saw Tom Riley, the night-shift PA (Psychiatric Assistant), conducting his hourly bed checks, going room-to-room with a flashlight to make sure each patient was safe (and breathing) in his or her own bed. As they passed in the corridor, he and Tom quietly acknowledged each other with a nod. Before Knott reached the nursing station, Tom called out to him in a loud whisper: "Doc! Doc, you gotta see this!"

He did a quick about-face and joined Tom Riley in the doorway of room 202. Tom turned on the overhead light and the room seemed to leap forward out of darkness. An emaciated elderly woman in a wispy white gown was marking on the wall with a red crayon. When Knott recognized the patient, he understood Tom's sudden animation. She was Elsa Loveless, the ninety-two-year-old resident of a nearby nursing home who had been transferred to Ridgewood after she lapsed into a near-catatonic state. In the week since her admission, she had remained completely uncommunicative and incapable of feeding herself. And now here she was, standing on frail legs and drawing on the wall, apparently oblivious to the presence of two men in her room.

"Miss Loveless?" said Knott. "Elsa?"

She gave no sign that she had heard him, and continued her work with the crayon.

"What the heck is that?" Tom pointed at the red confusion of squiggles, swirling lines, and blotchy shadings of the old woman's child-like drawing.

"I think she's writing a caption," Knott said. "Let her finish."

They watched in silence as she printed a single word beneath her artwork, the crayon clamped awkwardly in her gnarled claw-like fingers. When she was done, she turned away from the wall and began to slash at her wrist with the waxy tip of the crayon.

"That's really weird," Tom said, shaking his balding head.

"Let's get her back to bed," Knott said, gently taking hold of both her wrists. "Come on, Elsa. It's bedtime. We don't want you to fall."

She offered no resistance. After she was safely tucked in, the two men raised the metal bed rails, and then simultaneously returned their attention to the markings on the wall. Like patrons of an art museum trying to make sense of a mystifyingly abstract painting, they stared at the bizarre artwork of Elsa Loveless. The word printed beneath the helter-skelter sketch only added to the enigma of the drawing itself:

HELLING

"What does that mean, Elsa?" asked Knott. "'*Helling*.'"

A faint smile (or perhaps a grimace) appeared on her thin lips, then she closed her pale blue eyes and immediately began to snore.

"Considering that she was working in the dark and she's legally blind, I guess we can't expect it to look like much of anything," Tom observed.

"You're right. Still, I'd like to know what she *thought* she was drawing. And what prompted her to come out of la-la-land long enough to draw it."

"Well, clearly she's not going to tell us."

Knott took another long look at the mystery sketch, then said, "Tom, make sure that no one cleans that off the wall. Not without my say-so."

"You got it, Doc. Mind if I ask why?"

"Yes, I do."

Tom Riley shrugged. "Ooh-kay."

Knott hated to be rude, but in this case a rude response was better than a truthful one, and the truth was, he wasn't sure why he wanted the strange drawing left intact. He knew only that he did.

CHAPTER TWO

FROM THE FRONT PORCH OF HER HOUSE overlooking the hamlet of Widow's Ridge, Liza Leatherwood watched the sun climb higher above the mist-shrouded hills and wondered if she could survive another sleepless night. "Lord," she said, sighing. "I feel nea'ly 'bout as old as them hills."

A widow of sixteen lonely years, she had gradually fallen into the habit of talking to herself, finding comfort in the sound of her own voice, but here lately, the raspy sound of her vocal chords was just one more nagging reminder that she was becoming an old crone, withered, wrinkled and liver-spotted like a wizened witch from a child's nightmare. Her mind was still plenty sharp, but her old bones betrayed all of her eighty-nine years.

She shifted her trifling weight in the rocking chair, reached down and picked up the Mason jar of clear liquid from its resting place beside the rocker. Holding the pint jar to her drooping bosom, she unscrewed the metal lid and brought the rim of grooved glass to her lips. The smell of the spirits was so strong it took her breath away, causing her to delay the first sip. "If Wilbur was to see me now, he'd think I'd gone soft in the head," she said, referring to her late husband. She half-believed he *could* see her now. He had put so much of himself into this house that there were times when she could actually feel his presence round about her.

Wilbur Leatherwood had begun laying the foundation for the house the same day Liza agreed to marry him, back in the spring of 1938. The house was raised and furnished by midsummer, and they were married by a circuit-riding preacher on the tenth day of August. A week or so later, while Wilbur was working in the quarry, Liza's grandmother sat with the new bride right here on this same porch and told her the dark secret.

Though Liza's memory was not as keen as it once was, she could recall every word her grandmother had spoken that long-ago day. With the Mason jar of spirits forgotten for the moment, she closed her eyes and once again revisited the fateful conversation with her mother's mother.

"They's some things you need to know, now that you're not a child anymore," Granny said with heavy solemnity. Her weathered face lost all trace of her characteristic kindliness.

Thinking the old lady was about to tell her about the "birds and the bees," Liza said, "Mama already told me all that, Granny."

Granny shook her gray head. "I'm not talking about marital relations. Now you hush and just listen. Some things you think you know, ain't true. A long time ago they wuz some bad things happened hereabouts. Things so terrible that they're only spoken of in whispers or not spoken of atall.

"Things the menfolk don't know about and—God willin'—never will. You must never breathe a word of this to your husband, nor to any man."

Young Liza was chilled by the gravity of Granny's voice and demeanor. She could not imagine what her grandmother was talking about, but she was seized by a powerful yearning to learn of the forbidden—and tantalizing—secret.

"You know how our little hamlet come to be called Widow's Ridge?" asked the elder.

"Yes ma'am. 'Cause back during the Civil War, none of the men came home. They all died of grievous wounds or terrible disease, making widows out of all the married women of the little hamlet with no name."

"That's what you've been told, and you learned it word for word, but it's a made-up story. After what *really* happened, the womenfolk got together and come up with that cock-and-bull tale and repeated it so many years that it stuck. They did it to hide the truth. It weren't the war what killed all them boys."

"Then what was it, Granny?" Brimming with impatience, Liza squirmed in her hard seat.

The old woman shut her eyes and shook her head, as if trying to dispel thoughts too dreadful to bear. When finally she answered, the words issued from her tremulous lips like the mournful wail of a bereaved widow at her husband's wake. "The Helling," she lamented.

Taken aback by her grandmother's display of naked emotion, young Liza only echoed the words in a hoarse, questioning whisper. "The Helling?"

The rumbling whine of an approaching automobile intruded upon Liza Leatherwood's darksome remembrance, and she opened her eyes to see the sporty little car turning off the dusty road and motoring up the gravel drive which led to her house.

"Damnation," she spat, screwing the lid back on the Mason jar. "That man's determined to hound me to my grave."

Tires crunching the gravel, the sports car stopped behind Wilbur's ancient pickup truck (which hadn't been started in over six years), and Professor Alfred Thorn hopped out of the convertible, giving her the glad hand. "Hello, Mrs. Leatherwood," he called as he strode to the front steps. "I've got something for you."

Liza rocked forward in her chair. "You're wasting your time, Professor. I told you, I don't know anything about that twaddle."

Ignoring her comment, Professor Thorn stopped on the first porch-step and held up a fat book. "It's *The Complete Works of Nathaniel Hawthorne.* My gift to you, no strings attached."

"Everything's got strings," she contended. "Just because you can't see 'em, don't mean you can't get tangled up in 'em."

Thorn chuckled, thoughtfully stroking his white-whiskered chin. "Perhaps you're right," he said. "Nevertheless, I want you to have this. You did say Hawthorne's your favorite author."

"I did. And I likewise said I can't help you with your re-search."

"You did, indeed. And I have to take you at your word." He came up the steps and held out the book bound handsomely in brown leather. "Please, Mrs. Leatherwood, accept this as a tribute from one Hawthorne-lover to another. Nothing more, nothing less."

Relenting, she reached out and took the heavy volume with both hands. "Thank you kindly, Professor. I do love the way the man tells a story. I'm not a scholar but I love a good tale, well-told."

"I think the old scribbler would be pleased to count you among his devoted readers." Thorn gave her a warm, knowing smile.

"Your flattery's wasted on me, Professor." She balanced the book precariously on the knobs of her knees.

He laughed. "That's what I like about you, Mrs. Leatherwood. You always say what's on your mind."

"I'm too old to do otherwise." She removed her bifocals and cleaned the lenses with a handkerchief she pulled from the bosom of her dress. "And I'm not so foolish as to believe you drove all the way up here just to give me this book. So come out with it. What do you want now?"

He looked down at his feet, assuming the countenance of a scolded child—though Liza judged him to be in his mid-fifties. And right handsome in a rugged sort of way, looking more like a sportsman than a Professor of Anthropology at Dogwood Community College.

"Though I don't understand your reluctance to share your knowledge of the local folklore and legends, I respect your decision to keep it to yourself. But I would appreciate it if you would point me to someone of your generation who *would* be willing to help me with my project."

She put her glasses back on and gave him a closer appraisal. He was all business now, the scolded pup having yielded to the seasoned bloodhound.

"You see, Mrs. Leatherwood, I've already turned up some fragmented yarns of a 'Demon of the Dark Wood' and the 'Devil of Goat Head Hollow.' Most all of these folk legends have a common thread running through them, and they have much in common with the lore of faraway places and long-ago times. Hawthorne himself made reference to 'the Black Man that haunts the forest.' These stories and myths are an important element in most cultures, and sometimes they are linked to actual events, growing over the years to mythic proportions. And it's that convergence of history and myth that most interests me. *That's* the region I want to explore."

Liza leaned back and set her chair to rocking. "So you come up here to deliver me a lecture. Well, it was most gratifying, but I still can't help you. And I don't know anybody who can."

Thorn spread his hands in an apologetic gesture. "Forgive me for lapsing into lecture, but I'm convinced that Widow's Ridge is a hidden treasure trove of native myth. Over the years I've developed sort of a sixth sense about my fieldwork. I get a certain feeling—an actual tingling sensation—when I'm on the edge of discovery, and I've got that feeling right now. Forgive me if I'm overly passionate about my work."

"Passion can be the ruin of a man," she said, firmly entrenched in her role of Keeper of Secrets. "You'll not find your treasure round here. And here's a bit of hill wisdom you'd do well to remember: *A man who digs cursed earth, uncovers great sorrow.*"

"That's a good one," he said, beaming a big smile. "Better than a Chinese fortune cookie. I'll bet you're full of those old sayings. It would be a real shame if you took such gems to your grave."

"Professor, you're about as pigheaded as my Wilbur was. And I'll thank you not to speak of my grave before I'm dead and buried in it."

With a chivalrous bow, he said, "I beg your pardon. I meant no offense."

"I'll take none if you'll leave me alone now. I've got chores to tend to, and I don't have time to sit here yapping about old wives' tales and mountain superstitions. You'll not find your bogeyman round here."

"Once again, I'm humbled by your unabashed honesty," said Thorn. "I won't trouble you further. But you still have my card if you should change your mind."

"I won't."

"You take care, now, Mrs. Leatherwood. I hope you enjoy the book."

She watched him drive off, secretly saddened by his departure. The truth was, she liked the man and rather enjoyed being in the company of a gentleman of such scholarship. She regretted having to send him off so rudely, but she'd had no other choice. The one thing he wanted from her was the very thing she was sworn to keep to herself. She had sworn an oath before Granny and God never to speak of the Helling; she had kept that oath for a passel of years and she didn't intend to break it now that her remaining years on this earth were surely numbered in single digits. You didn't get into Heaven by breaking a sacred oath. On the other hand, Liza questioned the wisdom of taking such terrible knowledge to the grave. Would not her soul be tainted by carrying that sinful knowledge so close to her heart for so many years? Though she wasn't Catholic, she believed confession was a necessary means of unburdening the soul and cleansing the spirit. Dare she stand naked before her Maker with this guilty secret still in her bosom?

There had been times when she hated her grandmother for telling her of the Helling, times when she couldn't fathom why the old woman had deemed it necessary to impart the horrible secret to her innocent granddaughter; but as she matured, Liza came to understand Granny's motive. The elder had brought her into the sisterhood of truth and baptized her with the bloody knowledge so that she, Liza, would be forewarned against a recurrence of the abominable incident. "Forewarned is forearmed," as Wilbur used to say, usually in reference to matters of politics and weather. Granny had forewarned her so that she might be able to resist the "shrill and dark summons" if it ever came again.

And last night it *had* come. Howling out of the dark wood, the dreadful summoning had ripped the night with its evil cry. Piercing and irresistible, the demonic shriek echoed across hill and hollow, seeking resonance in souls pricked by its barbed waves of sound. Liza had been snapping pole beans at the kitchen table when the unearthly screech found her. As insidious tendrils of sound slithered around her, she stiffened her spine and felt the dribble of warm urine in her crotch. Even as she felt the commanding force of the shrieker behind the shriek, she found the will to clap her hand over her good ear to muffle the sound, and when the shriek finally ended in eerie silence, she crumpled forward to rest her head on the kitchen table, exhausted by the effort of resistance. The deafness of her left ear had undoubtedly saved her by diminishing the effect of the shrieking summons. Yet she instinctively knew she was far from safe; the next commanding cry would find her weakened and afraid. She didn't believe she had it within her to fend off the summoner a second time.

Drastic measures were required, and now that Professor Thorn was gone, Liza could get on with what she knew she had to do. She picked up the Mason jar, removed the lid and drank some of the potent brew (corn liquor Otis King brewed in his basement for his personal consumption). Liza had never been a teetotaler, but she couldn't remember the last time she had imbibed *spiritus fermenti*—which was all to the good because it meant that the brew would hit her hard and fast, numbing her senses and dulling the pain she was about to inflict upon herself. She didn't want to do it, but she could think of no other way to defend herself against the evil shrieker.

The Black Man of the wood.

When the jar was half emptied, she knew she was drunk enough to proceed. She pulled up the skirt of her long dress and withdrew the hatpin from the bottom hem, then she dipped the sharp tip of the long pin into the jar of spirits to sterilize it.

As she gazed out over the hamlet of Widow's Ridge and at the complex of new townhouses below it, she paused a long moment to listen to the singing of unseen birds, and then she raised the hatpin to her right ear and eased the point inside until it met resistance. Without further hesitation, she jabbed the pin deep and punctured the eardrum, just as her stern grandmother had long ago prescribed.

Abruptly, the birds stopped singing.

Liza Leatherwood's world slipped into ringing silence.

* * *

The idea was to empty his mind even as his body labored mightily to spirit him along the mountain trail, arms and legs pistoning on automatic pilot, gutting it out until the ache in his lungs and the fatigue in his legs disappeared and he achieved that Zen-like state known as the "runner's high," but this morning Rourke's mind would not be stilled. His thoughts were astir with the nagging disappearance of Judy Lynn Bowen, and he continuously turned it over in his mind the way a dog worries a bone, gnawing, gnawing, gnawing . . .

Lucy Fur, his Irish wolfhound, loped ahead of him, occasionally glancing back as if to say: "What's the hold-up, Hairless Master? I thought you wanted to run?"

When the pager clipped to the waist of his jogging shorts beeped, Rourke slowed to a walk, unclipped it, held it up to his eyes and saw the numerical message.

999: HQ's signal to get his ass to the nearest phone and call in for further instructions, *pronto.*

"Come on, Lucy," he called breathlessly to his dog. "Home, girl!"

The wolfhound responded immediately to his command, turning around and running past him, leading the way back to his house in Goat Head Hollow. Rourke turned and jogged after her, his mind racing to the conclusion that the emergency page had to be about Judy Lynn Bowen.

But he was wrong. The dayshift dispatcher told him that Sheriff Gladstone had been admitted to Dogwood General for emergency treatment of a head wound suffered in a domestic attack. Rourke was to report for duty ASAP, rather than wait for his 3-11 shift.

"How bad is it?" he asked, still breathing heavily from the morning jog.

"They don't know yet," said Alice Marsh, the nubile dayshift dispatcher. "They're taking X-rays now. Sheriff's conscious but confused. He's saying his wife did it to him. Whacked him over the head with an iron skillet."

"What! That's crazy! *Shirley Gladstone?* I don't believe it. The sheriff *must* be out of his head."

"That may be," Alice said, "but they haven't been able to locate Mrs. Gladstone to get her version of the story."

"Jesus," said Rourke, immediately thinking of the missing Judy Lynn Bowen.

"We've got two units looking for her now. Deputy Venture is still at the scene."

"Okay. I'll be in as quick as I can get there."

"Deputy Rourke? Doesn't this mean you're Acting Sheriff now?"

"Yeah," he said, suddenly realizing that he would be responsible for running the investigation of the assault on Sheriff Gladstone, as well as running the whole damned department. "That's what it means."

* * *

"Good thing the old man's got a hard head," said Deputy Carl Venture as he pointed a latex-gloved finger at the black iron skillet on the tile floor of the Gladstone kitchen. "That thing's heavy enough to crack open a skull and spill out the brains."

"Jesus, Carl," Rourke said. "We're talking about the sheriff here."

Venture shrugged. "I'm just saying . . ."

"Don't say it again." Rourke looked at the spatters of blood on top of the kitchen table and the pool of blood on the floor next to the overturned chair. Then he looked back at Carl Venture and said, "Tell me what we know."

"Well," Venture said, consulting his notebook, "when the sheriff didn't show up at his usual time, the dispatcher called his home, thinking maybe he'd overslept, that last night's thunderstorm might've knocked out his power. When she didn't get an answer—this was around nine-thirty—she decided to dispatch a deputy—yours truly—to his house. I arrived here at nine-forty-three, entered the house when nobody answered the door, and found the sheriff in his jammies, unconscious on the kitchen floor. I saw he was still breathing and tried to rouse him, and when I couldn't revive him, I called for the ambulance. The paramedics arrived at ten sharp—they made damn good time, didn't they?—and the sheriff came to as they were loading him onto the stretcher, at which point he said, 'My wife. She tried to kill me.' Then he was in and out of consciousness, mumbling incoherently mostly. But I did catch something he said as they were putting him in the ambulance. He said, 'Made her crazy. She couldn't help it.' Then they took him away."

"No sign of forcible entry?"

"Nope. Hard as it is to believe, it looks like it probably went down just like he said. His wife brained him with that fucking skillet, then hoofed it out of here for parts unknown. The family car's still in the carport, next to the sheriff's cruiser."

Rourke stared at the black skillet on the floor and wondered what could drive a sweet-natured God-fearing woman of late middle-years to do something like this.

"Sure makes you think, doesn't it, Rob?" Carl said. "Married to a woman for umpteen years and then out of the blue—whap!—she turns on you for no good reason. Bet it makes you glad you're still a bachelor, huh?"

"The only thing it makes me is sad," he replied. "Lift whatever prints you can off the skillet. We know Mrs. Gladstone's prints will be on it, and maybe the sheriff's, but we need to be sure no third-party's prints show up. At this point we can't rule out the possibility that someone else assaulted the sheriff and kidnapped his wife. The sheriff could be confused about what happened because of the blow to the head. For the time being, we have to consider him a questionable witness."

"Okay, Sherlock." Carl grinned. "You're the boss. For now."

Rourke gritted his teeth and let Venture's sarcasm pass. "I'm going to the hospital to see if the sheriff's clear enough yet to tell me what really happened. Until we get this thing nailed down, there will be no public comment other than 'Sheriff Gladstone is being treated for a head injury.'"

As soon as he was back in his cruiser, Rourke radioed the dispatcher and told her that he would be at the hospital for awhile. Then he added, "You did a good job of handling things this morning, Alice. You earned yourself a commendation. That will be my first official act."

"Why, thank you, Rob, I mean . . . Acting Sheriff Rourke." He could hear the playful smile in her voice.

"Unit Two, out," he said, wondering if she could hear the smile in his voice, as well. She was twenty-seven, and he was forty-two, but the fifteen-year difference in their ages hadn't prevented their ongoing mutual flirtation. Rourke recently had become hopeful that the flirtation could develop into something more serious, but as yet, he hadn't made any serious move in that direction. And just now, the timing didn't seem right for such a move. As Acting Sheriff, any romantic involvement with an underling might open himself up to charges of sexual harassment; not that he thought she would ever pursue such a drastic course, but as a public official, he had to be conscious of appearances, and even the appearance of impropriety could prove damaging to his future career (he wanted to be more than *Acting* Sheriff).

Pulling into the parking lot at Dogwood Medical Center, he pushed aside his thoughts of romance and tried to mentally prepare himself for interrogating his boss, The Honorable Rufus D. Gladstone, Sheriff of Arcadia County.

CHAPTER THREE

"I THINK I'VE LOST MY ANGEL!" Julie Archer said, jamming her foot on the brake pedal and bringing the van to a rough stop in front of the arched gateway of Mountview Villas.

"God*damn* it, Jools, don't *do* that shit!" said Angela Raynor, glaring at Julie through the smudged lenses of her dark glasses. She shifted her rump on the passenger seat and angrily adjusted the seatbelt strap so that it was no longer mashing her right breast.

"I've asked you not to take the Lord's name in vain, Angela. It's no wonder that Michael's deserted me, with all your cursing."

"Oh sure," snapped Angela, reaching for a cigarette, "blame *me* for running off your imaginary friend." She stuck the cigarette between her lips and lit it with a butane lighter. "I'm beginning to think this whole thing is a big mistake. I never should've let you talk me into moving up here in the god . . . the *gosh darn* hills."

"Thank you," said Julie, cool and perfunctory. "And Michael is not my imaginary friend. He's my guardian angel. My muse. And you know it."

"I know you *think* he is," Angela countered, blowing smoke through her flared nostrils.

Julie giggled. "You look like a dragon when you do that."

"Give me a break, woman. I'm in no mood for your melodramatics. It's already been a long day, my ass is numb from sitting so long, and I think I'm getting my period."

"Aha! PMS. I knew it." Julie smiled, doing her best to relieve some of the tension between them.

"Yeah, that's it. Post-Millennial Shock." Angela's deadpan expression collapsed around a grin, then she laughed in spite of her pique.

"Good one, Ange." Julie shared the laughter, forcing it a little.

Angela removed her dark glasses and ran a hand through her short blonde hair. "You don't really blame *me* for chasing off Mikey, do you?"

"Of course not. No guardian angel worth his salt would leave on account of something so trivial. Not unless I was the one blaspheming."

"He's probably just taking a little break," offered Angela. "You know, like he had to get out and stretch his wings or take an angelic leak or something. Oops! There I go again, offending the Heavens. I'm sorry. I'm just an unreconstructed heathen. Always was, always will be."

"That's all right. Michael enjoys your perverted sense of humor almost as much as I do."

"Yeah? He told you that?" Angela looked askance at her dark-haired friend.

"Well, he doesn't really talk to me," Julie explained. "Not with words. But I can sometimes feel his moods. And I can feel his laughter when you get off a good one."

Angela shook her head in mock wonder. "You're a trip, Julie Archer. A one-way trip, destination unknown. And like a fool, I'm along for the wild, crazy ride."

Julie turned her attention to the complex of brand-new townhouses beyond the gateway before them, encircled by walls of somber gray stone. "There's home," she said. "Mountview Villas, townhouse number six. And we're the very first ones here. Isn't it beautiful?"

"Kind of spooky, if you ask me. Which, of course, you just did. And I could do without those gargoyles squatting on that ugly wall like they're about to shit stones. But I'm sure you love that Gothic crap, being a famous horror writer and all."

"Yes, I do, as a matter of fact. Did I tell you I suggested those gargoyles to Daddy?"

"Only about a thousand times. At first Daddy Warbucks didn't like the idea, but you persisted and he finally saw the wisdom of your idea, blah, blah, blah . . ."

"You're such a smart-ass."

"And proud of it." Angela stubbed out her cigarette in the ashtray. "Well, Miss Archer, shall we cross the threshold of the illustrious estate and find our new abode, posthaste?"

"Yes!" Julie shouted cheerfully as she stepped on the gas pedal. The white van shot forward, carrying them through the arched entrance and onto the grounds of the complex of buildings her father had designed and built himself (under the auspices of his company, Archer Enterprises). Although the grand opening was scheduled for the first week in July when the first rent-paying tenants would start moving in, Julie's father had agreed to let his daughter and her roommate move in two weeks early; all they had to do in return was keep the swimming pool clean and chemically balanced until the groundskeepers and maintenance crew reported for duty a week before the grand opening. It was, as Angela had said upon learning of the arrangement, "a really sweet deal." Julie's father had already had their unit furnished, so all they had to do was carry their personal items from the van to the townhouse. The cable TV hook-ups weren't ready for service yet because the big satellite dish on the roof of the stately clubhouse needed fine tuning, but Julie didn't care about that anyway. She planned to spend much of her time working on her new novel (tentatively titled: *The Ravenwood Horror*), and in her off time, reading some of the classics of literature she'd never found time to read before.

Having promised never to disturb Julie when she was writing, Angela planned to work on her tan during the sunlit hours and audit a few night drama classes at Dogwood Community College before actually beginning her enrollment as a fulltime student in the fall. She had dropped out of the University of Georgia back in 2004, pleading lack of motivation, and went to work as a waitress at a Hooter's in an Atlanta suburb. There she had fallen in with some theater types and aspiring actors, and had gotten caught up in their enthusiasm for the stage and all things theatrical. "It's the thespian life for me," she was fond of saying, enjoying the odd looks of those who thought "thespian" had something to do with sexual persuasion. She harbored no grandiose plans about going to Hollywood and becoming a movie star; Angela wanted to be a stage actor, be it in summer stock, off-Broadway or diminutive dinner theaters. She wanted to play juicy roles in front of live audiences. Though her stage experience was limited to a minor role in her high school's inevitable presentation of *Our Town*, she wholeheartedly believed she had real talent, and Julie agreed.

Hazy sunlight glinted off the inviting blue-green water in the Olympic-size swimming pool as they drove past, prompting Angela to say, "Stop right here. I'm gonna take a baptismal dip. I'm serious. Stop."

"You're seriously disturbed," said Julie, stopping beside the pool. "We're in the mountains now, remember? That water's gonna be really cold."

Angela jumped out of the van. "Come on, you pussy, let's go skinny dipping."

"Not me. I'll give you two minutes, then I'm driving off. I want to get unpacked and settled."

Angela dashed to the pool, stripped off her shorts and T-shirt, shed her bra and panties, then dove into the water. Julie left the motor running, and impatiently drummed her fingers on the steering wheel. She surveyed the surroundings, checking to be sure that there was no one else around to see Angela's nude swimming exhibition. But of course there wouldn't be anyone else. They had the place all to themselves. Julie expected that they would have the run of the place until late summer when the units would fill up with college students from wealthier families.

Angela surfaced, screaming shrilly. "Jesus Christ! It's cold as a witch's tit!" She hopped out of the pool, threw on her shirt and shorts, and ran back to the van with her undergarments clutched tightly in her hand. Through chattering teeth, she said, "Yu-yu-you're ri-ri-right, it's cu-cu-cu-cold."

Julie drove slowly forward, following the narrow little street up an incline and stopping at its zenith so they could look down into the quadrangle behind the clubhouse. It was an elaborate rock garden with a bubbling fountain and imposing statuary, enclosed by thick sharp-edged hedges of dark green.

Forgetting her shivers, Angela cried, "Holy shit! An army of angels!"

"Surprise!" said Julie, laughing like a naughty child. "Mountview Villas, where the angels come to roost."

"How the hell did you talk your dad into *this*? It looks like a fucking cemetery."

"It does not. It's a meditative rock garden. The angels were done by world-famous sculptors. Cornelia, Dickinson, and even Father Brankin, who studied at the Accademia di Belle Arti in Rome. To name just a few."

"That must've set the old man back a pretty penny. But I have to admit, it does look angelic as hell. Very impressive."

"You want to get out and look?"

"Nah. I'm not in a meditative mood. Right now all I want is a hot shower and a hot toddy."

"You're hopeless," said Julie, goosing the gas pedal.

"Hey, can I help it if I do my best meditating on the porcelain throne? All those angels make me as nervous as a ho in church."

"Hopeless," Julie repeated, pretending to be offended.

Less than an hour later, the van was unloaded and all their things were inside the two-story apartment. Julie laid claim to the bedroom overlooking the quadrangle of angels, and Angela took the room across the hall with a towering view of the mountain's tree-lined summit. Both bedrooms had adjoining bathrooms, and Angela was warming up from her cold dip with a steaming shower. Julie had just finished setting up her workstation on the desk in her room (she could've turned the spare bedroom into a study, but she liked having her workstation close to her bed so she could get up and bang away on her laptop in the middle of the night if she felt like it—as she often did). She turned on the power to make sure everything was in good working order. With a low-pitched hum, the system came online, the screen glowing a dark blue.

"All systems go," she said to herself. But she knew that wasn't altogether true. Something was missing. Certain it was more than a silly superstition, Julie had come to think of her angel as her semisecret muse, and now that she no longer felt his benign presence, she was afraid she wouldn't be able to write without Michael at her shoulder, offering silent guidance and inspiration.

"Where are you, Michael?" she whispered. "Why have you deserted me?"

Julie's angelic guardian had been with her since prom night of her senior year in high school. That night as she was climbing into the backseat of a friend's Chevy, she felt a feathery touch on the back of her neck and was suddenly and inexplicably overwhelmed with a feeling of impending doom and abject sadness. Her date asked her what was wrong. And then she knew; and she whispered: "Death car." She got out of the car and tried to talk her friends out of their joyride, but they just scoffed at her and went ahead, leaving Julie and her sullen date on the curb. The four students in the car all died later that night in a head-on collision with a tractor-trailer. Julie realized that the feathery touch and the dire warning must have come from a guardian angel. From then on, she tried to keep herself attuned to the otherworldly realm of angels, and she gradually learned to sense the guardian's presence (it felt something like warm sunlight on a bleak winter's day). He never actually spoke to her; he communicated by means of angelic radiation, which Julie received as premonition, inspiration or validation. Of course, there had been times in the dozen years since prom night when Julie doubted the existence of guardian angels, and times when she thought she must be delusional for having believed that some divine entity was watching over her, but now she had no more doubts. Michael was real. And for some reason, he had left her alone and unprotected. Had she done something to anger him?

Yawning, she rose from her desk to stretch her kinked-up back and then decided to lie down on the bed for a catnap. She was a little road-weary from the trip from Atlanta and felt the need to recharge her biological batteries. She fluffed the pillow, stretched out on the bed and closed her eyes. The sound of running water from across the hall in Angela's bathroom was as soothing as the sound of a gentle rain on a tin roof, and Julie swiftly drifted into the seductive netherworld of sleep.

* * *

She wakes with a start. The computer's screen gives off an eerie green glow in the darkened room. She eases herself off the bed and sits at the desk. She reads the green letters on the black screen.

HE COMES

She hears the droning patter of Angela's shower and the hum of water moving through pipes. She gives her head a shake, trying to clear her sleep-fogged mind. "I didn't write this," she says. "Who did?"

Another line of green typeface appears on the screen.

MICHAEL

"You gotta be shitting me," she says in disbelief. Then she shouts: "Angela! How the hell are you doing this?"

She stares at the screen. "Michael? *My* Michael?"

YES

"This is not real. I'm dreaming is what this is."

DREAM REAL

"Whoa, what the fu—"
All the letters of the next two lines appear simultaneously.

HE CALLS
DONT ANSWER

"I don't understand," she says, her heart drumming against her rib cage. "What're you saying?"

More letters appear onscreen.

ZXXIALIERNVOSLDMKRPZXUY

"Michael? I can't read that. That's gibberish. Michael?"

When no new line appears, Julie begins to tremble with dread. Her teeth chatter, though she is not cold. "Michael? Don't leave me. Please!"

EOKJF;OUASDGVVPEROTU

With tears streaming down her cheeks, Julie places her hands on the screen and whimpers: "Why did you leave me?"

LSBADLKD PLACELAMLZXUFDARKNVNUONEMDCOMEST

The extraneous letters fade away and Julie reads the remaining words.

BAD   PLACE   DARK   ONE   COMES

Before she can speak again, the screen goes dark.

An oozing, suffocating darkness envelops her and she is drawn ir-resistibly into a black chasm . . .

* * *

Wrapping a bath towel around her dripping body, Angela lifted her mug from the bathroom counter and drank the last of her hot toddy, then sloshed some bourbon into the mug and drank it straight. She moved languidly to the bedroom window and gazed out at the forested moun-tainside and at the houses dotting the ridge above her. Hillbilly houses, she thought, inhabited by backwoods in-breeders straight out of *Deliver-ance.* Cow fuckers who tell you to squeal like a pig while they sodomize you. She snickered at her own childish cynicism, then amended the thought: Most of them are probably decent God-fearing people, the same as me—except for the God-fearing part. Though she had been raised in the Methodist church, she had decided early on that if there *was* a God, He would not be the wrathful figure of vengeance the pulpit-pounders liked to portray. No, He would more likely be an It, a cosmic intelligence underpinning everything from the infinitesimal to the infinite. Heaven and Hell were no more than constructs of the frail human mind, and Good and Evil didn't exist outside of human perceptions. Angela had learned that in Philosophy 101. Funny though, that Julie had taken the same course and come away with a totally different outlook. But then, no amount of philosophy could make Jools give up her guardian angel. Old Mikey was her angelic crutch, her soothing delusion. Angela didn't begrudge her that. Whatever gets you through the night, like that old John Lennon song said.

As was often the case, the bourbon put Angela in a philosophical state of mind, so she went across the hall to find an audience for her pregnant pontifications. But her would-be audience was curled up on her bed, catching a few afternoon Z's. "Sweet dreams, Jools," she whispered, and decided a nap wasn't such a bad idea. She went back to her room, tossed off the bath towel and lay down naked on her own bed. *Just a short nap, then I'll explore our new digs.*

* * *

The stone angels wear the pale blush of moonlight and Angela marvels at the way their blank eyes seem to follow her every move as she wanders through the garden of smooth stones. The walls of hedges enclosing the quadrangle are dark and sinister, yet each leaf is a sharply distinct spade-shaped spearhead, stirring imperceptibly in the night air. She doesn't know what possessed her to come out here—alone in the dark and wearing nothing but a towel—to walk among the spooky statuary of mythical beings, but she knows she has made a mistake in doing so. A terrible mistake. Because she now knows she is not alone. Something is moving with her, stalking her, just out of range of her peripheral vision. She feels its presence, its hunger . . .

She pauses in front of a winged fairy seated beside a fountain spouting water and she reaches out to touch the nymph's white-marble flesh. "If I had your wings I'd fly the hell outta here," she says in a voice not quite her own. She suddenly spins around on the axis of her bare heels, hoping to catch sight of whatever is stalking her. *There! Something moving in the moon shadows.* Something there but not there. A ghost?

Angela hastens along the stone footpath, looking for—but not finding—the way out of this haunted garden. The sound of weeping brings her up short. On its knees and bent over an altar of rosy marble, an angel with half-folded wings is weeping into the crook of its stone arm. "My

God, you're alive!" cries Angela. Then it dawns on her: "You're *all* alive."

Wings flutter stiffly, rustling the air. The night sighs with the collective breath of stony sentinels guarding the luminous rocks of mystical geometry. The weeping angel lifts its head. Tears of blood streak the perfect contours of its face. Rivulets of blood flow from the corners of its mouth, and Angela sees the half-eaten corpse of a human infant lying on the altar.

"That's my baby," Angela says, for she knows in her heart that the dead infant somehow evolved from the fetus that a doctor sucked from her womb within the grim walls of an Atlanta abortion clinic three years ago.

"No," says the carnivorous angel, "you gave it to me. She's mine now."

Turning to run from the guilty spectacle of gore, Angela encounters a new horror. From its gothic pedestal, an angel with mammoth musculature steps upon the earth and flutters great wings no longer made of stone. The alpha male of angels towers over Angela and looks down at her with a ferocious aspect. She wants to run but her legs feel like they've turned to statuary stone. Leering at her, the angel speaks in a voice hewn from granite: "Stone to flesh, flesh to stone."

Angela screams when she sees the enormous richly-veined phallus rising from his powerful loins. Cold hands throw her to the ground. The fierce angel falls upon her, wrenches her thighs wide and rips her apart with his ungodly phallus.

All she can do is scream. Then she turns to blood-streaked stone.

* * *

"Jools!"

"Angela!"

They each awoke screaming for the other. They met in the hallway and fell into each other's arms, seeking refuge from their bad dreams, but their desperate embrace offered little solace. They both sensed that some psychic boundary had been breached, that a dark river of nightmares had reached flood-stage and its clammy terrors were about to overflow the banks of the waking world.

They huddled head-to-head in the dim hallway, simultaneously laughing and crying, their tears a warm drizzle on Angela's bare breasts.

CHAPTER
FOUR

HE WAS KNOWN BY MANY NAMES.

In Goat Head Hollow he was called One-Eyed Jack, owing to the fact that he always wore a patch over his empty eye socket.

In the town of Dogwood he was known as The Rambler, or sometimes the Scrambled Rambler, because rambling was what he did and his brains were said to be scrambled (how else to explain his aimless wanderings over hill and dale?).

The inhabitants of the little hamlet of Widow's Ridge referred to him variously as The Wandering Hermit, The Monk (because of his solitary and ascetic lifestyle), Old Scout, or simply Old Edgar. Because the log cabin he called home was closest to Widow's Ridge, some of the more kindly-disposed ridge dwellers thought of him as one of their own, and a few even claimed him as their vagabond mascot.

To the students of Dogwood Community College he was known as Bigfoot, and to many of the younger children of this North Georgia hill country he was called The Bogeyman because he projected a rather frightening, piratical appearance, and because some parents used the specter of the eccentric rambler to scare their youngsters out of venturing into the woods and getting lost. "Stay out of the woods or the Bogeyman"—The Rambler; Old Edgar; Old Scout; The Mad Monk—"will get you," a parent might warn.

This man of many names had been christened Asa Edgar by his parents as they dipped their newborn boy into cold river currents. To this day Asa retained a vivid memory of that baptism, even though his mother had told him years ago that it wasn't possible for newborn babies to remember anything. His mother had been mistaken. He *did*

remember. But he hadn't argued the point; his father was a strict disci-
plinarian and not one to spare the rod, the belt, the switch, or whatever
was handy at the time of the boy's offense, and arguing with a parent
was most certainly a violation of the "Honor Thy Mother and Father"
Commandment.

As an only child, Asa learned to keep a lot of things to himself. He
saw things others in his rural orbit apparently didn't see, and he learned
to keep those things to himself as well, because he didn't like to be called
"Crazy Asa" by the other children in the one-room schoolhouse. Rather
than become a social outcast, he became a loner by his own choice, a
follower of his own inner lights. While the other kids played their silly
games, Asa took to the woods and found contentment in solitude. The
creatures of the woodlands were his companions, and the expansive
canopy of trees became the boundless cathedral wherein he worshiped
Great Earth Mother. With his mind afire with ecstatic visions, he grew
into manhood. When his parents died he sold their house in Widow's
Ridge and built himself a log cabin in the deep woods near the top of his
ancestral mountain. The Great Mother sustained him. Hunting, trapping
and fishing put food on his humble table, and when he needed money for
supplies, he did odd jobs for people in Widow's Ridge or in Dogwood.
Once, back in '89, he worked as tracker for Sheriff Gladstone and helped
the law track down an escaped convict who had taken to these hills.

Now he was sixty years old, and he could feel his life winding down.
While he maintained enough physical strength to meet the rugged demands of his chosen way of life, some of his inner fire had gone out of
him. Worse than that, Earth Mother no longer shared new secrets with
him. His visions no longer blazed so gloriously. It was almost as if the
earth itself were losing its magic. More likely, the loss of magic was his.

Asa sat on a hollow log beside a small stream of clear water. He
turned up the patch, uncovering his empty eye socket, then dipped his
hands into the stream and washed his face and bushy beard. The water
was cold but it did not refresh him. "Is this my weird?" he asked the
mountain stream. "To be hollowed out like a soulless ghoul?"

He could hear no answer in the gurgling flow.

"Mother? Why am I deaf to your songs, though my ears still work?"
He wanted to cry, to mingle his tears with the streaming tears of the
mountain, but there was no crying in him. He felt nothing but a crushing emptiness within his barrel-chested trunk.

Then it came to him. A long-forgotten conversation with his

birth-mother rose from the shallows of his timeworn memory, triggered by his utterance of the word "weird." Closing his eye, he saw the fire blazing in the hearth and heard his mother's reedy voice.

"Asa, it come to me tonight what your weird is," she said.

"What's a weird, Mama?" He knew from experience that whenever his mother got that faraway look in her eyes, she had been consulting her oracle. It was said that his mother was a witchy woman, but Asa knew his father wouldn't abide witchy doings, so he therefore knew his mother could not be a witch. She just knew how to read some things that others couldn't. She could read the stars, the clouds, tea leaves and even the bumps on your head, if she took a mind to.

"Your weird is your destiny," she explained. "It's what a body's put on this earth to do."

"Then what's *my* weird?" young Asa asked.

His mother gazed into the fire as though she might be reading something in the leaping flames. Finally she scrunched up her wrinkled mouth and answered. "Your weird is to be the sentry to these hills."

"Like a lookout?"

"That's right. A guardian, though you surely ain't no angel." Her thin lips formed a skinny smile.

"What do I look out for?" Blue-coated Yankees marched through his imagination. Of all the tales his mother told by the fire, he liked stories of the Civil War the best. Her shivery ghost stories gave him nightmares and he preferred not to hear them.

"Anything bad that might come your way. Anything that would harm you, your home or your people." Then his mother put a hand on his shoulder and said, "And most especially look out for the Beast that comes out of the earth."

"You mean like a bear? A mountain lion?"

"No, son. I'm talking about an evil thing that crawls out of the darkest pit to prey on the innocent."

"You're talking about the Devil!" Asa couldn't contain his sudden agitation. The fireplace suddenly became a window open to the fiery depths of Hell. If his mother's hands hadn't been on his shoulders, he would have jumped up and run out of the house.

"No. Satan is a fallen angel. This Beast is a *pagan god*. Older than the hills."

Asa instinctively grasped the concept of a beastly god, and he asked what he was supposed to do if he should see such a being.

"I reckon you'll know iffen the time ever comes. I pray to God in Heaven you will."

Then with an admonition never to speak of his weird to anyone else—not even to his father—his mother tossed another log onto the fire and that was the end of the conversation.

As Asa grew older, he more or less dismissed the idea of a beastly god, but the idea of being the sentry of the hills appealed to him and fitted well with his rambling way of life.

Now, Asa the old man looked upon the surface of the mountain stream and saw the ghostly reflection of the hearth fire his mother had laid that cold night so many years ago, and he shivered. "Is it my weird that's come upon me like the cold fingers of death? But I'm old and brittle. My wick is burnt short."

A mist formed above the fiery water, and within the mist he saw the nebulous face of his dead mother, saw her gaunt lips moving, heard the watery echo of her raspy words: "Your weird."

As the misty vision evaporated, Asa stood on creaking bones and sniffed the air for the scent of the Beast. His twitching nostrils picked up an odd earthy odor he couldn't identify, and he knew at once that the scent had been there for days, hovering just below his awareness. Age had dulled his sharp sense of smell. He squatted down by the stream, plucked two pebbles from the bottom and stuck a pebble into each nostril. Then he chose a larger pebble and stuck it in his mouth and sucked on it. Breathing through his mouth, the hard taste and smell of the earth filled his senses. After a few minutes he spat the pebble out and removed the smaller ones from his nostrils. He inhaled deeply, then sniffed the air again, his senses cleansed and suddenly keener. Beneath the earthy smell was the pungent, musky odor of a rutting beast, definitely not a deer or any animal with which he was familiar.

Downwind and a long way off from the origin of the smell, he picked up his hickory walking stick, put his eye patch down over his vacant socket, and ambled off to meet his weird.

"So, this is what a pagan god smells like," he said to the late-afternoon sky. A moment later the sky responded by dropping a dead sparrow at his feet.

CHAPTER FIVE

ROURKE OPENED AN ENVELOPE of headache powder and deposited the bitter grains on his tongue, then washed them down with a shot of filmy black coffee that had gone cold on his desk. The headache had come on during his visit to the hospital to see Sheriff Gladstone, and it had grown progressively worse as the day wore on. He tucked his chin to his shoulder and sniffed the armpit of his shirt, confirming that the stink was his own.

"Alice, I'm going home to take a shower and put on a clean shirt."

Alice Marsh looked up from the dispatcher's desk, her brow wrinkled with puzzlement. "A shower?"

"Yeah. And don't look at me like that. I'm not losing it, I just need a shower. When you paged me this morning I was out for my morning run and I didn't take the time for a shower. Now I'm beginning to offend myself."

"Why don't you wash up in the lavatory? I could help you with those hard to reach places." She winked and flashed him a provocative smile.

Ordinarily, Rourke would have delighted in her flirtation, but now he was not in the mood; the events of the day were weighing too heavily on him, and the burden of his responsibilities as Acting Sheriff only added to the onerous weight. He needed some time alone to think things through and sort them out. He grabbed his hat and headed for the door. "I'll be back in less than an hour," he said.

Alice plumped her lips. "You're no fun."

On the drive home he reviewed the conversation he'd had with Sheriff Gladstone this morning. With his head bandaged and his eyes blackened, Gladstone looked like a fat raccoon in a turban. The nurse warned Rourke that her patient was "off on a little trip to the Twilight Zone," and that he probably wouldn't make a whole lot of sense.

When Gladstone saw Rourke with his hat in his hand, he studied him with a lopsided expression, then said, "Ta hell ya doin' here, Robber, ya sick? Ya don't look so good."

"How you doing, Sheriff?" asked Rourke, standing at the foot of the bed.

"Me? Hell, I can't get myself up. You got your pocketknife with ya? Cut these damn ropes off me, will ya? I'm spoze to be fishin' the lake."

Rourke saw the leather restraints binding Gladstone's wrists to the hospital bed. Not a good sign. He moved to the side of the bed. "Sorry, boss, I don't have my knife with me."

"Shit, son, you outta uniform without ya got a knife." The lid of his left eye was droopy. His lips were cracked and caked with a chalky mixture of dead skin and dried saliva. A few pieces of white lint clung to the gray stubble sprouting from his chubby cheeks.

"Sheriff, I need to ask you a few questions. About what happened between you and your wife."

"Gladys? Woman's a goddamn saint, sho nuff."

"She is a fine woman," Rourke agreed. "But why would such a fine woman hit her husband over the head with a skillet?"

Gladstone's droopy eyelid twitched as a look of confusion twisted up his face. "Damnedest thing, I tell ya what's the truth! That yowling! On and on. It run her crazy. Right outside the house. Scariest thing I ever heard."

"What yowling?"

"Gladys . . . is she all right? I gotta see her. You find your pocket-knife?" Gladstone was becoming more and more agitated, yanking his arms against the wrist restraints. His face reddened and a wildness came into his eyes.

"Easy now, Sheriff," Rourke said, putting a hand on Gladstone's shoulder. "We'll find her for you. Everything's going to be all right. You just take it easy. Get some rest."

Gladstone sank back into his pillow, his eyelids fluttering, then closing. Thinking he had fallen asleep, Rourke tiptoed toward the door.

"Robber? Ya bring me them worms?" The croak in his voice brought to mind a huge bullfrog.

"Yeah, I got 'em," he said by way of humoring the man. "Get some rest now, and I'll meet you at the lake."

"Good boy," Gladstone said, closing his eyes again. "Teach ya how to bait a hook the right way."

That was the way Rourke left him. Gone fishing in the Twilight Zone.

And from there, Rourke's day hadn't gone any better. When he got back to the office, he learned that Sarah Melton was missing. The young schoolteacher hadn't shown up for her summer-school classes at Dogwood High, and subsequently the door to her duplex was found standing open, her car in the driveway, but she was nowhere to be found.

Then truck driver Clark Ellroy reported that after a week on the road, he had come home in the middle of the day to an empty house in Widow's Ridge; his wife Sybil was missing, and he suspected foul play "because she's a real homebody and she woulda left me a note if she was going somewhere."

First, Judy Lynn Bowen; then Gladys Gladstone; and now Sarah Melton and Sybil Ellroy. What the hell was going on? Three women missing from Widow's Ridge, and one, Gladys Gladstone, missing from Dogwood. Did they, Rourke wondered, have anything in common? Were they members of a secret cult? Victims of a mass kidnapping?

Rourke was at a loss; he could come up with no reasonable explanation for the disappearances, and he found nothing to link them except the coincidence of timing. If it *was* coincidence.

He drove up in front of his secluded house as the sun was edging toward the western horizon. Lucy Fur got up from her favorite spot on the front porch and trotted down to meet him.

"Hey there, girl," he said, dropping to one knee and hugging the wolfhound. "How's my Lucy?"

Lucy licked his face and made guttural whining sounds, expressive of her simple joy.

"How's my best girl? Huh?" He grappled playfully with her, then headed toward the house. He paused at the front door, looked back at the cloud-streaked sunset, and for some inexplicable reason, he felt gooseflesh crawling up his back. He shook it off and went inside for a quick shower. As much as he wanted this long day to end, he dreaded nightfall.

* * *

"Dr. Knott?"

The voice pulled him back from the monochromatic chaos, but the bizarre slashes of imagery stayed with him, even as he looked away from the wall-drawing above the empty bed and turned toward the person calling his name a second time.

"Alfred Thorn," said the tall man with the close-cropped hair, short white beard and amiable affect. "From the college?"

"Oh, yes. Of course," said Knott, stepping forward to shake the robust man's proffered hand. He remembered the man's face—it was hard to forget a guy who was the spitting image of Papa Hemingway—but he couldn't recall ever having spoken to him, nor could he recall the man's position at the college. "Good to see you."

"Some of my students still talk about you," said Thorn. "You made quite a dent on their impressionable minds. Your lectures on abnormal psych are becoming the stuff of legend."

"Well, that's certainly flattering. I think." The man's grip was powerful and Knott was glad when he released his hand.

"You don't remember me, do you?" Thorn continued to smile. His Hale-Fellow-Well-Met countenance made it clear that he was not the sort to take offense at being overlooked or forgotten.

"I remember your face," Knott admitted, "but I don't recall your department."

"Anthropology. In fact, I *am* the Anthropology Department. Diminutive but not insignificant." Thorn chuckled.

"So, Professor, what are you doing in our neck of the woods?"

"I'm here to visit one of your patients, a dear friend of mine. Sharyn Rampling. How's she doing?"

"I'm sure she'll be happy to see you."

"Oh, I'm sorry," said Thorn, bringing his hand to his mouth. "I shouldn't have asked you that. Patient confidentiality. I withdraw the question. Though she's like family to me."

"Well, don't let me keep you from your visit," Knott said in a polite attempt to send the professor on his way.

But Thorn didn't seem to hear him. He had shifted his gaze to the wall-drawing and was obviously lost in contemplation of the red jumble of lines and shadings. "Fascinating," he said. "Am I to assume a patient produced that, or is one of your staff experimenting with hallucinogens?"

Knott couldn't hold back his laughter. He was beginning to like Thorn. The man's good-natured humor was infectious. "The former, I assure you. As a matter of fact, a catatonic patient. She came out of it long enough to create this modest masterpiece. Even gave it a title, as you can see."

"Tell me, Doctor, what do you see in it?" Thorn continued to gaze into the drawing, fingering the bristles of his beard as if to stimulate new insights.

"I honestly can't tell you. It's just random slashes and swirls of crayon, yet . . . if you look at it long enough . . . there's a suggestion of . . . I don't know what. But there's something there that draws you into it."

"Quite so," Thorn agreed. "You could cut that off the wall, frame it and hang in The Metropolitan Museum of Art and those twitch-nosed critics would go ga-ga over it, comparing it to early Picasso." Thorn moved closer to the drawing. "You know, it does have something in common with certain cave drawings I've seen. A primitive archetypal quality, a resonance . . . Sorry. I got carried away there for a moment. So where is the artist?"

"In a rocking chair on the front porch. The nursing staff takes her out every day for fresh air. The worst thing for a catatonic patient is—"

"By God," interrupted Thorn, "I think I see it! Look here."

The professor stepped closer to the wall and pointed to a dense blob of color amid radiating squiggles and swirls. "See the face? The horns? And here, here's the body. And these globs of color down here are the feet. Hooves, I should say."

Knott was caught up in Thorn's enthusiasm and tried with limited success to follow his spirited explication of the drawing. "What do you suppose it is? The devil?"

"Maybe, but I don't think so. It's rather more like that creature of ancient myth, the satyr."

"Satyr," repeated Knott. "That would certainly give it a sexual connotation. A satyr being the male counterpart to the nymphomaniac, in traditional psychiatric terms."

"Yes, yes, and look here. This suggests an erect phallus, does it not?"

"Possibly." Knott's innate skepticism came to the fore and he suddenly felt that Thorn's interpretation was a little too tidy, too easy. Too disturbing. "But the patient is well past the age of raging hormones."

"Yes, but in the realm of mythical archetypes, timelessness rules. The ancient gods are ageless. As is the human spirit, if you believe in that concept."

For Knott, the spell of discovery was now broken. "Well, Professor, I'm afraid we just went beyond my area of expertise. If you'll excuse me, I've got patients to see."

"Surely," said Thorn, following the doctor out of the room and into the corridor. "I'm curious, Dr. Knott. What do you make of the title the old girl gave her work? *Helling.*"

Knott shrugged. "Well, it does look hellish, if not satanic. What do you make of it?"

"That's the really intriguing thing," said Thorn, lowering his voice and speaking in a conspiratorial tone. "I've been looking into the local folklore, just for my own amusement, in lieu of a summer vacation, and I just recently came across that term. The Helling is some mysterious thing only whispered about by some of the local antiquarians. Whenever I press for more information, the seasoned citizens inevitably clam up. It's as if they're sworn to secrecy. As if there is a sinister history here, buried beneath some cryptic legend."

Dr. Knott said, "So we may assume my elderly patient knows about it and was compelled to express it in her artwork. You're right, Professor, it is intriguing."

"Would it be all right if I took a photograph of that drawing?"

His first inclination was to refuse the professor's request. Instead, he said, "As long as you don't shoot any of the patients, it wouldn't be violating confidentiality. And of course the artist must remain anonymous."

"Excellent. My camera's in my car." Thorn was already moving toward the exit.

"Professor?" said Knott. "I'd like a print myself."

"You got it, Doc."

CHAPTER
SIX

SHARYN RAMPLING'S DAY BRIGHTENED considerably when Alfred Thorn walked into her room and flashed his Cheshire-cat smile. She snapped her book shut and stood to greet him. He engulfed her in a vigorous bear hug and she happily yielded to his hardy show of physical affection.

"How're you doing, dear?" he asked as they finally disengaged.

"Better, now that you're here. I think I'm going stir crazy. I'm not used to this confinement."

"But other than that, you're . . . okay?"

"I'm not crazy, if that's what you're hinting at. Dr. Knott says I probably just need my medication adjusted."

"Well, anything's better than an attitude adjustment, eh?"

Sharyn laughed. "You're the craziest one in the room, Alfie. Maybe you should check yourself in. I think there's a vacancy next door."

Thorn brought his finger to his lips. "Shhh . . . That's our little secret, Professor Rampling. I don't have the time for a good head-shrinking. I'm on the trail of something *verrry* interesting."

"Really," she said, smiling sardonically. "I can see it now. The cover story in *The American Journal of Anthropology*: 'How I Spent My Summer Vacation' by Alfred Thorn, Esquire, PhD, and all those other letters you're so fond of putting after your name."

"Touché," he said, clutching his hand over his heart. "But seriously, Sharyn, I *am* onto something."

"Well, have a seat and tell me all about it. As if I could stop you." She sat on the bed and waved him to the chair. "Anything to get my mind off myself."

He drew the chair close to the bed, sat down and leaned forward.

"You sometimes teach mythology, don't you?"

"Yes, but I'm hardly an authority on the subject. Last quarter they had me teaching Business English and Grammar, though I don't know the first thing about business."

Thorn waved off her disclaimer. "What do you know about the Great God Pan?"

"Oh, I was afraid you were going to ask me something I didn't know, something about some obscure Asian god or some such. Actually, I know quite a lot about Pan."

"Well?"

"Well, what do you want to know? Specific questions would be helpful. You're a brilliant man, Alfred, but I sometimes wonder how you ever got through all your schooling, with your bull-in-a-China-shop approach."

"Start with the basics. Pretend I'm an ignorant student who thinks Nike is just a brand-name shoe."

"Ha! All right then, class. Listen up and learn. You *will* be responsible for this material." She winked at Thorn, then proceeded with her mock lecture. "Now, keep in mind that ancient cultures borrowed liberally from one another to the extent that it is very difficult if not impossible to trace the origins of many mythological figures. Pan is no exception to that rule. He was one of the oldest of the Greek gods, and the Greeks claimed that Pan was the same as the Egyptian god Amon-Ra, the supreme god of the sun. Some scholars believe the legend of Pan actually began with Pancika, the Hindu fertility god.

"The Greeks were unsure of Pan's parentage. Some said Zeus was his father, others said Hermes sired him. But they all agreed that Pan was born with horns on his head and with the hindquarters of a goat. So, Pan was part anthropomorphic god and part beast. He was raised by wood nymphs called dryads. Even as a youth, Pan was a horny little devil, and he often subjected the nymphs to his lustful passions. I suppose you could say the nymphs brought out the beast in him. Our horny hero went on to become the god of woodlands and pastures, king of woodland beasts and ruler of the Arcadian satyrs. Satyrs, you will recall, were those half-man half-goat dudes with relentless erections and a taste for wine and orgies. They were the original party animals."

Thorn let loose a boisterous laugh. "Oh, you're good," he said. "You would have even the untamed students eating out of your hand."

Sharyn nodded and smiled appreciatively, then continued. "Pan was often identified with Dionysus, the Greek god of wine and revelry. Now

Dionysus, too, had his following of satyrs, but he also had a band of priestesses known as Maenads. Named after Maenalus, a holy Arcadian mountain where Dionysus shepherded his odd flock, the Maenads were 'wild women' whose drunken orgies usually ended with the killing and eating of male victims. Our hero had carte blanche carnal knowledge of these Dionysian Maenads. As far as I'm concerned—and more than a few scholars agree—Pan and Dionysus are virtually interchangeable, one and the same.

"The legend of Pan has had quite an impact on our culture. Many words and phrases we use today can be traced back to the god Pan. The best example is the word *panic*. Pan was said to have had a dreadful cry that could strike such fear in those who heard it as to cause them to—"

She fell silent with a shudder of cold revelation. The echo of the mysterious, animalistic cry that had so terrified her now reverberated along the paths of auditory memory.

"Sharyn? What is it? Are you all right?" Thorn moved to the edge of the chair.

She nodded, took a calming breath of air and forced herself to continue, though her own voice sounded hollow to her now as she recited from memory. "Caused them to panic and flee in terror. Uh, the Greek word for tragedy literally means *goat song,* after the horned and hoofed Pan. And then there's *panoply*, from ceremonial processions in the ancient City of Pan or Panopolis. But perhaps the most telling legacy of Pan can be seen in the traditional view of the Devil. That's right, boys and girls, Satan got his horns, hooves and wicked character from none other than Pan. Clearly, the medieval church used the pagan god as the prototype for their Ruler of Hell. And why do you think Satanists use the goat's head in their black ceremonies? That's right. Pan became the image of the Devil, and his satyrs became Satan's demons, thanks to a few brooding monks with too much time on their hands.

"As the centuries went by, Pan's reputation lost much of its bite. You've seen him in cartoons as a cute, harmless little guy playing his hornpipe as he dances merrily through the woods. Thanks to Romantic poets like Byron and Shelley, and to America's Disneyland mentality, Pan has been reduced to little more than a castrated cartoon. We should not forget that the *original* Pan was a dreadful god who inspired abject terror in the hearts of mere mortals. Any questions?"

Thorn softly applauded.

Sharyn stood and went to the window, trying to conceal her inner turmoil from her friend and colleague. Darkness was gathering outside, piling up like thunderheads before a storm.

"Are you sure you're all right?" Thorn asked.

"Yes, I'm just feeling a little shaky, that's all."

"Oh, shit!" He suddenly hammered his leg with his fist. "It was a panic attack that brought you here. I'm sorry, Sharyn. I'm a complete ass. I didn't mean—"

She rounded on him, startling him to silence with the swiftness of her move. "It's all right, Alfred. Stop coddling me. I *hate* that."

"Sorry," he said in a small voice.

Sharyn's sudden flash of anger had, for the moment at least, checked her fear. If anger was an antidotal defense against another attack of panic, then she was prepared to be one pissed-off bitch. "And stop apologizing," she added.

Thorn nodded meekly and seemed to draw himself in. The sight of such a big, strapping male cringing like a scolded animal amused Sharyn, but she didn't dare let herself laugh; she was determined to maintain her angry edge. It seemed to be her only real defense against the outer darkness and the dangerous thing it concealed.

"What's with this sudden fascination with Pan? And what is this 'verry interesting' thing you're so on about?"

"Ah, it's nothing, really. You know me. I just—"

"Don't bullshit me, Alfred. Tell me."

"All right." He laced his fingers over his lap and regarded her warily. "I've been digging into the local folklore and I think I might've struck paydirt. It all started with a conversation I had a couple of months ago with Howard Bently, our illustrious historian. You know Howard. A meticulous researcher, when he's sober. A crushing bore when he's in his cups. Well, one night over a bottle of his best scotch, Howard regaled me with his knowledge of local history, and to my great surprise and relief, he was anything but boring. He told me he had come upon some documents from the Civil War era suggestive of a hidden history of Widow's Ridge. The old boy referred to his documents as 'historical apocrypha,' and went on for the better part of an hour about some horrendous incident alluded to in one of these documents. He said he found proof that Widow's Ridge is *not* so named because its married women were widowed by the war. Howard is convinced that story was concocted to hide what really happened."

"What on earth does all this have to do with a character from Greek mythology?" Sharyn was having a hard time keeping the lid on her escalating impatience.

"Nothing, as far as Howard Bently is concerned. He deals in historical facts, not myth. But this is where I enter the picture. When Howard showed me the personal journal of Reverend John T. Waller, I made the connection myself. And since then, I've been delving into the local folklore and legend, looking for further connections. You see, Sharyn, when a community—or a society—conspires to hide a certain truth, that truth will inevitably find new avenues into the open. Even if it has to come out in the form of legend. Or myth. And I think that's exactly what happened in Widow's Ridge. In short, I think some educated, creative soul back in the eighteen-sixties reinvented a Pan-like legend as an alternative to a scandalous historical incident. The legend survived for over a hundred years, but now it seems that the current crop of elders want it to die with them. I've found no evidence that they've passed it along to their younger generations."

"Why would they want to let a legend die? Folklore is a big part of the heritage of these hill people."

Thorn shrugged. "I suspect it may be because we live in a time when myth and legend are no longer necessary. The wonders of technology have replaced the need for mythological wonders. Apollo is no longer a god, it's a rocket to the moon. The ancient world had all manner of gods, heroes and monsters. What do we have? Big Foot, alien abductions and a reanimated Elvis."

"I believe there are still things that go bump in the night," she said. "Even if they're just representations of the unknown."

"That's true, but these days it's the monsters we know that terrify us. The wacked-out kids who walk into their school and start blowing away their classmates with automatic weapons. The family man who kills his wife and kids, then takes his rampage public when he walks into a high-rise building and randomly guns down office workers. A suicide bomber with mind ablaze with religious delusion. The monsters we know are *us*. And they're all too human. We don't have to make them up."

Sharyn was beginning to relax a little. Her fear had subsided and her protective anger no longer seemed necessary, for the time being. Thorn's apparent obsession with some local legend had captured her imagination and stirred her natural curiosity. She wanted to know more. "So what was in the preacher's journal that led you to back to Pan?"

After a moment's hesitation, he reached into his shirt pocket and pulled out a small white envelope. "You can read it for yourself," he said as he gave it to her. "But be warned: some of it is rather grim."

She slipped her fingers into the unsealed envelope and extracted several sheets of folded paper. She sat on the edge of the bed and crossed her ankles.

"Those are photocopies of key pages of the reverend's journal," he told her. "Howard wouldn't let me borrow the actual journal, but he was good enough to let me copy some of it."

Sharyn unfolded the three pages and smoothed them on her lap. Reverend Waller's script was penned in bold cursive, embellished with fussily flamboyant strokes, but it was legible.

"While you peruse those, I'm going to see if I can prevail upon that pretty young nurse to give me a cup of coffee," said Thorn. "Would you like one?"

"No, thank you. Patients aren't allowed caffeine, and I don't need anything that might keep me awake tonight. You go ahead."

As Thorn eased out of the room, Sharyn switched on the lamp on her bedside table and began to read the excerpts from the journal of the long-dead preacher.

20 June 1866

Journey from Talking Rock uneventful. Sheltered last night at the Irving House. Brother Irving and his family being of Good Christian stock, it was a fortifying sojourn. Mistress Irving provided a delightful repast, though her apple cobbler sorely tested my ability to resist the sin of gluttony. The Irvings are recovering quite well from the ravages of The War. Their orchard will doubtless produce a bountiful crop. God has returned their son Jacob to the bosom of the family, and though he lost a leg and an arm to The Cause, young Jacob's faith remains strong. From the Lord all blessings do flow.

21 June 1866

Disaster has struck! A fearsome storm caught me on the trail North of Mt. Oglethorpe and unleashed a bolt of lightning which caused my horse to unsaddle me and to leave the trail in her bolt. The Lord was with me and saw that I sustained only minor bruises and bumps, but my horse broke her leg and I had to put her down with my Merciful pistol. Old

Abigail was a fine mount and I am saddened by her demise. I am now faced with the unpleasant prospect of traveling afoot. Though my arrival be late, I shall march into Dogwood with my countenance aglow with God's Glory.

22 June 1866

Holy Father protect me from the evil I have seen! My journey has taken me into a wilderness of depravity, lo! unto the very Mouth of Hell! A day's hike delivered me into the vicinity of the rustic little hamlet of no appellation which sits high on the ridge over Dogwood and environs. As I departed the trodden path to venture into the thick heart of the woods in order to partake of a cooling stream therein, I came upon a sight only Satan Himself could have rendered. Squatting on bare haunches like a feral beast was a denuded girl-child whose tender age could not have exceeded thirteen years. So enraptured was she in her ghastly act that she at first took no notice of me.

I hesitate to commit these words to paper, though I know I must. The child was tearing raw flesh from a severed human arm with her teeth and was devouring the bloody meat! Her golden hair was a nest of wild curls, the lower tresses streaked with the blood of the bodiless arm and hand.

My mind grappled for a rational explanation for the manifest obscenity. My mental grappling ended when the feral girl saw me and I in my turn saw the Bloodlust in her wild eyes. Thereupon she tossed aside the mutilated arm and sprang to her feet. While I was mindful of the danger to my person, my attention fixed on the sight of a gold wedding band on the marital finger of the masculine hand adjoining the severed arm. That gold ring brought home the Reality of the Abomination. The wild child regarded me fiercely, as with great hunger, and I knew she was taking my measure.

God forgive my murderous intentions, but I drew my pistol and aimed it at the child's budding breast. I don't know whether I could have released her soul from its Hellish bonds but I know that question will always remain with me. The girl scampered off into the underbrush, forsaking her ungodly feast.

After collecting my wits, I removed the wedding band from the dead hand and put it in my pocket in hopes of finding someone to identify its former owner. I buried the arm in the soft forest floor and marked the piecemeal grave with a flat rock shaped vaguely like Florida. I departed with alacrity, for I sensed the wanton stares of unseen watchers.

23 June 1866

Dogwood is abuzz with Rumor and wild speculation. Even the soberest of citizens have been seized by the unexplained abandonment of the neighboring hamlet on the ridge. I confess I am in part responsible for the uproar, but I believe I am blameless in my heart for I acted out of Christian Charity.

After my encounter with the handmaiden of Satan, I hastened to the nameless ridge village and found the place deserted, save for a handful of small children, hungry and terrified in their abandonment by neglectful parents, and one bedridden old woman who babbled incoherently about a murderous band of wild women, led by her hated daughter-in-law. The woman was plainly feebleminded, but her confused babblings were seized upon by the gossips of Dogwood and the fabulous tale spread like a fire in the wild. The orphaned children were rounded up and taken into the homes of charitable Dogwoodians. Search parties were formed and the surrounding hills were combed for any sign of the missing adult population of the ridge hamlet (which was said to number five and thirty).

The searchers are still out, but I could not join them. God forgive me! but I am afraid to venture back into those woods for fear that new horrors may await me there.

24 June 1866

I am a man of some education. I have devoted much of my life to study of Holy Scripture. I have taken it upon myself to spread the Word of God far and wide. Why is it that now words fail me? How is it then that I feel so inadequate, so ignorant in the face of Manifest Evil? If this be a test of my faith, I tremble with fear that I shall be found wanting. I am unable to sleep, unable to eat. This humble servant of

God grows weak, haunted by the vision of that feral child devouring flesh of her own kind. And now there are new visions to torment me. Though I did not see the dreadful sights myself, the descriptions of those who did have left their taint in my soul. The searchers found the dismembered remains of mass slaughter scattered in the woods surrounding the ridge hamlet. In most cases the flesh had been largely stripped from the bones, the limbs hacked away from the bodies as with an axe blade. As all the victims were male, we can now account for the menfolk missing from the hamlet, but what of the females? And what, Dear God, happened to the heads of the males? All decapitated, no heads found.

Could the feebleminded crone's tale be true? Did the women of the hamlet go on a murderous rampage and slaughter their own menfolk? Few here in Dogwood believe such. Yet the women remain missing and no one has posited a credible explanation for the Butchery. Would that this be but a dream and I a feverish dreamer!

Sharyn reread the last line, then folded the pages of photocopy and stuffed them back into the envelope, noticing a slight tremor in her hands.

"Well?" Thorn's voice startled her; she had been so absorbed in her reading of the dead man's journal that she had not seen him come back into the room. "You see why I connected the reverend's writings to the Dionysian myth of Pan, don't you?"

She nodded. "The Maenads."

"Exactly. The suggestion is too strong to ignore. A band of mad-women tearing male victims limb from limb and devouring them in drunken tribute to the horned god of the woodlands. Without question, the Maenads."

"But if your working theory is that the myth was used to cover up what really happened and to blame it on a woodland god, then what *did* happen? And what about the missing women? Were they ever found?"

"Oh yes," he said after slurping some coffee from a Styrofoam cup. "The women turned up all right. Most of them, anyway. According to Reverend Waller's subsequent entries, the womenfolk returned under cover of darkness and were found back in their homes the next morning. When asked where they had been, not a one of them seemed to know they had been gone for a number of days. A few of them related strange dreams of particular vividness, dreams of bloodshed and violence, but most of them said they remembered nothing at all, and even denied having been gone in the first place. And none of them seemed disturbed by the absence of their menfolk. Some claimed their husbands never came home from the war, others said their mates had been killed by wild animals."

He sat in the chair and crossed his long legs. "As to what really happened and *why* it happened, I haven't worked that out yet. That's why I've been trying to get more information from the elders of Widow's Ridge. But they're a tightlipped bunch of biddies. It was only by happenstance that Professor Bently found Waller's journal. He was going through boxes of old documents—letters and the like, donated years ago to the local historical society and then stored in the cellar of the Dogwood library and forgotten—when he happened upon the reverend's journal."

"Maybe the reverend was delusional," Sharyn hypothesized. "Or maybe he was trying his hand at fiction. Have you considered that?"

"Of course. But let's say the old guy *was* crazy as a shithouse mouse. That still doesn't account for what happened to the men of Widow's Ridge. Bently checked the official records of the Confederacy and the Death Registries of Arcadia County, but he found only one man from the ridge village who died in the war. Something happened back there in 1866. Something for which there is no official record. Just the journal of a circuit-riding preacher. An incident some refer to as 'The Helling.'" Thorn put down his coffee, leaned forward in his chair and took both of her hands into his. "Are you ready for the kicker, Sharyn? The amazing thing I saw in a room down the hall on my way to visit you?"

She nodded, though she wasn't sure she wanted to hear what he was about to tell her.

"An elderly catatonic patient, a female, drew a picture on the wall—in crayon, mind you—of a Pan-like figure and labeled it *Helling.* Dr. Knott said she came out of her catatonic state just long enough to do the drawing. Is that not fantastic? Check it out for yourself. Room 202."

She snatched her hands away and said, "I don't want to see it."

"Sharyn? What is it? Did I—"

"Alfred, you're my closest friend," she said as she moved to the center of her bed, leaned her back against the headboard and hugged her knees to her chest. "You know most of my personal history and you know that without medication, *I* would be crazy as a shithouse mouse. But believe me when I tell you, I am not having a manic episode now. I am not delusional. I'm *scared.* I admitted myself here because I heard something that literally scared the piss out of me, and I can't tell you what made that awful sound. All I know is that it was the most terrifying sound I've ever heard, and it caused me to have a *panic* attack. And now you come here with your stories of Maenads in Widow's Ridge, of mass murder and cannibalism."

"Sharyn, I—"

"No, I'm *not* crazy, but I have this irrational fear that maybe there *is* something out there right now, calling to *me*, perhaps trying to make me into one of his madwomen. Doesn't that sound crazy to you? It does to me, but I know *I am not crazy*." She rested her forehead on her knees.

Thorn worried his chin whiskers. His brow furrowed in concern. "What did it sound like? Describe it for me."

"Like a hundred wild animals screaming with one voice. Powerful. Compelling. Entrancing . . . It had a physical effect on me I can't adequately put into words. It clouded my mind, took away my will. It pulled at me like a magnet, but I was paralyzed with fear. Thank God."

"And your doctor says it's because you need your medication adjusted."

"Yes, that's his initial impression. But I don't believe that's it. I would like to believe it, but it just doesn't ring true. I've been on lithium a long time and I've had to have the dosage adjusted before, but I never ever experienced anything remotely like this. Not even when I was full-blown manic. I'm sure my lab-work will bear me out."

"Where were you when you heard this . . . call of the wild?"

"Home. Quietly reading poetry."

"And your house sits at the edge of the woods," he said. "And correct me if I'm wrong, but there's nothing *but* woodland between your house and Widow's Ridge."

"Right. Actually, I'm just outside Dogwood city limits. That new development—what's it called? Mountain Villas?"

"Mountview Villas."

"Whatever. I think it's a little closer to Widow's Ridge, but it's a couple or three miles off to the side of my house and a little higher up the mountain, so it's not really between me and the ridge. But what's your point?"

"I guess I don't have a point, love," said Thorn. "I'm just thinking out loud. Pointless speculation, I suppose. But still . . ."

"But still, you're entertaining the absurd notion that a mythological creature is alive and well, and living in those woods," she said. "I know. I am too."

"For the record," Thorn said with exaggerated bluster, "I am a man of science, and as such, I most certainly would not engage in fanciful speculation of that sort. But off the record?" He spread his large hands. "I'm thinking the same thing you are. Thinking but not believing."

A cold tingle ran up Sharyn's back and crawled into her scalp. She shuddered, then rubbed her arms as if to warm herself.

"For the sake of argument," he said, "let's play this out. Let's say there is an aeons-old god roaming our hills. Perhaps he's come from another time, or another physical dimension. According to the brightest minds of modern physics, such a notion is mathematically possible. So he's out there, issuing his call. But to what end? What does he want? What brings him to our world?"

"If we're talking about Pan, he wants orgies of beastly sex. He wants nymphs to worship at the altar of his loins. He wants to wield his celebrated phallus. The Horned God is a horny god."

"Has he come to recruit new Maenads? Is that the explanation for what happened in Widow's Ridge over a hundred years ago? Were the men of the hamlet slaughtered as sacrificial lambs to an old god? And has he come back for new offerings of sex and sacrifice?"

"I just remembered something else from my mythology course," she said. "Dionysus-slash-Pan was a savior-god, actually a forerunner of Christ. The blood of the men the Maenads murdered was used to fertilize the grapevine, which symbolically represented the god's physical incarnation. Dionysus was, after all, the wine-god. And blood-wine supposedly represents the human soul."

"So . . . the Horned God is here to collect sacrificial souls and to take them back into the bosom of Mother Nature, from whence we all come? Or is it that our hypothetical modern-day Maenads are out for blood to bring their god into their world, because so far, only his terrible cry is manifest, and he wants to come hoofing full-fleshed into the twenty-first century?"

"You know how crazy we sound, don't you?" said Sharyn. "This whole thing is preposterous. Isn't it?"

"Of course, it is. But if we're to believe Reverend Waller's account, something happened in eighteen sixty-six that made the women of Widow's Ridge slaughter their menfolk and subsequently cover it up with the story that the men all died in the Civil War. And layered beneath that story is the suggestion of Dionysian myth, this Helling. I suspect it was concocted to relieve the women of their guilt over what they'd done."

Sharyn said, "Unless it's not a myth."

A nurse's aide knocked at the door, stuck her head in and announced that visiting hours were over.

Thorn stood. Sharyn rose with him. She held his hand and kissed his cheek at the door. "Thank you, Al. Thanks for playing along. It did me a world of good. You always know just how to reach me. Who else but you could make me see how far-fucking-out my thinking was, and without belittling me. Pan, my ass."

She lightly kissed his lips.

He gave her a bewildered look, started to say something, then shrugged and smiled.

"Good-night," she said.

"Sleep well. I'll come back tomorrow," he promised.

When she was alone again, she went to the window and parted the curtain. Her reflection was a pale blur in the dark glass. Thunder tumbled down the mountainside and filled the hollow. Trembling, she hugged herself and tried to banish the stark image of a goat-footed god back into the realm of mythology.

CHAPTER SEVEN

Asa Edgar stepped out into the rain and shut his cabin door behind him. Lightning flashed above the mountain and a cannonade of thunder roused ghosts of displaced dead.

Asa could feel the electric crackle of restless souls in the stormwind. He smelled the ancient grave-scented sadness of homeless soldiers lost and wandering these black hills, bearing wounds grievously eternal. Overriding those familiar scents were the pungent odors of the Beast and the sour stench of Asa's own fear.

The hallucinatory word-images and ecstatic artwork contained in Asa's thick book by William Blake were fresh in his mind as he trudged through the night rain. As he had no television or radio, he usually spent his evenings reading either Blake or the Good Book, by firelight or by lamplight. Tonight had been no different. Tonight he had read passages about Blake's ancient god Urizen, and that strange poetry still sang in his breast, adding a cutting edge to his apprehension.

The lines of poetry were etched in flames in his memory.

Lo, a shadow of horror is risen
In Eternity! Unknown, unprolific,
Self-clos'd, all-repelling: what Demon
Hath form'd this abominable void,
This soul-shudd'ring vacuum? Some said
"It is Urizen." But unknown, abstracted,
Brooding, secret, the dark power hid.

Urizen and the Beast of the hills were becoming one in the center of his fear. And his fear was edging into the territory of deep terror, where Urizen's "dark power hid."

Asa did not want to go deeper into this wet darkness. He did not want to risk a dangerous encounter with the beastly god, but he was bound by solemn duty, having been charged to the task years ago by his mother. He was the sentry. The lone guardian of his ancestral hills.

"My weird," he whispered to the night, remembering the sharp pricks of his mother's magic needles and the cutting discipline of her special blade she employed to bleed the fear from him.

* * *

Rourke set the phone softly back into its cradle and muttered a curse.

"Mrs. Bowen must be a basket case by now," Alice Marsh said from behind the dispatcher's desk. "You handled that well."

Rourke grunted. He took a sip of lukewarm coffee. "I just can't figure it," he said. "Four women vanishing without a damn trace . . ."

"Venture called in while you were on the phone," she said. "Wanted to make sure his overtime's approved."

He nodded, thinking: *That prick.* "Call the hospital and see how the sheriff is doing."

"I just did. He's sleeping now. Still confused when he's awake."

Rourke rifled the pages of the four unofficial Missing Persons reports on his desk. "The only thing I know to do," he said, "is to see if Dudley Wallace can get his bloodhound to pick up Mrs. Gladstone's scent and track her down. That's assuming she set out on foot. And if this rain keeps up, the dog will probably be useless."

"You want me to call him?" asked Alice.

"No, I'll do it. I should've got him on this earlier, before dark, but I kept thinking Gladys would turn up."

"You had your hands full all day. And besides, nobody's been missing twenty-four hours yet."

He looked at his wristwatch and said, "Two more hours will make twenty-four for Judy Lynn."

The phone jangled as he was reaching for it to call Dudley the dog handler. He answered. The caller identified himself as William Archer, the owner and builder of Mountview Villas. Archer said he'd spoken to Sheriff Gladstone last week about checking on his daughter and her roommate, and he was calling now to report that the two young ladies had arrived there today, adding that he would appreciate it if a deputy could check in with the girls tonight, "just to let them know they're being looked after, since they're there by themselves."

"Yes sir," Rourke said. "We'll be glad to do it. I didn't think anybody would be moving in until the first of the month."

"I told Julie she could move in a couple of weeks early. She's a writer," Archer explained, "and she's anxious to get started on her next book in the solitude of the mountains. I figured she could keep an eye on things until the maintenance crew reports for work while she's working on her book."

"We'll keep an eye on them," said Rourke. "No problem."

He hung up, knowing he'd probably lied to the man. With the unexplained disappearances of four local women, Rourke knew that two girls living alone in Mountview Villas had the potential of becoming a big problem for Arcadia County's undersized sheriff's department.

"What was that all about?" Alice asked.

"Another damn headache," said Rourke. "Two girls—"

A rumbling boom of thunder shook the building, drowning his words.

* * *

Trey Knott pushed his plate aside and took a sip of wine.

Susan said, "You're awfully quiet tonight."

"Hmm?" He looked across the table at his wife.

"Something on your mind?" Her brows arched over her lovely blue eyes.

"I was thinking about a patient. This elderly catatonic took a crayon to her wall for some non-scheduled art therapy."

Susan smiled. "Must've been pretty interesting to preoccupy you so."

"It was pretty bizarre," he said. "Unsettling, actually. The anthropology professor from the college was so taken with it he took photos. Alfred Thorn?"

"Goodness, what was he doing there?"

"Visiting a friend."

"I didn't think catatonics did much of anything," she said.

"She came out of it long enough to color the wall, then she withdrew into herself again. She even labeled her work. 'Helling.'"

"And you're trying to make sense of it. Looking for a deep psychological significance?"

He shrugged, then smiled. "Thorn saw a satyr in it. With a huge erection."

Susan laughed. "A satyr?"

He chuckled. "Yeah, you know. Half man, half beast, with insatiable sexual appetites."

"Probably says more about Thorn than the artist."

"Maybe. But then I saw it too."

Susan smiled slyly. "Hmm, I think I can handle your appetites. More wine?"

"Better not. I'm still on-call."

"Then you'll have to settle for getting drunk on the wine of love." She teased her lower lip with the tip of her tongue, eyes sparkling.

Rain blew against the dining room window as the thunderstorm rolled over the house. Knott stared into his glass of claret and envisioned the swirling red chaos of the old woman's crayon drawing.

* * *

The lights flickered and Angela cursed. "The lights better *not* go out," she said.

"I love a good storm," said Julie, bending to the vanilla-scented candle's flame to light her cigarette.

"You would. Being a famous horror writer and all."

Julie sat back on the couch, crossed her legs under her and exhaled a stream of smoke. "I'm not famous yet, but this new book just might put me on the literary map. I'm going to make it *really* scary. I can't remember the last time I read a book that gave me the willies."

Angela chortled. "I can remember a couple of willies that were pretty damn scary. Before I changed my sexual allegiance."

"You were such a slut."

"You were nobody's idea of a saint." Angela cut her eyes at Julie.

"No, but I didn't screw Kenny Kleeber either." Julie squinted in the cigarette smoke.

"Hey, I was stoned. And he wasn't *that* bad in the sack. If his dick was as half big as his ego, it would've been great."

They both laughed. Angela sipped from her wine glass. Julie flicked ashes into the ashtray.

"I can't get that dream out of my head," Julie said. "Scared the shit out of me. I *loved* it. Now if I can just capture that raw fear in my novel . . ."

"You would've really loved mine. Getting raped by a statue! God. An angel with a giant dong. Where the hell did *that* come from?"

"What's really strange is that we had nightmares at the same time. I almost never have nightmares. I wish I could, you know, for my writing's sake."

"And it wasn't even nighttime. Wouldn't that make them daymares?"

"I think being here is going to be good for my writing," said Julie, drawing deeply on her cigarette. "There's a strong vibe about this place. A Gothic feel, a sense of old, restless spirits. I *love* these mountains. I feel like I belong here."

"It is beautiful up here. But I'm staying away from those damned angels."

"For God's sake, Ange, it was just a dream. You can be such a child."

"I've always had this thing about statues. They creep me out big time. I think it goes back to that wax museum in St. Augustine. I was six years old, and my parents dragged me in there and I freaked. All those wax dummies standing around like dead people with their eyes open was more than I could handle. And then one of them started moving. I pissed my pants and ran out of there screaming. They tried to explain later that it was animatronic. Didn't mean shit to me. I knew those dummies were all coming to life to get me. I've never set foot in a wax museum since. You couldn't drag me into one now. And stone statues have the same effect. That's why I hate cemeteries. I just know all those stone statues are a breath away from coming alive and coming after me."

"No wonder the dream freaked you," said Julie, turning sympathetic.

"Hey." Angela shrugged. "I won't bother them, maybe they won't bother me."

Julie stubbed out her smoke and stood. "I need to get some writing done. Will you be all right? By yourself?"

"Yeah, sure. I'm not six years old anymore." She flashed a wan smile. "I've got a play to read. Ibsen's *The Doll House*. If you hear voices, it'll just be me reciting lines."

"Unless it's those restless mountain spirits." Julie showed her teeth in a demonic grin and waggled her brows.

"You can cut that shit out right now. Maybe you like being scared, but I don't. Keep it to yourself."

Julie blew her a raspberry, then smiled, got up and started to her bedroom.

"Hey, don't forget we're getting up early in the morning to go grocery shopping," Ange said.

"Our first foray into Dogwood," Julie said, putting mock dreaminess in her voice.

"Hillbilly Heaven. Hold me back." Angela jumped up and bounced off to her room.

Julie sat down at her laptop and limbered her fingers. Rain ticked against the window. A flash of lightning illuminated the gathering of angels in the garden below. She shivered pleasurably.

* * *

Liza Leatherwood sat in her rocker before the cold fireplace and listened with dead ears to the ringing silence of the room. The deep quiet made her feel as if she were not fully in the world. Her loss of hearing heightened her remaining senses, sharpening them against the surrounding silence. She no longer clearly heard the familiar sounds of summer night on the mountain. She didn't hear the wind moaning around the eaves of the house or hear the rain pattering on the roof. She could feel the bone-deep vibrations of thunder but she heard them distinctly only in her memory. She felt the creaking of the wooden rocking chair but she scarcely heard it.

She regretted the incremental loss of her hearing and it made her sad to know that the remainder of her allotted time on the mountain would be spent in virtual silence, but she also felt a sense of triumph. The shrill call of the beast would fall impotently on her partially deaf ears. She would not be pressed against her will into the service of evil revelry and brutal slaughter. A woman her age probably wouldn't survive the Helling anyway and therefore wouldn't have to live with her evil deeds, but now, being immune, Liza no longer had to fear for her soul.

She unscrewed the metal lid, turned the jar up to her lips and sipped again of the strong spirits. Then she opened the leather-bound book in her lap and began to read another Hawthorne story.

She heard the great man's words in her mind and they resonated within her breast. Hawthorne's deathless voice soothed her for a time. Then her eyes grew tired and she shut the book and wiped away a tear with a lacy hankie.

* * *

With a delicious shudder, Alfred Thorn smoothed the photocopied pages of Reverend Waller's journal on his desk. His small office was a bubble of security, a cozy cubbyhole on this stormy summer night. He was the only person in the building, according to Sam Bellows, the nightshift campus security guard.

Thorn packed his pipe and fired it up, savoring the taste and aromatic tang of Prince Albert tobacco—the same brand his grandfather had smoked most of his life. There was no smoking on campus, but there was no one here to catch him at it and complain. He read the first line of the entry he hadn't let Sharyn see, but his mind wouldn't stay focused on the words. He kept seeing the fear in Sharyn's eyes and in the worry lines around her eyes' corners—fear he'd added to by showing her Waller's handwritten words and bringing up the subject of Pan. Now he wished he hadn't done it. He should've kept the visit light and just let her know he was there for her, but he'd let the excitement of discovery get the better of him and he had foolishly brought her into his search for the secret of Widow's Ridge.

"The Secret of Widow's Ridge," he said aloud, thinking it would make a fine subtitle for the scholarly article he intended to write for *The American Journal of Anthropology,* once he got to the bottom of the folk-loric mystery. Then he once again saw Sharyn's fear-constricted face and he winced. He shouldn't have indulged in such speculative fantasy in front of her. What the devil had he been thinking? He'd inadvertently provided her with raw material to feed her near-delusional thinking about some demon of the dark wood calling to her. How could he have been so insensitive? He didn't know much about bipolar disorder, but he knew that when the body chemistry was out of whack, the typical manic-depressive was prone to delusional thinking. He damned well should've known better than to contribute to Sharyn's unreasonable fears.

Thorn knew what the problem was. He was a man of science, but he still had a boy's love of science-fiction and the fantastic. He had never outgrown his love of the amazing tales of Edgar Rice Burroughs, H.P. Lovecraft and the like. That same love had led him into the fields of anthropology and archeology in the first place. Moreover, he believed it was important that he maintain a youthful sense of adventure in his work. Scientific pursuits tended toward drudgery, and the scientist had to take inspiration where he found it if he didn't want to become a drudge himself. Of course, he never let those fantasies creep into his actual work, and until now he'd always been able to keep the two worlds separate, but this current project was somehow different. This time the fantastic *wanted* to intrude upon the rational world—as it had in his searching conversation with Sharyn. He'd done her a terrible disservice. He needed to make amends. He decided he would take her some flowers when he saw her tomorrow and keep the visit carefree and cheery, with no shoptalk and no mention of anything upsetting.

His conscience somewhat assuaged by his future intentions, he reread the entry for June 26, 1866.

The missing women returned to their homes in the dead of night and were not discovered until the next morning. Most were naked, but a few wore blood-stained garments indicative of their participation in the Abominable Slaughter. The women were confused and could not explain their collective absence, nor could they explain the dried blood on their persons, beneath their fingernails and even in the hair of their privates. Nor were they the least concerned about the gore or about their memory lapses. When asked what had happened to the menfolk, not one of them could answer. But neither did they seem unduly concerned with the missing men. When at last they were told of the slaughtered remains found in the forest, they all seemed genuinely surprised, but not a single female seemed shocked. To a woman, they accepted the news of their Butchered men with a singular lack of emotion. The death of a family dog would've evoked more of a reaction than these women exhibited.

I talked to a few of them myself. There was a coldness in their eyes that unnerved me terribly. I could not look long into those dead eyes without fearing the Evil lurking behind them.

But the thing that terrified me most was coming face to face with the girl I'd previously seen eating human flesh. I remembered her well enough—her gore-smeared face will haunt me to the end of my days—but she recognized me not at all. Looking into her blank face convinced me that the women truly had no memories of their murderous rampaging.

I confess I was afraid to spend another night upon that ridge. A common burial ceremony was held for the recovered remains of the dead men. I prayed aloud over their graves and silently prayed for the souls of those women responsible for putting them there, and then I departed just before dark. I was more than willing to risk the Dangers of night travel than spend a night near those Possessed women.

Thorn leaned back in his chair and sucked thoughtfully on his pipe, conjuring a bucolic image of Liza Leatherwood. He was convinced the old girl possessed information he needed to further his investigation, but he didn't know how to get it out of her. She was a stubborn old bird, too sly to be manipulated into letting anything slip out. But Thorn could be stubborn too, especially when he was on the hunt for buried secrets. He decided he would try her once more before writing her off as a dead-end, a lost source. Tomorrow morning he would have a heart-to-heart with the woman, put his cards on the table, tell her what he knew and hope for the best.

Somewhere in these hills was an unmarked mass grave hiding the old butchered bones of the missing men of Widow's Ridge. If Thorn could find it and set up a dig, he might uncover proof that the mass murder Reverend Waller chronicled in his journal had actually happened.

*　*　*

Asa bent down to examine the gutted corpse. The thunderstorm had moved off toward Goat Head Hollow, leaving a cool drizzle and a light fog, but he was mostly dry inside his poncho. That was good because he knew a chain of storms was coming his way. He pulled the penlight flash from his pocket and clicked it on. He played the beam on the belly of the dead dog, a mongrel with a lot of German Shepherd in him. Something had ripped the mutt open from throat to anus and scooped out its innards. There was no sign of the missing entrails.

Asa stood up straight and sniffed the air. The rain had washed away much of the vile scent, but it was still strong enough to make him queasy and lightheaded. The Beast was ranging the hills tonight.

And it was hungry.

CHAPTER EIGHT

SHARYN RAMPLING WENT DOWN THE DIM CORRIDOR toward the nurse's station to ask for her prn sleep medication. It was after eleven but she wasn't at all sleepy. Remembering Al Thorn's story about the elderly female patient's drawing on the wall, Sharyn paused in the doorway of the room housing the only elderly patient on the unit, and looked into the room. The light was off but the light from the hallway partially illuminated the old woman's room.

Sharyn looked past the sleeping white-haired woman to the wall behind her and the red markings on it. There wasn't enough light filtering into the room for her to see any kind of recognizable figure in the markings; she was tempted to switch on the light for a quick peek. Her hand was on the switch when a voice startled her, making her jump back out of the doorway. She spun around to see the night nurse, Carrie Sanders.

"Did you lose your room, Miss Rampling?" asked the nurse.

"No. Of course not. I'm not that far gone. I was just trying to see what she drew on her wall."

Sanders smiled. "Looks like something a three-year-old would do. Bunch of scribblings all it is. You want your prn?"

"Yes, please. I can't get to sleep." Sharyn smiled apologetically. Then she followed the nurse to the small med room and waited at the half-door while the attractive black woman unlocked a metal drawer, found her sleep medication and dropped it into a tiny plastic cup.

Sharyn washed the pill down with a swallow of water from a miniature paper cup. "Thanks," she said. "I don't usually take sleeping pills but Dr. Knott thought they could help. He seems like a good doctor, but . . ."

"But?"

Sharyn shrugged. "I don't know if this is something any doctor can help me with."

"You feel like talking about it while you wait for your sleep med to kick in?"

"Oh, thank you, no. I'll go on to bed and read until I get sleepy."

"Okay then. 'Night."

"Good-night."

She padded back to her room, the old floorboards in the corridor creaking beneath the worn carpet. Behind the closed door of the room next to hers came the loud snore of a deep sleeper, and Sharyn wondered how the snorer could possibly sleep through that buzz-saw racket. Feeling a tinge of envy, she slipped quietly into her room, settled into bed and opened her book on the life of William Shakespeare. Because not much was known of the Bard's life, the book was loaded with conjecture and read more like a novel than a biography, but for Sharyn, much of it rang true. It was fascinating stuff, and it soon took her out of her nocturnal preoccupations and fearful concerns and transported her to Elizabethan England. Her eyelids grew heavy and she found herself rereading passages, compulsively determined to reach the end of the paragraph before shutting out the light and yielding to sleep without a fight. She glanced at the travel clock she'd brought from home. It was nearly midnight. Her eyes went back to the text and she resumed where she'd left off, though now her vision was a little blurry.

With a jolt, she opened her eyes and took another look at the clock. Now it was 12:45, and she still hadn't reached the end of the paragraph and hadn't even realized that she'd drifted off. She gave up, shut the book and turned off the bedside lamp.

She dreamed. Though she knew she was in the midst of a dream, she was no less terrified by the thing that came out of the red chaos on the old woman's wall and stepped brazenly into Sharyn's world. Towering over her, it moved with a jerky motion on oddly jointed legs, its heavy hooves clomping on the floor as it came forward, broad shoulders hunched and head extended as if to crane down for a close look at her with fierce eyes aflame with lust.

I want to wake up now, she said to her dreaming self. I don't want to see this.

But she couldn't wake up. All she could do was stand, trembling, in the dream room and subject herself to the creature's intensely lascivious scrutiny. When she saw the enormous phallus jutting from its lightly furred loins, its bulbous head bobbing above her belly, she screamed herself awake.

* * *

Rourke chased sleep. Sleep eluded him. The steady drone of rain on the roof should've easily lulled him into slumber but it hadn't. The rain only made him more pessimistic, more certain that Dudley Wallace's bloodhound wouldn't be able to pick up Gladys Gladstone's scent tomorrow morning.

It was after midnight, and he was tired and emotionally drained from his extended workday but his mind simply wasn't ready to shut down for the night. His thoughts flitted from Sheriff Gladstone to Judy Lynn Bowen and the other missing women, and then darted back to Gladstone's hard-to-swallow assertion that his wife had beaned him with the iron skillet, only to return yet again to the other women reported as missing. It was dizzying, the way his thoughts darted about like phantom fish in the opaque goldfish bowl of his skull.

When he tried to focus his thoughts, they went on the lam like wanted fugitives, skulking off in directions Rourke didn't want to follow, but did because he had no choice. And now he was a captive audience of one to the mental replay of the conversation he'd had this evening with Judy Lynn Bowen's fiancé, Josh Jordan.

The young man hadn't been able to contain his agitation, getting up from his armchair to pace in front of the hearth, occasionally stopping to look squarely at Deputy Rourke with pleading eyes and no words to adequately express his anguish. "Somebody took her," he said again. "That has to be it, 'cause she wouldn't just run off and not tell anybody, like that runaway bride that was all over the news awhile back. Somebody took her."

Rourke agreed, but he didn't say so. It was too early in the investigation to be so certain of it, but he was. The urine on Judy Lynn's car seat was the clincher. Something had scared the piss out of her and then . . . poof! She was gone. Taken. Spirited away, leaving behind a fiancé well on his way to becoming an emotional cripple.

Rourke's conversation with Judy Lynn's parents hadn't been any easier. Reverend Bowen had tried to be strong, the pillar of faith he was expected to be, but Rourke hadn't missed the fear in the preacher's eyes nor the tremor in his hands. Mrs. Bowen had done a better job of hiding her anxieties, denying that anything bad could've happened to her sweet daughter and asserting that Judy Lynn would turn up with a good explanation for why she'd disappeared. The Lord would protect her.

But the fact was, nobody Rourke interviewed had any idea what might've happened to the young woman.

She was just gone.

And Sheriff Gladstone was out of commission with a cracked skull, leaving Rourke solely responsible for investigating the disappearances. It was a make-or-break situation. If Rourke blew it, his chances of one day getting elected sheriff would be blown as well. He tried not to think about the future political implications; he knew his prime concern should be finding the victims—if *victims* they were—and determining exactly what had happened to them, but he was too tired to exert mental discipline, and his renegade thoughts refused to be apprehended.

He got up and went to the bathroom. Flicked the light on.

Lucy Fur roused herself from the oval rug on the floor at the foot of the bed and padded after him, giving him a questioning whine.

He reached down to scratch her head. "Am I keeping you awake, girl?" She licked his fingers.

"You sleep and I'll be the watchdog, huh? Why not? Can't dance. Can't sleep either."

He relieved himself with Lucy sitting on her haunches behind him, her head erect and ears at attention, poised to receive any command forthcoming from her master. He flushed the toilet and went to the sink, bent down and drank cool water from the faucet.

Lucy Fur whined, then suddenly scampered out of the bathroom with a soft *woof.*

Rourke wiped his mouth with the back of his hand and followed her.

She trotted to the bedroom window, on full alert now. She barked at the curtained panes, her barks sharply ringing against the high ceiling.

"What is it, Luce?" Rourke stood behind her in the long rectangle of light falling from the bathroom doorway.

She barked three times and then crept closer to the window sill. Her hackles were up, as if she sensed imminent danger.

Rourke cocked his ears to catch any sound outside that shouldn't be there but he heard nothing but the unremitting murmur of rainfall. Usually, the only time Lucy barked like this was when strangers had come into the yard; the occasional trespass of a raccoon or possum never warranted such an intense reaction.

Rourke slipped into his jeans and grabbed the Colt .45 semiautomatic and the flashlight he kept in the drawer of his bedside table.

"Stay," he said. Lucy obeyed, though Rourke could see she wasn't happy about being left out of the action.

He left the bedroom, went down the hallway and through the kitchen to the back door and stepped out onto the screened-in back porch he'd added onto the house a couple of years ago.

The heavy rainfall had cooled the summer night, and he shivered as he moved to his left, the side of the house his bedroom was on, and crept between the picnic table and the metal glider that furnished the back porch.

He clicked on the flashlight and shone the beam through the screen. The rain fell in slanting streaks, looking like a jeweled curtain in the cone of battery-generated light. Stepping close to the screen, he angled the beam left, toward the lawn outside his bedroom window.

He saw nothing but sheets of falling rain and wet grass that needed cutting. The hazy backwash of light from screen hindered visibility. If he wanted to be sure nothing was out there, he would have to go out into the rain. So be it.

As he started toward the screen door a movement caught his eye and he swung the light beam toward it.

At first he thought it had been a trick of the light because there was nothing there but falling rain, but then he saw it again. Or more accurately, he saw the *shape* of it, saw the rain painting the form of something that wasn't entirely visible—wasn't entirely *there*.

For a very brief moment Rourke thought he was seeing a special-effects movie illusion, the Invisible Man walking in the rain, the rain diverted just enough to reveal his shape. But this rain-made shape shining in Rourke's meager beam of light was not that of a man, not exactly. It was bigger than a man, at least seven feet tall. The contours of its upper legs suggested the hindquarters of a horse, though this was certainly a two-legged creature. It walked like a man on crooked stilts, yet there was a strange agility in the way it moved through the rain with otherworldly gracefulness.

Rourke went rigid with fear. There was a falling sensation in his belly, as if he were trapped in an elevator jerking him up and out of this world. His scalp tingled. His fingers around the handgrip of the .45 went partially numb and the gun felt impossibly heavy. He had the sudden urge to urinate, though he'd only moments ago emptied his bladder. His pulse quickened, thudding noisily in his ears above the sound of the heavy rainfall.

He was suddenly certain that he was seeing something man was not meant to see, witnessing an intruding life-form from some lost and ancient world. Surely the gods would punish him for seeing this.

He shook off the yoke of fear, cast out his outlandish thoughts, pointed his pistol at the moving shape and shouted: "Freeze!"

Later, he would feel foolish that he'd ordered the rain-thing to freeze, but right now all he felt was fear and the familiar fight-or-flight surge of adrenaline.

His finger tightened on the Colt's trigger.

The apparition halted in the rain. It turned toward him, and just for an instant Rourke saw—or thought he saw—the thing's goatish face. Eyes glittering like bright jewels below the surface of oil-black pools. A nose like an outcropping of eroded rock on a craggy cliff-face. A lipless gash for a mouth, teeth a luminescent green like the wood of young bamboo. Thick shoulders slightly slumped, suggesting nonchalant arrogance. A bulky torso growing out of the hips and legs of an indeterminate beast, the lower back arched at an odd angle for balance.

Its mouth opened wider and twisted up into what might've been a smile. Its eyes bore into Rourke, chilling him.

Then the curtain of rain closed on the creature and it was no longer there.

If it ever had been.

Rourke went out the screen door and into the rain. He followed the flashlight's beam to the spot upon which the thing had paused to look at him. He shone the light all around the backyard. The rainfall was so heavy he could scarcely see the big magnolia tree by the toolshed or the stone barbeque pit that resembled a Stonehenge-era throne.

There was no visible sign of the phantom intruder.

But beneath the scent of rain on the wet earth Rourke smelled the unmistakable musk of a feral beast.

He went inside to dry off. He carried with him the odoriferous spoor of something wild.

Lucy Fur caught the bestial scent and growled at him.

CHAPTER NINE

ASA TRUDGED THROUGH THE RAIN AND THE DARK. He'd lost the scent of the Beast, and now he was relying on his tracker's intuition to tell him which way to go.

Over the years he'd come to think of this inner sense as his Spirit Tracker. Whether tracking man or beast, Asa believed he had the ability to home in on his prey's spirit and go after it. In some ways, spirit tracking was more reliable than following the physical spoor of his prey, but employing his internal tracking mechanism took a lot out of him; it drained him very quickly, taking more out of him in mere minutes than did ranging for hours over treacherous terrain, so he didn't do it often. Each time he used it, he lost a little piece of his soul. If he relied on it too much it might kill him outright or leave him a soulless wanderer, a roaming ghoul. A being with no soul was a dangerous thing, like Blake's abominable void, a void to tempt a demon.

Asa glided over the wet woodland ground, scarcely making splashes in low-lying puddles, his body seeming to operate independently of his Spirit Tracker now. His focus ranged ahead of him, psychic sonar seeking a target, eyes seeing but not seeing the trees and brush immediately in front of him.

There.

Just to the left of a rain-slick outcropping of rock.

Just there. A void, a dead pocket of empty space that reflected nothing. A hidden hole in the world drawing him toward it, resolute waves of gravity pulling at him, *hungering* for him.

Time slips its moorage, casting Asa adrift on crests of chronological chaos, only to drop him in a bottomless trough between ghostly waves.

Every hair on his body stands on end. Static electricity crackles and sparks darkly in the rain. Electromagnetic fields overlap and intermingle. Asa wraps his arms around the trunk of a young white pine and presses his face to the bark, desperately holding on to the arboreal anchor amid the raging electromagnetic storm. And still the void exerts its irresistible pull, weakening his tenuous hold on the world.

He cries out to the earth: "Mother! Help me now!"

But the Great Mother is oblivious to his cries, and his grip on the tree begins to slip. The yawning void relentlessly wrenches him, intent on stealing him from the precarious cradle of the earth.

The tree slips from his grasp and he tumbles end-over-end toward the abominable void, mercilessly unmanned, an astronaut astray, falling sideways into a black hole.

* * *

Julie sat in the flickering light of two berry-scented candles and stared into the soft glow of her laptop's screen. A forgotten cup of cold tea rested on the desktop to her right. She tapped her cigarette against the ashtray to knock off a long ash, and then took another draw of smoke from the filter. Night nuzzled against the bedroom window with the spooky stealth of a prowling cat.

She stared at the blank screen, her mind similarly blank. She had never experienced that dreaded malady known as "writer's block" before, but here she sat, most certainly blocked. Her creative juices simply refused to flow. She'd been sitting here for . . . what? An hour? Hands poised over the keyboard, fingers ready to stroke the sensual entity of creativity that lived within her and to inveigle smooth-flowing verbiage from the mysterious word-spring. To no bloody avail.

She angrily stubbed out the smoking butt, sat back in a huff and sighed: "Michael . . ."

She suddenly hit the CapsLock key and typed: "DAMN DAMN DAMN."

The Ravenwood Horror was stuck in neutral. She'd written the first three chapters in an inspired rush of words and gripping images before leaving Atlanta, and now she couldn't resume her place in the make-believe world of Ravenwood Manor. It was as if she had been branded an intruder, turned away and locked out by the sentient manor house. Barred from her own creation.

Michael was AWOL and she couldn't write a word without him at her shoulder, guiding her through the manor's hidden passages and into forbidden rooms and deeper into the dark heart of the rambling old house. Her story was stalled. She was dammed up.

She heard the softest whisper of movement behind her. She stiffened in the chair. Her heart pounded.

Fingers touched her hair, pulling it off her neck. Warm lips touched the sensitive skin behind her ear.

Without turning, she reached back and stroked Angela's cheek. "Mmm, what are you doing still up?"

Angela withdrew her lips. "Trying to entice you into my bed."

"Don't tempt me." Julie swiveled the chair around and looked up at Angela, who stood with one knee cocked and a hand on her hip. She wore a baggy Vidal Sassoon T-shirt that tented over her plump breasts and erect nipples.

"Why not?" Angela nodded at the screen. "You don't seem to be getting anywhere with your book."

"That's exactly why not. I've got to work through this block. If I let it get the best of me, I may never break out of it."

Angela frowned and crossed her arms over her breasts. "You know what you are? A control freak."

"Don't be ugly."

"I'm not. You *are* a control freak. All novelists are. I guess you have to be when you're pulling all those strings, getting inside your characters heads, and unfolding the plot just the way you want it, but what irks me is when you try to do it in the real world, always with your hand on the control buttons, trying to make things happen the way you want them to. Well, here's a clue, Jools. The real world isn't like that. There ain't no control buttons."

Julie narrowed her eyes, then slipped her hand between Angela's thighs. As she suspected, Angela wore no underwear. She tenderly ran her fingers up the spongy lips until she found the hard little knob nestled in tiny folds of flesh. "What were you saying about control buttons?" Julie asked with a small laugh.

"Not a damn thing." She shifted her feet to widen her stance. Her breath came faster. "I was beginning to think you'd gone back to the dark side."

"The hetero side? No, it's not that. It's just that I'm *stuck*. Can't get no traction, can't get no satisfaction."

"What about your dream? As bad as it scared you, I would've thought you'd find a way to use it in your book."

"No," she said, withdrawing her hand. "Unfortunately, I dream in clichés. The otherworldly message coming through cyberspace has been done to death. And it wouldn't fit my story anyway. But it did spook me. It was almost as if Michael were trying to reach me through my dream. Trying to warn me."

"So then . . . my dream was those stone angels telling me they really wanna fuck me? I don't think so, Jools. A cigar is just a cigar, and bad dreams are just bad dreams."

"You know what Gail says." Gail was the lesbian art teacher who'd helped them discover the true nature of their sexuality. She was an authentic bohemian, heavily into the occult, and brilliant.

"Yeah, yeah, I know. Just because she's a card-carrying member of Mensa and her IQ is higher than yours and mine together, doesn't make her right about dreams and all that occult junk. The only time that New Age crap makes sense to me is when I'm stoned out of my mind. I think that says it all, don't you?"

Ignoring Angela's antagonistic answer, Julie said, "'Dreams are doorways to other dimensions, and they're every bit as real as the waking world.' That's what Gail says. And I happen to believe it. So did Carl Jung, Indian medicine men and lots of other cosmic pioneers."

"I don't want to argue with you, Jools. I want you to come to bed with me. You can believe what you want." Angela smiled lasciviously. "If you want to believe you're making love to an angelic being of divine light, that's cool with me if that's what it takes to get you off."

Julie turned laconic. "Sorry. Not tonight."

Angela stroked her cheek again. "*I'm* sorry. I didn't mean to piss you off."

"Didn't." Julie swung back to face the laptop. She back-spaced her triple-DAMNS into oblivion. "Sweet dreams, Ange."

"Slim chance of that."

Angela's bare feet whispered over the carpet as she retreated from the room.

Julie rubbed her palms together as if conjuring magic into her fingers, then held them over the keyboard, charged and ready to strike at the writer's block and beat it down to rubble.

The screeching seemed to come from a long way off and grew rapidly louder, as if the screecher were approaching at an impossible speed, covering vast distances of darkness in a matter of seconds.

Julie's fingers froze over the keyboard. Her eyes fell out of focus. Saliva suddenly swamped her tongue and drooled from the corner of her slack mouth. Caught in a Pavlovian paradox, she wanted to go to the screecher, and at the same time wanted to run and hide, wanted the shrill cry to cease before her head exploded.

The unceasing screech grew louder and louder. Julie's ears popped as if in response to a sudden altitudinal pressure change. She shivered feverishly. Her teeth clenched, then began to chatter.

The spiky sound wrought strange changes in spatial dimensions. The bedroom and everything in it shrank to postage-stamp size, then just as suddenly expanded to include the outside world of endless darkness—the realm of the terrifying screecher.

Julie lost control of her bladder and urinated in her shorts. The liquid warmth triggered deep spasms of arousal.

She rolled her chair backward and bolted out of it, bumping her thighs on the desk and spilling the cold cup of tea. She turned and stumbled toward the bedroom door, certain now that the way to the screecher was down the stairs and out the front door of the townhouse, certain that the screecher was waiting for her out there in the night and the rain. The surrounding walls wavered in and out of her sight as if they were unable to maintain solidity against the incessant shriek of the one calling her out. The carpeted stair steps were spongy, scarcely solid enough to support her bare feet as she descended them and made for the door.

As she reached for the doorknob, she half-expected her guardian angel to grab her by the scruff and stop her headlong plunge into the grasp of the thing waiting on the other side of the door.

She wanted Michael to stop her.

She *didn't* want him to stop her.

She turned the knob and threw the door wide. A rainy gust of wind hit her face, as did the overpowering odor of the unseen screecher.

Like wash on a clothesline, sheets of rain fluttered before her in the yellow glow of the porchlight, threatening to open like jeweled curtains upon a world beyond this one, to once and for all reveal the maker of the unrelenting sound that held her in its thrall. A painful fullness in her breasts yearned to be expressed, to be violently suckled.

A hazy shape appeared in the rain. Raindrops splashed off its wide shoulders as it came forward, growing taller with each jerky step.

"My God," she said, or thought she said, looking up at the looming shape.

Then Angela came through the doorway, pushed her aside, raised a pistol and fired. The screeching cry abruptly ceased with the firearm's sharp report. The shape in the rain began to dissolve, bleeding into the darkness and disappearing in a matter of seconds.

The rain-curtains closed.

"What the hell *was* that?" Angela pointed the handgun at the rainy darkness.

Julie didn't answer. She shuddered violently.

"You all right?" Angela put a protective arm around her.

"N-n-no. I'm-m not."

CHAPTER
TEN

ROURKE DROVE THROUGH THE STONE ARCHWAY of Mountview Villas, the Ford Explorer's headlights carving thin rain-streaked swaths out of the night. Only a few of the streetlights were on, and all of the buildings were dark except one at the back of the compound. He turned right on a narrow lane and drove toward the townhouse with the lighted windows and porch.

Not long after he'd seen—or imagined he'd seen—the rain-thing in his backyard, Rourke remembered the phone call from the Atlanta builder whose daughter and her roommate were already here at Mountview Villas, just the two of them in an otherwise vacant apartment complex. He had told the man he would check on the girls, but he'd forgotten them until he was crawling into bed. He'd made a mental note to pay them a visit in the morning.

But the backyard visitation had left him on edge, too restless to sleep, and the thought of some mysterious beast roving the night made it imperative that he drive to Mountview Villas to make sure . . . to make sure what? That there was no rain-thing lurking about? Well, yes. And just to be able to say he'd been true to his word and checked on them. The girls would no doubt be in bed for the night at this late hour so he wouldn't actually lay eyes on them, but he would do a drive-by, identify their vehicle and then feel better about things—maybe even good enough to be able to get some sleep when he returned home.

Because it was raining, he had the SUV's windows up and the air-conditioner running to defog the windscreen. The wipers flogged the glass noisily and the rain drummed on the Explorer's roof. Rourke nevertheless heard the unmistakable *crack* of a single gunshot as he drove toward the building with the Dodge van parked out front.

He accelerated, simultaneously powering the driver's-side window down so he could get a better fix on the next shot, if it came.

Then he saw the two girls huddled on the lighted portico of the townhouse. In T-shirts and little else, they both looked ready to bolt as he drove up to the curb in front of them. The dark-haired young woman stared blankly while the blonde shielded her eyes against the glare of the headlights and held a pistol in her other hand, keeping it down by her bare leg.

Out of uniform and behind the wheel of a civilian vehicle, Rourke knew he had to proceed with caution to avoid getting shot as a late-night miscreant. He opened the door and stepped slowly out of the Explorer with his hands raised, palms forward. Wearing a pullover shirt, blue jeans, and cowboy boots, he felt naked and vulnerable as he softly shut the driver's door with his foot and said, "Easy now. Don't shoot me. I'm Deputy Sheriff Rob Rourke. Mr. Archer asked me to check on you girls."

The dark-haired girl whined: "Daddy . . .?"

The blonde with the gun said nothing.

Rourke said, "What're you shooting at?"

Then the blonde spoke: "If you're a deputy, where's your uniform?"

"Hanging in the closet. I'm off-duty. Tell you the truth, I didn't remember I promised to check on you until I got home." He hoped his confession would break a little ice and make him less threatening to the girls—especially to the one with the gun. "What's going on?"

The blonde said, "We saw something . . ." Her words trailed off as she looked off into the rain.

"It was screaming," said the dark-haired young woman. "Screeching. It was terrible. It . . ."

Rourke advanced slowly. "Let's get in out of the rain and you can tell me about it. Okay?"

"You got some identification?" asked the blonde. She seemed more with it than her shaken companion.

He pulled his wallet from his hip pocket and held it out in front of him like a warrior's miniature shield as he went close enough for her to see his official ID. "Okay? Can we step inside now? I'm getting water-logged out here."

"Come on in," said the one with the pistol, which appeared to be a .25-caliber automatic with a pearl handle. She stepped aside and let him enter first. She showed good instincts, not letting him get behind her.

"What exactly did you see?" he asked when they were inside and the door was shut against the rainy night.

The girls looked at each other as if they were both unsure of what they'd seen. Rourke knew the feeling. He didn't know exactly what he'd seen in his own backyard.

"I don't know what the hell it was," said Blondie. "It was raining so hard and it was like . . . it wasn't all the way there. If that makes sense."

Remembering his rain-thing, he thought it made perfect sense. "Can you describe it?"

"It was just a big shape in the rain," said the dark-haired woman. "But that screeching sound scared the pee out of me. Literally." She blushed.

Rourke nodded uneasily. "Which one of you is Miss Archer?"

"I'm Julie Archer," said the blusher. "And this is my roommate Angela Raynor."

Rourke said, "Miss Raynor, would you mind putting your pistol down."

She stared into his eyes a long moment, then set the gun on the coffee table. "I have a permit."

He nodded.

"I didn't know you brought your gun," said Julie Archer, seeming a little more oriented and confident now that she was inside and in the company of an officer of the law—even if he was out of uniform and unarmed.

"Don't give me any shit about it either. What do you think would've happened if I didn't have it?"

"I don't know what would've happened. I'm not even sure what *did* happen. I've never felt so strange in all my life. Didn't you feel it?"

"Not like you did, apparently. Girl, you were zoned out. Why the hell did you go outside after hearing that god-awful shrieking?"

Julie shook her head. "I don't know. I was . . . like in a trance or something. Like it was calling me and I had to . . ." She shrugged.

A puzzle piece snapped silently into place in Rourke's mind. He pictured Judy Lynn Bowen leaving her car on Widow's Ridge Road and walking into the woods to answer the spellbinding call of something altogether wild. Something that defied rational description. Like the thing he'd half-seen in the rain. "And you shot at it," he said to Miss Raynor. "Do you think you hit it?"

"I don't know. I'm a pretty good shot, and I aimed center-mass, you know? But the damned thing just . . . disappeared. If I didn't know better, I'd say it was like some supernatural beastie out of Julie's books. She writes horror stories."

"What if it was?" Julie Archer widened her dark eyes.

"Don't *even* go there," said her roommate. "Not if you want me to stay here."

"But you just said——"

"I said if I didn't know better. I do. Know better. It was some kind of animal. Or maybe a shared hallucination."

"You don't know what it was and I don't either. So don't tell me what it wasn't, Angela."

Angela rolled her eyes and said to Rourke: "You'll have to excuse her. She also believes she has a guardian angel, who happens to be curiously absent tonight. She sometimes gets her spooky stories mixed up with reality."

"I do not." Julie crossed her arms over her chest.

Rourke said, "Keep your doors locked at all times and don't go out after dark. Is your phone turned on?"

Julie nodded. "And we have our cells."

"Any problems, call nine-one-one." He looked at Angela. "And don't you go taking pot-shots at anything. I'm gonna take a look around outside. Starting tonight, I'll have a deputy make nightly checks here. Okay?"

They both nodded.

"Good night, then, ladies. Welcome to Dogwood."

He went outside and checked the tiny front yard and the parking lot for blood, but he found nothing to indicate that the phantom prowler had been wounded. He hadn't really expected to. A rain-thing wouldn't bleed.

Would it?

*   *   *

Julie fired a furious look at Angela, who had just locked, bolted and chained the front door. "Why'd you shoot off your mouth about me to that man? Don't you *ever* put my business in the street again."

Angela met her fury with a cold stare. "I didn't put anything in the street. The man's a cop, for Christ's sake. He was looking out for us. Which is more than you can say for your alleged guardian angel."

"You didn't have to tell him about Michael."

"Cool it, Jools. Didn't you see the way he reacted when we told him what we saw? He already *knew*. Whatever that thing was, Deputy Dog knows something about it. I could see it in his bloodhound eyes."

Julie's eyes brimmed with tears. "I don't *know* what I saw," she said, shoulders slumping as she collapsed on the couch. "Or what it did to me. I've never felt anything so . . . so . . ."

Angela sat beside her and snugged an arm around her sagging shoulders. "It's okay," she said. "You're safe now."

"I don't feel safe. What if it comes back? What then? That sound did something to me. I was . . . I lost control. It called me and I couldn't stop myself from going out to meet it. Didn't you feel it?"

"Not like you did. I felt scared. Then angry. Tell you the truth, I felt sort of stoned and paranoid, like I'd smoked some kick-ass weed. But mostly I was pissed off."

Julie exhaled a shuddering sigh. Angela stroked her hair and added, "I'll tell you what I really felt. I felt like a mean-ass bull dyke ready to take down a lounge lizard for trying to put the moves on my woman. How fucked up is *that?*"

Julie snorted, then hiccupped. "You're not a dyke. You don't have a bullish bone in your bod."

"But I felt like I was shooting testosterone bullets, babe." Angela comically deepened her voice and said, "C'mere, little honey, and suck on my peashooter."

Julie chuckled. Then sniffled. "Let's go to bed. I want you just to hold me."

"Sure, baby. Go on up. I'm gonna make sure the back door and the windows are locked."

Julie stood unsteadily, chewed her lower lip, and then padded toward the stairs. Over her shoulder she said, "Bring your gun when you come up."

* * *

Rourke drove at a crawl through Mountview Villas' maze of narrow little streets, looking for any sign of a prowler lurking in the wet darkness. It was simply a matter of routine; he didn't expect to find a prowler too insubstantial to go bump in the night. Of course, it was possible that the young ladies had been stoned on illegal drugs and only imagined they saw something—or jointly hallucinated the thing in the rain, if that was possible. But what about the screeching they had described? Hallucinations didn't scream, did they?

Besides, Rourke had seen it himself in his own backyard. Or something very like it. He couldn't write that off as freaky coincidence. His rain apparition and the thing the girls had seen and heard were—or at least *could* be—one and the same. He'd lived all of his thirty-nine years in Dogwood, and he was familiar with all of the indigenous wildlife, but he had never seen the likes of that rain-thing anywhere, outside of illustrated books of mythology. Wildlife, indeed. How wild could it get?

He braked and rolled to a stop atop a small hill overlooking the hedge-walled courtyard in the center of the compound. The Explorer's headlights illuminated the eerie statuary standing in the slanting rain within the rectangle of dark green hedges, majestic stone angels and cherubic gnomes arrayed in mystic formation amid the Oriental rock garden. It was a creepy spectacle; it brought Rourke's thoughts back to mythological beings and creatures of fantasy.

He shut his eyes and tried to recall the image of the thing he'd seen (and smelled) behind his house. He visualized the shape the specter had made in the rain, but it was only that—a shape without distinct features. Like a shadow caught in a rain-streaked mirror, the shape refused to resolve itself into any distinct image. But its shape and the way it moved suggested . . . what? What kind of mythical creature?

The answer came to him in the image of a man with the hindquarters and legs of an animal. Half man, half beast. Very similar to bookish renderings of the mythological satyr. Or was it that other thing . . . the Minotaur? No, the Minotaur had the monstrous head of a bull, didn't it? This thing had been more akin to the satyr. Yeah, that was definitely the image his backyard phantom had left in his head. Satyr.

Sure, and Bigfoot's living in the basement with Elvis, both waiting for me to come home and fry them a couple of peanut-butter-and-banana sandwiches.

He opened his eyes. Took one last look at the spooky rain-beaten statues, then backed up and drove off into blowing torrents of rain.

CHAPTER ELEVEN

SHARYN SAT HUNCHED OVER THE TABLETOP-EDGE of a wobbly card table which had been pushed against the corridor wall, her hands clasped together as if to maintain a firm hold on her roiling emotions and keep a handle on her fear. She knew she was right on the edge of losing control. If she lost it, she would likely give in to the urge to run screaming down the hallway and would surely end up strapped to her bed, or stuck in the padded Quiet Room, shot full of heavy-duty tranquilizers and nodding off into Nightmare Land.

She couldn't let that happen. Strapped to a bed was the last place she wanted to be with that thing out there, surreptitiously stalking her in the corridors of night, creeping closer through the rain.

The night nurse was coming toward her now, gliding silently down the hallway on her white Nikes, white teeth glowing in a half-smile on her dark face.

Sharyn tried to return the smile, but the corners of her mouth wouldn't cooperate, stubbornly bent on preserving the toothy frown frozen on her face.

"Feeling a little better?" asked the nurse.

Sharyn nodded. Nodding was the easiest way to lie. If she tried to speak, her terror might come out in a manic rush of psychotic-sounding words. And she most assuredly was not psychotic.

"Don't you want to go back to bed and try to get some sleep?"

She shook her head. "Not yet," she allowed through clenched teeth.

Nurse Sanders looked at her wristwatch. "Let's give it ten more minutes. I'm bending the rules letting you sit up out here after curfew. Unless you're talking about what's going on with you. Nightshift coun-seling sessions are allowed under special circumstances."

Sharyn lifted her hands, spread her ten fingers and nodded. Ten minutes.

Ten minutes, then back to the cramped room where the nightmare waited in shadow, waited for Sharyn to shut her eyes and drift back into the lulling waves of sleep, and then the unrelenting undertow would pull her back down into the nightmare and that hideous beast with the enormous erection would have its way with her.

"Get a grip," she whispered to herself.

"Pardon?" said the nurse.

"Nothing." *Just the loony talking to herself.*

The nurse smiled reassuringly, then walked back to the nurse's station on her shoes' silent treads.

Sharyn tried not to think about those photocopied journal entries Al Thorn had let her read, but that was like trying not to picture a pink elephant when someone says, "Don't think about a pink elephant." In her case, the pink elephant had shape-shifted into a rutting god with a killer hard-on. And to make matters worse, Reverend Waller's handwritten words were floating in front of her eyes, snaky sentences undulating like underwater tentacles. She brushed them away as if swatting a fly. The cursive words broke apart in the air and the alphabet shower evaporated before falling into Sharyn's lap.

She stared blankly down the long corridor in front of her and listened to the steady beat of rainfall. She tried to slow her respirations, thinking that if she could control her breathing then she just might be able to get a foothold on the windswept plains of her psyche where her fears had gone to run as wild as untamed horses. She knew she was past the point of driving them off, but if she could assert enough control then she could at least ride herd on them before they dragged her off into a full-blown stampede of panic toward the inevitable box canyon of mental paralysis.

A ringing phone broke the relative silence, and a stab of fear as sharp as an ice-pick penetrated her chest. Phone calls in the middle of the night terrified her. When she was ten years old, a midnight phone call had delivered the bad news that her father had been gravely injured in an automobile accident. He'd died of massive head injuries before the next sunrise. Sharyn had feared late-night phone calls ever since, their shrill nerve-jangling rings always piercing her viscera, twisting in her belly like the cold steel blade of a carving knife.

The nurse's voice carried down the hallway, not overly loud but nevertheless as clear as the singing ping of a crystal goblet, and Sharyn listened to the one-sided exchange. As a rule, she didn't indulge in eavesdropping, but she made the exception this time because she thought it might take her mind off her own free-floating anxiety and semi-rational fear.

The upshot of the nurse's conversation was that an emergency admission was en route via ambulance to the hospital. Nurse Sanders efficiently repeated the information as it was given to her, no doubt writing it down as she did so. "Fifty-six-year-old female . . . extreme agitation . . . no history of mental problems or violence . . . attacked husband without provocation . . . oriented times four . . . required physical restraint . . ."

Welcome to the club, Sharyn thought. The Dogwood Society of Wacked-out Women, President Sharyn Rampling presiding. Get out of line and I'll gavel your skull.

She smiled to herself, feeling a smidgen better than she'd felt only moments before. *I despaired of my lack of shoes until I met a man with no feet.* The grass wasn't greener on blighted ground.

Sharyn had never been married, but it wasn't difficult to imagine the impulse to do violence to any man who happened to be handy when the megrims in your head went from melancholic to vitriolic and you just had to fire-all-your-guns-at-once and explode-into-space because you were fucking-A born-to-be-wi-i-ild.

Uh-oh, bad sign.

Free-associating old rock songs to the flight-of-idea bugaboos bouncing off the interior walls of your skull, like that red-rubber-ball bubblegum bullshit you couldn't get out of your head for days after you heard it on the oldies station, Randy & Spiff doing their hokey DJ comedy all-along-the-watchtower but you can't-get-no no-no-no- no-satisfaction because nothing is even a-little-bit-funny while your conscience-explodes and harmonicas-play-skeleton-keys-in-the-rain . . .

Double uh-oh.

Whenever Bob Dylan wailed in her echo-chamber cranium she knew she was revving up to barrel off the tracks because only a crazy person or a magic-mushroom eater could truly understand old Bob's lyrics, and now they were making perfect sense to her—as if he'd written them all those hard-driving road-weary years ago with Sharyn Rampling in mind, *for this very moment*, at this desperate stopover along the bloody rails to hell.

Until this moment she hadn't believed that her recent panic attack could be a precursor to a manic episode. None of the other signs signaling the onset of mania had been present. She had been taking her meds just as prescribed. Of that, she was certain.

But now those old familiar feelings were creeping in around her mind's edges, jabbing her like little cartoon demons with pitchforks, taunting her with the promise of wild and crazy times ahead if she would just give in and go with the scattershot momentum of her gloriously soaring disease. Soon she would be making lists of things to do, drawing up detailed plans for world peace or diagramming ingenious inventions guaranteed to prevent AIDS, cancer, and PMS. Then there would be absolutely no fucking doubt that, yes indeed, she was cycling, roaring like a crack-cranked Hell's Angel on a monster Harley, toward the manic pole of her disorder. But until those things actually transpired, she would refuse to believe that what was happening to her was due to her psycho-biological disorder.

Unless and until she did something outrageously characteristic of her condition, Sharyn was not going to accept that what was happening to her now was simply psychogenic.

There *was* something out there in the night. She'd heard its terrifying cry. She'd dreamed flesh onto its ancient bones. And now she could feel it drawing closer. Stalking her.

She knew in her racing heart that these hospital walls were not strong enough to keep it out.

Nothing was.

*   *   *

Trey Knott was taking a middle-of-the-night leak when he heard the thing scream. The eerie cry was so startling that it stopped his urine midstream, and he just stood there with his pee-shooter in his hand, his ball sack tightening, drawing up as if trying to squirrel away precious nuts.

Knott shivered, astonished by his visceral reaction to the sound. He stared into the commode and just for the briefest moment he actually feared that whatever was making that horrendous noise might come screaming up through the sewer pipes, fly out of the toilet and latch onto his penis or throat.

Feeling suddenly dizzy, he leaned his left palm against the wall to steady himself as the hair-raising scream (the hairs on his forearms stood on end as if pulled erect by static electricity) went on without end.

Finally, the screechy scream faded out beneath the rattling hum of rainfall on the roof. Knott blew a sigh of relief and continued to relieve himself, urine nosily splattering and babbling in the porcelain bowl's water. He shivered again—this time as a biological response to the body heat lost with the urine.

Sharyn Rampling's attractive face flashed into his mind, and he remembered her dubious account of the unseen screaming beast that had sent her into a panic. But now her story didn't seem suspect, not in the least. Hadn't he just heard the same unearthly cry himself? And a god-awful cry it was, as unnerving as a wildcat's yowl and as grating as giant fingernails raking across the world's noisiest chalkboard.

Knott had been awakened ten minutes earlier by a phone call from Ted Devine, his erstwhile golf buddy and ordinarily a level-headed guy, but tonight Ted had been beside himself with worry about Mrs. Ted's bizarre, uncontrollable behavior. Ted had already called 911 for an ambulance, and he wanted Knott to admit his wife Dani to Ridgewood and be her attending physician. "You're the only headshrinker I trust," Ted had said with a nervous laugh.

"Where is Dani now?" Knott had asked.

"I had to lock her in the closet."

So Knott had phoned the hospital to give admission orders, and then went to the bathroom to empty his full bladder. Which he was still doing now, peeing like a stud horse because he'd had that extra glass of iced tea with his late supper.

Then the screaming resumed, screeching nails grating on Knott's nerves—nerves that were beginning to unravel. He wanted to put up his piss-pistol, run to the gun cabinet to grab his shotgun in case the screamer tried to enter the house, but this time he couldn't stop pissing. Couldn't stop shivering. Moreover, he was unable to move; the scream had frozen him to the floor, robbing him of voluntary movement.

He heard Susan's wrenching moan from the adjoining bedroom, and he *had* to run to her to see what was wrong, but he couldn't because he couldn't hold his water, couldn't stop shooting the golden stream into the bowl—no more than he could've stopped ejaculating in the middle of a bone-rattling orgasm.

Then he regained a semblance of voluntary muscular control and he called out: "Susan? What is it?"

She said something but he couldn't make out her words over the gurgling splash of his urine, the roaring drumbeat of rain and the incessant screaming of something somewhere out there in the night.

And still he couldn't stop peeing. *C'mon, c'mon, hurry up, goddammit.*

He heard a rustle of movement and the urgent staccato thumps of bare feet on the floor of the darkened bedroom.

"Susan! Wait!"

Finally he squirted his bladder's last measure into the toilet, slipped himself back into the folds of his pajama bottoms and dashed out of the bathroom without taking time to flush. He saw his wife's naked backside disappear from the bedroom doorway as she darted into the hallway.

Where the hell was she going in such a hurry and in the middle of the night?

He went after her, calling her name again. He slapped at the wall-switch as he ran by it, and the living-room light came on. He caught up to her as she was going out the front door, going toward the source of that raw call of the wild. He grabbed her right shoulder to stop her. She swung around and smacked his jaw with her left fist and jerked her shoulder out of his grasp. Momentarily stunned, he stood and watched as she ran out into the rain. He wasn't stunned by the force of Susan's blow but by the fact that she'd delivered it without hesitation. She wasn't a violent person. She didn't even like to watch PG-violence in movies. Her sudden violence was proof that she wasn't herself. Proof that the shrill screaming was driving her mad. With ten years of practicing psychiatry behind him, Knott knew all about madness, but this was beyond his experience. He knew nothing of madness brought on instantaneously by sound. He'd seen nothing in the literature that even hinted at such an improbable theory. But he knew in his gut that he was witnessing that very phenomenon firsthand.

Just as he knew that the thing that had sent Sharyn Rampling running to seek refuge in the hospital was out here, right now, calling to his wife. Only Susan wasn't running away from it—she was running toward it.

"Susan, no!" he shouted as he started out the door after her.

The house was atop a shady hill in Goat Head Hollow, and their nearest neighbors, Sam and Mary Ann Stribling, lived a mile down the blacktopped road in a refurbished farmhouse, so Knott didn't have to worry what the neighbors would think if they saw him chasing his naked wife through the rain. Nobody was around to see the rowdy spectacle.

What worried him, of course, was what would happen when Susan reached the screaming thing. Whatever the hell it was, it was calling her out for a reason. A reason he couldn't begin to fathom because he knew of no creature in nature that could exert a hypnotic influence on human beings. According to folklore, some snakes were said to be able to hypnotize their prey, usually birds, but science said otherwise.

At the far edge of the slanting yellow rectangle of light spilling from the front door and across the front lawn, Susan lost her footing on the wet grass and went down on her hands and knees.

Knott ran toward her, eyes scanning the surrounding darkness for the maker of that eerie sound. Though it most certainly originated out here in the night, he couldn't get a fix on it. It was almost as if it were coming from high-end surround-sound speakers hanging in the sky, highest-fidelity speakers powered by a monster mega-watt amp.

Whatever and wherever it was, he didn't see it. He skidded to a stop on the slick grass and clamped a hand on Susan's shoulder as she was rising to run again.

She yelped, then turned her head and snapped her teeth at his hand, catching a sliver of skin on his little finger and ripping it, making him snatch his hand off her.

Then she was up and running again.

He tore off after her, his long legs making up for his lack of speed, and when he was close enough he leapt forward, wrapped his arms around her torso and rode her to the ground.

She twisted and squirmed in his arms. She screamed, enraged beyond reason. He exerted more pressure, remembering the bear hugs he and his boyhood pals had administered to each other, the hugger doing his best to make the hug-ee pass out.

Her scream became a stuttering wheeze as he forced air out of her lungs. He squeezed harder still. He began to talk to her in low tones, lips close to her ear, hoping his voice might have a soothing effect. "Easy, baby. Easy now. You're okay. Relax. Relax now. I've got you. Don't fight me, Susan. I love you, I love you, I love you . . ."

She thrashed her legs and jerked her head from side to side, otherwise immobilized by his crushing hug. After awhile she was still.

My God, have I killed her?

The shrieking of the thing in the darkness grew furiously louder, angrier, and Knott feared that his eardrums would implode, but then it finally relented, trailing off in the distance and dying away in the steady sound of the rainfall.

* * *

Asa Edgar clawed the ground and tried to hang on to the flaccid skin of the earth around the rim of the black void, but the pull of the sucking hole was too strong and his fingers only raked oozing lines in the mud as he slipped backward into the hellish pit. His long graying hair was charged with static electricity, spiking straight out in all directions, and his skin tingled as each tiny pore opened in involuntary sympathy to the hole that was trying to devour him.

He didn't know how long he'd been grappling for desperate purchase at the rim of the hole. His sense of time was askew, his mind afire with all-consuming fear. The muscles of his shoulders and arms ached as if he'd been at it for hours, fighting for more than survival, and he now knew he'd finally reached the end of his worldly tether and the limit of his endurance. He had lost the battle.

The slick rim of the hole fell away and he slid backward into subterranean darkness.

A wall of cool stone broke his fall and sent thrumming jolts of pain running up and down his spine. Then the world seemed to right itself and Asa found that he was sitting on the floor of a cave, his back resting against a concave wall. Though it was dark, he could see pale shapes round about him, womanly forms. The cave was rife with the palpable scent of feminine musk. And lurking below that smell was the familiar scent of the Beast.

He slowly raised a hand to flip up the eye patch and uncover the empty left socket. He often did this to improve his night vision. He didn't understand how it worked—how an eyeless socket could increase his remaining eye's ability to see in the dark—but somehow it usually did. He figured it had something to do with his Spirit-Tracker sense, in effect a *seventh* sense. It didn't work every time, but this time it did.

He looked warily at the women sitting still as statues in the cave. They were all naked, all ghoulishly staring straight ahead at nothing he could see, their eyes as dull as snowflake obsidian. Zombified. In the thrall of the Beast?

There. Did that one with the long teats just twitch her face?

Remembering his penlight, Asa reached inside his muddy poncho, snaked fingers into his shirt pocket and dug it out. He clicked it on and shone the thready beam in the face of the woman he thought he'd seen twitch her facial muscles in a sort of grimace.

She did not react to the light. Her face was as blank as her eyes. Her shoulders were slightly slumped, and her reddish hair was a misshapen bundle of snarls. Her pretty face was just beginning to show age in the furrows in her forehead and in little sparrow tracks around the corners of her eyes. Something about her was very familiar to Asa. He was sure he'd seen her before, somewhere.

He played the light in the faces of the other women, one by one. These weren't statuesque wood nymphs. They were ordinary women who lived nearby. Or had, until the Beast stole them away and brought them here. But to what end?

A young woman with an upturned nose, firm breasts and wheat-colored hair suddenly turned her head toward the light, and her eyes lost some of their blankness. "Help me," she said in a small voice.

Taken aback, Asa was speechless—as he often was in the company of females. That these women were naked only added to his tongue-tied silence. He worked his mouth but all that came out was a raspy grunt.

"Please," the woman said. A tear trickled down her dirty cheek. "I wanna go home."

Then it dawned on him that Earth Mother had brought him here to save these women, to steal them back from the Beast. The Void hadn't been trying to eat him after all. But how could he get them all out? The three other naked ladies remained spellbound. Could he stand them up, chivvy them out and prod them along like cattle? Perhaps he could, if they could walk in their dazed condition. He would need the help of the one talking to him, the young one with the upturned nose. He knew he had to overcome his shyness and speak to her. He took a deep breath that sent a jagged bolt of pain up his backbone.

"What's your name?" he asked her, his gruff voice amplified by the cave's acoustics and chased by ghostly echoes.

For a moment the blank look came back into her eyes and Asa feared he was losing her, but then he understood that she'd turned her gaze inward in search of her name. She was only partly here in this world; much of her mind remained in the netherworld where the other women no doubt were, sent there by a creature powerful enough to strike them dumb with awe and turn them to flesh-and-blood stone.

"Judy," she said with the childlike innocence of a three-year-old, "Judy Lynn Bowen."

"I'm Asa. Asa Edgar. Think you can you help me get these other ladies out of here, Miss Judy?"

"I . . . I don't know." She glanced at the others. Her lips trembled and she looked as if she were going to cry. But she didn't. She looked back at him and slowly nodded her head. "Yes," she said just above a whisper, sounding more grownup now. "We have to go before he comes back."

Asa pulled his poncho off over his head and offered it to her. "Put this on," he said, covering his empty socket with his eye patch, "'Fraid the others will have to go in their birthday suits."

She glanced down at her nakedness and blushed. She accepted the wet poncho and slipped into its relatively dry interior. "Thanks. Asa."

He nodded, then stood up stiffly, doing his best to ignore the sharp sparks of pain shooting from the base of his spine down the backs of his legs.

Bracing her slender hand on the cave's wall, the girl rose shakily to her feet. A look of uncertainty crept into her face as she glanced at Asa. Then her eyes widened with terror and she said, "He's coming back!"

Asa listened keenly but he heard nothing but the rain falling outside the cave. "How do you know?" he asked.

"I *feel* him. He's close!" She trembled, biting her lower lip.

Asa took her at her word. He had little doubt that the young woman was somehow still attuned to the creature that had clouded her mind and psychically imprisoned her here with the other stolen women.

"Then we have to be quick," he said, already moving toward the three women sitting spellbound on the cave's floor. "Help me get them on their feet."

With a panic-stricken expression clenching her otherwise attractive face, she bent to a matronly woman with gray hair, slipped her hands under the woman's arms and firmly raised her to her feet. "We have to go, Miz Gladstone," she said.

Asa had a wealth of questions he wanted to ask Judy about the Beast, but those would have to wait. Now the only thing that mattered was getting the ladies out of the cave before the monster returned.

CHAPTER
TWELVE

KNOTT FOLLOWED THE AMBULANCE through the diminishing rainfall. He sat hunched over the wheel, leaning forward as if that paltry few extra inches could actually improve visibility through the rain-smeared windshield. The wiper on the driver's side needed a new blade, and Knott silently cursed himself for being lax in maintaining his Jag.

Procrastination is a symptom of repressed anger, his psychoanalytic mind nagged.

Fuck off, he told his inner shrink.

He wasn't angry. He was scared. Afraid of his wife's anger, her rage. Most of all, he feared for her wellbeing.

"Come on," he said, glaring at the ambulance on the road in front of him. "Speed it up, asshole." Okay, so maybe he *was* angry. So what?

He wanted badly to unleash the horsepower under the Jaguar's hood and burn up the winding road with speed, though he knew there was no reason to do so. He didn't need the cold, analytical voice of his inner headshrinker to tell him that the impulse to gun the horses was his pent-up anxiety looking for release. Getting Susan to the hospital ten minutes sooner wouldn't make a significant difference. She was safely strapped to the stretcher in the back of the ambulance, with an EMT in attendance; she was in no position to harm herself or others.

The white hand-towel wrapped around his left hand was blotchy with blood from the stigmata-like wound in the soft flesh of his palm. Susan, in her rage, had caught his hand in her mouth and bitten a chunk out of him. That was the moment he'd realized he couldn't handle her at home and called for the ambulance to transport her to Ridgewood after he'd wrapped her in a bed sheet to restrain her. He was past caring how it might look to others when they learned that esteemed psychiatrist Dr. Trey Knott had admitted his own wife to the funny farm.

Can't even keep his own wife sane, a faceless voice mocked, *so how's he going to help his patients? Better set his own house in order before he meddles in our domestic affairs and in our blooming heads.*

Screw that, he thought. Susan was in trouble. Helping her was the only thing that mattered now. If his reputation suffered a temporary setback, so be it.

Before the ambulance pulled up in front of his house he'd phoned ahead to alert the nursing staff and give verbal admission orders for Susan. He was thankful when Nurse Sanders answered. She was the best nurse on staff and the one least likely to make him feel uncomfortable (or idiotic) when it came time to explain what had precipitated Susan's violent episode. Sanders would take it all in, nodding with sympathetic understanding—even though he himself was at a loss to understand just what the hell had happened. Yes, he'd heard the shrill, disembodied shrieking that had presumably set Susan off, and no, he didn't know what the hell it was, but he saw the effect it had on his wife.

It was the same sound Sharyn Rampling had described, undoubtedly the same shrill screaming that had driven her in a panic to seek admission. But what the hell made that sound? What creature in nature possessed the power to cloud human minds and affect human behavior with its cry? And why hadn't that eerie cry affected Knott in similar fashion? True, he had felt *something*—something he didn't exactly know how to put into words—but he hadn't gone berserk. Hadn't turned violent. He'd felt fear, but he'd been afraid for Susan, not for himself. Still, that sound had disturbed him deeply, viscerally. And it had momentarily paralyzed him. It disturbed him now just thinking about it. He feared that its echo might be trapped in his skull. How crazy was that?

When the ambulance pulled up in front of the hospital, Knott pulled into a designated "Doctors Only" parking space in front of the paved walkway leading from the main building to the small cafeteria on the right. He was standing impatiently by the ambulance's rear door before the driver got out. The rain had dwindled to a light drizzle, and the night was unusually cool for this time of the year.

The other EMT opened the rear door from the inside, and Knott saw his wife belted to the stretcher. The blue robe he'd managed to get her into before leaving home hung open at her thighs, revealing her long shapely legs but thankfully it covered her privates, concealing the fact that she wore no underpants. Dressing her in the robe had been hard enough; he hadn't risked getting kicked by trying to force her into a pair of panties. Just wrestling her into the robe had been a chore, given her surprising strength and ferocity.

As the Paramedics unloaded the stretcher, Knott flipped open his cell phone and called the nurse's station to tell Nurse Sanders that he was downstairs with his wife. Sanders said they were ready to receive the patient. Then she asked if he still thought the leather restraints were necessary.

"Yes, I'm afraid so," he said, then pocketed the phone and jogged up the front steps to hold the glass doors open for the stretcher-bearers. As they carried Susan past him, she shot him a look of undiluted hatred and snapped her teeth at him. He tried to say something comforting to her but a shaky catch of breath in the back of his throat held him silent.

* * *

Sharyn was still seated at the card table when the ambulance attendants brought the woman in on a stretcher. She was surprised to see Dr. Knott accompanying them. He glanced down the hallway at Sharyn but didn't seem to recognize her. He had already looked away by the time she raised a hand in greeting.

To avoid returning to her room, Sharyn had agreed to unburden herself to Nurse Sanders, but then the first emergency admission arrived and Sanders had her hands full with getting the new patient admitted and sedated. The woman had walked in with an EMT on each arm. The deer-in-the-headlights look on her face had made Sharyn avert her eyes.

This woman strapped to the stretcher was a different story. She had the look of a wild animal. Her eyes were predatory, and she was actually growling at Dr. Knott, who looked as if he were on the verge of crying.

Nurse Sanders touched Knott's shoulder and said, "I'm so sorry, Dr. Knott. You know we'll take special care of her."

Knott nodded and watched as the Paramedics rolled the woman into the room next to the nurse's station, the only room on the unit with an observation window visible from the station. Psychiatric intensive care.

Sharyn surmised that the ferocious-looking woman was Knott's relative—perhaps his sister, or possibly his wife. The poor guy. That had to be a bitch, admitting your own family member.

Sanders and Tom the mental health tech trailed the stretcher into the room. Knott remained in the corridor, looking lost and forlorn. He looked up at the ceiling, and then turned his head and looked at Sharyn. This time he recognized her and started toward her. He wore jeans, a blue shirt with the tail out, and a pair of cordovan loafers and no socks. She thought he looked much younger in casual clothes. He gave her a wounded smile as he stopped at her card table.

"Can't sleep?" He pulled out the straight-backed chair opposite her and sat down.

"I don't want to sleep," she confessed. "I had a booger of a bad dream."

"I can up the dosage of your sleep medication. But there's no guarantee you won't have nightmares."

"No thanks. I'm not sleepy anyway." Sharyn sensed that he had something he wanted to say to her and that he was unsure how to broach the subject.

"Are *you* all right?" she asked, glancing at the blood-stained towel wrapped around his hand. Turning the tables on her shrink gave her a sense of power, though she was sincere in her inquiry. She had never been one to engage in one-upmanship with a therapist.

The question startled him, but he quickly recovered. "I'm fine," he said, though he clearly wasn't. "I heard something tonight that . . . made me remember your description of the sound you heard. It was . . . I'd never heard anything like it. I don't know if I should even be telling you this . . ."

Sharyn stiffened her spine. "You *heard* it?"

"I heard *something*. So did my wife. That's her they just brought in on the stretcher."

"My God. It . . . did that to her?"

"Apparently." His face reddened. "She's never had any problems before. Behavior problems. But when that shrieking started she ran outside naked. In the rain. She turned violent when I tried to stop her. That awful sound went on for at least five minutes, and when it finally stopped, Susan didn't come out of it. And now she still wants to take another bite out of me. Unless it's one hell of a coincidence, that animal cry triggered this wild behavior in her. I can't help but think it's the same sound that brought on your panic attack."

"She did that," Sharyn said with a nod at his injured hand.

"Yes. She was like a crazed animal. I don't know what to make of all this. I've never heard of any kind of animal cry that can instantly make someone go berserk. And if that's really what happened, why didn't it do the same to me? Or to you?"

"When your wife ran outside," she asked, "did it seem like she was running *to* the . . . shrieker or that she was trying to run away from it?"

Knott shrugged. "I couldn't tell where the noise was coming from. It seemed to be coming from everywhere. Maybe Susan could. I don't know. But my sense about it is that she was running toward it, and that the last thing she wanted was me—or anyone—trying to stop her. Because that's when she turned violent."

Sharyn stared at the makeshift bandage on Knott's hand. She took a breath, then said, "I know of something very much like this. In literature. Not medical literature. In mythology. You've heard of the Greek god Pan?"

"Yes?" He raised his brows in anticipation.

"Pan was said to have a shrieking cry that could terrify all who heard it, animals and humans alike."

"Pan," he said, his voice suddenly flat with skepticism.

"That's right. Pan. The god. Part man, part beast. A very powerful figure in mythology. Not at all like the modern-day emasculated representations you've probably seen of him."

"I shouldn't be discussing this with you," said Knott, straightening in the chair as if he were about to get up. "I'm sorry. I apologize for my unprofessional lapse. If you want to change doctors—"

"Cut the shit, Doc. Something really fucking weird is going on here and you know it. Don't hide behind your damned shield of professionalism. That won't do me or your wife one bit of good."

Knott leaned forward and lowered his voice. "You expect me to believe a character from Greek mythology really exists? That he's come to Georgia to—"

"No, of course not, but I think we have to at least look at the possibility that the myth might've been based on a real-life . . . thing, whatever the hell it is. Some myths are based on real events and actual people. Pagan religious practices . . ." Sharyn caught herself shifting into a higher mental gear and took a deep breath to tamp down the urgency she felt, lest the good doctor think she *was* manic. Then she went on, slower. "My friend and colleague Alfred Thorn is looking into Widow's Ridge folklore that seems to have parallels with Dionysian myth. Dionysus is closely identified with Pan. Some scholars believe the two are virtually interchangeable. The point is, Professor Thorn has found evidence that something happened in Widow's Ridge in the late eighteen-hundreds that suggests a correlation to Dionysian myth."

"The Helling," said Knott. "I spoke with him yesterday and he mentioned his . . . research."

"Right, right. He told me about the old lady's wall drawing. Another pesky coincidence? Or synchronicity again?"

Knott's eyes seemed to dim, as if a curtain had come down behind them. "I'm sorry, but I just can't accept this . . . speculation as a serious explanation for what's happened to my wife. Or to you."

"Sure you can. You just don't want to because this isn't something your pharmaceuticals can make go away. You *heard* it! You know something's out there."

He stood, avoiding Sharyn's eyes. "Excuse me. I have to check on my wife."

"You'd better get real, Dr. Knott. If Al Thorn is right, this thing that can't exist killed half the people in Widow's Ridge a century and a half ago. And now it's come screaming back."

CHAPTER THIRTEEN

Asa had a woman in each hand, his fingers exerting just enough pressure on the backs of their necks to guide them where he wanted them to go. It wasn't easy because the zombified ladies wouldn't move under their own steam; he had to gently push them forward to get them to shuffle along on their bare feet. If he pushed too hard or fast, they would slip on the wet ground and stumble and fall, but if he was too slow in leading them away from the magnetic pull of the cave, the Beast would surely catch them.

Judy Lynn Bowen was faring a little better with her charge, as she could use both her hands to marshal the chunky gray-haired woman over the wet ground and around brushy obstacles.

The rain had stopped and the trees were scarcely visible in the night's gathering mists. Lines of William Blake's poetry ran through Asa's mind as he shepherded the naked women blindly through the dark.

. . . they buried her in a silent cave. Urizen dropped a tear; the Eternal Man Darken'd with sorrow.

He wasn't exactly sure what the words meant; he wasn't even sure who or what Urizen was, but from his repeated readings of Blake he was pretty sure that Urizen was a misguided demonic god or a demigod responsible for the fall of the material world and giving form to the likes of the Beast. Asa often got the Bible and Blake's illuminated epics mixed up, but their passages usually served to soothe him, so he rarely bothered to sort them out in his head. Even the appalling passages about vomiting out *scaly monsters of the restless deep* somehow gave him succor; the act of naming the terrors made them a little less terrifying.

But now his terror mounted, filling his breast with contradictory urges. Though the monster's smell wasn't getting stronger, he didn't doubt Judy Lynn's insistence that it was drawing near, returning to the cave in which it had stashed the women for its nefarious purposes—whatever those might be.

"Hurry!" she said over her shoulder. "He's almost here!"

Then Asa knew it was too late to escape. He knew he wasn't *meant* to escape. After all these years, he was finally coming face to face with his weird. It was his destiny to meet the Beast and do battle with the savage fiend. Running away was no option. His *weird* was *here*. He could not run from his destiny. He knew not to try.

"You go," he said. "Leave the lady and get away from here as fast as you can." It was better to save one than to lose them all.

"I can't just leave her," she said, her voice thick with confused emotions.

"Yes you can. Go now! Run! Don't look back."

She dropped her hands away from the older woman and then dashed into the mists.

Asa unsheathed his bone-handle hunting knife and stepped boldly forward, putting himself between the women and the thing coming at him out of the mist.

* * *

She ran through the dark as if guided by a divine hand, or perhaps by an inner light, preternaturally benign, that prevented her from slamming into a tree or tripping over limb or rock. She didn't know where she was going, other than *down*.

Down was good. Down would take her off the mountain and away from the screaming beast.

And it was screaming now, shrieking in the distance behind her, but she didn't slow down, didn't respond to its shrill call. Not this time. She would not give in to its evil summons. Never again would she give up her humanity to the stinking bestial creature. Never! Not after the horrible things it did to her.

Despite her fierce determination to resist the otherworldly cry, Judy Lynn could feel her resolve weakening in the sound-wave assault of the echoes chasing her down the mountainside and through the fog. She clamped her hands over her ears as she ran, and though having her arms thus elevated threw off her balance, she managed to stay on her feet by slowing her pace.

Until a thin tree branch slapped her across the face at the exact same instant her left foot came down in a slippery patch of mud.

She twisted and tumbled headlong to the ground, throwing her hands in front of her just in time to save her face from a bone-crushing impact. The fall knocked the air out of her lungs, and for a long moment she felt as if she were suffocating. Her ears rang, but that was to the good; the ringing muffled the distant (but nonetheless insistent) cry of that hellish devil. She lay still and waited for her lungs to replenish their ration of air.

Never again would she make fun of Josh's father for his hellfire-and-brimstone sermons.

The Devil was real.

From the horns on his head to his cloven hooves, he was as real as real could be. And he had come up from Hell to torment her, to corrupt her soul and make her perform unspeakably evil acts. And even if nobody believed her, she knew she had to tell people what she'd seen and what had happened to her . . . and to the others—those poor women stranded back there with nothing to protect them but that crazy old one-eyed geezer, Old Edgar. *Asa.*

But he saved my life. If the creepy old man hadn't found the cave and shined the light in her face, she might've remained there at the mercy of the Devil. And everybody knew Old Scratch was merciless. Asa's little light had somehow brought her back to herself, and now the poor old man was back there wrestling with Satan, sacrificing himself so that she could live.

With the notion that Asa's penlight had been imbued with holy power and had fired a blessed beam of angelic light into her eyes, Judy Lynn took a painful breath, pushed up and resumed her descent.

The fog thinned as she went lower. She no longer heard the Devil's howl. The moon was visible now through breaking clouds and she could better see where she was going.

The road was down there somewhere. If she kept going, she would eventually find it and then she would hike back to the safety of houses and electric lights and place herself under the protection of God-fearing Christians. If she could keep the blessing of divine grace round about her.

And then she would warn them that Satan had come to these mountains.

* * *

"Urizen!" he shouted. He brandished his knife before the Beast. Then the words came, unbidden, from his memory: "I will cast thee out if thou repentest not, and leave thee as a rotten branch to be burned with Mystery the Harlot and with Satan for ever and ever." Words of Blake, though somewhat paraphrased, nevertheless shouted with all the baritone authority Asa could muster.

The Beast stepped forward through sinuous strands of ghostly fog, its hooves scarcely touching the ground. Asa blinked his eye to clear his mist-blurred vision. The thing standing tall in front of him didn't appear to be completely in this world, its shadowy form merely outlined by the mist. While the creature wasn't transparent, neither was it solidly there. It came to Asa that the Beast had one foot in this world and one foot in some other, which probably explained why he'd had such a hard time catching wind of its musk. Even now, its scent wasn't strong. But the thing's undeniable presence and harsh aura of menace sent Asa's pulse into overdrive.

Save for the sound of rainwater dripping from the trees, the woods were unnaturally quiet. The moon broke through the clouds and lent a pearly sheen to the short-furred flesh of the Beast's hindquarters. Two hornlike protuberances growing out of its wide forehead made Asa wonder if this thing before him now was Beelzebub himself, ascendant from Hell. But no, that couldn't be; his mother had specifically told him that the Beast he was to be on the lookout for was *not* the Devil—not a fallen angel. It was an ancient god, one from among the panoply of deities that populated Old World mythology. He *knew* this creature. He'd seen its likeness in library books, though none of the illustrations had captured this thing's terrifying aspect, nor its ferocious presence.

Asa widened his stance and braced himself for battle. He tightened his grip on his hunting knife's haft. As much to confound the Beast as to calm his vaulting anxiety, Asa bellowed more of Blake's words: "'For he stove in battles dire, in unseen conflicts with shapes bred from his forsaken wilderness of beast, bird, fish, serpent & element, combustion, blast, vapor and cloud.'" The words strengthened him.

The Beast pierced him with a gaze of cold fury, as if Asa's belligerent tone had enraged it. It came forward on those curiously bent legs, moving with unnerving animalistic grace.

Asa extended his arm and jabbed the air with his knife. "Come on, you stinking pig! You'll not touch these ladies! I am the sentinel to these hills. I'll gut you like a—"

His words broke off midstream when two new women appeared, wraithlike, in the fog, one on either side of the Beast. The fiend had abducted two more to add to his captive harem. One young, the other middle-aged. Both sturdy specimens. Both shockingly naked.

The Beast opened its wide mouth, and at first Asa thought the thing was actually going to grin at him, but then the lower jaw elongated, the dark maw widened, and the Beast issued a strident cry that put the hairs up on the back of Asa's neck and unleashed a dribble of urine in his britches.

The powerful ululation saturated the night air, sonic waves solidifying into shimmering images called forth from the realm of ancient gods. Asa saw them hanging in the air like pictures on a gallery wall, frozen glimpses of a bizarre and timeless place ruled by ruthless gods like this one now standing before him. The cry rose in volume and pitch until blood trickled from Asa's ears, then it quavered, sharply decreased in pitch, and finally faded to a puling glissando that left Asa frozen in clammy fear.

The two women standing abreast of the Beast went into rhythmically convulsive contortions, as if dancing to maddening music only they could hear. Their faces twitched and contorted as well, their comely features transforming into hideous masks of rage. Then they came prowling forward in the slinky manner of stalking cats. Possessed and prowling.

Asa heard a shuffle of movement behind him and realized that the three ladies he was trying to protect were also making ready to attack him.

The Beast was using the women as chess pieces, frenzied pawns driven to violence by the cunning god's commanding cry. Asa was doomed from the start; he could not raise a hand against females. It was a cardinal rule ingrained by his strict upbringing. He would let them tear him apart rather than fight back. His only chance was to take down the Beast and hope that would break the malevolent spell woven over these females.

But it was already too late. The women attacked, launching themselves upon him, clawing and biting as they took him to the ground. With unnatural strength, the five females savaged him. He struggled to throw them off without hurting them, but they fought with the relentless ferocity of a pack of starving wolves. In the disorienting mêlée, Asa lost the knife, and one of the women snatched it up and planted the blade in his throat.

His dying scream gurgled in his throat, and he finally saw that it was his weird to sacrifice himself to this band of madwomen.

CHAPTER FOURTEEN

KNOTT DROVE THROUGH THE FOG, holding the Jag's speed to an impatient crawl for fear of running off the road. Though he knew the road to his home in Goat Head Hollow quite well, he didn't trust his memory or his instincts to keep him from losing the blacktop in the fog and plunging down the mountainside.

The fog inside his skull was the real problem; it made everything seem unreal, it rendered his perceptions unreliable. As a man whose vocation required a firm and decisive grip on reality, Knott was unaccustomed to feeling so *at sea*, so lost in mental fog as to be unable to navigate or circumvent the dangers he knew were there though he couldn't yet see them—like the shrieking thing in the fog.

From the moment he'd left Susan strapped to the bed in her assigned hospital room, he felt like an imposter. A fraud. He wasn't a real doctor, he was a psychiatric quack. His wife had lost her mind and he had no clue as to how to help her find herself. He was going home, abandoning Susan to insanity—or whatever the hell it was. He'd told himself it would do no good to stay the rest of the night with her; the IM medication he'd ordered for her would zonk her out for hours, so she probably wouldn't know he wasn't there. Susan was in the capable hands of a competent nursing staff. For now, she was safe.

But that wasn't the issue. What disturbed him so deeply was the fact that he could find no rational explanation for what had come over her with such a frighteningly rapid onset, and he certainly wasn't ready to buy into Sharyn Rampling's wild theory.

But I heard it myself. There was something out there making that god-awful noise that made her crazy. I felt it too. Not to the extent Susan did, but I definitely felt something . . . unnatural. Supernatural?

And what if it was still there, waiting for him? What if *he* succumbed to the thing's crazy-making cry next time? What if—

The dark shape darted into the road ahead of him, floating in the fog and flapping shiny bat-like wings. He stomped the brake pedal and cut the steering wheel hard to the right, narrowly evading a skid into the roadside ditch by cutting back to the left. The Jag lurched to a stop. He shifted into reverse and backed up, trying to catch sight of the figure in the rearview mirror.

A woman in a dark slicker, not a bat-creature. She had been flagging him down, not flapping wings.

She slapped her palm against the driver's-side window. Knott powered down the window.

"Help me," she said, panting hard.

"What's wrong? Are you hurt?" He saw that she was on the edge of untamed hysteria, that her hair was a mass of wet tangles festooned with leaves and twigs, as if she'd been rolling on the forest floor. Her face was streaked with mud. There was wildness in her eyes.

"We have to help them," she said, rushing the words. "He's come back. Please . . ."

"Get in," he said. "I'm a doctor." Realizing how inane that sounded, he added, "I can help you."

He caught a glimpse of her bare legs below the folds of the poncho as she ran in front of the headlights and circled around to the passenger's door, and he got the impression that she was naked beneath the muddy slicker, which was much too big for her.

She threw open the door and climbed onto the seat. She slammed the door and locked it.

"I'm Dr. Knott. What's your name?"

"Judy Lynn Bowen," Her lower lip poked out in the manner of a pouting infant bewildered by a personal injury it can't understand.

"What happened, Judy?" He pulled onto the narrow shoulder of the road and shifted into Park. He turned on the hazard flashers.

"Judy Lynn. Nobody calls me just Judy."

Knott smiled reassuringly. "All right, Judy Lynn. What happened? Who is it we have to help?"

"Those women . . . he took 'em and did terrible things to us. He's . . ."

"He took you too?"

She nodded.

"Who did?" Knott noted the bloody lacerations on her bare legs, the sort of scratches you might get by running through the woods, but she didn't appear to have any serious physical injuries—none that showed. Her serious wounds were apparently psychological.

"I don't know *what* he is. Some kind of monster. With horns like the devil. But the devil's not real, is he? But this thing is. Real. But he's not . . . he's here but not here, you know?"

"No, I'm afraid I don't. I'm not following you. Start at the beginning."

"You don't understand. We have to get help. The cops. He's right up there." She pointed at the wooded mountainside rising steeply on the right side of the road.

Knott glanced out at the lush darkness and his old fear of the dark once again reached out of the past to twist his nerves into an insidious knot. He shook it off.

"Did he rape you?" he asked.

In the green glow of the dash lights, her face suddenly turned demonic, and just for an instant Knott feared that she might attack him in a fit of paranoia. Then her face softened a little, and she said, "Yes. He did, but not, you know, like a regular rapist. It was . . . worse. Not that I've ever been raped. He did things to us, to *me,* that I . . . I can't talk about it now."

What were the odds, he wondered, of a delusional woman flagging down a psychiatrist on an otherwise deserted mountain road? Delusional or in shock, or both. But still . . . in light of what had happened to Susan . . . and with the sound of that screaming cry fresh in his mind, Knott wasn't absolutely sure that Judy Lynn Bowen was delusional. He briefly wondered what Sharyn Rampling would make of this girl's wild tale.

"I think we have to get out of here," she said with renewed urgency. "He could be coming after me. I don't think Old Edgar could fight him off."

"Who's Edgar?"

"You know, the one-eyed wanderer. Old Edgar, the crazy hermit. Would you please just get us the fuck out of here?"

"All right." He pulled onto the blacktop and executed a tight U-turn. He shut off the hazard lights as he accelerated toward Dogwood. "I'm going to take you to the hospital. They will examine you and clean up your cuts. I'll call the police and have them meet us at the emergency room and you can tell them what happened."

"No, that'll be too late! We don't have time for that. Those women—"

"I'm calling the police right now," he interrupted, hoping to quell her mounting agitation. He pulled his cell phone from his pocket and punched his speed-dial number for the county police. As psychiatrist, he often had dealings with the Sheriff's Department, calling upon deputies to transport patients hospitalized by court order or to serve commitment papers. When the dispatcher answered, he said, "This is Dr. Trey Knott. I've just picked up a young woman on highway twenty-nine, about two miles east of Goat Head Hollow. She says she was abducted and raped, and that her abductor is still on the mountain with—" He moved the cell away from his mouth and asked the girl, "How many women?"

"Three others."

He nodded, then continued. "With three other women."

"He had us in a cave," Judy Lynn said.

"No, she doesn't need an ambulance. I'm taking her to Dogwood Medical myself. If you can have an officer meet us there, he can talk to her then."

He folded the phone and dropped it in his shirt pocket.

Judy Lynn said, "I don't know if the cops can do any good. I mean . . . what happens if they shoot the thing? He's like a ghost. Bullets prob'ly go right through him. I shit you not. He's like nothing in this whole wide world, nothing you've ever seen before. Huh. You think I'm a nutbag, right? Or on drugs. Yeah, sure, I know. But I swear to God I'm not. That thing is *real*."

"I don't think you're a nutbag. You've had a traumatic experience and—"

"I'm marrying Reverend Jordan's son, for cripe's sake. You think he would let his son marry Psycho Girl? No fricking way, Doc." She folded her arms across her chest. She seemed very small-breasted beneath the voluminous poncho. "I'm supposed to marry him. He may not want me after . . . this. God."

She began to cry. She hugged herself as if trying to contain her overflowing emotions. Her shoulders shook. Her tears made streaks on her muddy cheeks that reminded Knott of war paint.

"I'm c-c-cold," she said, shivering. "C-could you turn on the heater?"

He turned the heater on and angled the vents toward her. She nodded appreciatively and hugged herself tighter, hunching her shoulders and tucking her chin to her chest. When her crying subsided, Knott said, "Did this thing that took you make a screaming sound, sort of like a wild cat?"

She looked at him with surprise-widened eyes, then she narrowed them in suspicion. "How did you know that?"

"I heard it earlier tonight, outside my house."

She nodded knowingly, jaw firmly set. "That's how it gets you. Like it hypnotizes you or something, you know? God, I can't get that sound out of my head. It's like it's stuck there, still . . . doing something to me." She shivered harder.

Knott's imagination went to a place he didn't like. His usual left-brain dominance gave way to intuitive right-brain speculation, and he was off on a magical mystery tour of possibilities—none of which he found reassuring. Some otherworldly creature was abroad in the night, roaming the hills with single-minded intent, issuing his irresistible call to the unsuspecting women who happened to reside within his newfound territory—his sphere of diabolical influence. But to what purpose? Why, to stash the women in a cave and psychically violate them, of course. To commit serial acts of supernatural rape. The formidable entity had the power to turn a gentle woman like Susan into a raging hellion, and he asserted that power by means of an ear-splitting cry. The creature's call was so compelling that those victims it summoned would try to tear apart anyone who tried to stop them from going to him.

So why didn't Sharyn Rampling heed the creature's call and rush to his side? This was Knott's left-brain voice trying to interject down-to-earth logic into his internal dialogue. Right-brain, with its peculiar power to see the big picture, the gestalt in the mosaic, had an answer ready: *Because her medication and/or the biochemical/genetic configuration characteristic of her disorder interfered with the process, her neural receptors having been altered by years of taking lithium. Instead of being seized with a compulsion to answer the call, Sharyn withdrew into a fortress of fear.*

Knott squeezed the steering wheel, his fingers expressing only a small measure of his mental stress.

Right, and the Tooth Fairy, the Easter Bunny and jolly ole St. Nick are waiting in your office for their next group therapy session, Left-brain mocked.

He wanted to query the girl further, even though his professional judgment told him not to do it; as unstable and agitated as she obviously was, a moving vehicle was a dangerous place to ask probing questions that might make her want to throw open the door and bail out.

But he had to learn all he could from her before he turned her over to the ER physician at Dogwood Medical, who would examine her for physical injury and for evidence of rape, and then probably recommend transfer to Ridgewood for a complete psych evaluation with a full battery of psychological testing. Knott couldn't wait; he had to know now. Susan was in trouble, and he needed all the pertinent information he could gather in order to understand her condition and determine the right course of treatment.

But what was the treatment for something like this? The *Diagnostic and Statistical Manual of Mental Disorders* would be of little use. Knott knew he was on his own this time, flying half-blind by the shiny seat of his pants. He could toss the holy DSM-V out the window this time.

Driving slowly through the fog, he kept his eyes on what little he could see of the road in the diffuse headlight-beams and said, "I would like to ask you a few more questions, if you feel up to it."

"I know you," she said, somewhat defiantly. "You're a psychologist."

"Psychiatrist," he gently corrected her. "That means I'm a medical doctor."

"I'm not crazy!"

"I know that, Judy Lynn" he said. "I'll be honest with you. I have a personal interest in what happened to you because my wife heard that thing's cry too, and it . . . did something to her. I'm trying to understand what happened to her. So I can help her."

"What did it do to her?"

Though he felt he was betraying a personal *and* professional confidence, he told the truth. "She ran out of the house naked and turned violent when I tried to stop her."

He glanced at her. Saw her nod.

"It called her out," she said. "Just like it did me. I hit a deer and ran in a ditch, and I was waiting for the wrecker when I heard it. I . . . I pissed my pants I was so scared, but then . . ."

"Then what?"

"Then I wasn't afraid anymore. It was like I was in a trance, you know? I left the road and walked into the woods to go to it. I *had* to go to it. I *wanted* to. Like nothing else mattered. And even after it stopped that screaming I went right to it, like there was an invisible rope pulling me. Then I saw it standing there and I got really scared again because I knew what I was seeing couldn't be real, but it sure as hell was. *Real.* It looked like something cut out of a Grimm's fairy tale book because it was too scary for little kids to see. It was . . . I don't *even* know how to describe it."

"Try. Please."

"It had these short horns on its head and its legs were like an animal's, a giant goat maybe. It looked sort of like that Pan dude, but . . . evil. Like an X-rated version, with that big . . . ugh."

"Big what?"

"Big hard-on. Pointing right at me. I wanted to run away when I saw it, but I couldn't. It made me keep going. And when I got closer I saw that it . . . he was like a . . . Whaddya call those things? Like in the movies, a *hologram*. Like it wasn't really there. But he was because then he *touched* me."

"Touched you how?"

"With his hands. They were cold and damp like really thick fog. Not solid, exactly, but I could feel them anyway. Like being felt up by a ghost."

"He touched you in a sexual way?"

"Well, *yeah*. Whaddya think, with a giant woody like that? *Of course* it was sexual. And I . . . couldn't help it . . ." She trailed off and began to weep softly.

"It's okay," he said. "You're safe now. He can't hurt you again."

"You don't know that! You don't know what he can do! You weren't there. He can do anything he wants. If he wants your wife, he'll come back and take her. And there's nothing you can do to stop him."

He wanted to tell her he didn't believe that, but he held his tongue; she believed it, and he didn't want to get into a pointless argument with the traumatized young woman. And the truth was, he was afraid she might be right. If she wasn't delusional and there actually was an otherworldly being he had to contend with, he needed to learn all he could about his foe and understand how it exerted its sinister will in the real world.

"So . . . it . . . he raped you then?"

She didn't answer.

"Judy Lynn?"

"It did *something* to me. I can't remember exactly. It's like it was a dream. A nightmare. But not. I'm not sure what all he did to me. But I still feel it. He . . . I think he put something *in* me. And it's still there."

She touched her fingertips to her forehead, then added: "Here."

"What do you think it is?" he asked. He was accustomed to questioning delusional patients, so this question came out as a matter of routine.

"I don't know," she said with a sob that wrenched his heart.

CHAPTER
FIFTEEN

LIZA LEATHERWOOD LAY ABED and listened to her blood.

The digital clock on the nightstand had extra-large numerals but when she turned her head on the pillow to look at them, all she saw was a red blob of light floating in the bedroom's darkness. She could've put on her glasses to bring the glowing splotch into focus, but she didn't bother. She knew she was well into the wee hours of morning; she didn't need a clock to tell her that. Time told itself within her weary bones.

Unable to sleep, she listened to her blood pulsing through her thin veins. Since she'd punctured the drum of her good ear with the hatpin, the internal sounds of her biological machinery were louder than the sounds of the outside world. This was both a blessing and a curse. The cry of the dark man of the wood couldn't claim her now, but the thudding of her age-worn heart kept her awake and reminded her of the frailty of her used-up body.

Her blood sluggishly whispered to her that Death was in the neighborhood, drawing nearer with each beat of her pulse. Even if the Grim Reaper didn't come for her tonight, he would come soon enough to still her heart and take her soul to wherever it was that souls went, once the body called it quits forever. Soon enough, *she hoped.* Her great fear was that she would suffer a stroke and lie immobilized for hours—or days—trapped in a withering husk, helpless to do anything but contemplate the unforgiving reality of her lonely end.

Miss Liza?

The gravelly voice startled her. She held her breath and tried to listen to the silence-steeped room. Her weak eyes searched the darkness.

"Who's there?" she croaked.

The Beast . . .

She *knew* that gruff voice. She sat up and stared at the dark shape hovering over the foot of her brass bed, softly backlit by moonlight streaming softly through the window.

"Asa? Asa Edgar, what the devil are you doing in my bedroom?"

Set the women on me.

"Asa, what in hell are—" She all at once realized Asa's voice had spoken inside her head, not out there in the gloom of the room. The shape shone with a faint luminescence, pulsating with each beat of her heart.

They've killed me, Asa whispered despondently.

She fumbled for the little pull-chain hanging from the shaded lamp on the nightstand, found it and pulled the switch. She blinked in the sudden light, her eyes dry and sandpapery. Between blinks she glimpsed Asa Edgar's mutilated face and torn-open throat. His one-eyed stare held her briefly, then the light in his eye dimmed and his tall form faded, receding into the out-of-focus background of the room.

Ghost tree, he said in a voice as empty and cold as a plundered grave.

Then he was gone. Gone from the room and gone from her head.

"Oh Asa . . ." she said with a low moan. Overcome with grief, she clutched at her breast as if to hold back the profound sadness and deep futility that encroached upon her heart.

The man had done occasional odd jobs for her since Wilbur died, and she had grown fond of the eccentric rambler who called himself sentinel to these hills. When she'd learned that he regularly read the works of William Blake, she had introduced him to the tales of Nathaniel Hawthorne. Many an evening had they sat on her porch while she read aloud to him. The stories from her old paperback copy of *Twice-Told Tales* always seemed to touch him deeply, as if they satisfied some deep hunger he felt but couldn't express. One October evening a year ago he'd brought his big book of Blake to show her the strange artwork and read some of the man's poetry to her, but she hadn't been able to make much sense of it. When she asked him to explain what he'd read, Asa blushed and admitted that he didn't really understand much of it, but that the words soothed him and scratched an inner itch he hadn't known he'd had.

Theirs had been a peculiar friendship, characterized by unspoken emotional needs and by long periods of silence spent gazing out at the hills. Liza had never spoken a word about the secret history of Widow's Ridge, nor had she ever mentioned the Helling, but somehow old Asa must've known about the area's shameful past. Why else would his ghost come calling to tell her the Beast had returned? He hadn't come just to bid her a final farewell. He'd come to warn her. And to tell her something about the ghost tree.

Set the women on me, he'd said. There was no mistaking the implication of those words. None at all.

The Helling had begun again. The beast of the dark wood had finally returned to have his way with a new generation of womenfolk and to demand sacrificial blood of innocent males. But why had Asa mentioned the ghost tree? And how had he known about it?

* * *

The ringing phone rescued Rourke from a disorienting nightmare. He sat straight up in bed, breathing hard and sweating. In the dream he'd been running from an unidentified wild animal, and his pulse rate now raced accordingly. It took several scary moments to realize he was in his bed and not fleeing the relentless beast.

He grabbed the cordless phone from its base, thumbed the Talk button and said, "Rourke."

The caller was Dean Elwood, the part-time nightshift dispatcher. "Sorry to wake you, deputy, but we thought you'd wanna know Judy Lynn Bowen turned up. They've got her at Dogwood Medical. Says she was abducted and raped. She's apparently okay physically, but her mental state is questionable."

Rourke was having trouble processing what he was hearing. Coming out of his nightmare-induced fight-or-fight mode, he glanced over his shoulder to make sure nothing was pursuing him, but all he saw was the blank bedroom wall. "Questionable?"

"Well, yeah. She says she was raped by a monster. Of the supernatural kind." Elwood chuckled softly. "I'd say that qualifies as questionable, wouldn't you, Rob?"

If you'd seen what I saw, you wouldn't think so, he thought, but what he said was, "So it would seem. We have a man with her?"

"Roger that. Deputy Sipes took her statement and he's waiting for the docs to determine disposition. Ask me, I'd say take her to Ridgewood for some intensive psychiatric care."

"Tell Sipes I'm on my way."

Rourke hung up and jumped into his uniform. Lucy Fur was in the hall, pawing the bottom of the bedroom door and knocking it against the doorframe. Before going to bed, Rourke had banished her from the bedroom because the encounter with the thing in the backyard had left her agitated and in a high state of canine alert. When he'd returned from Mountview Villas, Lucy bared her teeth and growled at him again, leading Rourke to conclude that he still carried the scent of the phantom in the rain.

He pulled on his boots, strapped on his gun belt and opened the door. Lucy Fur whined and submissively lowered her head as if apologizing for her earlier misplaced expressions of hostility. Rourke reached down and ruffled the fur on the back of her neck. "It's okay, girl. We've all had a rough night."

He grabbed his hat and went out the door. As he walked to his car through moonlit mist, he made several glances over his shoulders to make sure nothing was coming up on his flank.

* * *

Judy Lynn Bowen was sitting on the side of the gurney when Rourke swept aside the pale-blue privacy curtain and entered the cloth-walled cubicle. She looked up fearfully, her eyes bloodshot and misty. Wounded. A blue and white hospital gown that was too big for her hung loosely off her left shoulder. Her straw-colored hair was a nest of tangles. Her bare legs bore scratches and bruises that, at first glance, looked as if they might've been inked by a psychotic tattoo artist. To Rourke, she looked like a lost child, perhaps raised by wolves and just now rescued from the wilderness. Feral and afraid.

"Judy Lynn, I'm Deputy Rourke," he said, removing his Stetson.

Relief flushed some of the fear from her face as she took in Rourke's uniform, her eyes lingering on the pistol holstered on his hip. It seemed to Rourke that she was reassured by the gun, that she fully expected he might have to use it to defend what was left of her honor and her innocence. "Are you up to a few more questions?"

She shrugged, then sullenly pulled the gown up to cover her bare shoulder. "I guess."

"I know you've already talked to Deputy Sipes, so I'll keep it short. You must be anxious to get home."

Judy Lynn nodded, eyes downcast. "If they don't send me to the crazy house."

"You think they don't believe your story?" He moved a little closer, but not close enough to crowd her and make her feel cornered.

"How could they? I can't hardly believe it myself, you know? You won't believe me either."

"You might be wrong about that. Try me."

"Can you make them let me go home?" she challenged, looking him in the eyes. A tear trickled down her cheek.

"That'll be up to the doctors and your mom, but I might be able to give them a push in the right direction." He gave her what he hoped was a knowing smile.

She shrugged, then shook her head as she absently stared at the floor tiles. "What's the point? They don't even believe I was raped. I was, though. Even though there's no physical evidence, I *was*. By a monster. I don't know if he was a ghost or demon, but I know what he did to me."

"Can you describe him for me?"

She glanced up sharply at him, clearly surprised that he was taking her seriously enough to ask for a description of her ghostly rapist. "Yeah, if you promise not to make fun of me behind my back."

"I wouldn't do that. I promise you."

Judy Lynn closed her eyes and took a deep, shuddering breath. Keeping her eyes shut tightly, she said, "He was part man, part animal, like something out of a scary fairy tale. He had horns on his head, like the devil, and hooves for feet. His legs were like horse's legs, but thicker. I don't think he had a tail, though. I didn't see one. He had a face like a goat-man with a mossy beard, and his teeth looked like they were made out of brown wood. His eyes . . . they were so dark I couldn't see what color they were, but sometimes they shined and then they looked red. He had a great big woody . . . erection. Greenish purple. And he smelled like . . . like a barnyard, only sweet, like rotten meat. But the thing is, he wasn't really there. I mean, he was, but he wasn't. Like he was made out of electricity or dirty light. When he touched me, it wasn't like a man touching me but like being touched by, I dunno, frozen fog? That's why they didn't find any physical evidence that he raped me. Because he's not *physical*. He is but he's not." She opened her eyes. "Crazy as hell, huh? Bring on the straightjacket."

"No, it's not crazy. Fantastic maybe, but you're not the first to see something that can't be explained."

Then Judy Lynn Bowen changed. From the illusion of the lost, feral child something else emerged—something wantonly adult, bold and dangerous. She fixed him with a gaze so penetrating that he took a step backward and tensed his muscles as if anticipating an attack.

She suddenly cried, "You saw him! You did, didn't you. You saw the son of a bitch."

Taken aback, Rourke wondered how she could know that. What had she seen in his eyes that gave him away? "I didn't say that," he said, raising his empty hands in front of him.

"You did. You saw him." She smiled. It was a strange smile, sensual and blatantly seductive. Her tongue flicked out to moisten her dry lips. "You know I'm not crazy."

"I saw something," he said, trying to maintain an air of skepticism. "But it was raining too hard to get a good look at it."

"Son of a bitch, you did." Then her face collapsed around a crescent frown and her tone turned angry. "But you won't tell anybody because you're afraid they'll think you're crazy too. You're too chickenshit to tell the truth."

"I just told you, didn't I?" He folded his arms across his chest, his hat dangling from his fingers.

"Yeah, well I'll tell you something I didn't tell anybody else," she said, jutting her chin defiantly. "I know what he wants. I know what he wants us to do. He showed me. He put pictures in my head. And he'll make those other women do it, if you don't stop them."

Rourke had debriefed Sipes when he first arrived at the hospital, and Sipes told him that Judy Lynn claimed the "monster" was holding three other women captive in a cave near Widow's Ridge, so Rourke knew what she meant by "those other women." She'd recognized Gladys Gladstone and Sarah Melton, but she hadn't recognized the third woman.

"I'm listening," he said. "Go ahead."

She flashed him a whorish smile and said, "I'll tell you if you make them let me go home. Otherwise, forget it. You'll just have to wait and find out when the bodies turn up."

"I can't *make* them do anything. But if you have foreknowledge of a capital crime, you have a legal and moral responsibility to report it. If you don't, you could be charged with conspiracy to commit murder. Do you understand what I'm saying? You could go to jail if you don't tell."

"Yeah, I get it. But I'm crazy, remember? They can't hold me responsible. Hell, I hallucinated the whole thing, don't ya know? I'm the psycho chick who ran off into the woods because she was afraid to get married. That's what they're all thinking. I'm just another ditzy runaway bride."

"That's not what I think. I know something bad happened to you. Something that wasn't your fault. But you have to tell me what—"

"Judy Lynn," bellowed Mildred Bowen as she stepped brusquely inside the privacy curtains, totally ignoring Rourke. She handed Judy Lynn a clean set of folded clothes. "Put these on, honey, I'm taking you home."

"Mrs. Bowen," he said, "I need a few more minutes with your daughter if—"

"Not tonight," said the older woman. She was a tall, angular woman with a chiseled jaw and severe eyes. She looked every bit the hard-shell Christian she was. "I'm taking my baby home. She's been through enough hell for one night."

"Thank God," said Judy Lynn, "I'm dying for a cigarette." Then she smirked at Rourke, and he marveled at the way she'd changed before his eyes from a lost little girl to a mockingly sly *femme fatale*.

"She needs to get dressed," Mrs. Bowen said, "so you'll have to step outside now, officer."

Rourke nodded, set his Stetson on his head and reluctantly started away. Then he turned back and said, "Remember what we talked about, Judy Lynn. I'll be in touch real soon."

She puckered her lips and kissed the air, effectively kissing him off.

CHAPTER SIXTEEN

ROURKE SAW TREY KNOTT HUNCHED over a medical chart at the ER nursing station, his brow knotted with concentration as he scribbled a notation. The doctor looked up when Rourke approached the large horseshoe-shaped counter. Knott's face was haggard, his eyes bloodshot. If Rourke didn't know better, he might've thought the good doctor was coming off a bender.

"You're sending Judy Lynn home?" Rourke asked.

Knott nodded and closed the chart. "She's not a danger to herself or to others, therefore she's not a candidate for commitment."

"What'd you make of her wild story?"

Knott leaned back in the chair and folded his arms over his chest. "To tell you the truth, I don't know what to make of it. Confabulation, maybe. But I don't think she's delusional. She's certainly suffered a psychological trauma of some sort, but the ER doctor's exam revealed no evidence of forcible intercourse. Unless she was raped by a man with a very small penis and who was careful enough not to leave ejaculate, she wasn't raped at all."

"She tell you about the other women in the cave?"

"She did." Knott absently fiddled with the ball-point pen in his right hand.

Rourke leaned his forearms on the countertop. "She identified two of them to Deputy Sipes. Both women have been reported as missing."

Knott abruptly leaned forward. "That certainly lends credence to her story. I suppose you'll have to take a search party up the mountain to look for that cave."

"We'll need your help with that, since you're the one who found Judy

Lynn. You can show us exactly where you picked her up?"

"Close to it. I remember there was a Watch For Falling Rocks sign near the spot where she ran in front of me."

Rourke nodded. "I know it's been a long night for you, but we'll need you bright and early—which is only a couple of hours from now."

A heavyset nurse sat down at the opposite end of the desk and opened a chart.

Dr. Knott stood and motioned for Rourke to follow him out of the nursing station. They walked far enough down the corridor to be out of earshot of eavesdroppers. Knott's expression turned grave. "There's something you should know, Rob," he said, keeping his voice just above a whisper.

"Okay." Rourke leaned close so as not to miss what Knott was about to impart.

"The hypnotic cry she says she heard? I heard something just like that a few hours ago outside my house. It affected my wife. She ran out of the house, like she had to answer the call. When I tried to stop her, she became extremely violent and I ended up having to hospitalize her."

"Whoa. That's . . . I'm sorry to hear it, Doc." Rourke immediately thought of the two young women at Mountview Villas. And about the rain-thing he'd seen with his own disbelieving eyes. In his mind's eye he saw Mrs. Gladstone beaning the sheriff with an iron skillet.

Knott wasn't done. He said, "A patient of mine also reported hearing a similar sound that sent her into a state of panic. As much as I hate to admit it, I think something is out there, something with the ability to influence human behavior with its cry. What the hell could do that, Rob?"

"Damned if I know. But I think I may've seen it tonight. Whatever the hell it is. It was raining hard and I didn't get a good look at it, but what I did see was . . . I don't know what it was, but it was like nothing I've ever seen before."

"What did it look like?"

"Like I said, I didn't get a good look at it."

Knott gave him an appraising stare, then after a moment of thoughtful silence, he said, "You know the wildlife in our area, right?"

Rourke nodded.

"Do you know of any animal whose cry can turn people wild?"

"There ain't no such animal," said Rourke. "There's no such critter anywhere in the world, as far as I know."

Knott nodded and then said, "Not in *this* world."

* * *

While Dr. Knott finished his paperwork, Rourke slipped back to the exam area where he'd interviewed Judy Lynn and found the hospital gown she'd left on the exam table. With a pair of banding scissors, he cut off a swatch of the gown and stuck it in his pocket.

A few minutes later, Rourke raised HQ on the cruiser's radio and told the dispatcher to call in all law-enforcement and fire-department personnel, including the roster of volunteer firemen. "I want a search party ready to go at first light," he said. "No stragglers. And send a deputy to Asa Edgar's cabin to bring him in for questioning."

Knott was in the passenger seat, talking into his cell phone. "How's my wife?" he asked. After a pause, he said, "Call my cell if there's any change. Thanks." Then he closed the phone and stuck it in his pocket.

"How is she?" Rourke asked as he drove out of the hospital parking lot and into the street.

"Sleeping. I hope to God she's all right when she wakes up."

"She'll be fine," said Rourke. "She's got a damn good doctor."

"Thanks," Knott muttered. "Normally, it's not sound practice for a psychiatrist to treat a close family member, but . . ."

"But this isn't your normal situation."

"No, it's not."

Rourke adjusted the rearview mirror, not because there was anything to see back there other than the trailing blanket of fog glowing red in the cruiser's taillights but because he needed to do something with his hands besides steer the vehicle. He tended to fidget whenever he was nervous or uncomfortable, and right now, he was both. His nerves were still quietly thrumming from his backyard encounter with the phantasmal creature, and being at such close quarters with a man whose wife was psychologically reeling from a strange encounter of her own, Rourke couldn't help but feel a stab of sympathy for the husband.

His stomach growled, and he realized he might be able to level things out with a comforting plate of food. "What say we grab some grub while we have the time? That truck-stop just off the Interstate serves up a good breakfast. Good coffee, too."

"I'm not really hungry, but I suppose I should eat something."

"When you walk in and smell that hot griddle, you'll find your appetite quick enough. The truckers say the Trucking-A is where you go to find a lost appetite."

Knott grunted.

Rourke gunned the engine and turned the wipers up a notch to clear the fog off the windscreen.

They rode in uneasy silence toward the Interstate. The fog blotted out the surrounding mountains. Rourke's stomach growled.

* * *

Sharyn sat on the edge of the bed and opened the dummy book, *Smuggler's Nook*. She'd purchased it on a whim from an Atlanta novelty shop several years ago, thinking at the time that she might one day have cause to use it, and sure enough, that day came when she reported for her current admission to the hospital. When the staff checked her belongings for sharps and drugs, they didn't find what she'd secreted in *Smuggler's Nook*.

She opened the hardbound volume, thumbed to the hidden compartment in the back of the book and extracted her cell phone. Cell phones were considered contraband at Ridgewood; they were deemed non-therapeutic for the treatment milieu. There was a pay phone out in the hall, but middle-of-the-night calls were prohibited, so Sharyn used her cell to phone Alfred Thorn.

He answered sleepily on the fourth ring. "Y'ello."

"Al, it's me," she said, speaking as quietly as she could. "Sorry to wake you, but—"

"What's wrong?"

"Nothing's wrong with me," she said, a little too loud and too assertively. "But things are happening. Things related to what we talked about earlier."

"What, the mythology?"

"Yes. Dr. Knott just admitted his own wife here. He told me she turned violent after hearing a mysterious cry in the wilderness. He heard it too! He told me so himself."

"Good lord."

"I couldn't wait to tell you. I knew you'd want to know right away."

She heard him yawn. Then he said, "Yes, well I could've used another hour of sack time. I was up rather late. And there's not anything I can do right now with this information. Is there?"

"Uh, no, I guess not. I'm sorry. I couldn't sleep and you're the only one I could talk to about this."

"It's all right, dear. I'm waking up." He yawned again. "So Dr. Knott told you about his wife? Why would he do that? Hardly seems professional."

"That's how shook up the man was. He *heard* it, Al. I mean, my God . . ."

"Yeah, I got that."

"I told you I'm not nuts."

"Never doubted it."

"What are we going to do?"

"Well, I'm going to keep digging until I find out what's buried beneath the local legend. And you're going to keep yourself together until we get the whole thing cleared up."

"You're not getting it, Al. There's something out there, something *real*. This isn't an academic exercise. It's not something you can 'clear up' with facts. Don't you see that?"

"Sharyn, I have no idea what sort of animal can make a sound that drives people . . . wild—if that's what in fact happened—but I can't believe it will turn out to be any kind of supernatural beastie. I'm sorry, I just can't."

"Goddammit, Alfred, get your head out of your journals and smell the feces before you end up wearing it." She realized she was nearly shouting and lowered her voice. "I'm sorry, but you're not grasping the reality of the situation here."

Thorn's heavy sigh sounded like a stiff gust of wind in the cell's tiny earpiece. He said, "Listen, love, I never should've showed you those journal pages or told you about my project. It was totally insensitive of me and I humbly apologize."

"You're pissing me off, Alfred. Stop treating me like a mental invalid and hear what I'm saying. This thing is real. It's having a real effect on real people. And apparently we're the only ones with a clue as to what's really happening. We have a responsibility here."

"To do what? Tell everybody to beware the ancient god of the woodlands? Just because we're both tenured doesn't mean we can't make ourselves look like fools in the eyes of our colleagues and in the community at large."

"Yeah, well fuck you, Al. I'm thoroughly disappointed in you. I never imagined you'd be the one to let me down."

"Calm down, Sharyn. Calm down and just listen. I'm not letting you down. I'm trying to protect you from yourself. I don't know what it is you think we should do, but whatever it is, I seriously doubt it would be to the good. Now, I've been trying to figure out what possibly could've made the womenfolk of Widow's Ridge turn on their menfolk and slaughter them, and so far I haven't come up with a single plausible idea. You seem to be convinced that it was a Dionysian creature with supernatural powers, but I'm not ready to make that leap myself. Not yet, anyway. You're approaching the whole thing from a position of panic, and I'm trying to use my allotted powers of reasoning. I mean, how do you know that Dr. Knott's wife doesn't have a history of mental problems or that she might've gone ga-ga even if they hadn't heard that mysterious cry? I'm just cautioning you against jumping to unfounded conclusions, that's all I'm doing. Don't you see that?"

"Yes, I see. I see very well. Good-bye, Al."

Sharyn folded her phone and tossed it on the bed. Then she went to the window and gazed out into the night fog.

The startling knock on her door twisted a loop in her stomach. She spun around to see Tom the nightshift PA sticking his balding head into the room.

"You okay?" he asked. "I thought I heard shouting."

"I'm fine," she said. "I was talking so loud in my sleep I woke myself up. Sorry."

He nodded, then withdrew his head and softly closed the door.

Thankful that he hadn't seen the cell phone, Sharyn retrieved it and returned it to the secret slot in *Smuggler's Nook*.

Then she sat on the bed and wept tears of angry frustration.

* * *

She stood before the great haunted tree and gazed up at the moon-frosted limbs bending upward in warped supplication. Crossing her wrists over her chest, she clutched the hand-knitted shawl tighter over her thin shoulders and shivered against the fog-damp air of predawn.

The two-mile walk from her house to this secret burial ground had made her calf muscles burn with a bone-deep ache and knotted a stitch in her side. The hike left her winded, dizzy, and wondering if she'd lost her marbles or had finally slipped into senility.

But she knew it wasn't senility that had brought her here. The appearance of Asa's wraith in her bedroom and his ominous utterance of "ghost tree" had done it.

She wondered if Wilbur—God rest his soul—was looking down on her now, his eyes ghosted by the loneliness of deathless existence.

Liza was of two minds about what happens to a person after death; sometimes she was all but certain that the spirit was apt to linger in the very places a body haunted in life, but there were those other times of gnawing doubt when she was sure that death was eternal oblivion, simply a ceasing of existence. She hadn't given much thought to death as life's greatest mystery until Wilbur passed. Once he was in the ground she spent the ensuing weeks ruminating on just that: *When a person passes away, where does he pass away to?* Was there truly some ghostly part that went somewhere else, or was the decaying carcass in the ground all that remained? Was there an eternal soul, or was there nothing at the end of worldly life but the eternal sleep in soil?

There was a time when the thought of absolute oblivion chilled her to her aching bones, but in recent years she had come to think of oblivion as blessed relief, a final end to human suffering. When your body grew frailer with each passing week and you lived each day with the aches and pains of old age, it was hard not to see death as a welcome deliverance into nothingness.

But now, as she gazed up at the massive live oak planted more than a hundred years ago on the small burial site of the victims of the Helling, she knew without a doubt that the spirits of the dead were trapped within that tree. As surely as the oak's roots held those skeletal remains in their twining embrace, the ghosts of the murdered men lived within those oddly bent limbs and massive trunk. She could feel their tortured presence. Their twisted souls reached out to her with spectral fingers, but she remained just out of their clammy reach because they were imprisoned, held back by the great weight and mass of the mighty oak.

She shuddered so hard that her false teeth rattled in her head. She inched forward, shuffling her feet and extending her right hand to touch the rough bark of the trunk. She closed her eyes. The palm of her hand tingled, then quickly turned cold, so cold she felt as if she were touching a coarse wall of ice. A frigid current ran up her arm, traversed her thin shoulder and settled in her breast, centering there like a wintry void that turned her chest into a ribbed ice-box.

Then she understood exactly why Asa Edgar's wraith had directed her here.

CHAPTER
SEVENTEEN

"I THOUGHT YOU GRADUATED from the graveyard shift, darlin'," said the nightshift waitress at the Trucking-A's diner. "You get yourself demoted?"

"No, not yet," Rourke said with a wan smile. "You're looking good, Marlene."

"I wish," she said, waving off the compliment. But she really did look good for a woman in her early fifties. Her figure still curved in the proper places, her face retained much of its youthful attractiveness in spite of the lines etched there by years of cigarette smoking, and she somehow made her modified beehive hairdo work to her advantage.

Marlene pulled an order pad from the pocket of her rumpled pink uniform and licked the point of her stubby pencil. "What'll you gents have?"

Without looking at a menu, Rourke said, "We'll both have the Eighteen-wheeler Breakfast Platter and a pot of coffee."

"How do you want your eggs?"

Knott said, "Scrambled for me, please."

"Over easy," said Rourke.

Marlene jotted the order on her pad, then stuck the pencil behind her ear. "All right. I'll be right back with your coffee."

"Thanks, Marlene," said Rourke, propping his elbows on the table and interlacing his fingers under his chin.

Knott said, "Marlene's the archetypal truck-stop waitress."

"Uh-huh," Rourke said, though he wasn't entirely sure what "archetypal" meant. He said, "She's a honey."

"I wouldn't say that too loud. Somebody might think you're sexist."

"What? Honey? I didn't mean—"

"Oh, I know," said Knott. "But we live in hypersensitive times. A man can't be too careful."

"Yeah. I guess you're right. But Marlene would take it as the compliment I intended. She's about the most politically *in*correct person I know."

"I don't doubt it. A place like this must be a bastion of outdated sentiments and old-fashioned values."

"Yeah. The Truck-stop Time Forgot."

Knott allowed himself a mirthless chuckle.

Rourke glanced around at the other customers seated in booths or hunkered at the lunch counter. At half past four o'clock in the morning, the place wasn't crowded, and except for the tipsy young man and woman in a corner booth, they were all big-rig drivers with vacant faces and thousand-yard stares. Weary road-riders making a welcome pit-stop along their Southeastern routes.

Marlene brought a pot of coffee, wordlessly filled their cups and then sashayed to another booth.

"You want to tell me what you think you saw?" Knott asked.

Rourke heaved a sigh. "Like I said, I didn't get a good look at it."

"But you saw enough to make you doubt your eyes."

Rourke cocked a brow. "Did I say that?"

"You didn't have to. I read it in your face."

"What I get for taking a shrink to breakfast," Rourke said, smiling.

"Come on, Rob, let's not play games with each other. This is serious."

Rourke took a sip of black coffee. "Okay. If you swear you won't try to have me committed."

Stone-faced and stolid, Knott waited for Rourke to get on with it.

"A goddamn devil. Horns, cloven hooves, the works. That's what I *think* I saw. But it was . . . what's the word? Immaterial? Like a ghost, like it hadn't completely materialized in our world. The rain outlined it, but I had the impression the thing wasn't getting wet. Know what I mean? Like it was walking along in some other place that I only got a glimpse of. Like a window into another world. Is that crazy enough for you?"

"And it didn't make a sound?"

"Not a peep. It stopped and looked right at me, though. I think it sort of smiled at me. Not a friendly smile either. More like a predator grinning at his dinner."

Then he added, "If it hadn't been for my dog, I might've thought I imagined the whole thing. She went a little wild barking at it, and then at me just for getting close to it. Lucy Fur was my reality check."

"Lucifer? What—"

"My dog's name. First name Lucy, last name Fur."

"Cute." Knott pinched the bridge of his nose. "But I have to wonder if you have some sort of preoccupation with Satan that might've influenced your interpretation of what you saw in the rain."

"Hell no, Doc. I don't believe in Satan, and I certainly don't have a preoccupation. This is exactly why I didn't want to get into this with you."

"Sorry. It's my training. I had to ask."

"Yeah, okay. I get that. And it's my training that makes me ask if you and your wife are having marital problems. Was tonight the first time you ever roughed her up?"

Knott gave him a cold stare. "I didn't rough her up. I had to restrain her for her own protection. I've never laid an angry hand on Susan. Never. And I resent it that you would—"

"Hey, I believe you. But I had to ask. You got your training and I've got mine. No offense."

"Fair enough. None taken."

"Damn," said Rourke, "that reminds me, I've got to line up a tracking dog for the search. Excuse me." He pulled his two-way radio off his belt and called HQ. When the dispatcher responded, he said, "Call Dudley Wallace and confirm him and his dog for the search party."

Knott said, "I could show you a very effective technique for improving your memory."

Marlene saved Rourke from making a defensive smart-ass comment when she plunked their breakfast platters on the table and said, "There ya go, guys. Enjoy your breakfast."

* * *

Sharyn was almost asleep when *Smuggler's Nook* chirruped like a mechanical insect. She got out of bed, grabbed the book and quickly seized her cell phone. "Hello?"

"Sharyn, it's me," said Thorn. "I couldn't get back to sleep with the thought of you being mad at me. I'm sorry if I—"

"Forget it, Al. It's all right. But don't call my cell while I'm here. I'm not supposed to have it. If they hear it ringing, they'll confiscate it."

"Right. Sorry," he muttered. "Listen, I've been thinking . . ."

"Oh Lord."

He laughed half-heartedly, then said, "The hitch in my working theory is this: What could make a group of women go on a rampage and slaughter their menfolk? When you take away the supernatural catalyst of a Dionysian figure, what would make the women behave so violently? Something in the well water? Some contaminate that only affected females? Or were the women secretly practicing black magic and performing rituals that worked them into a state of frenzy? "

"A hillbilly witches' coven," Sharyn reflected.

"Yes, but that just doesn't feel right. My imagination fails me. I can't come up with a reasonable hypothesis for their motive."

"You *know* what I believe. But you're too goddamned stubborn to seriously consider it. I'm not saying it's supernatural. More likely, it's a life-form unknown to modern man. A very old one that just missed extinction. Maybe it hibernates for a century and a half, and then wakes up to do its thing. I don't know, but whatever the explanation, it's awake now and it's doing it again. But you won't believe it until you hear it or see it for yourself. I'm telling you, Al, it's out there and it's *real.*"

"Bigfoot with Pan-like shriek. Hmmm."

"Don't mock me."

"I'm not. That's what you're suggesting, is it not? Or something along those lines."

"You know what your problem is?" Sharyn caught her voice rising with her level of anger and lowered the volume. "You're hamstrung by a *National Enquirer* mentality. You're letting your self-doubt stop you, already imagining the ridicule your colleagues will heap on you. Just do the goddamn science, Thorn. Stop worrying about your precious reputation. It will take care of itself if you do your job."

"What does that mean? *National Enquirer* mentality? I don't follow."

"Don't be dense. I mean you're afraid of being ridiculed for uncovering a fantastic truth. Afraid your work will be front-page news in the tabloids and ignored by the scientific community."

After a long silence, Thorn said, "It *could* happen that way, you know."

"Sure it could, but a real scientist wouldn't let that stop him. Follow Galileo's example. Screw the establishment. Answer your true calling and do the damn work. Don't fear persecution."

Thorn's windy sigh made static in the earpiece of her cell. He said, "I'm doing the work, but I'm working without a net here. I have to feel grounded. It's all about the ground for someone in my field of endeavor. The ground gives up its buried secrets of human culture and development. The ground makes it all real. Man doesn't exist in a vac—"

"Alfred? I know what archeology and anthropology are, and I know all about working without a safety net. I *lived* that way until I got regulated on medication. What do you think bipolar disorder is? There's a deep end at either pole and no fucking safety net. I've gone off the deep end more than once, so you don't need to tell me what it's like. Okay? I've been there. So don't expect much sympathy from me."

"I'm not asking for sympathy. I'm just saying—"

"Take the plunge, Al. Or forget the whole thing and retreat to the classroom."

A knock on the door gave her a start. "Gotta go," she whispered into the cell and then hid it under her pillow. The door swung open and the night nurse stuck her head in.

"Still can't sleep," said Nurse Sanders.

Sharyn shook her head.

"Who were you talking to?"

"Myself. Don't worry, I'm not hallucinating. I live alone and I talk to myself sometimes," she lied. "I'm good company."

"Why don't you turn your light out and lie down? You won't get to sleep sitting up and talking to yourself."

"I will. Thanks." She turned off the bedside lamp and slid under the bedcovers.

Sanders gave her a curt smile, then withdrew and quietly shut the door.

Sharyn sighed in relief. Realizing how tired she was, she relaxed and let herself sink into the softness of the bed and closed her eyes.

A moment later she was asleep.

CHAPTER EIGHTEEN

JULIE ARCHER AROSE AT FIVE-FIFTEEN, made her toilet, and went downstairs to the kitchen to brew a pot of strong coffee. She sat at the kitchen table and waited for Mr. Coffee to work his java magic. It was an older deluxe model, red-plated with a softly glowing green clock-face that seemed to stare at her like a malevolently mystic eye from a fifties horror flick.

She fashioned her fingers in the sign of the death-dealing phallus against the evil eye—*mal occhio*—to ward off any bad juju. Then she quietly laughed at herself for being creeped out by a green-eyed Mr. Coffee.

But she was without her guardian angel, and that was no laughing matter. Not when there was a supernatural entity loose in the hills.

Before falling asleep in Angela's protective arms a few short hours ago, Julie had promised herself that everything would be all right in the morning and that she would feel *normal*. But now that morning had come, she didn't feel at all normal.

Her thoughts were dark and drear. Darkness still held sway over the land and over her. Come sunrise, things might look better but she didn't think so. The darkness that cloaked her heart would not be easily banished by sunlight. That infernal shrieking had seeped inside her and deposited something there, some numinous substance that was eating away the layers of her humanity. Beneath those layers something wanton and wild was awakening. She could feel its eagerness to get out, to be born. To come screaming out of her.

"Stop it," she whispered. *Stop thinking such morbid thoughts.*

She hammered the kitchen table with her fist and bolted out of the chair, making a physical show of her determination to remain in control of herself and her thoughts. She poured French-roast coffee into a large mug and took a sip, hoping to fortify her resolve with caffeine. Even as she did her best to ride out her emotional turmoil, the horror writer within stood back and observed from a place of detachment, looking for a way to use this profound experience in a story. If she could capture just a smidgen of the terror she felt and translate it into the language of fiction . . .

The thing inside her twisted and kicked like an infant in the womb. Julie clutched her belly and doubled over. The mug of coffee slipped from her grip and clattered on the tile floor, snapping off the ceramic handle.

"*Jesus*," she said with a gasp. She had to lean on the kitchen counter to keep from falling down. Then another cramp wrenched her intestines and she hobbled as fast as she could go to the downstairs bathroom. She threw the lid up with a bang and plopped her rump down on the cool seat.

Just a bad case of the runs, she told herself. *Not a wild thing ripping its way out of me.*

Not yet, anyway.

* * *

Fearful that something had followed her home from the haunted burial ground, Liza Leatherwood mounted the steps to her front porch and collapsed in the rocking chair. Her heart thudded so hard that she feared she might be in the early stages of a heart attack. She couldn't seem to catch her breath. Predawn darkness deepened, swirling round about her like the black robes of Grim Death. *No, no, no, not yet, please, not yet.*

A glowing shape appeared out of the wispy fog in the front yard and hovered above the grass like a slender white cloud. It glided toward her. As it neared, it slowly resolved itself into the shape of a tall man with craggy features.

"They Lord," she said. "Wilbur?"

She rocked forward, clutching a hand to her old dugs and squinting behind her bifocals for a clearer look. Yes, it *was* Wilbur. There was no mistaking his noble homeliness or the kindness shining in his eyes.

"You come to take me home?" A mournful groan escaped her lips. "Oh, sugar, I can't go just yet. I do want to, but . . ." She had to pause to catch her breath. "I got something I have to do first. Then I'll come directly. Hear?"

Wilbur's ghost shimmered, guttering like a lanky candle-flame above the porch steps.

Liza's heartbeats lost some of their frightening force. She breathed a little easier, knowing her time on earth wasn't quite over. She reached out with a gnarled hand and said, "Please? Touch me, Wilbur. Before you go."

The specter extended his long fingers and touched Liza's hand. A current of cool warmth made her fingers tingle. Bittersweet memories flooded her consciousness, a profound sense of nostalgia gilded with sensual tensions she'd thought she would never feel again. Touching death, she knew her nine decades of life were but a brief tick of Heaven's cosmic clock, and she was deeply aggrieved that she and her beloved husband couldn't have had a larger allotment of time together.

Wilbur withdrew his spectral hand. His face was a sad ghost-mask of regret.

"Wait for me," said Liza, sobbing. "I'll be coming soon."

Her late husband withdrew and disappeared into the fog.

Three dark shapes crouched like unmoving gargoyles in the front yard and watched her with luminous eyes.

* * *

Judy Lynn Bowen had to use the cordless phone to call Josh because she'd lost her cell phone the night she hit the deer and met *him*—the dark god of the mountains.

She sucked hungrily on her cigarette, the ninth from the fresh pack of Virginia Slims she was chain-smoking her way through, greedily drawing the smoke into her lungs as if it could satisfy the intense lust that burned within her.

But of course it couldn't. Tobacco was a poor substitute for what she really craved. Which was why she was phoning her fiancé at so early an hour to tell him she had returned to the world.

Her mother had wanted to take Judy Lynn home with her, but Judy Lynn assured her that she would be fine at her own home, so her mother reluctantly dropped her off at the rented house in Widow's Ridge. Judy Lynn intended to feed her fierce appetite as soon as possible, and she didn't want to have to worry about the ruckus she might raise in her enthusiastic feasting.

Josh answered his cell, his voice slack with sleep. "Hello?"

"Hey, baby, it's me."

"Judy Lynn! Thank God! Where—"

"I'm home. I need you to come over. Right now. I need you, Josh. I need you so bad." She touched her bare breast, pinching the taut nipple.

"What time is it? Six? Where've you been? Are you okay?"

"I will be when you get here. Hurry, baby. I'm dying for you to touch me."

"I'm on the way."

She hung up, stubbed out the Slim and fired another one. Then she lay back into the pile of pillows, spread her legs and ran her fingers between the sodden lips of her sex. She shuddered pleasurably. She sucked down more smoke. She spread her thighs wider, slipping her fingers deeper.

"Hurry, you prick," she said, "I can't wait much longer."

She set the cigarette in the ashtray so she could use both hands for pleasuring herself. As good as one hand felt, it wasn't enough. Nor would two hands be. Neither would Josh be. He was a good lover, but she was different now. She'd been touched by a pagan devil, and that touch had awakened feelings she never knew she had. Feelings she was only just beginning to understand.

She shut her eyes and the mouth of the mountain cave opened to her. She entered into its glowing darkness and fell on her knees before *him*. He stamped his hooves like a horse straining at the bit. His humongous erection quivered just above her head and she got the crazy idea that he was going to knight her with his throbbing wand and initiate her into his royal court. She gazed up into his eyes but quickly looked away, instinctively knowing that if she looked too long into those oily black orbs she would surely go mad. After a momentary relapse into the terror she'd felt when she first heard his shrieking summons, she bravely parted her lips and drank the sweet blood-wine from his engorged fount. The effect was immediate. A luminous river of lust flowed through her, around her, and then she was riding those wine-dark rapids through a timeless land of dark miracles, a realm inhabited by ancient gods and servile humans. The river spat her onto the shore and she found herself stumbling into a circle of naked revelers, wild women capering around a great roaring fire. She danced with them as they whooped and stomped, shaking primitive weapons at the night sky. Bare breasts bouncing, they danced themselves into a frenzy of unspeakable lust. Then he came out of the fire and took them one by one, ravaging them with his tireless member, savagely plundering them until they cried mercy. Then, having no mercy, he took them again with his great glistening staff.

She rode the swollen waves of her orgasm back to the reality of the bedroom and opened her eyes. The cigarette in the ashtray's groove had burned down to the filter and gone out. The first faint light of dawn nuzzled softly against the windows. She floated on a magical bed that she hoped would provide conveyance from the torture of covetous longing.

Josh stood at the foot of the bed, his boyish face a mask of shock at seeing his betrothed asprawl on the twisted bedcovers, her swollen labial folds gleaming with silvery mucus.

"Jesus Christ, Judy Lynn. Couldn't you wait for me?"

"Fuck me, Josh. Fuck me harder than you ever have."

He grinned uncertainly. "What the hell's got into you?"

"You wouldn't believe it if I told you. C'mere, stud." She cocked her knees, slipped the backs of her wrists along her inner thighs and waggled her fingers in welcome.

He unsnapped his jeans and stepped out of them. He pushed his jockey shorts down his long legs and then kicked them into the air, laughing.

He crawled onto the bed and let her slender beckoning fingers guide him to the core of her outrageous craving.

He rode her with abandon until he realized it was she who was riding him from below, humping him with frightening violence. When he faltered, she raked his buttocks with her fingernails, drawing trickles of blood. When he tried to pull away, she held him in place by wrapping her legs about his hips and squeezing him with strength that bordered on superhuman.

Her rushing bloodstream carried the echo of the pagan god's shriek, and it entranced her anew. She dug her nails deep into her lover's taut ass cheeks and he cried out in protest. His pain and his sudden terror fanned the flames of her volcanic passions, and when they finally erupted she sank her teeth into the pliable flesh of his throat and drank deeply of his arterial ejaculations.

He struggled desperately for his life, thrashing between her muscular thighs, but to no avail; she'd depleted too much of his energies. Her vice-like leverage was too precise, her strength insurmountable. His final convulsions brought Judy Lynn to orgasm.

When he was dead, she released him, rolled his slack carcass off her, took his wilted cock in her mouth and chewed it off at its root.

CHAPTER
NINETEEN

THE SMALL CARAVAN OF CARS AND PICKUP TRUCKS followed the police cruiser up the mountain road; a second cruiser brought up the snaking motorcade's rear. Blue lights flashed from the racks atop both official vehicles and lit the convoy at both ends, lending the illuminated fog a stroboscopic pulse of veinal blue.

The lead cruiser pulled to the side of the blacktop and parked on the shoulder in front of a Watch For Falling Rocks sign. The trailing vehicles followed suit and parked along the side of the road.

Rourke stepped out of the lead cruiser and waited for the others to disembark. Knott stood beside him, arms habitually folded across his chest. Neither man spoke.

Low-hanging clouds blanketed the mountain and leached much of the color from the chilly dawn. Though it was June, the mountainous elevation would keep summer's heat in check until later in the morning, when the cloud cover would burn off and the hills would turn as steamy as the lowlands.

Headlights winked out. Car doors creaked and slammed. Male voices tested the fog-muffled air with short bursts of extraneous comment and glib witticisms. Cigarette lighters made firefly flashes in the fog. Someone coughed and spat. Someone farted, drawing a few hoots and catcalls.

The men moved tentatively toward Rourke, who pointed at a leafless maple tree that stood in a small clearing above the road and said, "Form up by that dead tree and keep your voices down."

Rourke strode across the road and climbed a low embankment to the clearing. Knott trailed after him. A few minutes later all the men who would make up the search party had assembled themselves in a loose rank facing Rourke, who stood in a wide stance with the dead tree at his back. A few of the men had rifles, a couple had shotguns and one had a machete. Most were unarmed.

"All right," Rourke said, holding up his arms to catch their undivided attention. "You know why we're here, so knock off the grab-ass and get serious. Everybody with a gun step forward."

Six men moved forward, forming a provisional front rank.

"You six will form a wide skirmish line and move up the mountain. Nobody should be walking in front of you. The rest of you will stay well behind the guns. I don't want anybody catching a bullet in his ass. Keep about a twenty-yard interval between you and the men to your left and right as we sweep up the hill. We're looking for a cave where the missing women may be stashed. If you run into a bad guy, we want him alive, so don't get trigger happy."

"I don't see how we can find anything in this fog," someone said.

One of the volunteer firemen said, "I've been all over this mountain and I never came across a cave."

Rourke said, "That's why we have to do a thorough search. If there is a cave, it'll be hard to see."

"Where's Dudley's dog?" another man asked. "He can sniff out any-damn-body."

"There he comes now," said Travis Tate, pointing down at a black SUV coming up the road.

"Hell, I didn't know the mutt could drive," said Dave Deets, part-time deputy and perennial clown.

"Deputy Rourke, is it true that you got the tip about women held captive in a cave from an escaped abductee?" The inquirer was Arvin Sheets, editor of *The Dogwood Weekly*. He nervously rubbed a hand over his bald head as if he were polishing a beloved bowling ball.

"Abductee? Hey now, nobody told me we was huntin' aliens," Deets quipped.

"Arvin, are you here to help with the search or as just a reporter?" asked Rourke.

"Both of the above. Though I take umbrage at your 'just a reporter' remark."

"Yes, it's true, Arvin," Rourke said with an edge of warning in his voice, "but I'm not at liberty to make her name public."

Sheets scowled, then put away his notepad and pen. As an after-thought, he said, "Well, maybe you can tell me this. Is Dr. Knott here for some on-the-scene counseling in case we find the missing women?"

"This is not a damn press conference, Arvin," said Rourke, resting his hands on his hips. "I don't have time to field your questions. I'm trying to field a search party."

With his tracking dog leading the way on a short leash, Dudley Wallace came up the embankment.

Rourke said, "No smoking beyond this point. Dudley's dog has a sensitive sniffer, so put out your smokes."

With minimal grumbling, the smokers field-stripped their butts.

"The dog goes up first so we won't contaminate the scent-trail," Rourke went on. "The weather's in our favor. The sun should burn off this fog pretty soon but until it does, keep your eyes extra sharp."

Dudley Wallace approached Rourke and greeted him with a nod. He said, "Sit, Pogo," and the German Shepherd immediately obeyed his master and sat beside Dudley's right heel, tongue lolling.

Rourke reached into his pants pocket and brought out the small swatch of the hospital gown Judy Lynn had been wearing in the ER. He had cut off a section of the gown's sleeve, figuring the lingering scent of Judy Lynn's armpit would be enough to put the dog on the scent-trail she'd left when she came down the mountain to the road.

He handed the fragment of cloth to Dudley and said, "This has the girl's scent. Her back trail should lead to the cave where the women are supposed to be."

"So we're not looking for the girl," said Dudley.

"No, she's safe at home. She escaped, came down the mountain and flagged a ride."

"Then that's where Pogo should start."

Knott said, "I can show you the spot. I was the ride she flagged down."

Dudley and the dog accompanied Knott down to the blacktop. When they were in front of the Falling Rocks sign, Dudley held the gown fragment under Pogo's nose and said, "Find!"

The dog immediately set to the task, sniffing the ground as he pulled his master along with the leash. After less than a minute of scent-searching, Pogo obviously had the trail and started back up the mountainside with Dudley in tow. Man and dog circumvented the gathering of men in the clearing and made a beeline into the trees above them.

"All right," Rourke said to his search party of sixteen men, "front rank move out. And keep your intervals."

Knott rejoined Rourke and they hastened after Dudley and Pogo, staying close behind the skirmish line of armed men.

"And a dog shall lead them," muttered Knott.

"What's that?" Rourke looked askance at the doctor.

"A bunch of grown men following a dog. Seems a little strange, that's all."

"*Strange* is the name of the game," Rourke said with a brittle laugh.

CHAPTER
TWENTY

JULIE SAT LOTUS FASHION at the sculpted feet of a lofty stone angel. The marble pedestal beneath her rump was hard and cool, but it wasn't all that uncomfortable to one accustomed as she was to the discipline of meditation. Though she'd been a little scared in coming here alone, now that she was here she felt as if the small fog-kissed army of angels would protect her from the thing that had called her out last night. Though made only of stone, they were nevertheless angels, and thus should afford her some measure of protection in the same way a crucifix protects one from evil; such symbols had power if you believed in them. And she did. She *had* to. Otherwise, last night's terror would still be with her and she wouldn't have been able to set foot out of the apartment to come here in search of her guardian angel and for some semblance of security and peace of mind.

"Michael? Are you here?" Her voice echoed hollowly within the hedges and ricocheted redundantly off the garden of rocks and statuary, changing its timbre so much as it traveled its erratic course that it was scarcely recognizable as her own. "Please answer me. Give me a sign. Michael, please? I need you." Treble-edged echoes haunted her voice.

Here among the angels, Julie found it a little easier to disbelieve her earlier suspicion that something dark and inhuman was growing inside her, yet she needed reassurance from Michael.

But her guardian kept his stubborn silence, leaving her to face her fears alone.

"You shouldn't be out here by yourself. Not after last night."

She looked around to see Angela walking toward her in a man's blue-and-gray flannel shirt, bare-legged below the long shirttails. Julie patted her chest as if to quiet her startled heart. "You scared me."

"Sorry. I woke up and you were gone. You should've left a note."

"Sorry."

"We're a sorry pair, aren't we." Angela smiled as she sat beside her on the pedestal. She looked warily up at the angel towering over them, fingered the top button of her shirt and said, "Stop staring at my tits, you stone-faced pervert."

Julie laughed. Then she planted a kiss on Angela's cheek. "I think you're going to have to be my guardian angel since Michael's derelict in his duties. Would you?"

"Thought you'd never ask." Angela slipped her arm around Julie's back. "Guardian Angela, at your service."

"You saved my ass last night."

"That's 'cause I love that pretty little ass."

"I know. And I love you too. I don't know what I'd do without you."

"I do. You'd get your tit in the wringer and your ass in a sling. Just for starters."

"And you'll save me from myself." Julie said with skeptical inflection.

"Absolutely."

She placed a hand on Angela's bare thigh and caressed the soft stubble. "Ange, what did you see last night?"

"Same thing you did."

"Then you saw the devil. 'Cause that's what I saw. Sure as hell."

"That was your over-developed imagination, babe. All I saw was a shape in the rain."

"You must've seen more than that or you wouldn't have shot at it."

"I shot at it because of that fucking noise it was making. That screaming cry. Whatever makes a sound like that *has* to be dangerous."

"Then you really didn't get a good look at it."

"No, and I didn't want to either."

"It was the devil."

"There's no such thing, Jools."

"How would you know that?"

"Because I'm not a rightwing Christian moron. I think maybe you should switch to writing romance or mystery. All this horror crap is warping your mind."

"That's a mean thing to say. The Christian thing too . . ."

Angela shrugged. "I'm just saying . . ."

Julie jumped up and stalked off.

Angela went after her. "Hey, wait up. Don't be such a pussy."

"Leave me alone, dyke."

Angela caught up and put her hand on Julie's shoulder, and Julie rounded on her, drew back a fist and threw it at Angela's face. Angela blocked the punch with her forearm and stepped backward. "What the fuck's wrong with you?"

"Don't touch me!" Hot tears of anger leaked from Julie's eyes, though she didn't want to cry, certainly not after her lover had called her a pussy.

Angela held her open hands in front of her. "Okay, okay. Chill out. I won't touch you."

Julie started away again.

Angela hastened to her side and said, "Just because you're pissed at me doesn't mean I'm not going to protect you. Whatever that thing was, it's still out there somewhere and if it comes around again, I won't miss next time."

Angela pulled her compact pistol from the breast pocket of her flannel shirt to show she was serious.

"You can't kill the devil," said Julie, surprised by the force of her own conviction.

* * *

Drunk on her lover's flesh and blood, Judy Lynn fell into a dreamlike limbo between this world—the world in which she now lay on bloodied bed sheets—and the other one, the realm from which her rutting god had come in all his terrible glory, entering through the hidden circle of magic stones at the precise midsummer moment the sun stood still to claim that longest day as his own and to perfume the subsequent nights with his potent musk. Her blood understood that the imposing god would hold sway over the woodlands he trod like a ghostly shepherd, gathering his wayward flock for worship at his loins and to suckle them with his intoxicating phallus. She and the others were his chosen ones, his holy servants baptized in the blood-wine of his lust and spiritually primed for the impending ritual of his *becoming*.

The shock and revulsion she'd felt when he made her kill the stray dog and eat its raw entrails was blessedly behind her now. That grisly initiation, she now knew, was but a foretaste of the butchery and feasting that was to follow. Her palate had been primed, the godly seed planted in her soul, and in these moments of half-sleep when her surface mind relinquished the mental field to the throbbing under-mind, she *knew* what her god had planned for her and the others.

She opened her eyes. The low-watt bulb in the bedside lamp cast a dingy pall over the bedroom and lent a sepia hue to Josh's naked, mutilated corpse.

"My God," she said as she absorbed the gruesome boudoir tableau. The remnant of her displaced, humane self screamed from its submerged position that she should be appalled by what she'd done: murdered her fiancé in a frenzy of bloodlust. But the screaming complainant had already been subsumed by a new order of self. She was no longer Judy Lynn Bowen, descendent of backwoods hillbillies. Now she was *so* much more. She had become a vessel for the pneuma of an alien divinity older than humanity; she had the ability to see the world with new eyes; she had glimpsed another world on the other side of the thin skin of this one; her innermost desires were made flesh; her congress with the godly intruder had enhanced her physical and mental powers so much that she divined she was becoming something more than human. Much more.

She got out of bed, licking the last of Josh's blood from her lips. She caught a glimpse of herself in the dresser's mirror. The sight of her blood-slicked nakedness thrilled her anew, sent her heart leaping for her throat.

No, that was not Judy Lynn Bowen in the looking-glass.

"Jude," she said to her reflection. "That's who you are. Judy Lynn died on the mountain. We're Jude."

As she dragged Josh's body down the wooden steps to the basement, she felt a pang of regret that she wouldn't be getting married after all, but the little belch of remorse fled in the face of a larger truth: she was to become the bride of a god whose carnal appetites knew no bounds.

She in her turn would become a goddess, a being both bestial and celestial. A fabulous creature *in the flesh*.

CHAPTER
TWENTY-ONE

THE FOG WAS LIFTING. It hung in the trees, leaving a few wispy patches close to the ground, where the uneven ranks of searchers moved through flourishing undergrowth and trees, some of the men softly cursing the rising landscape as they went, others maintaining a stoic silence merited by the seriousness of their undertaking. A young woman had been kidnapped and raped; other women might still be on this mountain, held captive in a cave by an unknown pervert, a deviant fiend or worse. This was serious business, not some good-old-boy outing to be capped off with beer-drinking and good-natured shit-shooting.

When Knott's cell phone chirruped, Rourke shot him an angry look.

"Sorry," said Knott, whipping out the little phone and flipping it open, "but it could be about my wife."

Rourke nodded. He couldn't blame the man for his concern; he was a doctor and had to be available to his patients and hospital staff.

"Yes," Knott answered, keeping his voice down, "this is Dr. Knott."

Rourke looked ahead at Pogo pulling his master up the steep gradient, and just for a moment it seemed that the animal had the human on the leash.

"How is she?" Knott asked his caller. He listened to the answer, his face expressionless, and then replied: "Good. Take her out of the restraints and tell her I'll be in later this morning. Thank you."

"Your wife's doing better?" asked Rourke.

"Yes. She's a little groggy from the medication but apparently the episode is over."

"Glad to hear it."

Rourke's radio crackled with the garbled voice of the dispatcher. He pulled it off his belt and responded.

The dispatcher said, "Unit six couldn't locate Asa Edgar. He wasn't at his cabin. Over."

"Copy, HQ. Out." Rourke clipped the radio back on the gun belt and glanced at his wristwatch. It was three minutes past eight. Though the sun wasn't yet visible through the thinning mist, the forested mountainside was brightening by degrees; nevertheless, the trees and thickets seemed bent on retaining an ominous gloom.

An unseen crow cawed in a nearby tree, its cry brittle and hollow. The insistent cawing raised gooseflesh on Rourke's arms and neck, and he got the notion that the bird was simultaneously warning them away and announcing the search party's presence to a sinister culprit higher up the hill—the rain-thing he'd seen last night.

Rourke shook off his creepy chills and said, "Why don't you go see to your wife. We don't really need you here, you know."

"No, I want to see this through. Susan's in good hands. If we find any women up there, I might be of more use than you seem to expect."

"I didn't mean it that way," said Rourke. "I just thought you might want to be with Susan. I'm sure we can get along without—"

An eerie cry sounded in the distance, piercing the sodden atmosphere.

Rourke froze, as did Knott; as did all the men, stopping in their tracks. The only man not brought up short by the cry was Dudley Wallace, whose dog suddenly tried to break free of the leash and go charging up the mountain. Hanging onto the leash with both hands, Dudley went stumbling after the canine, issuing commands Pogo summarily ignored.

The screaming cry went on for a full minute. The armed men nervously readied their weapons as if fearing an imminent enemy charge. Others exchanged nervous glances and appeared to be on the verge of running back down to their vehicles and driving away fast.

Then the cry trailed off, and the landscape was steeped in silence. No birds sang. No insects whined. The mountainous terrain was eerily still.

Knott broke the silence. "That was different from what I heard last night. A different . . . song. But the singer's the same."

Rourke knew they didn't have time to discuss what they'd just heard. He'd lost sight of Dudley and the dog, and he was sure Pogo was carrying his master straight to the maker of that spooky cry. He was equally sure that Dudley would not willingly let go of the leash and abandon his beloved dog to the screaming creature. Rourke instinctively knew that whatever had made that sound was incredibly dangerous, and he was certain the other men knew it as well. They couldn't let Dudley face the thing alone.

He chopped the air with the edge of his hand and shouted, "Move out! Double-time! Let's go!"

Like an unhorsed and unreconstructed Civil War general, Rourke led his reluctant troop up the mountain. Knott jogged beside him, swept along by the momentum of fearful urgency.

A dark shape charged out of a thicket in front of them, growling as it raced along, its belly close to the ground. Dave Deets raised his shotgun but the thing was on him before he could aim and get off a shot, clamping its teeth on Dave's groin. Screaming, he toppled backward, and the pit-bull sawed its head from side to side, snarling as its teeth tore at the man's genitals.

Rourke drew his pistol as he ran toward Deets. From the corner of his eye he saw two more dogs burst from the forbidding undergrowth, both of them coming at full speed, their ears laid back for battle.

A shotgun boomed. A rifle cracked. A fourth dog crashed out of a bramble bush and leapt at a rifleman's throat.

Rourke turned and quickly aimed at the black mongrel that was coming directly at him. He squeezed the trigger and his .38 popped a shot that kicked up dead leaves and dirt beside his charging target. When the black dog was no more than ten yards away, Rourke fired again. The slug struck the mutt's head, immediately dropping him. Then Rourke returned his attention to Dave Deets and the dog that was now savaging Dave's throat.

Like a base runner sliding home, Rourke slid in beside Deets, jammed the .38's muzzle under the pit-bull's belly and fired two quick shots. The dog yelped through clamped teeth but did not relinquish its ripping grip on Dave's throat, which was horribly awash with blood.

Rourke stuck the muzzle against the pit-bull's skull, angling it away from Deets, and fired once more. The dog fell dead on Dave's chest. Rourke pushed the canine's corpse off Deets and pressed his hand into the ragged gash in the man's throat to stop the bright red blood from jetting into the air.

The other armed men had put down the remaining two dogs by this time, but not before one of the mutts had taken a chunk of flesh out of Harvey Carson's forearm.

Deets was already losing consciousness—whether from loss of blood or from shock, Rourke didn't know.

"Doc! Help me here!" Rourke shouted.

But Knott was already there, bending over the bleeding man and pushing Rourke's hand away so he could determine the severity of the wounds.

"He's bleeding out," said Knott. "There's nothing I can do."

"Just stop the bleeding, for Christ's sake," Rourke said.

"How? I can't put a tourniquet around his neck without choking him to death. The man needs immediate surgery. Out here there's nothing I can do."

"So we just let him die?" Rourke said through gritted teeth.

"We don't have a choice. His artery is shredded."

"Clamp it off."

"With what?"

"Jesus, I don't know," said Rourke. "There must be something—"

Rourke dug a hand into his jeans for his keys. He pulled them out and quickly shed his keys from the little metal ring. "Use this," he said, handing the ring to the doctor.

"I can't do it with that," said Knott, staring at the silver ring.

"Try, goddammit. Hurry!"

Some of the other men had crowded around to see the condition of their fallen fellow. A few of them lurched away after getting a good look at Dave's ruined throat and savaged groin.

Knott put the ring back in Rourke's hand and then sat on the ground beside Deets and put his fingers into the wound, trying to find the artery he would have to clamp off to prevent Deets from dying.

In a matter of seconds his hands and wrists were covered with blood. "I'll need another pair of hands to do this," he told Rourke. "Damn! Too slippery. Wait. There, I've got it, by God. I'll hold the artery while you clamp it off with the ring."

Rourke knelt on the opposite side of the patient and used his thumbnail to spread open the double rings of metal.

"See it? The little white worm-looking thing? Clamp it off right in front of my finger," Knott instructed.

As Rourke brought the ring close to the spurting artery, his thumbnail slipped out and the tiny gap in the rings closed. "Shit!"

"That's okay," Knott said, "open it again. Don't panic."

"I'm not," Rourke snapped.

Someone suddenly shouted: "Look out!"

Someone else cried out a muffled curse that was cut short by a loud thump.

Rourke glanced up to see a large brown bird—*a fucking hawk!*—attached to a man's face, the predator's talons digging into fleshy jowls amid a flurry of fluttering wings.

"Holy shit!" someone shouted.

"Get it off!" cried the man with the hawk on his face as he stumbled to his knees.

In the commotion, the artery slipped from Knott's fingers. Blood spurted, but with less force now. "We're losing him," said Knott.

Dave's eyes rolled up into their sockets, and his body shuddered.

"God*dammit!*" Rourke shouted.

"It's too late," said Knott, solemnly shaking his head. "He's too far gone."

"Bullshit," said Rourke, forcing himself to ignore the man struggling to get free of the hawk's talons. "Try again."

"He's gone, Rob," Knott said.

Arvin Sheets had managed to get hold of the hawk's wings, and he yanked the bird downward. The talons ripped free of its prey's face, slashing the flesh open. The hawk broke free of Arvin's grip and flew off into tatters of fog. Someone fired a futile shot after the hawk.

The man with portions of his face badly shredded was Billy Barker, a volunteer fireman and ne'er-do-well, whose exploits with married women were the stuff of local legend and provided the punch-lines for more than a few ribald jokes in Dogwood's bawdier quarters. His rugged handsomeness was said to be irresistible to ladies of all ages, sizes and shapes. Rourke caught himself wondering if Billy's bloody lacerations would become alluring scars to further tempt the young man's female prey into future illicit liaisons. The kid sure wouldn't be getting much action before the ugly wounds healed.

"Think you can do something about *his* wounds without killing him?" Rourke asked Knott.

Knott glanced at Billy Barker, then shot Rourke an angry look. "Don't be an asshole," he said. He wiped his bloody hands on his jeans and started toward Billy.

Rourke grabbed Knott's arm, and said, "Sorry. You didn't deserve that. I just . . ." He shrugged and glanced at the dead man at his feet.

"I know. Forget it."

"What the hell's going on here?" Arvin Sheets wore an expression of dismay as he addressed the question to his comrades. "Hawks don't attack people like that. And those dogs—"

"It ain't natural," said Harvey Carson, nursing his wounded forearm. "That weird cry called 'em down on us, sure as shit. What the hell *was* that thing? Weren't no wildcat, that's for damn sure."

"By God, I think you're right, Harv," said Arvin. "As unbelievable as it is, I think you're right on the money. That thing ordered the attack. Don't you think so, Rob?"

Rourke didn't answer; instead, he drifted away from the clot of men and used his two-way to call for an ambulance and for the coroner. "Dave Deets is dead," he said into the radio, "but don't mention his name to anybody. All you know is we've had one fatality and a couple of injuries."

Another eerie cry sounded from the upper reaches of the terrain. This time it came in staccato bursts that brought to Rourke's mind a cartoonish wildcat with a stutter. The odd cry brought the cawing response of countless unseen crows; the crows' raspy caws raised new gooseflesh on Rourke's arms and puckered his anus. Every man in his company of searchers stiffened with palpable fear, sensing what was coming next.

"Holy shit, here they come!" someone shouted.

A murder of crows swooped down out of the fog in attack formation.

A shotgun blast greeted them.

And still they came.

CHAPTER
TWENTY-TWO

LIZA LEATHERWOOD CAME AWAKE with a shudder. A muscle spasm in her lower back brought a whimper to her phlegmy throat. A film of fog blurred the lenses of her bifocals, trapping a tiny piece of faded rainbow there, but she nevertheless saw that the dogs still sat in her front yard, keeping their evil vigil. Three dangerous-looking mongrels with dead eyes and dark, mangy fur. Watching her.

"Lord," she said with a guttural moan. "I'm too old and feeble for this nonesuch."

Her trek to and from the haunted tree had exhausted her, and she'd fallen asleep in the front-porch rocker before sunup. Now daylight filtered through the thinning fog, and she judged that she'd slept for at least an hour in the chill air. Her arthritis pained her something fierce, especially in her fingers and in the joints of her arms and wrists. She wanted to get up and go inside the house for some pain medicine and to escape the malicious gaze of those dead eyes, but she couldn't find the energy to make a single move. Moreover, she was afraid that the dogs wouldn't let her out of their sight. No doubt they had followed her from the spirit-haunted tree, in unholy service to the Demon of the Dark Wood. Their vile master somehow knew what she intended to do, and he would do his damnedest to stop her. She wondered if the bugger also knew how stubborn she could be once she set her mind to do something.

"Aye," she said for the benefit of the hounds, "when I make my mind up to do something, by God I do it. And it'll take more than the likes of you ugly fleabags to stop me."

Trouble was, she couldn't do the chore herself—she wasn't physically able. She would have to get somebody else to do it for her. But that was all right, because she knew just the man for the job. All she had to do was get up, go inside, pick up the phone and call him.

When the spasms in her back subsided, she drew in a big breath, braced her knotty hands on the flat arms of the rocker and pushed up to a tentative standing position. She swayed a little, keeping her eyes on the three dogs. They didn't move off their haunches, but they did seem to sit up a bit straighter, as if alerted for action.

Liza knew they could be on her before she had time to pull the screen door open. They would very easily bring her down and tear her up, if that was their intention; she didn't doubt that it was, if she made the wrong move.

So she had to outfox these baleful hounds. Confuse them and throw them off guard. If she could do that, then she just might make it into the house. If not, she would end her life as little more than a warm pile of raw dog food.

Feeling only slightly steadier on her feet, she hobbled on stiff legs to the edge of the porch, and avoided looking into the mutts' eyes as she began to recite: "'The Lord is my shepherd; I shall not want.'"

She reached up and lifted a wind chime off its little nail. She couldn't hear its delicate tinkling but she knew the dogs did. She gently shook the chime so that the six slender cylinders sounded against one another, and went on with her recitation. "'He maketh me to lie down in green pastures: he leadeth me beside the still waters.'"

Her voice grew stronger with each line of the psalm. The verses resonated within her as they never had before. Tears formed in the corners of her eyes. "'He restoreth my soul: he leadeth me in the paths of righteousness for his name's sake.'"

All three dogs cocked their sharp-edged ears toward her. Liza read indecision in the body language of the biggest mongrel, the alpha mutt— or so she thought. She increased her voice's volume: "'Yea, though I walk through the valley of the shadow of death, I will fear no evil: for thou art with me; thy rod and thy staff they comfort me.'" *What I wouldn't give for a big rod right now. I'd crack me some doggie skulls.*

She shook the wind chime harder. In spite of her impaired hearing, now she heard a faint tinkling: the wind chime sounding a world away. "'Thou preparest a table before me in the presence of mine enemies: thou anointest my head with oil; my cup runneth over.'" *And I'm about to pee in my britches. Lord, give me strength to see this through.*

The alpha mutt's tongue lolled out and it stood up on all fours. Its two companions also got to their feet.

Liza virtually shouted the last lines of the psalm, delivering the words with as much evangelical spirit and Bible-thumping cadence as she could muster: "'Surely goodness and mercy shall follow me all the days of my life: and I will dwell in the house of the LORD for ever.'" *But right now I'm going in my own damn house, thank you, Jesus.*

She suddenly flung the wind chime high into the air, and it arced over the grass and came down behind the dogs. Involuntarily, they tracked it with their dead eyes. Though they were surely under the influence of a demon, they were still dogs, and thus they did what dogs do. What dog could resist a thrown object?

"Fetch!" she shouted, but she didn't wait around to see if they obeyed. She spun on the balls of her feet and made a hobbling dash for the screen door. She thought she heard a bark behind her, followed by a snarling growl.

She grabbed the thin rusted handle and yanked the screen door open. She felt the vibration in the floorboards behind her as one of the dogs leapt onto the porch. Then she was through the doorway and spinning around to slam the heavy oak door. She caught a terrifying glimpse of a dog flying at her, its teeth bared and shedding threads of saliva, its eyes finally alive with unnatural hunger.

The door slammed on the leaping dog, the impact rattling the dark oak in its frame. She turned the key and locked the door for good measure. She didn't know if demonic dogs could turn a doorknob, but she was taking no chances.

Her heart pounded to beat the band, and she was so emotionally and physically drained that all she wanted to do was crawl into her brass bed and pull the covers over her head, but she knew she didn't have that particular luxury.

She had a phone call to make. And a bargain to make, as well.

Casting wary glances at the curtained windows as she moved through the house, she went into the bedroom, picked up the volume of Hawthorne, opened it and found the business card she'd been using as a bookmark. Then she sat on the edge of the bed, picked up the phone and dialed Alfred Thorn's cell phone number.

She couldn't be sure, but she thought she heard—or felt—the dogs knocking and scratching at the front door. There was no doubt that she heard the mournful howling—which began a moment later—right outside her bedroom window. Not even a punctured eardrum could've stopped that ungodly sound.

* * *

Thorn answered his cell with his usual, "Thorn here."

". . . hear me? Professor? I can't hear a damn thing. You there, Thorn? Speak up!"

Thorn recognized the voice of Liza Leatherwood, who was apparently so hard of hearing that she'd started talking before he'd even answered his phone.

"Mrs. Leatherwood," he said, almost shouting to be heard. "I'm here. Can you hear me?"

"Is that little buzzing noise you? Lord, I don't know," she said. "If you're there, I got a deal for you. Come up to my house right now and I'll tell you what you wanna know. And you better bring a gun, 'cause there's some wild dogs plaguing me. You hear?"

"Yes," he shouted into the tiny mouthpiece, "I hear you. But I don't understand. What—"

"Better hurry, though. The dogs are trying to get at me. Hear? I'll tell ya where the bodies are buried. Just drop what you're doing and COME RIGHT NOW!"

There was a hollow click and she was gone.

Thorn was seated in his study with a thick volume of mythology open on his lap and a mug of steaming coffee on an antique end-table at his elbow. He closed his phone, and then shut the book, wondering if the old girl had finally fallen to senility.

Wild dogs? Well, he mused, it was possible. But why had the woman suddenly changed her mind about telling him what he wanted to know? Had she been speaking metaphorically when she said she would tell him "where the bodies were buried," or had she meant it literally? Dare he hope for the latter? With the hopeful thrill of discovery rising in him, Thorn bolted from his leather chair and went to the roll-top desk, where he kept a .45 caliber semiautomatic under lock and key.

Five minutes later he was backing his restored 1976 Triumph TR6 out of his driveway, the loaded pistol on the seat next to him. The wide-eyed boy in him was lighting out on a fantastic adventure involving demon dogs and a forbidden burial ground; Thorn the man suffered a nagging disquiet that communicated the need for caution. The mature Thorn remembered keenly the old woman's warning: *A man who digs cursed earth, uncovers great sorrow.*

CHAPTER
TWENTY-THREE

ARVIN SHEETS YELPED AND DANCED LIKE A MADMAN, stomping and kicking his feet as he tried to dislodge the two fox squirrels that had simultaneously run up his legs, each little rodent now a moving lump under each leg of his trousers. His shambling clog dance might've been funny but for the terror etched in his face and the earnest curses he yelled between yelps.

"Drop your pants!" shouted Rourke, keeping a wary eye on the sky. He was ready to drop to the ground and cover his head if the crows launched another attack.

Arvin unbuckled his khaki pants and pushed them down to his ankles. His scrawny legs bore bloody scratches and at least three deeper wounds where the bushy-tailed devils had bitten him. One of the squirrels was hanging by its claws from the crotch of Arvin's boxer shorts, and the other one was clinging to the pale flesh of the man's inner thigh as if clinging to the bark of a spindly tree. Arvin slapped the squirrel off his thigh, and then pushed his boxers down, dislodging the second rodent. Both squirrels ran across the ground and scampered up the gray trunk of a tall pine.

"Jesus God!" Arvin shouted after he'd inventoried his bloody wounds and made sure his manhood was still intact. "Do squirrels carry rabies?"

Rourke surveyed the human ruins of his search party. The men were scattered about the landscape as if a giant hand had flung them like unwanted litter. Some of them still hugged the ground, where they'd dropped during the crows' aerial assault. A few stood with shoulders hunched, dividing their attention between the fog-streaked sky and the ground, aware that the next attack might come from either quarter.

Rourke avoided looking at Dave Deets's corpse. He wasn't yet ready to accept that the man was actually dead—and that he must bear some of the responsibility for the death. He caught himself silently cursing Sheriff Gladstone for allowing his wife to knock him out of commission, and then quickly chided himself for thinking so childish a thought. Gladstone, he was sure, would've handled things the same way, and the search party would've ended up in the same sorry state as it had under Rourke's leadership. No one could've anticipated a concerted attack by the indigenous wildlife, so Rourke was blameless—or so he told himself.

"That thing called the tune," said Knott, who had come to stand beside Rourke. "You know that, don't you? It commanded them to attack."

Rourke nodded. "Sure as hell seems that way. What the hell *is* that thing? I mean, what are we dealing with here? It's just not . . ."

"Possible," Knott finished the thought. "But there's no other explanation."

"It doesn't want us to find the cave," said Knott.

"What the hell?" said Billy Gatlin as he absently wiped blood from the gash in his cheek, put there by the beak of a furious crow. "What the hell? What the fucking hell?"

"Shut up, Billy," said Dan Wilcox, a fulltime fireman who stood six-three and had the sculpted physique of a professional bodybuilder. "You're losing it, man. Don't be such a pussy."

At the sound of approaching footsteps in the foliage above them, everyone looked anxiously in the direction from which it came. Dudley Wallace came out of the undergrowth, carrying Pogo in his arms. The dog's head hung limply from the crook of Dudley's elbow, bobbing in time to its surviving master's footsteps. Dudley's arms were covered with blood; Pogo's throat had been horribly mutilated. One of his eyes was gone.

"They killed him," Dudley said as he came closer. "Them goddamn dogs got the best of him. I tried to stop 'em but—" His voice broke in a heart-rending sob. Then he saw the human corpse on the ground and immediately paled. "My God, what happened?"

"Dogs."

"And crows. And a fucking hawk."

"And fucking squirrels," Arvin added as he buckled his pants.

Dudley bent down and laid Pogo on the ground. "Something's up there," he said, looking at Rourke. "Did you hear it?"

Rourke nodded.

"Let's go get the sumbitch," said Dudley. His cheeks regained some of their former color, but his expression was as grim as a gray tombstone.

Rourke said, "Anybody who's not up for it can wait here for the ambulance. The rest of us are going after that fucking thing."

* * *

Knott fought the urge to call the hospital for a status report on Susan. It had only been an hour since the charge nurse had phoned him with the welcome news that Susan appeared to be back from her excursion into madness, but the improbable attack of the animals and the chilling cry that had signaled the assault left him in a state of mounting anxiety. At its root was the certainty that Susan would not be safe as long as the maker of that uncanny cry remained at large. As badly as he wanted to get in his car and drive to the hospital to be by his wife's side, to hold her hand and anchor her to reality, he wanted even more to charge up the mountain to find and exterminate the unknown creature; he knew that the key to Susan's cure was in finding a way to eradicate the cause of her "illness." Knott intended to do just that.

Holding a dead man's shotgun in the crook of his right arm, he trudged beside Rourke, leading the ten other men who were willing to proceed up the forested face of the mountain in search of the monster and the women alleged to be in its insidious thrall.

The higher they went, the thicker became the mists of low-hanging clouds. Pearly moisture caressed their faces and fogged their eyes. The trees and undergrowth were thick with gloomy shadows, and Knott imagined faces in them, small-animal faces with empty sockets from which the all-seeing mystery-beast watched the trespassing hunters. He shivered.

To dispel the phantasmal image and the feeling of being watched, he thought of Susan. He imagined her naked on their bed, knees bent and thighs parted to exhibit her bearded sex. She slowly slipped two fingers of her right hand below her belly and parted the red, swollen lips to show how wet and ready she was for him. The tantalizing image made his penis grow fat with lust. He dropped a hand over his crotch to surreptitiously shift his growing erection to one side.

"What's that smell?" asked Billy Barker. "Smells like . . ."

"Cum," said Dan Wilcox.

"Like wet pussy," offered Harvey Carson. "Goddamn! I'm horny as a billy goat. What the fuck . . . ?"

Knott smelled it too. And *felt* it. For all their crudity in expressing it, the men were right: the air was rife with the intoxicating musk of sex.

"Must be some weird kind of plant," Wilcox said.

"No, *it's* doing it," said Arvin Sheets. "It's another defense mechanism. A distraction."

"Well it's sure as shit working," said Harvey. "All I can think about is getting laid. Them women in that cave better look out if we *do* find 'em."

Knott and Rourke exchanged worried glances. "He could be right," Knott whispered. "This thing apparently has more than one way to affect behavior. Another weapon in its arsenal. We could be a real danger to those women."

"Are you serious?" asked Rourke. "How could—"

"Don't you feel it?" Knott said, no longer able to whisper. "Aren't you . . . stimulated?"

Rourke blushed. Then said, "This is crazy. I feel like we're all caught in the same crazy nightmare."

"Yes, but it's not our nightmare. It's his. *Its*."

"You honestly believe it can make us resort to rape? I'm sorry, Doc, I don't buy that."

"Think of the consequences if you're wrong."

"So, what? We should give up, turn around and go home?"

"I want to get this thing as badly as you do, but . . ."

"But what?"

Knott shrugged. "I don't know. I'm afraid we might be walking into a trap. That we're up against something so . . . bizarre we don't know how to defeat it."

"I don't know about you," Rourke said, somewhat belligerently, "but I know I'm not a rapist. I just don't have it in me."

"One thing I've learned in my practice of psychiatry is that none of us knows the extent of the darkness that lives within until it comes out into the light. I believe we're all potential murderers and rapists. Don't forget, humans are animals. Civilized, but nonetheless animals. We're high-functioning primates."

"Some of us believe we're made in the image of God." Rourke eyed the wooded landscape above them as if he expected the Devil to suddenly appear and whisk them to Hell.

"Animals, just the same. Mammals with carnal urges and instincts," said Knott. He didn't want to be having this conversation, not now. Not here. Not with that brawny scent of sex in the air and his penis in a state of semi-arousal.

"Get your hands off me, faggot!" Wilcox all at once shouted.

"I just wanna touch it," said Billy Barker, his voice slurred and thick.

"Goddamn queer!" Harvey Cox said with great vehemence. He balled his fists.

Rourke turned to the squabbling men and said, "Hey! Knock it off. Get a grip."

Arvin Sheets already had a grip: he'd unzipped his pants to unlimber his phallus, a look of ecstasy on his face.

"What the fuck?" someone said in obvious disgust.

Knott tightened his fingers on the shotgun. Tension—sexual and otherwise—charged the atmosphere. An explosion of violent lust seemed imminent. Knott feared it as much as he wanted to see it, feel it, taste it. He thought he should try to intervene, but nothing in his psychiatric experience had prepared him for emergency group therapy in the field with armed men driven to the brink of sexual frenzy. Still, he felt he should try.

But Rourke beat him to the punch. He drew his pistol and fired a shot into the air. "I said *knock it off*. I'm Acting Sheriff, and if any of you sons o' bitches want to test my authority, step up and I'll shoot you where you stand, by God."

"Easy, Rob," Knott said under his breath. As much as he admired the way Rourke was handling himself, he feared that the deputy was perilously close to abusing his vested authority in a lethal way.

If Rourke heard him, he gave no sign. He said, "Put your goddamn dick back in your pants, Arvin. Or I'll blow it off."

"I bet you could too," Wilcox said with an ugly smirk. "I bet you could blow him off real good, you cocksucker. You ain't the fucking sheriff."

Knott stepped between the two men. "Time out," he said, keeping the shotgun angled at the ground so no one would misinterpret his intentions. "We can't let things get out of control here. Everybody take a deep breath and just step back from the edge, okay? We are not the enemy. That screaming thing up there is, and it's doing this to us. Fight *it*, not each other."

"Fucking headshrinker, go back to your loonies," said Wilcox. "You don't belong here, you pussy motherfucker. Unless you wanna bend over and take it up the ass."

Rourke shoved Knott out of the way, stepped forward and hammered his pistol against Wilcox's head. The big man went down in an ungainly heap, his bulked-up muscles no defense against cold, hard steel.

Rourke turned to the others and said, "Here's what you're gonna do.

One at a time, march down the mountain, get in your vehicle and go home. As of now, this search party is disbanded. You go first, Arvin. Now. Move!"

Arvin zipped his fly and started down. He glanced back with a look of embarrassed confusion.

"Billy, you go next," Rourke ordered. Billy complied, fingering his penis through his jeans as he went.

One by one, under Rourke's watchful eyes, the men headed back to the road. Knott was spellbound by Rourke's manliness and his assured command of the situation. He caught himself imagining Rourke joining him and Susan in bed; pictured Rourke's naked body between Susan's thighs; saw him pumping her with abandon, his muscular buttocks beautifully taut; saw Susan at last unmasked, her face stark with naked lust. The mental picture made his pulse race and his penis throb. He tried to banish it from his mind.

"Okay, Doc. Your turn."

"What about him?" Knott pointed down at the unconscious Wilcox, hoping to distract attention he feared his erection would draw.

"Fuck 'im. He's not going anywhere for awhile. I'll pick him up on my way down, if he's still here."

"You're going up there by yourself?"

"Yeah. This looks like a one-man job after all."

"I'm going with you. I'm all right."

Rourke stared hard into Knott's eyes, and then said, "I'm not so sure about that."

"What makes you think you're the only one strong enough to resist this . . . spell? Besides, you don't know what's up there. What if it sets more dogs on you? You need another gun. And maybe we can help each other fight the effects of this stinking scent."

"Or maybe it goes the other way and we end up shooting each other."

"Life's a crap-shoot," said Knott, attempting a smile. "You can't win if you don't roll the dice."

"All right, high-roller. Let's go then. But if you start acting hinky, I'll put you down."

"I know. And I'll do the same for you."

Rourke smiled and holstered his pistol. "You're all right, Doc." He offered his hand.

Knott accepted it. Until that moment, Knott never knew a handshake could be so sensual.

CHAPTER
TWENTY-FOUR

THORN'S STOMACH GROUSED AT HIM because he'd neglected to feed it breakfast, but he disregarded the gastric rumblings as he drove up the winding road to Widow's Ridge; he was far too eager to get to Mrs. Leatherwood's house than worry about the nuisance of an empty stomach.

She was going to tell him *where the bodies were buried*. If she was true to her word, he could have the physical evidence he needed to proceed with his anthropological explication of native myth versus native history, and he would finally have something substantial to boost his flagging career, and more importantly, to relieve his middle-age ennui. He knew this was his chance to make a significant mark in his chosen field.

He hoped to God the old lady hadn't been speaking metaphorically about buried bodies. Something in the way she'd said it—her matter-of-fact tone, perhaps—told him she'd meant it literally. If so, then Thorn would finally "make his bones."

He chuckled at his pun.

"Bones make the man," he quipped for his own amusement, nearly giddy with excitement.

Of course, even if he found the burial grounds, there was a good chance that the bones would've long ago become dust. Much depended on the acidic content of the ground and on the mineralization and remineralization of the bone tissue. If luck was with him, at least some of the bones would now be fossils. If he was *extremely* lucky, some of the fossils would bear the marks indicative of a violent end. Even so, any forensic evidence would be circumstantial, at best, and Thorn would have to rely on Widow Leatherwood's oral history to lend credence to his thesis.

As he turned on the wipers to clear fog from the windshield, a deer dashed into the road directly ahead of his convertible, and he reacted by slamming his foot on the brakes and wrenching the wheel hard to the right. He knew his little sports car would not fare well in a collision with a full-grown deer, and his determination to avoid a devastating impact led him to cut the wheel too sharply, and the TR6 headed toward the ditch on the right. He compensated quickly and cut back to the left. The car fishtailed and then rode the grassy shoulder of the road, the right wheels skimming the rim of the red-clay ditch as he braked and finally rolled safely to a stop.

He glanced to his left to see the graceful whitetail bounding into the woods on the left side of the blacktop. He blew a whistling sigh through his teeth, relieved that he wasn't nose-down in the ditch. But his relief wasn't absolute; from some dark place inside him came the notion that the deer had deliberately tried to stop him. Such suspicion was ridiculous, of course. Though Sharyn wouldn't think so. Sharyn and her over-imaginative ideas about the pagan god of the woodlands . . .

Thorn gazed into the woods on his right. His skin prickled up and down his arms. He sensed someone watching him from within the foggy gloom of greenery. Someone or some *thing*.

He floored the gas pedal, pulled back onto the road and sped away. He glanced uneasily in the rearview mirror to make certain nothing was coming after him.

* * *

Sharyn took her breakfast in her room rather than in the hospital cafeteria. Though the nurse had strongly encouraged her to join the small group of patients trustworthy and well enough to dine in the cafeteria, she'd begged off, claiming a headache she didn't really have. She simply wasn't ready to venture outside the relatively safe haven of hospital walls.

She ate all she could stomach of the eggs and greasy bacon strips, then chased it with black decaf. Then she dressed in jeans and an oversized blue T-shirt and ventured down the hall to check on the condition of Dr. Knott's wife. She wanted desperately to talk to the woman and compare notes, so to speak. She also felt a responsibility to let Mrs. Knott know that she wasn't crazy—that there truly *was* something out there with the power to fog women's minds with panic, or lust, or even the urge to commit violence.

When she'd glanced in the doorway last night and seen Susan Knott strapped to the bed in leather restraints, Sharyn had thought: *There but for the grace of a genetic biochemical flaw go I.* She was more convinced than ever that her bipolar disorder (and maybe her lithium) had saved her from becoming a female berserker in response to the pagan call to madness. The question now was whether intense fear and panic were preferable to the alternative. She couldn't deny that a darker part of her *wanted* to give in to the godlike entity's call to brutal bacchanalia. Were she to surrender to the manic phase of her disease, stop taking her meds, and let it take her to the extremity of its polarity (as she'd been so many times tempted to do), the likelihood was that she would likewise end up strapped to a hospital bed, *in extremis.* There were, of course, worse and more dangerous places to end up, and there was never a shortage of low souls wickedly lascivious enough to take you to those depths of depravity and degradation. Sharyn had come very close to that end before her first hospitalization and subsequent diagnosis; had in fact narrowly escaped a gang-bang. The forbidden territory of her psyche was always well within reach, ever tempting her to breach its ephemeral gates, follow skewed inner pathways into the outer world and partake of prohibited delights and sweet terrors of the flesh—to wallow in her inherent wantonness. That such indulgence might be fatal only served to sweeten the sexual pot and raise the spiritual stakes. Sharyn always had the easy option of damning herself, and this certainty shaped her life and gave it layers of dangerous ambiguity to which "normal" people apparently had little access. She was blessed with that curse.

As she came to the doorway of Susan Knott's room, Sharyn's heart-rate accelerated. Her short walk down the corridor had taken an inordinate length of time. She felt as if she'd been walking for hours; her legs trembled with fatigue and she was short of breath. Had she blanked out? Succumbed to a petite fugue state? She wasn't sure. What she *was* sure of was that she was at the threshold of a fresh panic attack. She feared confrontation with the woman, and she also feared the no-longer-latent wildness within herself. Though she had no concrete reason for thinking so, she nevertheless thought—feared—that being in the company of the woman on the other side of the door might be extremely dangerous, that she and Susan Knott might fuel one another's ferocity and both go spiraling out of control. But she knew she had to risk it; if it meant drifting into the orbit of the woman's madness, so be it. She raised her fist and rapped her knuckles on the door. Without waiting for a response, she turned the doorknob and entered the room.

The woman was sitting on the side of the bed, gazing out the second-storey window. Her back to the room's doorway, she didn't bother to turn around to see who'd come into the room.

"Excuse me," said Sharyn, doing her best to suppress the tremor in her voice.

"I know you," said Susan Knott. The hospital gown hung open below her shoulder blades, the two lower ties undone. Her skin was creamy white and blemish-free. Sharyn moved forward, suddenly seized by the urge to touch the other woman's smooth flesh.

"You do?" said Sharyn, crossing her arms below her breasts to keep from touching the woman's inviting skin.

"You're my sister," said Susan. Her voice was throaty and somehow terribly seductive.

"No, I'm Sharyn Rampling. Your husband's my doctor, for the time being."

"You think I don't know my own sister?" She laughed, as if privy to a secret joke.

"If you'd turn around and look at me," said Sharyn, "then you'd see I'm not . . ."

Then it struck Sharyn that the woman didn't mean she was her biological sibling. "Yes, in an odd way I guess we are. We're both here for the same reason, aren't we?"

"Did you see him?" Susan Knott half-turned, putting her left hand on the bed behind her and leaning some of her weight on it as she looked up. Sharyn was pretty sure she'd seen that same vampish gesture in an old black-&-white Hollywood melodrama.

Their eyes met. Each read recognition in the other's eyes. The wildness within Sharyn leapt forward to show itself in her face, taking her breath away in the process. She gasped when she tried to speak. Clutched a hand to her bosom, and tried again. "No," she managed to say, "I didn't see him. I think I wanted to when it called but . . . I was afraid."

Susan nodded. Her lips formed a half-smile. "I can smell him. He's close now. Coming closer. We don't have long to wait."

"What is he?" Sharyn asked. She took a step closer and rested her thighs against the side of the elevated bed. "Do you know?"

Susan Knott's tongue flicked out to moisten her lips. Her eyes brightened by an inner fire. "God," she said.

"God," Sharyn echoed.

"A *real* god, not the one in Sunday-school fairy tales. God with a righteous cock."

Now Sharyn smelled it too: the musk of a rutting beast. Though Susan

Knott hadn't got close enough to see her god, she nevertheless carried its indelible scent on her person. And a maddening scent it was! Sharyn flushed with insidious heat. Her flesh prickled with sudden, unbearable desire. Her nipples stiffened against the cotton of her bra. She squeezed her thighs together, the friction bringing a warm surge of wetness down there. Her breath caught in her throat. "That's . . . an odd thing to say," she said, her voice gone husky. But was it, really?

"He's coming. They can't keep us from him by hiding us away in the crazy house. He's coming for our flesh and nothing can stop him. And when he comes inside us, we'll wear his flesh."

Sharyn had to get away from this madwoman, or else go mad herself. Already she felt herself drawn into the maze of the woman's ambiguous words, tossed and battered between poles of meaning. She wanted to turn around and march out of the room, but she couldn't make her legs move, couldn't resist the urge to touch Susan's tantalizing skin. She reached out to take the enchanting woman's offered hand. Static electricity arced and snapped between their fingertips just before they touched.

And then the woman was pulling Sharyn onto the bed, groping her breasts and running a hand roughly between her legs. Sharyn tried to voice a protest but what came out was a moan of passion. She slipped her hands inside the hospital gown to cup Susan's small breasts and caress their rigid nipples.

Sharyn sank into the mattress, dizzied by desire, hungry to taste the other woman's body. Sex with another woman was nothing new to her. She'd had a drunken sexual experience with another female when she was a sophomore at the University of Georgia, and thereafter had enjoyed physical relations with both sexes. Nonetheless, the lust she felt now was stronger than any she'd ever known. She kneaded the lithe breasts in her hands as Susan, moaning, straddled her hips.

Susan reached behind her neck, untied the gown and shrugged it off her shoulders. Then she leaned down and fed a breast into Sharyn's rooting mouth.

"He's coming," Susan said, throwing her head back. "Coming . . ."

Sharyn shifted her attention to Susan's other breast. She took the long nipple in her mouth and vigorously sucked it, occasionally teasing the areola with the tip of her tongue. She could taste the lingering musk of the otherworldly beast and it drove her to heady distraction, unleashing fresh waves of lust low in her belly. She echoed Susan's ecstatic cry: "Coming . . ."

As sharp and clear as the facets of an exquisite diamond, the realization that she wanted the bestial god to come informed her passion and drove her to the edge of screaming release; the orgasm, when it came, would be but a minor prelude to the dark god's advent and to the perverse revelries that were sure to follow in his phallic wake. Sharyn was no longer afraid; novel desire had burned the old fears and reactionary taboos to ashes. Now there was nothing to stop her from throwing herself into the purifying flames of sexual alchemy.

Susan's foot found its way to Sharyn's sex, bare toes teasing her inflamed vulva through the denim of her jeans.

"God," Sharyn said, moaning the word as a prayerful imprecation.

"Damn," said Susan with a sinister laugh.

A sharp rap on the one-way-glass window to the nursing station did not stop the lovers' illicit exploits. Sharyn scarcely heard it, all her senses effectively befogged by the smoky heat of carnal delirium. She unfastened her jeans and pushed them off her hips to give Susan access to her pussy.

Susan took immediate advantage; she trailed kisses down Sharyn's belly and then buried her mouth between her swollen lips and lapped at the silky wetness.

Sharyn tangled her fingers in Susan's thick hair, closed her eyes and gave herself over to a darkening maelstrom of lust. Swirling images appeared on the undersides of her eyelids. She saw a ring of glowing stones, and beyond the pulsating circle of light she saw startling snatches of a world made of fire. It was no surprise that the fiery visions throbbed in time to her racing heartbeat. The inner and outer worlds were coming together in her, and at the heart of the consequential third dominion was a roaring furnace of refiner's fire. Carnal heat fueled the fire and quickened the spirit. Immutable flames threatened to consume the tenuous walls dividing coexisting realms of reality and unreality, and she was poised at the delicate nexus, flesh-petals opened wide to receive what was coming.

A dark shape appeared in the wall of fire, and it came forward, flames dancing on its form without burning it. Surely this was a god, glimpsed now because there were pictures hidden in the scent Susan carried in her pores, vision-giving pheromones Sharyn hungrily absorbed as their bodies intermingled.

The sharp rapping of skin and bone on glass became more insistent but it seemed worlds away and had nothing to do with her. And even if it did, whatever business the old world might have with her paled in the blood-red firelight that haloed the god stalking through sacred flames. More than she'd ever wanted anything, she wanted that holy fire to engulf her. Wanted the blazing god to fill her, to fuck her yielding flesh until her soul ran red with blood.

Overwhelming sensations brought revelation. Sharyn's detached inner eye—the neutral observer that had always been present as dispassionate witness to the wild swings between the poles of her disease—saw and made sense of what was happening now. Dr. Knott had withheld her medication, and the chemical hurdle that had perverted her response to the call of the goat-man was collapsing now, making her vulnerable to forces older than humanity. The echo of the goat-man's seminal summons and his enchanting scent hung in the ether, ineradicable and irresistible.

Susan's mouth found Sharyn's clitoris and tongued it with dagger-like precision, sending Sharyn closer to the great wall of fire burning at the border of two worlds. And closer to orgasmic cataclysm. The duality of her disease could not survive such devastation—or so she fervently hoped. If she survived, she would live to see the final reconciliation of the two halves of her battered psyche: this was the goat-man's unspoken promise to her. This was revelation.

Rough hands suddenly wrenched Susan off Sharyn.

A man's angry voice said: "This is inappropriate! Control yourselves!"

Sharyn opened her eyes and saw Susan Knott floating in the air above her, held aloft by a big black man with giant, muscular arms. But Sharyn was too close to climax to control herself. She shut her eyes and gave herself to the consuming fire.

CHAPTER
TWENTY-FIVE

"GODDAMMIT, JOOLS, LET ME IN!" Angela pounded the fleshy part of her fist on the bedroom door. Then she kicked it, growling in frustration.

Hunched naked over her laptop, Julie said, "Go away." Then her fingers resumed their mad dance on the keyboard, tapping letters magically onto the screen. Since returning from the garden of stone angels, she'd sequestered herself in her room, desperate to vent the teeming stuff in her head and her gut. The damn of her writer's block had finally collapsed, unleashing a crashing cataract of creativity that she captured as quickly as her fingers could fly, transposing the flood of images to the bright page.

She was writing the bones. Writing down the flesh. The blood. The viscera. All that was in her had to come out or it would surely poison her. She was writing to preserve her sanity. Writing for her life.

She'd stripped off her clothes as she wrote; she didn't pause to analyze her sudden need to be naked. It simply felt right to keep physical encumbrances to a minimum. She was midwife to her own birthing. The sonic seed implanted in her psyche last night had already come to term, and the hour of birth was now at hand.

With *The Ravenwood Horror* aborted and forgotten, she was free to tell this new tale with a *tabla rosa* mind. But the slate didn't stay blank or pristine for long; the words and images spewed forth in sick gouts of blood and black fluids, letters like bird tracks in the pornographic gore.

"Julie, please," said Angela at the door, "I'm really worried about you now. Why have you locked me out?"

"You're sweet," Julie said, her lover's distraction truly trying her patience now. "But you have to leave me alone now. I'm *working*."

"But we were supposed to go into town, remember? For groceries?"

"Goddammit, woman, go away!"

Ange kicked the door again. "You know what? You're a first-class bitch. You want me to go away? Fine. I'm fucking outta here."

Julie made a guttural sound in the back of her throat that wasn't quite a growl. She hammered a fist on the desk, then jumped up and went to the door. She unlocked it and threw it open. "Angela, wait . . ."

But Angela was no longer there.

"Angela? I'm sorry," she said to the empty hallway. "I just need a little more time alone. If I don't get this stuff down now . . ."

She heard the front door slam. She went to the top of the stairs, and stood there a moment, debating whether she should go after Angela. A few seconds later, she heard the van crank up and drive away, tires screeching.

"Be a bitch, then," she said.

Then she returned to her writing to resume the scene wherein a slatternly madwoman has sex with a big black dog. She'd never written of such perversity before, certainly not with Michael looking over her shoulder, but that was of no consequence now. She no longer needed a guardian angel.

She'd found something more suited to her purposes. Something dark and primal, mysterious and terribly exciting. A godly *thing* that was changing her from the inside, out.

* * *

Rourke was the first to see the dark mouth of the cave, partially hidden behind a twisted thicket of vines. He put his hand on Knott's shoulder and then pointed at the cave's entrance. The physical contact with his companion heightened the extraordinary sexual tension he'd been trying to ignore. He snatched his hand off Knott's shoulder, and then brought his index finger to his lips to urge silence and stealth. Knott nodded. They crept as quietly as they could toward the cave.

Rourke drew his pistol, momentarily relieved by the physical rush of unambiguous masculine power. He unclipped the flashlight from his belt, aimed it at his face and clicked it on to makes sure the batteries were good. They were.

Knott brought the shotgun up to his shoulder as he moved toward the cave. He handled the gun with the aplomb of an experienced hunter.

The sun was a hazy ball of fire above the breaking fog, but the woods seemed somehow darker now, filled with sinister shadows. The scent of sex was stronger this close to the cave, and Rourke reckoned that they were walking into a trap set by the devious creature of unknown origin. He sensed that his law-enforcement experience and tactics would be of little use here. He didn't want to go into that granite maw of darkness, didn't want to step into its throat; the horrors within would surely swallow him.

Then he recognized an underlying smell: the coppery odor of fresh blood, mixed with the suffocating smell of raw flesh. He glanced to his right, looked down, and saw blood spatters and scattered pools of blood. Something—or someone—had been recently slaughtered on this ground, but there was no evidence of animal skin or body parts.

He silently prayed that this was only the blood of a large woodland creature.

He froze a few feet from the entrance. Knott glanced his way, eyebrows raised. Rourke steeled himself as best he could, then nodded to Knott and together they went into the cave.

The hairs on his arms stood at attention as he moved into the electromagnetically-charged air. He raised the flashlight in his left hand and braced his pistol-holding right hand on his left wrist to synchronize the aim of gun and flashlight.

"Oh Christ," said Knott, who was the first to see the abomination on the floor of the cave.

Rourke saw it then and put the beam of light on the two rutting figures. The woman was oblivious to the presence of her disgusted spectators. On her hands and knees, she stared blankly at the cave wall in front of her as a large brown dog went about his business of humping her from behind. The mongrel's ears were laid back, his teeth bared in a wicked canine grin as he fucked the dazed woman.

"No!" shouted Knott as he stepped toward the dog and raised the shotgun as if to hammer the mutt's head with it.

"Wait," Rourke said. "I'll do it so there's no chance he can bite her." He cautiously walked up to the dog and stuck his gun's muzzle an inch from the side of the dog's head. The mongrel cut his yellow eyes at Rourke but he was too deep into the throes of bestial lust to pull out of the woman and escape with his life. The dog whined and humped faster, its tail flagged over its furry flanks as if to protect its genitals.

Rourke cocked the hammer, angled his aim so that there was no chance of hitting the woman with the shot, and squeezed the trigger.

The dog's head flopped to one side and hung limp even as his flanks made two, three final thrusts into the woman, then the mutt convulsed and fell still, draped as limp as an animal skin over human haunches.

"God," said Knott, his face starkly pale in the dim light.

Rourke shone his beam about the cave to confirm that there were no other occupants. "Where are the others?" he asked.

"*He* took them," said Knott. "And the son of a bitch left this poor woman just to taunt us. Do you know her?"

"Sarah Melton," Rourke said. "A schoolteacher."

Rourke holstered his gun and then bent down and peeled the dead dog off Sarah Melton's fleshy rump. She looked back at him and growled, her eyes ablaze with rage. He tossed the reeking dog to the ground and backed away from the furious woman.

Knott intervened, kneeling beside her but taking care to stay out of range of her teeth. He said, "Sarah, it's all right. We're here to help you. You're safe now. I'm Dr. Knott and this is Deputy Rourke. We—"

She made a mewling noise and shifted her weight so that she was offering her "hindquarters" to the doctor. Rourke realized he should've brought a blanket to cover her with, but in her present state of mind keeping her covered wouldn't have been easy anyway.

"No, Sarah," Knott said, exercising the patience of a man accustomed to dealing with deeply disturbed individuals. "This is not appropriate behavior. I want you to stand up now. Take my hand, Sarah. Take my hand and stand on your own two feet."

Knott straightened up and extended his hand.

Sarah cut angry eyes at him and snarled, baring her slight overbite.

"I don't think"—Rourke started, but didn't finish his thought because the woman suddenly lunged at Knott's hand, snapping her teeth and just missing his fingers when he snatched his hand away.

Undaunted, Knott spoke again in the calm but firm voice of the therapist: "Sarah, I won't allow you to bite anybody. You need to get control of yourself right now. You're a human being. Act like one. You are not a beast of the field. What would your students think if they could see you acting like a wild animal? Now stand up and walk out of here with me."

The woman whined, reminding Rourke of a scolded dog. She hung her head and crawled forward a few feet on her hands and knees. Then she lifted a knee and let go with a loud fart, which she followed with maniacal laughter.

Rourke neither heard nor saw what happened next between the

madwoman and the psychiatrist because a pulsating circle of light at the cave's doorway and its accompanying subterranean hum completely captured his attention. Immobilized by the sight, he could do nothing but gaze, slack-jawed, into the center of the glowing circle. The ordinary world of daylight outside the cave undulated like a sheer window curtain in a soft breeze, intimating a darker world behind its thinning veneer. He glimpsed—or thought he did—many sets of watchful eyes in the shadowy world. Animals' eyes, he was sure. Then the center of the circle opened out into a widening vista of ancient ruins, stone columns and mausoleum-like structures overrun with leafless vines and odd tentacle-like creepers.

Rourke felt suddenly sick. Inner darkness crowded his vision and he was sure he was going to pass out. His ears rang. Something was pulling him out of himself, hollowing out his chest and draining his essence. He was all but certain that he was dying. He threw out a hand to brace himself on the wall of the cave but his hand *went through* the granite as if it were made of water, and he fell to his knees, caught in a whirlpool of physical sensations the human body was never meant to experience, nor designed to withstand.

That the world was not made of solid stuff somehow didn't much surprise him. It seemed now that he'd always suspected as much, though he wasn't the sort of man given to contemplating such abstract concepts. Solidity was illusion. The very stuff of reality was elusive. Illusory. Which probably went a long way in explaining how Rourke was sinking into the malleable stone floor of the cave.

"We have to go." The voice came from very far away; its words held no meaning for Rourke as he slowly sank into layers of stone.

Something seized his shoulder and tugged at him.

"Come on, man! Get up!"

He looked up through the haze of porous rock and could just make out the flesh-knitted face of Trey Knott. Then Rourke was rising out of rock and stumbling to his feet, the stone floor of the cave solid beneath them.

"Did you see?" Rourke said, letting Knott lead him out of the cave.

The glowing circle was gone. The hum was still there, though it was very faint now. Rourke's entire body was singing, vibrating at a frequency only he could hear.

"More than I wanted to see."

Knott had Sarah Melton off her hands and knees and on a leash, muzzled. Rourke did a double-take and saw that the woman had a leather belt in her mouth, notched tightly behind her head, and that Knott was controlling her with it, directing her out of the cave as well. "I had to muzzle her," he explained, "to keep her from biting me. I know how this looks but what else could I do?"

Rourke nodded, taking this in stride. What would've seemed shockingly extraordinary a couple of hours ago was now merely a matter of course. A naked woman on a leash made perfect sense, given the bizarre circumstance of *this* morning.

"Are you all right?" asked the doctor.

"I don't know what *all right* is anymore," Rourke honestly answered. "What the hell just happened here?"

If Knott had an answer, he kept it to himself.

CHAPTER
TWENTY-SIX

THORN HAD NEVER SHOT AND KILLED an animal larger than a rabbit, and that single experience had soured him on killing for sport and turned him against hunting altogether, so the proposition of shooting dogs was not a pleasant one—never mind that these mangy monsters crouched outside Widow Leatherwood's house were the antithesis of Man's Best Friend.

Shoot them he would, if he had to.

He drove up in front of the house and sat on the horn, giving the mutts a steady bleat he hoped their sensitive ears could not long tolerate. The dog on the front porch turned its head, cocked its ears and gave Thorn what he supposed was a look of irritation. The larger and more ferocious-looking mongrel got up from its post at the corner of the porch and came toward the Triumph with ears laid back and teeth bared in a slobbering snarl. The third dog at the other corner of the house didn't so much as glance Thorn's way, but maintained its low-bellied crouch and kept its gaze locked on the house.

Laying off the horn, Thorn picked up his .45, put the car in reverse and wheeled into a position that gave him a clear shot over the driver's-side door at the approaching hound. The fact that he hadn't taken time to put the convertible's top up meant that he couldn't afford to miss what he was shooting at; with a muscular leap any one of the dogs could be on top of him and at his throat.

He sighted on the approaching dog's black head at a spot midway between its close-set eyes. The dog was coming straight on and so unwittingly offered itself as a more or less fixed target. When the snarling mongrel was less than ten yards away Thorn fired. The dog's head nodded once and then the beast lost its legs and went down in a dead heap of muscle and fur.

As Thorn lowered the pistol the other two dogs left their posts and charged the car, coming at him from two different directions. He snapped off a hurried shot at the one on the left and missed. He gunned the engine and the TR6 shot forward across the lawn and out of the dogs' paths. He turned hard to the right and cut a wide circle, just missing a willow tree at the edge of the yard. There he braked, drew a bead on the nearest beast and fired. The .45 slug took the dog in the flank, spun the surprised mutt in a half-circle and deposited it in a mound of bloodied fur and exposed flesh and bone.

The last dog righted its charge and took a running jump at Thorn. In a panic he got off three rapid shots, the last hitting the airborne dog in the belly and knocking it off course. The dog banged headfirst into the driver's door and dropped to the ground, yelping.

Thorn leaned over the door and finished the gut-shot mutt with a blast that blew apart the dog's skull and spilled its brains on the grass.

Exhilarated by his four-wheel dogfight, Thorn drove a victory circle around the bodies of his canine enemies before parking in front of the house and jumping out to pound on the widow's door.

"Not bad for a schoolteacher," Mrs. Leatherwood said from behind the screen door. "Come on in, dogslayer. I have a lot to tell you and little time."

When she opened the screen for him he saw the rifle hanging from her left hand. "My late husband's twenty-two," she said. "I had to shoot the door a few times to keep 'em from tearing it down and coming in after me."

She stepped aside and he entered. She shut and bolted the door. She suddenly rounded on him and said, "Since you were here last I've gone deaf so don't waste your time asking me questions. Just sit and listen to what I tell you and nod every now and then so I'll know you understand."

Thorn nodded. She led him down a creaky hallway and into a small parlor hung with dark floor-length curtains that looked as if they belonged in a larger, better-appointed room. One wall was taken up with unvarnished bookcases interspersed with paperbacks, hardbacks and a few spiral-bound recipe books. On one shelf books shared space with homey knick-knacks, copies of *Reader's Digest* and small-framed photographs yellowed with age. The room smelled of musty books, fragrant lavender and mildew.

"Have a seat, professor," she said, waving him to a loveseat with upholstery embroidered with red and pink roses. She collapsed heavily into a stuffed armchair and groaned. "Oh me."

Thorn perched on the edge of the loveseat, eager to hear what she had to say. He had many questions he wanted to ask but didn't because they would quite literally fall on deaf ears and go unanswered.

"Thank you for getting rid of them hellhounds," she said with measured weariness. "The Dark Man of the Wood surely sent them to torment me."

Good Lord, the old girl's gone daft. And she looked as if she'd aged years since he last saw her.

She must've caught the alarm in his face because then she said, "Hear me out before you go to thinking I'm a crazy old bat."

He dutifully nodded and leaned back in his seat. The excitement of the dust-up with the hounds of hell was already deserting him; in its place was a sharp pang of empathetic melancholy. Sitting in this sad room with this glum old woman was nearly more than he could bear, suggesting as it did that he would similarly end his days as a lonely old man, all alone in an equally somber room. He quailed at the image of so bleak a future and averted his eyes.

Liza Leatherwood went on: "When I was a young girl my grandmother sat me down and told me about the Helling—the very thing you've been pestering me to tell you about. She swore me to secrecy and it pains me to have to break my vow now, but I've come to know something my granny didn't. It would be sinful if I was to keep it to myself, sure enough. Which is why I have to tell it to you. But before I do, you have to promise me one thing. You have to swear to me that you'll cut down a tree and remove the stump. Tear it up by the roots. You understand?"

"Yes, no, I mean—"

"Say it," she said with a fierce look. "Swear you'll get rid of that tree."

"I don't understand. What's a tree has to—"

"Are you deaf? I told you I can't hear worth a damn. Now raise your right hand and get ready to swear you'll get rid of the tree."

She got up, walked stiffly across the room and held a Bible in front of him. Thorn hadn't noticed the Bible until now; it seemed to have appeared as if by magic.

"Put your left hand on the Good Book," she instructed, "and swear it."

He put his left hand on the Bible, raised his right hand and said, "I swear I will get rid of the tree."

She nodded, her face losing some of its tension.

Outside a crow cawed bitterly, as if protesting Thorn's vow to fell a tree.

"I don't expect you to do the cutting yourself," she said. "Better to hire it done. I 'spect you'll find a tree-removal outfit in the phone book. But you have to be there to make sure it's done proper. Nod to show you understand."

Thorn nodded, wondering how much he would have to go out of pocket in keeping his odd vow.

The woman returned to her chair and to her story. "Here's the thing, professor. There really is a Dark Man of the Wood, just like Hawthorne wrote about. Only worse. The one hereabouts is more demon than man. I don't know if it's the same one Mr. Hawthorne told of. More likely there's more than one of 'em in the world. This one showed up in these hills back in eighteen-sixty-five. Far as anybody knows, that was the first time. Those that saw it—or *remembered* seeing it years later—said it was part goat, part man, with horns and cloven hooves like the Devil. Maybe it *was* the Devil. It sure enough brought a heap of evil when it came."

Thorn opened his mouth to speak but she shushed him with a wave of her hand and a stern look. "According to my granny, it cast a spell on the womenfolk of what's now Widow's Ridge with its ungodly cry. It called 'em out and they had no choice but to go to him. Evidently, its cry clouded men's minds too, 'cause most of 'em didn't do anything to stop their women. In most cases though, it was sly enough to call the women when the men weren't about.

"What happened when they went to him, my granny didn't know. She said that most of the women either couldn't remember or were too ashamed to say what it did to 'em. But whatever it was, it was most unnatural—if you catch my drift. However the demon did it, it turned the women into raving killers. They lured the menfolk into the woods for some sort of orgy and slaughtered every one of them in some sick ceremony to honor the goat-man. Granny hinted that some of the women turned cannibal and actually ate parts of the men. When it was all over, the women returned to their homes like nothing had happened—or like they'd all had the same bad dream.

"When folks in Dogwood got wind of it, they went looking in the woods and found the remains of the murdered men. Nobody could figure out exactly what had happened or who'd done the butchering, so they ended up burying the body parts they found in a common grave

about two miles from where we sit. A circuit-riding preacher said a few
words, and not long after, somebody decided to plant an oak tree on the
gravesite as a kind of memorial. Because they never found all the body
parts or any of the heads, nor knew for sure who they'd buried there,
they didn't put up grave markers."

"That's the tree you want me to remove! The one on the gravesite."

She silenced him with a scalding look. Then she continued her tale.
"Folks took to calling our little settlement Widow's Ridge, and rather
than pass on the story of the shameful slaughter to the next generation,
the women concocted the story that all the murdered menfolk had been
killed in the Civil War, hence the name Widow's Ridge. Folks in these
parts went along with the fiction, I guess, because they preferred it to
the truth. Nobody wanted to think about what might've transpired out
in those woods. Made 'em too uneasy, I reckon. Better to think of the
dead men as war heroes. A dozen men, all told."

She paused to stare off into the dim room and to pick a speck of lint
from her dress. Then she continued. "Three nights ago—or was it four?
I've been so out of sorts here lately, I can't be sure—he came back. The
goat-man. I heard its cry. It was just the way my granny said it would be.
She warned me that it would come back someday and that I would know
its shrill cry when I heard it. I knew it for what it was, all right. It was
like nothing I'd ever heard in all my long years. If I hadn't already been
deaf in one ear I'm sure I woulda gone out to meet him. Most women
can't resist the call. Very young children and the mentally afflicted can,
but not without going some kind of crazy—or so my grandmother said,
and I reckon it's true. Anyway, hearing that cry scared me so bad I took
a hatpin and punched a hole in the eardrum of my good ear so if I heard
it again I wouldn't go crazy.

"So he's come back and he's gathering a new band of women to do
his murderous work. But here's the thing, professor. *I know how to stop
him.* I won't bother to tell you how I know 'cause you wouldn't believe
it if I told you. That tree you're gonna cut down? It's haunted by the
souls of the men that were killed more'n a hundred years ago. That oak
tree's been their prison for all those years. When you have it cut down
and the roots pulled up, their spirits will be released and then in their
pent-up rage they can drive off the demon. Before you ask how I know
this, I know because I *saw* it. Vengeful spirits are powerful like nothing
else on this earth."

She paused long enough to give Thorn an appraising stare. He tried to keep the incredulity he felt from his face because he didn't want to upset the old woman further. From her haggard appearance, he didn't think she could take much more adversity.

She said, "You don't believe it. Well, that's fine. You don't have to, so long as you keep your promise and take down that tree."

"I will keep my promise," he said, speaking slowly so that she might read the words on his lips.

"Oh, I know it's hard to believe," she allowed. "Over the years I doubted it myself. I knew my grandmother believed it with all her heart and soul, but the one thing that didn't make sense to me was: Why here? Out of the whole world, why would the demon pick these hills to do his mischief?"

Thorn nodded. He was wondering the same thing. Even if you could accept the rest of it, that was the one question that weakened the whole argument. *Why here?*

"Well, I studied on that a lot, down the years," she said in a tone Thorn could only think of as professorial, "and I've yet to come up with a good answer. Some folks say there was a witch lived hereabouts back before the Civil War and that she had truck with the spirit world, household gods, demons and such." She shrugged. "I never met a witch so I don't have an opinion on that. Asa Edgar's momma was a healer with some strange ways and notions but she wasn't what I'd call a witch. More likely, there's something about the land itself that invites the demon or makes it easy for him to come into our world. I've read something about 'ley lines' and how they have strong magnetic energy that makes them places of power, and I think something like that would be the more likely answer. But who knows? All I know for sure, the creature is real and he's come again."

Thorn had first heard of the mystical powers of ley lines from his students and had subsequently researched the subject just enough to satisfy himself that it was nothing more than a brew of New Age fantasies, shaken not stirred with a jigger of science.

"Remove that tree and you'll find your bones under it," she said. "You need to do it today, professor. Yesterday woulda been better."

He nodded.

"And take your gun with you. You'll probably have to shoot some more evil curs, of one sort or another. The goat-man won't leave without a hard fight."

CHAPTER
TWENTY-SEVEN

SHARYN SAT ON THE EDGE OF HER HOSPITAL BED and hugged her knees tightly to her chest as if to contain her humiliation, but of course she couldn't. The nursing staff had caught her acting out her bizarre sexual fantasy—she *hoped* it was fantasy, rather than something more disturbing—and now, half an hour later, a shameful blush still burned her face like a blistering tattoo.

She harbored no illusions about her sexual orientation; she was undeniably bisexual. She came down (and came) in both gender camps. Much the same as her psyche vacillated between mania and depression, her sexual desires vibrated along a continuum between male and female, and on the whole, she found the overall symmetry satisfying. She didn't consider it in any way abnormal, and she had little patience with those pompous self-appointed guardians of morality who saw homosexuality as a sinful aberration. She was the way she was because of her genetic makeup and none but the grossly ignorant could believe there was such a thing as a sinful gene. Had genetics played no part in the matter, she thought she would've chosen of her own free will to "go both ways," rather than to limit herself to a solitary sex.

The shame she now felt was due to her lack of control in the presence of Susan Knott. It had to have appeared to the nursing staff that Sharyn had taken advantage of a seriously disturbed patient—and maybe she had. But no, that wouldn't wash, because Susan Knott had been the instigator, or more accurately, the catalyst.

But that wasn't right either.

Sharyn knew that the true catalyst was the Dionysian entity that had set this whole bizarre business in motion, and was even now exerting its insidious influence. It wasn't fantasy. It wasn't delusion. It was reality.

Hyper-reality.

And she hadn't been strong enough to resist it. *That* was the real source of her shame. She should've recognized that she was being manipulated from beyond and should've gotten the hell away from that woman before . . .

"But I *wanted* it to happen," she said aloud. "I knew exactly what was happening and I didn't care."

She shook her head violently. Then she pounded her fists on her knees. "Damn you," she whispered, though she wasn't sure if she was damning herself or someone else.

She clamped her eyes shut and rested her forehead on her knees. Unfamiliar emotions welled up within her, and she was overcome with a strong sense of dislocation. Without actually moving, she felt herself transported to some other place and time. The cramped little hospital room was a cave. The cave was embedded in an ancient woodland. Mythical creatures skulked with nefarious purpose about the shadowy landscape. Dark energies of lust and baser urges charged the rarefied air; Sharyn's inner sea of stormy emotions swelled sympathetically, and she could do nothing but wait for the brutal waves to break on the eroding shore of her sanity.

* * *

After they'd seen Sarah Melton secured in the back of the ambulance, Knott and Rourke waited for the coroner to arrive. Forty-five minutes later, Rourke was driving Knott back to the medical center to pick up his car. The cell phone's sober ring-tone broke the uneasy silence.

Knott flipped open his cell and answered the call. Though he had come to rely heavily on the high-tech gadget in recent years, he'd always felt fumble-fingered when opening the little thing with his big hands and had on more than one occasion dropped it in the process. He didn't drop it this time. He fingered the correct little square on the pad and answered: "This is Dr. Knott."

The dayshift charge nurse told him that there had been "an incident" with Mrs. Knott, and then went on to describe in clinical detail Susan's inappropriate physical contact with another female patient, Sharyn Rampling.

When he'd heard enough of it, Knott interrupted the nurse and told her he would get to the hospital as soon as possible. He angrily tapped the END button and broke communication.

He glanced over at Rourke, who sat wearily behind the steering wheel, staring at the road ahead as if lost in thought. Knott was relieved that the deputy gave no sign that he'd overheard any of the nurse's side of the conversation.

Though it went against his psychiatric training, Knott was nevertheless deeply ashamed of his wife. When dealing with his patients, he assiduously guarded against making moral judgments, but this was his wife, for God's sake! He winced when he realized the extent of his anger with her, and then he was ashamed of himself. Susan was in no way to blame for her behavior, he knew. Unnatural forces were at work here. He'd directly felt their effects up on the mountain, so how could he hold his wife accountable for her aberrant behavior when he knew that something very powerful was pulling psychic strings and orchestrating the vilest of acts and most absurd follies? He could not.

His mind's fresh images of what had happened to the search party offered further evidence of diabolical influence. The whole scene might've been comical if it hadn't been so deadly. Seeing a group of manly men in the throes of homosexual panic wasn't an everyday sight, to be sure. His own state of arousal on the mountainside had been unlike anything he'd ever experienced, and he'd hated feeling that he was not completely in control of his faculties. Still, he'd fared better than some of the other men, and he supposed that was a function of his willpower and his training to remain detached in the face of madness.

He glanced again at Rourke's grim countenance. "Are you all right?" he asked the deputy.

"I would be if I could get these damn pictures out of my head. You saw the same shit I did. How do you deal with that? You got any professional secrets for that sort of thing, Doc?"

Knott did a quick mental run-through of appropriate responses but all he could say was, "No."

Rourke's knuckles blanched as he tightened his grip on the wheel. Then he said, "Sarah Melton . . . Think she'll ever be the same?"

"Like she was before all this happened to her? Impossible to say, at this point. I don't know how much she'll remember when she comes out of her dissociative state."

"*If* she comes out of it."

Knott waited a beat, then he said, "There's a complication in my wife's condition that doesn't bode well for any of those exposed to . . .

this thing. That was the hospital that called a few minutes ago. The staff caught my wife sexually acting out with another female patient. She's not . . . she's never been anything but a straight-laced heterosexual. How can one's sexual persuasion change overnight?"

"So . . . those guys on the mountain could be affected the same way? *We* could be? Long-term?"

"I don't know. We just don't know what we're dealing with. What this thing really is."

"Yeah. Well, whatever it is, I have to catch it. And kill it. And you have to do what you can to clean up the mental mess it's made."

"Want to switch jobs?" Knott asked in an attempt to lighten the mood.

"No way, Doc. I'll leave the head-cleaning to you. All I want is one clean shot."

CHAPTER
TWENTY-EIGHT

THORN FOUND THE TIP TOP TREE SERVICE in the yellow pages and made the call. A man named Carl explained that he could fell the tree with a chainsaw and use a stump grinder to shred the stump in a matter of minutes.

"I'll pay you a hundred dollars extra to do it today," Thorn said.

Carl said he reckoned he could get to it before dark, no problem.

Thorn gave him directions to Mrs. Leatherwood's house and Carl agreed to meet him there at three o'clock. That would give him time to recruit the students he needed for the dig. He spent the rest of the morning calling his students and getting tools and the necessary equipment together. If there were indeed human remains buried beneath the tree, he would then notify the authorities. He didn't anticipate a legal problem with an archeological dig, but it was wise practice to cover his bases.

He called the cell phones of six students who would be eager to assist him with the dig but he was unable to reach one of them. That was okay. Five would do.

He made notes on Liza Leatherwood's incredible tale, writing it up without making any judgment of its veracity. The main thing now was uncovering the remains. With any luck, the bones would speak for themselves.

* * *

Rourke dropped Knott off at his car in the Medical Center's parking lot. "I hope your wife gets better," he said. *Before she gets worse,* he thought to himself.

He was too tired to think his way through to his next move. He needed sleep, at least a couple of hours to belay his physical and emotional exhaustion. He was in no condition to tackle the official paperwork for which he was responsible. How the hell was he going to write up what had happened to the search party without sounding like a raving psycho? A few hours of sleep should clear his mind, but he was in charge now. His fellow deputies would be looking to him for leadership. Sleep was out of the question.

He drove back to the Sheriff's Office, wondering how he could get the other lost women away from a thing with apparent supernatural powers—and how he could prevent other women from being taken.

* * *

Jude—the former Judy Lynn Bowen—was sleeping in her dead lover's blood when the god called her out. Sated in every possible way and drunk on dreams of glorious debauchery, she came to crystal-clear consciousness immediately, rose from the basement floor, and went outside to answer the divine summons. She didn't fret that she was stark naked and covered in blood. She was beyond such concerns. She wasn't worried that neighbors might see her walking from the back door to the woods. Her god—her bestial bridegroom—was awesomely capable of handling such incidentals.

The morning light hurt her eyes and she was glad when she stepped into the shadows of the woods to drink the darkness down. Her body quivered pleasurably in anticipation of being once again in *his* presence.

A short distance into the trees, she paused, unsure of which way to go. He called again. A short high-pitched whistling shriek only she and the neighborhood dogs could hear. She went toward the sound, eager and unbearably excited.

A small band of women waited beneath a willow. They were naked except for leafy vines tied around their waists and laurel makeshift wreaths on their heads. Some of them held walking sticks, and two of them were armed with club-like tree branches. A tall woman with unusually long breasts held a machete in her left hand and a laurel branch in her right. Most of their faces were familiar to Jude, but like her, they had sloughed off their dull identities in order to serve *him*.

A knot of jealously twisted in Jude's belly and rage suddenly seethed just beneath her outward calm. She did not wish to share her god with these women. They were not as worthy as she. Had they killed for him? Had they given up everything to serve him? Were they all to be his brides? No! She would fight them to the death, if she had to. *She* was the chosen one, the youngest, the prettiest, surely the most desirable.

She stood still and worked out in her mind how she might take the machete from the bitch with the long tits and show them all that *she* was the special one. And the toughest.

But then a woman with long red hair stepped forward, placed a laurel wreath on Jude's head and kissed her full on the mouth, slipping her tongue past Jude's lips. The other six women surrounded her and closed on her in a bizarre group hug. Jude's jealously and rage drained away, replaced by an intense feeling of peaceful well-being. Feminine hands groped her, caressing her breasts and slipping past the lips of her sex. Some of them licked Josh's blood from her skin while others chewed her blood-matted hair. She shut her eyes and yielded to their kittenish ministrations.

They took her gently down and took turns between her legs, lapping up her womanly juices. When the ritualistic initiation was over, the bestial god appeared before them and they took turns kneeling at his feet, sucking down his sweet semen.

Now Jude understood that no single woman could satisfy his prodigious needs. Without her sisters to share carnal duties, the god's lustful demands would surely kill her. They were his band of brides. It could not be otherwise.

When it was her turn to swallow his intoxicating nectar, she did so with devout relish. She soon fell back on her haunches knowing that tonight was to be the nuptial celebration. Tonight she and her new sisters would honor *him* with the bloody revelry he demanded. And at last their group marriage would be consummated.

* * *

As soon as Knott stepped onto the unit, the three staff members at the nursing station lapsed into an uncomfortable silence. They looked at him as if they didn't know what to say. He needed a shave, a shower and a change of clothes. He knew he looked more like a patient off the street than a doctor. The irony being that his wife was the patient.

"How's Susan?" he asked, folding his arms across his chest.

With a glance toward the observation window, the dayshift charge nurse said, "She's resting quietly in her room."

Knott kept well away from the window. He didn't want Susan to see him yet. "And Miss Rampling?"

"Also in her room. Quiet, but . . . spooky."

"Spooky," he repeated. "Can you be more specific? In clinical terms?"

"I'm sorry, Dr. Knott, it's just that . . . I don't know how to put it in clinical terms. The way she looks, the way she looks *at* you is just plain spooky. Her eyes have this wildness in them, but her behavior's been nothing but appropriate since . . . the incident."

Another nurse chimed in, "It's like she's right on the edge of losing control. But what makes it so scary is the way her personality changed. I knew her when she was here the last time and now she's like someone else. Almost like she's possessed."

"I wouldn't use that term, Sandra," the charge nurse gently admonished her underling. "I think—"

Knott cut her off: "I'll see Miss Rampling first. Don't let Susan know I'm here."

* * *

Sharyn Rampling was seated on her bed with a book in her lap. She looked up as he entered the room, and the faraway look in her eyes made him doubt that she'd actually been reading.

"Morning," he said. Saying *Good morning* would've been dishonest, and he wanted to avoid superficial niceties and game-playing. A good therapist sets the example and hopes the patient will follow it. He sat in the armchair and crossed his legs. He didn't have her medical chart with him; the chart could be seen as a symbolic barrier between them and he knew she was savvy enough to note its absence. "I understand you've met my wife."

She narrowed her eyes as if trying to read his face. She said nothing. He said, "You want to tell me about it?"

A slight smile crossed her lips. "Are you sure you want me to, Doctor Knott? It gets pretty kinky. It could be hard for you, you know, to maintain your professional detachment."

"I'm not pretending that I don't have a personal interest in this, Sharyn. We both know better. I haven't spoken with my wife yet. I wanted to get your perspective first. Please tell me what happened."

"I'm sure you read our charts."

"No, I didn't. I got a brief verbal report from staff. All I know is that you were in Susan's room and that you engaged in sexual activity with her."

"You make it sound so cheap," she said with a coy little smile.

"I don't want to interrogate you. Just tell me how it went down."

She laughed. "Went down? Is that a Freudian slip or a deliberate use of sexual euphemism to . . . prime my pump?"

He felt his face redden. He bit back an angry response and said nothing.

"All right, Doc, I'll give you the blow by blow, but I can't promise I won't get aroused by it. You probably will too. You sure you want to risk that? Who knows where that might take us?"

"Something very dangerous is going on here and if we can't get a handle on it, we won't be able to protect ourselves. This goes way beyond what's happening with you and Susan, but you're part of the big picture and I need you to help me understand it. We don't have time to play games."

"But it *is* a game, don't you see? We're being played. Your wife and I are game pieces. You are too, in your own way. You're the knight the queen sacrifices in service to the king. That's it in a nutshell. That's all you need to know. The game's afoot and there's nothing you or I can do to stop it. Not that I'd want to, not anymore."

Knott sighed involuntarily. "So what happened between you and Susan was orchestrated by . . .?"

She twitched her nose and a look of alarm suddenly came into her face.

"What is it?" he asked.

"I *smell* him," she said, losing a measure of her condescending composure. "His scent is on you."

"Him?"

"Don't play innocent. You know who I'm talking about."

"Your woodland god. Pan. Or Dionysus."

"Where have you been?" She said this sharply in a scolding voice.

Determined to keep the dialogue on track, he ignored her question and asked, "What precipitated your encounter with Susan?"

"The scent was on her too, but not as strong as it is on you right now. But it was more than that. It was the way she looked at me, and in her words as well. We *connected*. There was this unspoken subtext. It was, I don't know, *biblical*. You know, like *Whenever two are gathered in my name, I am there too.* Something like that. But we sure as hell aren't talking about Jesus. Now you tell me. Where have you been? The scent wasn't on you last night. Something happened, didn't it? Something big."

"I went along with a search party," he said. "We found one of the missing women."

Her eyes widened. "How . . . was she?"

"Dazed, disoriented. Abused."

"God." The old fear flashed in her face, then quickly vanished. "It's really happening now. We're living the myth. Or it's living us. Any way you slice it, we're fucked."

Then she hungrily sniffed the air, taking in as much of the lingering scent of the beast as she could, and gave him the most demonic grin he'd ever seen.

* * *

Knott entered his wife's room, his heart rapidly knocking against his ribcage. He did his best to keep his voice from shaking as he said, "Susan? I need your help."

She was lying on the bed with her eyes shut and her hands folded over her abdomen. Except for the hospital gown she wore, she might've been a pretty corpse dolled up and laid out for viewing. She didn't move.

Knott went a step closer to the bed. "Susan?"

Her eyelids fluttered, then opened.

"How are you?" he asked softly.

"You're the doctor," she said, "you tell me."

"I don't honestly know. I need you to help me understand what's happening."

She sat up slowly, regally. She looked at him, her face serene. "You don't have it in you."

"Don't have what in me?" He fought the urge to cross his arms over his chest.

"Understanding. You're not equipped for it. You'll never see beyond all your psychiatric nonsense. Those silly shadows on the walls of your pathetic little cave."

"I believe I can if you'll help me. Give me a chance. I'm here as your husband, not your physician. Please."

"But you're not my husband. That marriage was a sham, a cheap imitation. I've already moved on, little man. I don't expect you to understand. But don't worry, I'm sure you'll find a new cavewoman to replace me. A cute little thing with perky tits and a worshipful smile. Like that tight-assed little nurse with the great big crush on you."

"Why do you feel this need to hurt me, Susan? You were never like that before."

"That's just it. *Before.* This is after. And it's nothing like before. I don't need a headshrinker. And I certainly don't want to be married to one."

He didn't let his feelings show in his face. He soldiered on, undaunted. "Do you understand what happened to you last night, why you were compelled to run outside naked?"

"Go away, Trey. Really. This is boring. Go play doctor with patients who might actually need you. I don't."

"I'm not going away. I won't desert you, Susan."

"Don't do me any favors, you stubborn ass. Stand there all day then. You won't get another word out of me." She zipped her lips in pantomime.

Outside the window a blue jay raised a ruckus. Susan turned her face toward the window in rapt attention. She nodded as if she understood the bird's hostile squawking.

Knott stood there a long moment, then said, "I'll see you later, Susan." He paused in the doorway and said, "I love you."

CHAPTER TWENTY-NINE

AT FIRST, JULIE WAS ONLY DIMLY AWARE of the rustling movement downstairs. She came out of her writing trance long enough to identify it as the sound of Angela putting away groceries, bumping about the kitchen, slamming cabinet doors in an apparent display of anger. That woman sure can hold a grudge, Julie thought. That was okay. She would make it up to her later, make her understand that a writer *has* to write when the deep channels finally open up and the words and ideas come flooding forth with single-minded vengeance. And the writing was good. The best she'd ever done. What she had here was not just another horror tale. No, this was serious literature. This was art of the highest order. Once she'd opened herself to the darkness within, the words flowed out of her and onto the page with frightening ease. Almost as if someone else were dictating the sentences. The way the story was writing itself, it would almost be an act of plagiarism to put Julie Archer down as the author.

Footsteps on the stairs. *Damn.*

A knock on the door. "Jools? I don't like this. I don't like being locked out."

"Sorry, Ange. I can't stop now. I'm in the zone. You have to leave me alone for now. I'll make it up to you, I promise."

"If this is how it's going to be, I might as well go back home. Fuck this shit." She kicked the door.

"Please, Angela. Try to understand what this means to me."

"I know exactly what it means. It means you're a selfish bitch."

"Go! Away!"

"Fuck you, no!"

Julie stood up and faced the locked door. "You're spoiling everything."

"No, Julie, you are. And you know what? I'm not going to let you. No fucking way."

Angela began to batter the door, probably throwing her shoulder against it.

"Stop it! You'll hurt yourself, goddammit!"

She didn't stop. She threw herself against the door again and again.

Julie started sobbing as she went toward the door to unlock it. The door came open with a sharp crack of metal and wood and Angela crashed to the floor. Julie shrieked in surprise. She hadn't thought it would be so easy to break down the door.

Angela jumped to her feet and Julie fearfully backed away. Neither of them paid notice to the crow cawing right outside the window. Angela's eyes blazed at Julie's nakedness, her face a twisted mask of madness.

"Daddy's gonna kill me," Julie said with a glance at the splintered wood where the door's top hinge had been.

"*I'm* gonna kill you, you bitch." Angela grinned maniacally as she advanced.

The crow cawed louder still.

Julie looked around for something to use as a weapon.

Angela was on her before Julie could grab the hardback dictionary off the desk.

As Angela bulled her to the floor, Julie thought she could hear the eerie shriek from last night's phantom visitor in the rasping cry of the crow. She stopped struggling and gave in to Angela's rough sexual assault. Soon she was shrieking in orgasmic abandon. All the darkness that was inside her came out in a violent rush and Julie gave it expression in ways that would've shocked even the most jaded connoisseurs of extreme horror.

* * *

Leaving word that he was not to be disturbed for anything short of the end of the world, Rourke retreated to the solitude of Sheriff Gladstone's office in hopes of catching a badly needed catnap. He was so tired he couldn't think straight. He felt as if he'd become one big throbbing raw nerve. He figured a twenty-minute immersion in the blessed unconsciousness of sleep was just the soothing balm he needed to get him through the tribulations and trials of the coming hours. With a glance at his wristwatch, he sat behind the sheriff's big desk for a soporific timeout.

He leaned back in Gladstone's chair, propped his boots on the desk, pulled his hat over his eyes and tried to surrender himself to peaceful slumber. He gradually tuned out the low voices and ringing phones in the next room—in effect, turning off the world—and drifted away.

Out of dreamy darkness came Alice Marsh, her eyes as flinty and flirtatious as the eyes of a ruthless love goddess, her plump lips pursed in the pout of a succubus sent to suck a man dry and leave him shriveled and spiritually impotent for eternity. Trapped behind a desk in a dank chasm, there was no place to run. Not that he really wanted to, because what man could resist such a woman's otherworldly charms and daring sexual advances? Alice relieved him of his pistol, stroked it seductively, ran her tongue around the rim of its muzzle, smiling all the while, and then she peeled off her uniform, jumped on top of the desk and performed a series of unnatural acts with the glistening gun. He watched her through his hat as she moved her hips in provocative gyrations, each thrust threatening to dislodge his sanity. Like a vaudeville vixen whose time center-stage has ended, she suddenly directed his attention stage-left, where a monstrous dog was fornicating with a faceless woman with scrawny blood-streaked flanks. "Jesus God, I can't watch this," he complained, "I'm an officer of the fucking law." Alice smiled and said, "From your lips to God's dog's ear, fucking law."

Coming awake all at once, he yanked his feet off the desk, removed his hat from his face, and catapulted himself out of the chair.

"Christ," he said, wishing he could disown his unwanted erection. "No rest for the fucking wicked."

* * *

Fresh from a steaming shower, Knott collapsed naked onto the bed and covered his eyes with a forearm to block the daylight seeping in around the bedroom's closed curtains. His body was weary but his mind would not rest. It insisted upon replaying grisly images of the search-party fiasco and of the subsequent horror he and Deputy Rourke had witnessed in the cave. Most disturbing of all was the cruel image of Sarah Melton with that demonic dog humping her from behind and the physiological effect that god-awful mental picture was having on him right now.

As much as the act of bestiality shocked and sickened him, so did it now arouse him. The hot shower had coerced a semi-erection from him, and the vivid memory of the dog violating the dazed woman now brought his hard-on to full term and forced him to consider the possibility that he himself was a sexual deviant. (How else to explain why he should be so aroused by such a vile act of perversion?)

He covered his erection with a pillow and told himself that he was still feeling the unnatural effects of his circuitous encounter with a supernatural being. Surely that had to be the explanation. Didn't it? While it relieved him of some responsibility, the idea was far from comforting; that such an entity could have so devastating an effect on his wife, his marriage and himself (not to mention its effect on all those other poor souls) was in itself shocking and dispiriting. Knott had never before in his life felt so helpless, so defenseless—so at a loss as to how to proceed from this untenable point.

As a man who doubted the existence of God, Knott was duly surprised at how quickly he'd come to accept as fact the existence of a mysterious creature with seemingly supernatural powers. While he supposed it was possible that the entity's ability to wreak all manner of havoc on human lives was a rare but naturally occurring phenomenon, he didn't really believe it was. Having been affected by some measure of the thing's influence and having witnessed its more overwhelming effect on others, Knott was inclined to believe the unknown creature was, in fact, some sort of supernatural being. And even if the thing was not *super*natural, it most certainly was *un*natural—as unnatural as sexual intercourse between different species.

God, but he wished he could get that obscene image out of his mind!

He lifted the pillow for a peek at his penis. *Shit! Still raging hard.* He was tempted to flog the damned thing into submission, to punish it for its lasciviousness, but that would be more of a lewd reward than punishment.

He got up, made himself an icepack and went back to bed with the icy remedy applied to his insistent organ. It hurt like hell at first, but soon enough a cold numbness set in. His erection ebbed, and finally he was able to go to sleep. He took with him the dream-image of Susan as the sweet-natured person he'd married, rather than the coldhearted run-with-wolves woman she'd recently become.

* * *

Julie Archer read aloud the words she'd just written. The lines of dark characters on the laptop's glowing screen came alive in her mouth and she tasted each pungent word, slowly savoring the supple language and getting inside the word-spawned images, wallowing in them much the same as she had wallowed and bathed in her lover's warm blood.

Angela's blood was cold now. Her eyes were glassy, the left one already gone a little milky, reminding Julie of the clabbered eyes of Mister Whiskers the morning she'd found the beloved housecat dead and stiff as a stuffed animal in a taxidermist's shop.

Julie so loved the taste and the sound of her own words that she read them again, this time employing drama-queen inflections in her oral presentation.

"'The demon had me pinned to the floor, using her elbows like vices to keep my bent legs immobile as she buried her face between my naked thighs and nipped the tender lips of my sex with her wretched teeth. She had the ungodly strength of ten bull dykes on steroids and I was helpless in her clutches. She looked up at me over my dewy pubic mound and the pale expanse of my flat belly and said with her Hell-coal eyes burning into me: "You belong to me, bitch. There's no fighting it."

"'There was such evil greed in her eyes that I had to look away. I stared at the door she had knocked half-off its hinges to get at me and I tried my desperate best not to respond to what she was doing to me with her teeth and spirited tongue. But it was no use. Her demonic proficiency had my poor pussy foaming at the mouth with lust and I knew then I was on a one-way slide to Hell, lubricated by my own wanton juices.'"

Julie liked that last line so much that she had to read it again. She knew a tight-assed editor would accuse her of overwriting that last bit, but Julie knew better now than to ever heed the advice or give credence to the opinions of ignorant editors, snooty critics or detractors of any sort. It had happened just the way she wrote it. She was *there*, for God's sake, she ought to know! This wasn't fiction. This was real-life reportage, gussied up in fictional trappings, of course, because it was going to be disguised as a novel—not presented as a true and felonious confession. Her poor pussy *had* been foaming at the mouth. And she *had* nearly lost herself (her writer's self) to Angela's bullying seduction. But in the end it was her orgasm that saved her. It was the orgasm that had released the dark power within her and allowed her to fight back with deadly vengeance. She had seized Angela's head with both hands and gave it such a powerful twist that it felt like she'd wrenched the bitch's head off her neck. She could still hear the loud snap it made when Angela's vertebrae ruptured. Her orgasm went on long after Angela fell limp between her legs. She rode those dark orgasmic waves like a cosmic surfer tapping the deepest source in all creation.

What she'd done to Angela's body later was done strictly for the sake of her art. For *story*. The story she was then already composing in her head. To make sure the demon stayed dead, she had to cut out its heart and eat it raw.

So she did. With a kitchen knife, a metal meat tenderizer to crack the ribs, and tongs to remove the heart. Her detailed graphic description of that anatomical dissection was sure to become the stuff of hardcore horror legend. What other horror writer had sacrificed so much for his/her art?

Julie pulled a stringy bit of cardiac tissue from between two lower molars, flicked it at the wall, and then went on with her dramatic reading.

CHAPTER
THIRTY

THORN BRAKED IN FRONT OF THE LEATHERWOOD HOUSE and killed the engine. He hopped out of the Triumph and threw up a hand in greeting. Liza Leatherwood was sitting dead-still in her front-porch rocker. She was dressed in black, as if waiting to go to a funeral. Even though she'd obviously taken pains with her makeup, the heavy application of cosmetics could not hide her haggard countenance. Thorn couldn't help thinking that the old woman looked like she might be a stand-in for a fanciful funeral's guest-of-honor corpse.

She rocked forward and gave him a severe look. "Did you do it, professor? Did you keep your promise?"

Stepping onto the porch, Thorn said, "I did." Then he remembered she was all but deaf, so he vigorously nodded his head. He pointed to his wristwatch and then held up three fingers. "Three o'clock. He'll be here." He pointed down at the ground. "Right here. In about ten minutes." He held up ten fingers.

She rocked back and nodded.

Thorn had been obliged to offer the man at the tree service a hundred dollars extra to do the job today rather than get to it later in the week. He figured it was a good investment, as he was eager to get at the ground beneath the "haunted" tree. The actual archeological dig wouldn't begin until tomorrow, but Thorn had recruited two male students, Todd Beasley and Jason Darby, to meet him here and be ready to start digging up the dead roots as soon as the Tip Top Tree man felled the tree and removed the stump. They were hearty, strapping young lads and should be able to get the roots out of the way before nightfall.

A dirty white Toyota pickup truck came up the driveway. Jason Darby waved from the driver's window as he parked beside Thorn's Triumph.

Before she had a chance to ask, Thorn told Mrs. Leatherwood (in words and pantomime) that the boys were going to help dig up the roots.

The Tip Top Tree Service truck arrived a moment later, towing what Thorn assumed was a stump grinder. The tree man had explained on the phone that the stump grinder could reduce the stump and underlying roots to mulch in a matter of minutes. All Jason and Todd would have to do was shovel that mulch out of the way and dig up any peripheral roots, preparing the ground for tomorrow's more careful dig.

"You want to ride with me?" Thorn asked the old lady, pointing at her, then himself and finally at his car.

With a nod, she stood up and started—wearily but with great dignity—toward his vehicle. He offered his arm but she ignored it and went down the porch steps unassisted.

When she was settled in the passenger seat, she said, "I'll tell you how to go. It's not far. Is this little car safe?"

"Yes ma'am," he said, and then remembered to nod.

"I thank you for getting rid of them dogs."

He nodded again. He hadn't taken time to bury them but instead had dragged them into the woods and left them for the buzzards.

The three vehicles caravanned down a two-rut road that wound its way along the mountain's outer contours and deeper into shady trees. Ten minutes later they were there, and Liza Leatherwood pointed a bony finger at a tall, all but leafless tree, its limbs black and twisted against the summer sky.

"There it sets," she said hoarsely. "The ghost tree. You'll find your bones under it, but the poor souls left their bones a long time ago and are trapped in the tree. Bones don't matter to nobody but you."

Thorn cut the engine and opened his door to get out.

Mrs. Leatherwood said, "You brought your gun like I told you?"

He opened the glove box and extracted the .45. "Thanks for reminding me," he said by way of humoring her. He didn't expect that he'd have to use it again. Just the same, he was glad to have it. Those spooky dogs had thrown him quite a shock in the way they'd tried to attack him. He could almost believe Mrs. Leatherwood's characterization of them as devil dogs.

"I have to do something before he commences to cut it down," she said, opening her door.

Thorn moved quickly around the car to give her a hand out of the passenger seat. She took his hand and stood with a groan. Then she moved stiffly toward the tree, which stood forlornly on a weedy shelf of mountain ground.

While the Tip Top man got his chainsaw from the back of his truck and Jason and Todd unloaded picks and shovels from the Toyota pickup, Liza Leatherwood walked out onto the narrow lip of land, reached out her hand and rested her palm lightly against the tree's thick trunk.

She muttered words Thorn couldn't make out, and then she pulled what looked like a pruning knife from the folds of her black dress and used both hands to stick its curved blade into the bark. She withdrew the blade, placed her palm on the cut and shut her eyes, looking as if she were trying to commune with the tree—or with the spirits allegedly trapped within it.

Todd and Jason joined Thorn in front of the Triumph. "What's she doing?" Jason asked.

Thorn said, "Showing respect for the dead. Which is exactly what I want you boys to do when you start digging. As far as you're concerned, this is hallowed ground."

"Aye, aye, Skipper," said Todd, leaning on the handle of his shovel.

Mrs. Leatherwood leaned in closer to the tree and kissed it, then she turned and walked back to the car.

As Carl the tree man approached the tree with his chainsaw, Thorn suddenly had the feeling that unseen eyes were watching them from the shadowy woods. He touched the butt of the pistol stuck in the waist of his jeans and kept his eyes on the woods beyond the haunted tree.

* * *

Sharyn no longer felt the fear that had driven her to seek refuge in the hospital. The fear had been usurped by intense anticipation, a bone-deep expectancy, born of the furtive knowledge that a momentous event was impending, hanging over her like a fierce blade—not a sword of Damocles, but rather a sword of shining truth. If the truth turned out to be terrible, then *tough shit, deal with it.*

She knew she could. Deal. With anything. The thing that had happened between her and Susan Knott was a revelation. Mental doors had slammed shut behind her as spiritual doors opened in front of her. Whatever was going to happen, it was going to happen soon. Tonight. It had to. She couldn't remain on this razor's edge of anticipation much longer.

Her skin nearly jumped off her bones when the ponytailed med nurse knocked on her door and came in with the dose of lithium Dr. Knott had ordered. "Your lithium levels were good," the nurse explained, "so we're starting you back on it."

Sharyn cheeked the medication and discarded it after the nurse left the room. When the call came again, she would answer it unimpeded by the mind-dulling drug. This time, nature would take its course. She would follow her nature, if not her *bliss*. She and Susan would go together into that dark night of bright possibilities, and no manmade psychotropic concoction was going to stop them.

Before the med nurse had left the room, she told Sharyn that Dr. Knott would be in to see her again later in the evening. Sharyn had smiled with the tablet chipmunked in her cheek. Was it too much to hope for? That the good doctor would be here when the last call came? How fitting that would be! How salaciously seductive! The unkindest cut of all, yes. Karma comes calling, Doc, and you'd best not be standing in the way when it does.

She went to the window and looked out. Harsh sunlight gave everything a sharp edge. The dark green leaves on the magnolia tree were leafy blades thirsty for blood-rain. The lawn below was a blanket of tiny blades, sunny green teeth to chew you up and spit you out before the ground drank your blood. The natural world was a cruel world. Red in tooth and claw. It demanded brutality. Survival depended upon it. Victory belonged to the quickest, the cruelest. That was the way it was, would ever be.

Deal. And let the sacred cards fall where they may.

She looked up at the westering sun, the all-seeing eye of fire.

She didn't have long to wait now.

She could feel it coming on hot summer currents, riding waves of inevitability.

"The goat-man cometh," she whispered to the room, unable to keep a big grin off her face.

* * *

Rourke was doing paperwork when Alice Marsh entered Gladstone's office, saying, "I know it isn't the end of the world . . ."

He gave her a puzzled look.

"Remember? You said don't disturb you unless it's the end of the world?"

He nodded, remembering.

"But I thought you'd want to know that two more women are missing. Marian Kemp and Charlotte Champion."

Rourke bit his lip to keep from cursing. He wanted to set a good professional example now that he was in charge and Sheriff Gladstone's condition was not much improved. Seeing Alice in a tight uniform tailored to show off every seductive curve of her body, his thoughts were anything but professional.

"Here are the call notes," she said as she put two handwritten forms on the desk.

He caught a whiff of her perfume and vividly recalled the musky scent that had assaulted the search party. "Thanks," he said.

As she headed for the door, he said, "Wait. I've been meaning to ask you. Have you heard any strange noises outside your home?"

"No. Just the usual noisy neighbor stuff. Why?"

He shrugged. "There've been reports. Some sort of weird wild animal cry."

She studied his face a moment, then came closer, leaned her thighs against the desk and spoke in a low voice. "Rob, what really happened on the mountain this morning? The guys aren't themselves. They're . . . sheepish. They all have this whipped-dog look in their eyes and it's like they're afraid to speak of what happened. I mean, I know a poor man was killed by a pit bull but this is . . . something else."

"When I figure it out, I'll let you know."

Her mouth fell into a deep frown. Her eyes misted.

"I didn't mean to sound so snappish," Rourke said. "Things happened up there that I can't explain, and I just don't know how to talk about it yet. I'm sure it's the same for the other guys. You had to be there, you know?"

Alice nodded. "Well, if you ever want to talk about it, I'll buy you a beer and you can give it your best shot, okay?"

"Okay. Thanks." He tried to smile and felt as if he'd suddenly grown heavy jowls that weighted down his lips.

"You'll find that I'm a good listener. If you ever take the time."

"I will," he said. "Soon as all this has blown over. I promise."

"Good. It's a date, then."

"Yeah, I reckon it is."

Pausing at the door, Alice looked back and caught him staring at her backside. She smiled, winked, and went out.

As soon as the door snicked shut, Rourke felt his face flush flame-red with shame. *Busted, you chickenshit hump. Thinking with your peckerhead instead of your brain. And you damn well know why. Because you're shit scared. Because that monster on the mountain got the best of you. The rain-thing, the screechy-thing, the mind-fucking thing almost made you his bitch and you don't know how to fight it. Because you've been avoiding the truth: you're a poor excuse for a cop, much less Acting Chief. You're clueless. Out of your league. Just sit back and lick your wounds, lick your balls, stroke yourself silly because you can't fight this fiend with the unearthly power to control wildlife and cloud men's minds with insane lust.*

He rubbed his face with his hands, the coarse stubble bristling and reminding him he hadn't shaved since yesterday.

"What the fuck can I do?" he asked his hands.

You could shave. Or maybe you could get it up long enough to stick it in Alice Marsh but you're impotent when it comes to fighting the monster. Face it, Deputy: You're fucked.

He had recovered one woman—poor Sarah Melton—and Judy Lynn Bowen had escaped on her own, but both women were, in very different ways, mental casualties.

Rourke had considered calling in the FBI but hadn't because the women hadn't actually been kidnapped. How could he explain to a federal agent that a supernatural being was using some sort of mind-control to abduct area women? He couldn't, not without sounding like a complete idiot or tinfoil-hat kook. The FBI was out. This was entirely Rourke's problem. A problem he couldn't solve. The ball was in his court but he couldn't even see the net, much less take a shot.

He reached down and drew the pistol from his holster. He stared at it. The so-called *equalizer.* Felt the gun's cold dumb weight.

If I could just get close enough. I could end the bastard's reign of sick terror. Failing that, I could go out with a bang.

CHAPTER
THIRTY-ONE

THE BEAR MOVED THROUGH THE UNDERBRUSH with agility that belied its five-hundred-pound bulk. He was ranging far from his usual territory, moving toward the place into which the sun would soon sink for its dark sleep, answering the powerful call the wind had carried to his sensitive ears before sunup.

The bear had never heard that sound before, yet it seemed familiar, resonating with internal thunder and spurring him on like thorns in his massive flanks long after the call had ceased.

He had paused in his long journey only long enough to drink from a cool stream and to eat small portions of sweet berries and tender roots. He had ignored the small female bear he encountered along the way and had gone on without mounting her.

Now he was nearing the end of his trek. He sensed his destination before he saw it. He heard the weak chattering voices of humans in the distance, just over the next rise. He caught their fleshy scents. The few times the bear had come upon men, he had slipped away unobserved, instinctively knowing that the hairless creatures were best avoided. But now something stronger than instinct drove him. It was that thorns-in-the-flanks feeling that urged him on and angered him. To overcome his fear of men, the anger bloomed into rage.

Even when the shrill noise of the shiny thing one of the men held in his hands started up, the bear did not shy away or change course. The ugly whining noise grated on his ears, infuriated him, and drew him toward the man with the noisemaker.

The bear broke cover and charged the man making the offending noise.

* * *

Liza Leatherwood sat slightly slumped in the passenger's seat of the professor's sporty little car and held her breath as the tree man touched the chainsaw's speeding belt of teeth to the bark of the haunted tree. Thorn and the two boys from the college were standing about twenty paces behind the man with the chainsaw.

Liza had seen many a tree felled in her time. Before Wilbur died, she'd watched him take down three pine trees behind their house with his new chainsaw, so she knew how it was done. She knew the tree man would cut a huge pie-slice wedge out of the trunk in the direction he wanted the tree to fall and then when enough of the trunk was sawn away he would cut through on the opposite side of the tree and then stand back and let gravity finish the job.

"Lord, I hope this works," she said, her words unheard over the chainsaw's racket.

The spirits trapped in the tree had told her it would work. The ghosts of Wilbur and Asa had lingered long enough to facilitate her communication with the imprisoned spirits, otherwise she probably wouldn't have been able to receive the otherworldly message.

The message was clear enough. One of the original wild women had planted the seed given her by the dark man of the wood in this unhallowed ground, and from that seed this cursed tree hand sprung. As long as the tree stood, the souls of the slaughtered men would remain imprisoned. Take the tree down and their souls would at last be freed, and their righteous rage would be strong enough to drive the goatish god away and break his supernatural hold over the current inhabitants of this hill country. As far-fetched as it seemed to her, Liza had to believe in the hard-won wisdom of the spirit world; she had to believe it would work.

She prayed that it would.

The sun's shadows were growing long, and she shielded her eyes with her hand because the bright rays hurt her tired eyes. In the ear with the punctured drum, the chainsaw sounded like the buzzing of a mosquito.

She blinked her eyes. She squinted behind her bifocals. What was that coming out of the woods? At first she thought it was another devil dog, but as it charged clear of the underbrush and trees she saw the thing for what it was: a huge bear!

Transfixed by the terrible beauty of the great lumbering beast, she sat frozen in a long moment of pure awe. Then a harsh shudder ran down her spine and the spell was broken.

The others hadn't yet seen the black beast. She shouted a warning but no one could hear her above the chainsaw's steady whine.

She threw open the door and half-stumbled out of the car.

The bear was coming up on the professor's left, gaining speed as it ran toward the haunted tree. Liza knew then that the goat-man demon had sent the bear to prevent the felling of the tree. She knew this as sure as she knew her own name. As sure as God created Heaven and Earth.

She ran with one arm outstretched toward Thorn. Her clunky shoes and arthritic bones made her movements painfully awkward. She wasn't running, she was *shambling*, doing the Old Folks' Shuffle as if on wooden legs and locked ankle joints. Her heart was a fluttering hummingbird trapped in her chest, wings beating in panicked desperation.

The black bear was less than five yards away from Thorn and the two boys. Liza shouted, "Hey!"

Professor Thorn turned his head her way just in time to see her stumble and fall to the hard ground. Her head landed on her outstretched arm, knocking her bifocals off her face.

What she saw from down there was a maddening blur of violent motion colored with heartbreaking splashes of blood.

* * *

When Thorn saw Mrs. Leatherwood trip and fall, he immediately started toward her, to help her up. He hoped her brittle bones weren't broken. People her age often died of medical complications resulting from broken hips and such. Her face was a scrunched-up mask of wrinkles, eyes wide, mouth working soundlessly.

As Thorn dropped to one knee beside her, Todd Beasley flew into the edge of his field of vision, tumbling through the air as if doing an acrobatic cartwheel in the sky, a rooster-tail of blood growing from his head.

Thorn turned and saw a giant bear charging toward Carl the Tip Top Tree man. Wearing protective goggles and a yellow hardhat, Carl was bent to his work with the chainsaw and didn't see the massive beast bearing down on him.

Thorn shouted a futile warning. Then he remembered the pistol under his belt. He drew the .45 and took quick aim at the bear's enormous hindquarters.

He fired just as the bear plowed into Carl and knocked the man to the ground with stunning force. The chainsaw hit the ground and chewed dirt as it sputtered and died.

Thorn fired again as the bear swatted a big paw at Carl's head and shoulders. Then Thorn was walking toward the black-furred beast, firing shot after shot into its flanks and ass.

The bear roared as it turned toward Thorn. It was the most terrifying sound he'd ever heard. It communicated all the rage of the animal kingdom. It said: *I'm going to rip your flesh apart and crush your bones in my teeth!* It said: *I'm going to devour you in all your parts and shit your sorry remains in the dirt!*

"Kill it!" the Leatherwood woman yelled.

"Jesus Christ!" blurted Jason Darby. Then he threw down his shovel and ran toward the Toyota pickup.

Carl the tree man's head hung at an odd angle, partially detached from his neck. The bear's claws had easily ripped through the man's flesh, severing tendons and blood vessels but missing the vertebrae. Carl's eyes were wide open and still blinking, as if his head didn't know it was living on borrowed time now, effectively estranged from its body.

The bear's close-set beady eyes locked on Thorn. It let loose another terrible roar and then came lumbering toward him, gaining speed and quickly eating up the meager distance separating Thorn from a grisly death.

* * *

Marlene Tew was already exhausted. Her feet hurt, her lower back was achy, and she was getting a booger of a headache. And the busiest hours lay ahead of her. The Trucking-A was a popular stop, not just for truckers but for motorists in general and even for the locals who wanted a tasty meal in homey surroundings. What this meant for Marlene and the Trucking-A's other waitresses was hour after hour of fast-paced table hopping, modest tips and few opportunities to slip out back for a cigarette or to collapse in a chair and put your feet up.

This afternoon the boss had called Marlene in to cover Karla's evening shift because Karla hadn't shown up, hadn't even called in sick. It wasn't like Karla to not show up without calling in, and Marlene was concerned for her old friend and co-worker, but the job kept her too busy to do much worrying. She had her designated tables to work, and it was her practice to never get behind, never to let the orders pile up on you. That was the only way to keep from getting worn to a frazzle in this job. Keep up! Stay ahead of the curve. *Never* get behind the curve. She didn't exactly understand what that phrase meant, *behind the curve,* so she'd given it her own interpretation. Like a NASCAR driver, you wanted to stay ahead of the pack if you wanted to win the race. Behind a curve in the track, with other cars ahead of you, was where you didn't ever want to be.

Right now she was ahead of the curve. It was too early for the supper crowd. There were thirteen diners, mostly men, except for a family of vacationers on their way to Florida, and most of the men were truckers. Sometimes Marlene would see a female trucker but not that often.

Of course, it was a damn site easier to keep up on the nightshift, and having worked all night last night, she hadn't had her usual allotment of sleep—and no unwind-time at all—before having to put on a fresh pink uniform and return for the extra shift. So she was already exhausted.

And totally unprepared to face the bizarre horror that was about to turn the Trucking-A's down-home restaurant into a slaughterhouse.

It began when the crazy-eyed topless chick burst through the door with a crooked hickory walking stick in her hand. On her head was a wreath woven from a honeysuckle vine. Her cut-off jeans appeared to be blood-stained, as did her thighs and ankles. She didn't utter a word as her wild eyes swept the entire room, as if quickly counting heads.

Kenny the fry cook looked up from his griddle and shouted: "Hey! You can't . . ." His words trailed off as two, no, *three* more wild women in various stages of undress filed in through the front entrance, coming to stand with the first one. One of them had an ax. One had a machete. The other had a pick-ax. All of the blades were blood-streaked.

Marlene dropped her tray of food and it hit the floor with a sharp clatter. Her heart pounded with trip-hammer force, making her eyes jump in their sockets. When the woman with the honeysuckle wreath raised her hickory stick and let out a warbling war cry, an involuntary trickle of urine soiled Marlene's panties, and she began to tremble all over.

There was a brief moment of relief when Marlene told herself that this had to be a bizarre protest by animal-rights activists or a bit of guerilla theater staged by crazed vegans to shock the meat-eating customers. But her relief died when she smelled this band of wild-eyed women. It was an overpowering feral scent that put unwanted pictures in Marlene's head, pictures of unspeakable acts of brutality and sexual perversions of the worst kind imaginable.

No, these women weren't here to protest anything. They had come to do violence. They were here to inflict deadly wounds. These were modern-day warrior women.

When six more of their tribe streamed in through the front entrance and the last one in locked the door and turned the CLOSED sign outward, Marlene turned and ran toward the double swinging-doors to the kitchen, intending to slip out the back door, jump in her car and get the hell out of there. She stopped short, her heels skidding to a halt, when a naked woman with a baseball bat exploded through the swinging doors and bashed the head of Skinny Jenny, the newlywed waitress who weighed ninety pounds in her stocking feet. Jenny went down with her tray of hot food, blood from her scalp spattered on a side-dish of fries.

A big trucker Marlene knew only as Big Bob jumped up from his plate heaped with a T-bone steak and potatoes and advanced toward the woman with the baseball bat. His pinched-face expression suggested a man afflicted with severe constipation. "Give me that bat, you crazy bitch," Big Bob growled.

The crazy bitch gave it to him. An off-the-shoulder shot right across Big Bob's prominent jaw, the bat cracking with a homerun sound, and Big Bob staggered backward, stunned, his lower jaw hanging at a strange angle, his eyes red-rimmed and instantly bloodshot. He lowered his head, hunched his thick shoulders, and snorted; Marlene could see that he was going to charge the batter like a mad bull. But Big Bob was too slow. The crazy bitch cocked the bat and swung again, this time connecting with the side of Big Bob's head, just behind the left ear. The big man dropped to his knees, then toppled forward onto his face.

Marlene had been backing slowly away during the one-sided bout between Big Bob and Crazy Bat, and now she bumped into the lunch counter. She glanced down. Saw the steak knife resting on the edge of a gravy-smeared plate piled with well-gnawed chicken bones that hadn't yet been bussed. Without giving thought to the consequences, she snatched up the steak knife and held it out in front of her with both hands as if wielding a heavy sword. She pointed it at Crazy Bat and hoped it would discourage the wild woman from coming any closer. *Go bat somebody else and leave me alone.* But of course, she didn't. She leered at Marlene, laughed demonically, and then slammed the bat down on the counter just to see Marlene flinch.

Seeing the woman up close, Marlene realized that she *knew* this woman, by sight but not by name. *She goes to my church!* Usually on the arm of a distinguished-looking portly man with graying hair. With her face dirtied, her hair disheveled, her long legs streaked with dried blood and breasts bared, she looked more like an Amazon jungle woman than a churchgoer. Nevertheless, Marlene said, "You go to my church. Sweet Jesus, don't hurt me." It was a desperate thing to have to say, and it was said to no effect whatsoever.

Crazy Bat again smacked the bat on the countertop. Again Marlene jumped. The woman glanced at Marlene's nametag and said, "Jesus ain't here, Marlene. You serve the wrong god. Too bad for you. Marlene."

Marlene was dimly aware of violent commotion in other sections of the restaurant. She heard the disturbing sounds of blows being struck, of blades chopping into live flesh, going *ker-chook! ker-chunk!* And the screams, Jesus! the screams and the pitiful cries for help! A little boy crying for his mama—one of the vacationing couple's towheaded twins. The shouted curses. The whimpers. The desperate pleas. She couldn't think about that now. She had to concentrate on getting away from the woman with the bat and getting the hell out of this . . . abattoir.

The wrong god. What the devil did that mean? The woman had said plain as day that Marlene served the wrong god. *Ask her! Put her off! Distract her with the question and then run for it.*

"Whaddaya mean, I serve the wrong god?" she asked, her voice quaking with mortal fear.

With a casual flick of the bat, the woman knocked the knife out of Marlene's hands. "Wanna see?" Crazy Bat asked with mad glee. "Wanna see?" Then she chivvied Marlene behind the lunch counter, made her place her hands palms-down on the countertop, and proceeded to use the bat to hammer Marlene's hands to the countertop with steak knives.

Marlene passed out when the second knife pinned her left hand to the counter. She couldn't have been out for long, because when she came to, the slaughter was still going on. She was a captive witness. She watched in a painful daze. It was almost as if she were watching a movie. Drunk-sick and watching a snuff film. Bodies sprawled across tables and on the floor in pools and smears of bright blood.

Only one man remained alive. A tall trucker with a CAT hat sitting sideways on his head. He'd taken an ax away from one of the wild women and split her head with it, and now the other women had him backed into a corner and were menacing him with their weapons. He swung the ax but the females stayed just out of his range. The woman with the honeysuckle wreath in her hair poked at him with her hickory stick and he swatted it away. A weaponless woman with short blond hair pegged him with a bottle of hot sauce, right between his eyes. He swung blindly, and the women swarmed over him and wrestled him to the floor.

Marlene shut her eyes after a fat woman with a huge heart-shaped ass planted a meat cleaver in his throat. She tried to shut her ears to the ungodly sounds coming from the killing corner, but of course it wasn't possible to shut your ears. Your ears were defenseless when your hands were pegged in place with knives and helpless.

Marlene drifted in and out of consciousness. At one point, she felt an overwhelming presence and was suddenly certain that if she opened her eyes she would see the powerful god she'd neglected to serve, but all she saw was a wicked bunch of gluttonous women hungrily eating the raw flesh of severed limbs.

CHAPTER
THIRTY-TWO

IN RECENT YEARS LIZA LEATHERWOOD had sometimes imagined how
Death might take her, how she would finally succumb. She'd never
believed that she would die peacefully in her sleep. She doubted that
anyone *ever* died peacefully in sleep. Death might find you abed, in the
middle of the night, but there was no way you could sleep through it.
There had to come that moment when you found yourself in Death's
cold grip and you *knew* your time on earth was up. When your heart
stopped or something vital exploded in your brain, there had to come
that moment of panic or regret when you realized you were about to be
evicted from your body and that your body was only hours away from
the undertaker's table, days away from burial or cremation. Dying peacefully in sleep was nothing but a tall tale people told themselves, hoping
to take comfort in the myth.

But of all the ways Liz imagined Death would claim her, she'd never
dreamt that Death would come in the guise of a ferocious bear. Yet,
there the bear was, charging down on the professor, chuffing like a steam
engine as it closed in for the kill. If Thorn couldn't stop the giant beast
with his little pistol, the bear would surely take her after it was done
with him. It was to be her punishment for daring to interfere with the
Dark Man of the Wood's unholy plan.

The tree remained standing, the souls still imprisoned within it,
and the man who'd tried to cut it down lay dead, nearly decapitated. It
galled her that she might die in such abject failure. Her own noble plan
had come to nothing. The goat-man would win and have his way, and
Liza's pitiful soul would journey from this mortal realm bearing that
failure. She would have to stand before God in shame, knowing that her

failure had needlessly cost many innocent lives.

She found her bifocals and slipped them on, and then pushed herself up into a kneeling position so that she could bear solemn witness to Thorn's demise (she owed him that much) and so that she might offer a final prayer for forgiveness before the beast savaged her.

Liza had to admire the man's bravery. He stood his ground, aimed his gun and didn't shoot until the bear was less than five yards away. Bam! Bam! Bam! Three rapid shots that should've hit the animal dead in the face, but Liza couldn't see if they did. The bear didn't slow down. And then it was too late anyway, because the bear was right on top of the professor.

"Lord . . ." Liza began her last prayer.

Then the miracle happened.

Professor Thorn turned on his heels and let the bear go past him like a bullfighter waving the bull by with his red cape in a graceful veronica. But Thorn had no cape, and the bear didn't actually go by. The bear crashed headlong into the ground like a locomotive that has run out of track and must plow into earth like a doomed Leviathan.

Liza raised her clasped hands to the sky, shook her doubled fists and said, "Thank you, Jesus!"

* * *

Rourke was cruising a back road near Widow's Ridge when the dispatcher radioed the report of a bear attack on Haunted Tree Trail. One fatality, and one severe injury. EMS was already en route.

He turned around, switched on the emergency flashers and gunned the engine as he headed for Widow's Ridge Road.

Haunted Tree Trail was the Department's unofficial designation for the dirt road that dead-ended at the "haunted" tree. The place was a popular make-out spot for horny teenagers, and on weekends it was a routine checkpoint for patrolling deputies. You had to show the colors to keep the kids honest, to keep them from going too far. The kids understood that if you caught them with their clothes off or if two heads weren't visible when you put the spotlight on their car, they would be in for an embarrassing police escort to their respective homes, where they would be made to confess their fumbling sins to their parents.

But now it wasn't even dusk, so Rourke doubted that the victims of the bear attack had been teenagers out for a little early park-and-spark action. Besides, if you stayed in your vehicle, you shouldn't be vulnerable to a bear attack.

Rourke radioed the dispatcher. "Who called in the bear attack?" he asked.

"Professor Alfred Thorn," the dispatcher said.

"He say what they were doing out there?"

"Negative."

He sped past the old Leatherwood place and turned onto the twin ruts of Haunted Tree Trail. With the wild-animal attacks on his search party still sorely fresh in his mind, he was obliged to wonder if the bear attack might've been—for whatever reason—directed by the same "supernatural" entity, Rourke's new nemesis.

The trail was bumpy and Rourke slowed down. Even so, the cruiser's shock absorbers were stressed to the max. The trees and thick undergrowth encroached upon both sides of the trail as if they meant to overtake and obliterate it.

When the top of the fabled tree came into view, Rourke recalled some of the silly stories he'd heard about it in his youth, spooky tales suggesting that tree's twisted trunk and gnome-like limbs resulted from an ancient witch's curse. Of course, he'd never believed any of them, but there had been that one time when he, a senior in high school, had parked near the tree with his sweetheart Cheryl Tatum and she swore that she heard eerie voices coming from the tree. Cheryl, normally a levelheaded girl, was so frightened by those voices that she refused to go near that "creepy place" ever again. She was crying as he drove them away in his restored Impala. "They sounded so angry," she said of the spirit voices. Rob asked what they had said. "Nothing in words," Cheryl answered. "Just angry screaming."

Now, as he pulled up and parked the cruiser behind the Tip Top Tree truck and got his first hurried look at the mauled victims of the bear attack, memories of Cheryl Tatum and her spirit voices fled and Rourke steeled himself for a close-up look at the decedent.

Alfred Thorn and an old woman in a long black dress watched as the two paramedics loaded a stretcher bearing a bloodied victim into the EMS vehicle. The biggest black bear Rourke had ever seen lay dead in the dirt, gunshot wounds evident in its head and face. Rourke slid out of the cruiser and joined Thorn and the old lady he now recognized as Mrs. Leatherwood.

"What the hell happened here?" he asked.

Thorn looked at him as if he were a dim-witted student and said, "Isn't it obvious?"

Then the Leatherwood widow rounded on Rourke and said, "Tell him he has to cut down that tree! You tell him!"

"A man is dead!" Thorn shouted at the old lady, as if this explained his apparent reluctance to do her urgent bidding.

"For God's sake, make him finish that tree!" Mrs. Leatherwood implored. "More people will be dead if he don't."

Rourke looked at the haunted tree and saw that a wedge had been cut from the heart of its trunk and that it wouldn't take much work to finish the job. Then he glanced at the partially decapitated corpse lying at the foot of the tree, a chainsaw resting close to the corpse. "Calm down and tell me what're you doing here and what happened," he said. "You first, Professor Thorn."

The EMS vehicle sped off to deliver the injured man to the medical center.

A few minutes after Thorn launched into his sketchy story of buried bones, murder and ancient myth, Mrs. Leatherwood said, "Lord help me," and marched stiffly toward the tree. She bent down, picked up the chainsaw, and said, "How do you start this damn thing?"

* * *

Carrying the head of the man she'd decapitated with an ax, Jude followed her sister-brides out the back of the restaurant and into the woods behind it. Two of their number had fallen in the furious revelry so now they were eight, each bearing a severed male head. Jude knew no remorse, felt nothing for their two dead sister-brides. Judy Lynn Bowen might've mourned the loss, had she not been reborn as Jude. Jude's higher calling did not allow for such human weaknesses as remorse, guilt or horror. Such emotions were transformed once you were washed in the blood. Remorse became joy. Guilt became pride. Horror became ecstasy.

They moved without words through the deepening woods, ranging with alacrity over hill and dale. Blood-sated yet still hungry, they moved with animal sureness to answer the summons of their beloved master—their betrothed. His call had never been so urgent as it was now. He *needed* them. He commanded them to run faster.

Answering the summons singing in her blood, Jude ran as hard as she could. She quickly outdistanced her sisters and grinned with prideful pleasure as she led the wolfish pack.

* * *

Knott parked his Jag in front of Ridgewood and went inside to see his wife again and his other patients. After a shave and a vigorous scrubbing in the shower, he felt presentable, but the miasmal residue of that mysterious creature still clung to him as stubbornly as the stench of a skunk's spray, although it was subtler and not as rank. It wasn't unpleasant exactly, but it conjured unwanted images of that cave and of unspeakable depravity. He'd splashed on extra cologne in hopes of covering it up.

He decided to see Sharyn Rampling first again because he didn't wish to give the appearance of providing his wife special treatment. Maybe it was silly but it seemed the right thing to do.

As soon as he walked onto the unit, he knew things were getting out of hand. A female patient in the seclusion room was shouting curses and banging her fists on the padded door, demanding to be freed. A middle-aged man in pajamas was arguing with one of the nursing staff, threatening to sue the hospital if he couldn't get his street clothes back. Down at the end of the hall, two young female patients were engaged in a shouting match in a disagreement over who was next to use the pay phone. The shorthanded staff was doing its best to put out these little fires before they could erupt into a behavioral conflagration. Knott ignored the uproar and went directly to the door of Sharyn Rampling's room. He raised his hand to knock and then hesitated. He was suddenly inexplicably afraid. He did not want to enter this room, intensely afraid of what might lie in wait on the other side of the door. He wanted to run back to his Jag, drive away from this place and put this waking nightmare behind him forever.

Thunder rumbled and the lights in the dim hallway flickered.

Knott's fist remained frozen inches from the dreaded door.

* * *

Something was wrong. She felt it in the muggy air of her room. She felt it like a knot twisting low in her belly. Where before she had been certain of her place in the coming fantastic events, now she felt an acute uncertainty, as if the world were turning the wrong way, leaving her to spiral out of control, far afield from her rightful place in that world.

Sharyn knew she was cycling. But this time it was happening too fast. She hadn't been off her lithium long enough to feel *this* manic so soon. But it was *more* than that. What she was experiencing now had more to do with the goat-man god than with her chemical imbalance.

Things were going so wrong. Things outside herself. An encompassing wrongness. Smothering her. She couldn't sit still for it. She had to act.

Susan Knott. Yes, she needed to be with her now. Susan would reassure her, tell her what to do, or at least give her a sign.

She jumped up from the bed and snatched the door open. Freshly shaved and showered, Dr. Knott stood in the doorway with a raised fist, and Sharyn recoiled as if she expected him to strike her down.

"Sorry," he said. "I didn't mean to startle you. I was just about to knock."

Backing away, she said, "I can't . . . I can't talk to you now."

"Why not? What's wrong?" He came into the room and softly shut the door.

She blurted: "I want to sign myself out."

"I don't think that's a good idea, Sharyn."

"I can't be here anymore. I have to go."

"It will be AMA," he said. "Against medical advice. Your insurance probably won't pay if you leave that way."

"I don't care. Get the papers ready. I'll sign them. I have to go."

She would've said anything to get him to leave her alone. She was afraid he would see the mania smoldering behind her eyes. Perhaps she would sign herself out! But not before she saw Susan Knott once more.

"All right," Dr. Knott said, "but first tell me why you feel you have to leave."

Then she smelled the scent of the beast again. It remained on him beneath the aroma of expensive cologne, the same scent she'd smelled on Susan, but stronger. A dizzying, maddening scent that sent her spiraling faster toward chaos. The creature's persistent scent no shower could wash away. Further proof—as if she needed it!—of the existence of the demigod behind ancient myths.

"I just told you, I can't talk now. I'm done talking. Please get out of my room, Doctor. My AMA papers, don't forget. Please. Now, okay? I have to go. Talk, talk, talk, I'm all talked out and more's the pity."

"Did you take your lithium today?" he asked, cocking a brow.

"Yes, yes, I took the damn stuff, now get out before I . . . I . . ."

"Before you what?"

Sharyn didn't get a chance to answer because the door suddenly burst open and Susan Knott shoved her husband from behind, making him stumble into the unmade bed.

Still in a hospital gown, Susan glared at him and said, "You thought you could slip past me, Dr. Freud? Give me the old Freudian slip again? Well, fuck you, Doc! You never could slip anything by me. I know all about your harem of nurses. And I don't doubt you fucked more than a few of your patients, using your godlike position to seduce defenseless women. You're a pig. A *male chauvinist pig*. But guess what? You're all done. It's time to take this pig to slaughter!"

Susan shot her hand out and jabbed something into her husband's neck. Then she yanked it out and jabbed it in again. Blood spurted from the first puncture. Knott fell backward on the bed and his wife went after him, relentlessly stabbing at his throat.

Sharyn watched, fascinated by the violence. After the third or fourth jab, she understood that the weapon Susan was using was a pink plastic toothbrush handle sharpened to a lethal point.

Dr. Knott's complexion went swiftly from angry red to ghastly white as his blood ejaculated into the air and in thready spurts onto his wife. He slapped at her but his defensive efforts were ineffectual, weakened as he was by shock and rapid blood-loss.

His eyes rolled up into their sockets and he lay still. Susan straddled him and began to lap and suck blood from his wounds. After a long moment of noisy slurping, she smiled up at Sharyn, licked a bit of gore from her upper lip and said, "Join me?"

Sharyn returned the smile and said, "Yes, thank you." Then she fell upon the wounds, feeling as if she had regained at last her proper place in the world.

CHAPTER
THIRTY-THREE

JULIE ARCHER HAD THOUGHT NOTHING COULD STOP the demonic flow
of her words onto the laptop's screen and into the electronic file. Not even
the slow seep of her menses leaking onto the seat. (Any other time she
would've gotten up for a Tampax, but then, any other time she wouldn't
have been writing naked. And anyway, this wasn't any other time. This
was NOW.) Not even the fierce thunderstorm blowing up right outside
the window overlooking her Garden of Angels had deterred her. She owed
it to herself, to her art and to Angela for her sacrifice to keep working,
to keep the inspired narrative going full-tilt boogie, baby, like a ghost
train bound for hell. Nothing could stop her.

But the summons, when it came, proved Julie wrong. The shrill call
superseded everything, dashed all previous concerns. It was the wild card
that trumped all others. The wildest card.

The summons said: Ditch the fiction and come taste real horror!

The summons said: You've always had a taste for horror.

The summons said: Come or die.

Julie closed the laptop, glanced longingly at her dead lover on the
floor, then went downstairs to collect the biggest kitchen knife in the
silverware drawer before dashing out into the rising storm to answer the
irresistible call to sublime action.

* * *

"We're in for a big blow," the coroner said with a wary nod at the threatening sky. Storm clouds hung low over the mountains like overripe fruit
ready to fall to earth. Thunder rumbled in the western sky. The weather
leached light from the late afternoon and lent the landscape a pallid blush.

Rourke absently nodded, distracted by Mrs. Leatherwood's persistence in pestering him. When he'd taken the chainsaw away from her, the old woman had gone into hysterics, and his attempts to reason with her had fallen on deaf ears. Thorn had said, "Save your breath, deputy, she can't hear worth a damn."

"Why does she want that tree cut down?" Rourke had asked.

"Long story," Thorn had cryptically replied. "Not one you would believe."

Then Dave Sikes the coroner had arrived in his black station wagon to discharge his official duty and pronounce the corpse dead of a bear attack. "Didn't know we had bears this big around here," Sikes had said of the dead animal.

"Me either," Rourke had muttered, keeping an eye on Mrs. Leatherwood to make sure she didn't have another go at the chainsaw.

And now, having got her second wind, the old lady was at it again, berating both he and Thorn for failing to fell the haunted tree.

Thorn said in a loud voice, "I *will* finish the job, Mrs. Leatherwood, but we have to wait until they remove the body. Understand?"

Then the professor turned to Rourke and said, "Those bones, if they're there, will be of the Civil War era. That's why I'm here. After the tree's removed, this will be the site of an archeological dig. The coroner may have to come out here again in a day or two, if I have any luck."

"What makes you think they're buried there?" Rourke asked.

"Mrs. Leatherwood says they are." Thorn lowered his voice and added: "She also thinks the spirits of the dead will be freed when the tree is cut down and that they will drive off some mythical boogeyman. I believe her about the buried bones, though."

"Boogeyman . . ." echoed Rourke.

"Yes, she believes—"

"Mr. Sikes, let's remove the body," Rourke said with authority. Then to Thorn, he said, "As soon as the body is clear, I want you to take that tree down."

* * *

She was so tired, all she wanted to do was shut her eyes and go to sleep, perhaps never to wake. But she knew she had to see this through to the end. She had to see the tree cut down at last. Only then could she rest.

She was back in the professor's little sports car, surprisingly comfortable in the bucket seat. So comfortable that it was hard to keep her eyes open. Thorn had put the canvas top up to keep the rain off her, but so far they'd had no more than a light sprinkle of big splattering drops.

As Thorn picked up the chainsaw, Liza looked round at the dark woods with the expectation of seeing more minions sent by the Dark Man to prevent the felling of the tree and the release of trapped souls. Where the bear had failed, the next assault might succeed. She looked but saw nothing sinister lurking in the woodsy shadows. Her bifocals weren't as effective as they used to be. She regretted that she'd put off a visit to the eye doctor for a new prescription. Just the same, she could see well enough to recognize new dangers when they came. And they *were* coming. The withering sensation in her heart told her so.

* * *

They ran and ran. The mountainous terrain was torturous but still they ran, ignoring the cuts and scrapes on their bare feet and naked flesh. The running had been too much for one of them (the oldest and heaviest among them: the sheriff's dowdy wife) and she had succumbed to an overtaxed heart, but the rest of them ran without falter, with Jude leading the way.

The booming thunder seemed to drive them on, adding urgency to their calling.

Jude's lungs were on fire and her limbs were heavy with fatigue but she didn't let herself slow down. Her mind was steeled, her resolve firm as her tits. She was already thinking of herself as First Bride to their omnipotent groom. Damned if she would allow one of the others curry his favor ahead of her. She was going to be the first to present him with the vital offering of a dead man's head.

The world of houses, streets, cars, phones, power lines, humdrum people and humdrum places—that world was no longer *real*. The dark woods were real. Judy Lynn's make-believe civilized world was gone, as was Judy Lynn the pretend person. Reality was Jude running to meet her eternal beloved. Running was reality. Reality was running, running through an Eden-like paradise, running away from mundane cares and workaday concerns. Running to a reward older than mythical Eden. Jude ran for all she was worth. She ran after the ultimate blood-promise of deliverance.

Ax in one hand, dripping head in the other, she darted across the forested earth, dodging trees and patches of briar, skipping over rotting logs and skirting grabby vines, cross-country running for glory, for glorious release.

She jogged around strange shapes of kudzu-covered statuary and then there *he* was! So gloriously tall, so utterly masculine, standing atop a wide pedestal-like stump of a bygone tree, his cloven hooves more perfectly formed than any sculpted masterpiece in a museum, his legs and hips fitting together at so odd an angle that they gave his thick muscular torso the graceful arching contour of a wood-carved hero affixed to the prow of an ancient warship, fearlessly facing waves of a storm-roiled sea.

His face! So noble in its goatish aspect, yet so strikingly human in his eyes and in the pleasing physiognomy of his high forehead. The two stubby little horns jutting from his head were, to Jude's way of thinking, absolutely adorable.

She dropped the ax and fell to her knees before the towering god. Holding the severed head in both hands, she extended her arms and offered it up, her blood-smeared breasts heaving as her lungs fought for air.

He cut her with his dark eyes and she could feel him looking into her hard-laboring heart. She trembled. He reached down and took the offered head. He held it in front of his face and studied it, his wide nostrils flaring, twitching. Then he pressed it between his big hands and crushed it nearly flat, the snapping of bones muffled by the head's skin and scalp. He dug the yellowish talons of his thick fingers into the fracture and pulled the skull apart as if tearing into a hard-shelled melon. Then he buried his mouth in the pulp of brain-fruit and devoured it. When he was done, he tossed the broken skull-rind away and licked his thick lips and wiped his goatee.

The other women came straggling in, huffing and puffing with exertion. They were such a ragged-looking band that Jude was suddenly ashamed of them. But then as they dropped one by one to their knees at the foot of the stump and held up their offerings, she knew it was all right, that he would accept their worship and what they offered.

With a flourish of his hand, he gave them to understand that they were to place the offered heads on the stump by his feet. This they did, so that he was soon encircled by the unsightly assortment of dead men's heads.

He began to sing. His song was not shrill like his summoning cry but was softly melodic, middle-pitched and piping, seeming to harmonize with the birds' singing as smoothly as it did with the percussive cawing of nearby crows.

Then he began to dance, hooves clopping the wooden pedestal without breaking the circle of severed heads. As he danced and sang, his purplish penis hardened and rose to shocking proportion, and Jude was reminded of a snake charmer enticing a serpent to rise and undulate to his piped rhythms. His terrifying cock bobbed heavily between his furry loins. Jude's breath caught in her throat.

He danced. The women stared, entranced. Jude's hips began to move with his rhythm. Before her eyes, the goatish god grew more distinct, increasingly vivid as if he were finally coming fully into this world so that he might lord over it as its intended master.

Jude knew what was coming next. He would dance himself into a frenzy of lust and would ravage her and her sister-brides. It wouldn't be like before. This time it would be totally physical, not like being fucked by a misty ghost but by an in-the-flesh man-beast. His magic wand of a cock would wash away her worldly sins, transform her, turn her into a goddess.

She was going wet between her legs. Her nipples hardened and yearned for his rough touch. She knew his singing and his clopping jig were having the same effect on the other women, but she was determined to be the first one fucked. She deserved as much. She'd earned it, hadn't she? She'd given up so much! Gave up her life, her lover. And she was the youngest of all the women, the one with the most life to give up. He *had* to take her first, to honor her sacrifice and her youth.

Then an ugly sound intruded and wrecked everything. It came from another part of the woods, distant but close enough to sour his magical song. Jude knew what was making that awful blat and whine: a chainsaw. Some redneck son of a bitch was violating the hallowed wood. Ruining the sacred ceremony!

The effect on the man-beast was immediate. His face turned ferocious. His eyes blazed with wrath. His dance turned violent. His hooves struck harder, faster. And then he crushed the skulls encircling his feet, stomped them one by one until all the heads resembled lumpy pancakes, covered with hair and vile ooze. He suddenly stopped dancing, opened his mouth impossibly wide and loosed a shriek so shrill and terrible that it nearly made Jude lose control of her bowels.

She knew right away that it was a call to arms and a declaration of war. She and her sister-brides seized their weapons and raised them to the thundering sky. The man-beast leapt down from his pedestal and started running toward the sound of the chainsaw.

Jude and the others ran after as their beloved goat-man led them into battle.

CHAPTER
THIRTY-FOUR

JULIE WASN'T USED TO SO MUCH PHYSICAL EXERTION. Though she possessed a slender frame, her sedentary vocation as writer had in no way prepared her for jogging cross-country through hilly landscapes of thick woods. Running naked with the knife, she felt somehow as if she were playing a role in an archetypal fairy tale. In fact, an old nursery rhyme tune was looping through her head: *See how they run, see how they run/They all ran after the farmer's wife/Who cut off their tails with a carving knife . . .*

She added her own spin: *Cut off their heads with a carving knife. Cut off their heads . . .*

She stopped a moment to catch her breath, bent over with her hands on her knees, her breasts pendulously hanging, heaving, aching. Then she was running again, going toward the caller, though the call had been too far away to hear with her ears, she'd heard it with her spirit's ears. And with her blood.

Thunder crashed all around her. Raindrops pattered on a carpet of dead leaves and pine straw. She became aware that someone was following her. Chasing her? Chastening her? Calling her off?

Michael?

Never mind Michael, she told herself. Too late for that—for the guardianship of angels. He'd had his chance and he'd let her down, left her in a lonely lurch. She'd been called by one more powerful, called upon to abandon the horrors of imagination, to leave behind the tired tropes and trappings of bookish horror. Now was the time to plunge your hands into the blood and guts of real life, plunge up to the elbows into bowels of reality, dive whole-heartedly into the bleeding thick of it, for once and for all, and most especially for the sake of the Dark One calling you on.

Julie Archer was running to meet her destiny. Buoyed by this knowledge, she ran faster, and the pain of exertion sloughed off and fell by the wooded wayside, left behind like her old identity and her misguided stabs at life.

* * *

Rourke watched as Thorn worked to complete the job begun by the dead tree man. From the assured way the professor handled the chainsaw, Rourke knew the man must've felled a few trees in his time.

A tug at his sleeve. Rourke turned. Mrs. Leatherwood was beside him, pulling him toward her lips. Just for a moment he thought she was going to kiss him, but then she was shouting into his ear: "You've got to get rid of the stump too!"

He nodded. He believed her. Believed she knew exactly what she was talking about. Thorn would have the tree ready to fall in minutes, and Rourke wasted no time in getting the motor-operated stump grinder off the little trailer behind the Tip Top Tree Service's truck and ready for action. He had never operated a grinder but he'd seen them in operation and knew he could do a serviceable job with it. He started the grinder's motor and stood ready. It was a boxy robotic-looking piece of equipment on squat wheels. It stood waist-high and possessed a blade-like disk with teeth designed to eat up a stump and turn wood quickly into mulch.

Through the noise of the grinder's motor and the chainsaw's whine, Rourke thought he heard the same beastly cry that had set off the animal attacks on the search party. But no, he couldn't have heard any such thing amid this machine-made clamor. And even if he had, it wouldn't matter. He and Thorn had their respective jobs to do and accomplishing them was their best defense, according to Old Lady Leatherwood. She believed this with such intensity that he made her beliefs his own. Having seen the beast—the rain-thing—with his own eyes, it wasn't difficult to believe. He had failed to defeat the creature with the ordinary means at his disposal. Extraordinary means were all that was left to him now. They *had* to work.

Thorn glanced up from his work and gave Rourke a nod, signaling that the next go with the chainsaw would bring the tree down. No more than five yards away from the tree, Rourke nodded back, his hands on the controls of the humming stump grinder.

Dave Sikes leaned against his van, smoking a cigarette as he watched over the dead man while waiting for the ambulance to arrive and remove the corpse from the scene. The shaken young man who had come along to help the professor with his initial dig finally emerged from the Toyota pickup and was keeping a wary distance from the hulking bear's carcass. He announced that he was going to drive to the hospital to see how his injured friend was faring, then he got back in the truck and drove off. Mrs. Leatherwood was leaning against the front of Thorn's sports car, arms folded across her chest, chin jutting with the unmistakable authority of an old-timey schoolmarm.

As Thorn began his final cut, a band of bare-breasted women armed with primitive implements came screaming out of the woods, running straight at the man with the chainsaw.

"Jesus Christ," Rourke said, not knowing whether he'd just uttered a prayer or a blasphemous curse.

* * *

"He needs us," Susan Knott said as she wiped blood from her mouth and chin with the back of her hand.

Sharyn Rampling looked at the dead doctor on the floor and knew *he* no longer needed anything.

"We have to go to him," Susan said with pressured speech.

Sharyn understood then. Susan was talking about *him*. Pan. Dionysus, or whatever name the ancient entity might go by now in this modern world. Not that *he* needed a name. He was beyond naming. Her thoughts were racing so fast it was hard to stay with the slowly unfolding events. Was she drunk on the dead man's blood? Drunk on feminine power in service to a masculine god? What was this aching emptiness she felt in her chest. Was it remorse at having had a hand in the doctor's death?

Susan bent down and dug keys from her husband's pocket. "We'll take his car. It's fast. A Jag. We have to hurry. Don't you feel it? He needs us."

"We're locked in," Sharyn reminded her blood sister.

Susan smiled. "We're stronger than they are. We'll *kill* our way out if we have to. Ready?"

Sharyn nodded. She *was* ready. With the taste of one kill still on her tongue, she realized that her aching emptiness was actually hunger for more mayhem. She hadn't struck the killing blows but she was nonetheless complicit in the gory deed.

* * *

Wearing the dead man's protective goggles, Alfred Thorn caught movement out of the corner of his eye as the chainsaw's teeth tore into the tree on the side opposite the gaping wedge sawn in the trunk. The tree listed toward the vacant wedge and Thorn peered through the smudged, sweat-rimmed goggles to see a handful of naked and semi-naked women running toward him.

He pulled back the chainsaw and straightened up to face the female chargers.

My God! Maenads! It's all true! Sharyn was right!

He understood in a flash that they intended to stop him from felling the tree. The old woman had been right too, in her assertion that someone or something would go to any length to try to protect the tree's integrity. And here they came, armed and wild, bearing down on him. Was that war-paint streaking their skin? No, it was blood!

All right, Alfred old boy, this is life or death. Defend yourself!

There came a moment of indecision wherein he couldn't decide if he should drop the chainsaw and draw his pistol or use the saw to fend off his attackers. In the end, he chose to stay with the chainsaw because he doubted that he would be able to actually shoot a woman. With the saw he might be able to keep them at bay or scare them off. Even a wild woman would have to think twice before running into the dangerous teeth of a chainsaw. He held it up in a threatening gesture, absurdly reminding himself of the murderous "Leatherface" in that Texas Chainsaw movie he'd seen back in the seventies.

But the women did not slow their charge. There were six, no, *seven* of them and they all were about to converge on him. He bent his knees a bit and went into a crouch with his whirring weapon held high in front of him. He decided to use the saw only defensively; if a woman ran into its teeth, it would be her own fault, not his.

When the closest woman was no more than ten feet from him with a machete raised over her head and her face twisted into a mask of pure rage, a gunshot popped off and she went down. She slid headlong at his feet, forsaking her machete and grabbing her thigh, screaming.

Thank God the cop had no compunction about picking off attackers with well-place non-lethal shots. After all, these women weren't in their right minds, weren't responsible for their reprehensible actions.

Distracted by a redhead with a sling blade, Thorn didn't realize how close the woman with the pickax was until she swung it at his head. He reacted on reflex and tried to parry the blow with the chainsaw. The saw's spinning belt of teeth sliced into her thin wrist and took off her hand, and the pickax struck Thorn's left shoulder a glancing blow.

More gunshots sounded above the chainsaw's whine. And then came a loud cracking noise as the tree began to fall on its own, toppling toward the ground in maddeningly slow motion.

A boom of thunder unleashed a sudden heavy downpour of rain.

A heavyset woman bringing up the rear of the disorganized formation of women froze, looked up at the tree coming down on her and then tried to scamper out of the falling timber's path, but she was too fat and sluggish, and the tree crushed her into the earth, its leafless limbs snapping hollowly and gouging the ground.

Thorn saw the ax blade as a gunmetal blur just before it chopped into his right shoulder, the shocking force of the blow knocking the chainsaw out of his hands and him to the ground. The chainsaw's motor sputtered and died. Gritting his teeth at the excruciating pain, he looked up at the ax-wielding young woman and saw her cock the ax over her shoulder for another blow.

His last thought before the ax fell: *This is it, I'm dead.*

* * *

When the tree hit the earth with a ground-shaking thud, Jude felt the volcanic fury of her master mounting toward eruption. Though he was well behind her, concealed by woods, she could feel how incensed he was that she and her sister-brides had failed him, and his fury fed her own frenzy. Her first ax-blow had knocked the chainsaw man down and bloodied his shoulder. Now she would have off his head with a vengeful strike.

She cocked the ax over her shoulder and swung it with all her might.

But something went very wrong. Something hit her chest with the force of a mule's kick, taking her breath away and knocking her backward as the ax flew from her hands. She staggered to stay on her feet. She looked down and saw the hole in her chest, just above her left tit.

I'm shot, she thought as the rainy world dimmed and her ears began to ring. She tried to catch her breath but couldn't. Her knees buckled. Her bestial rage drained away as if farting and spewing from the bullet-hole in her chest.

Then she was on the ground, tasting the earth. The rain was cool and almost soothing.

Cleansing.

This wasn't happening to her.

This was happening to a stranger.

This isn't me.
I'm Judy Lynn Bowen.
Judy Lynn.
Judy . . .

* * *

Rourke recognized Judy Lynn Bowen just before he squeezed the trigger. Had he hesitated in that flash of recognition? Probably. But it didn't matter. That dangerous thing he'd glimpsed in her eyes when he spoke with her in the hospital had surfaced to take control of her. He'd *had* to shoot her to save Thorn's life. Deadly force had been necessary. A clean shoot, any way you looked at it.

Now that Thorn was down, the remaining women turned their murderous attention on Rourke. They advanced in a strung-out line, brandishing their crude weapons.

"Stop!" Rourke shouted. "I *will* shoot you."

They didn't heed his warning. They stalked forward.

Behind the women something big and shadowy emerged from the tree line. Rourke knew at once what it was.

The rain-thing.

But this time it was more than an invisible-man outline in the downpour. Now it was solid and very much in this world.

And it was coming at him in a weird gallop that chilled Rourke's blood and made him want to turn and run.

* * *

Liza Leatherwood saw the dreaded beast come out of the trees, and her bladder let go with a dribble of pee. She'd watched in horror as the helling women tried their damnedest to stop the felling of the spirit-haunted tree. When the tree finally fell, relief washed over her, and she thought she could hear the spirits' angry voices above the low rumble of the stump grinder's motor. But the stump remained, the tree still attached to it by a tough skin of bark.

And now the beast of many a nightmare was *here.* Just as foretold. Here to fight for a foothold in this world. To have his way with frail humanity.

The deputy had his hands full with the mad hellers. That coroner feller had jumped into his van and driven away, the coward. It was up to her to finish the job.

Help me, Wilbur, she pleaded as she moved toward the chainsaw. She moved more sprightly than she'd moved in years. The rain fogged her bifocals and made everything look as if it were inside a melting cube of ice, but she could see the chainsaw well enough. "Give me strength, Lord," she said as she bent down and picked it up. It was heavier than it looked and the handle was slippery due to the rain, but she was determined to do what had to be done. She yanked the starter cord. The saw sputtered but didn't start.

The deputy fired two, three more times, but Liza kept her attention on her task. She yanked the cord again. This time the motor started and the vibration shook her arthritic bones something fierce. She pulled the trigger and the belt of saw-teeth cycled round the metal blade.

Then she bent low, ignoring the pain in her lower back, and guided the blade into the V-shaped swath of tree bark. Sawdust flew into the rain. *Please, Lord, help me do this.*

Then the saw cut through and the tree rolled free of the stump.

She dropped the chainsaw in the mud. She looked up to see the half-man/half-beast knock the deputy to the ground with a powerful sweep of its muscular arm.

The beast glared at her with its goatish face. It gave an angry shriek and danced toward her on hellish hooves.

CHAPTER
THIRTY-FIVE

SHARYN FOLLOWED SUSAN KNOTT down the semi-dark corridor toward the nursing station. The thunderstorm had knocked the power out and the emergency generator had kicked on to power a meager allotment of lights. A staff member was passing out supper trays from the food cart but took no notice of the two women striding with dark purpose toward their freedom. Susan was still in her bloody hospital gown, held together by three ties on the back and flapping open to reveal that she wore no panties. Sharyn admired her shapely ass and wondered if the woman worked out to maintain her pleasing physique. This was just one of many thoughts racing through her head with dizzying speed.

A middle-aged male patient standing in his doorway said, "Hey, nice bum, baby."

Sharyn shot him a warning look. She half expected Susan to round on the cretin to scratch his eyes out or rip his tongue from his offensive mouth, but Susan didn't slow down.

"Yours ain't bad either, honey," the cretin said in a consoling tone to Sharyn.

Sharyn gave him the finger and kept walking. She felt strong. There *was* power in sisterhood, especially when the sisters were in service to a greater power. A daemon. An undying demigod. How amazing that the myths of Pan and Dionysus were based on an actual entity! *Imagine the lecture I could give now to those quacking mush-headed students. "We have a very special guest today, students. A living legend, come to fuck you stupid in an orgy of bloody sex .One way or another you're all going to get fucked."*

Susan turned into the nursing station, grabbed the charge nurse by the throat and said, "Give me your keys, bitch. Give me any shit and I'll snap your neck."

Sharyn stepped into the chart-lined cubbyhole, grabbed a ball-point pen off the desk and brandished it like a dagger. "Do it," she said, reinforcing Susan's demand. "We're not playing, I promise you."

The nurse nodded her head the best she could and then reached into a pocket and pulled out a set of keys. Susan snatched them away and shoved the nurse to the floor.

A blond female Mental Health Tech sitting at the desk grabbed the phone and her voice boomed over the intercom: "Doctor Strong! Doctor Strong to the Adult Unit!"

Sharyn knew there was no Dr. Strong on staff. "Doctor Strong" was the hospital's code for a psychiatric emergency, usually signaling that a patient was acting out and was in need of being forcibly restrained. All available staff were supposed to rush to the designated location and help subdue the out-of-control patient or patients.

Susan grabbed the phone out of the blonde's hand and began to pummel her with it, cracking it against the young woman's head and smashing her nose. Sharyn menaced the floored charge nurse with the ball-point and said, "Stay down, goddammit."

Then the world dropped out from under her. Sharyn had to lean against the desk to keep from falling. The sensation of falling overwhelmed her. She was falling out of phase, falling out of step, falling, soon to crash to the earth like a toppling tree. *What's happening to me?*

Susan continued to batter the blonde with the bloodied phone. Sharyn wanted to tell her to stop before she killed the girl but her tongue was glued to the roof of her mouth, stuck there by bitter bile as viscous as the fluids of extreme sexual excitation. And still she felt the falling. Falling into a dark void, their escape plans falling to ruin. Falling too was her fated calling, her response to the daemon's irresistible summons. Now there would be only a calling to accounts. Now there would be hell to pay. The *helling* wasn't supposed to be this way, was it? Her mind raced to catch up to events gone wrong, far-away events whose effects were undiminished by distance.

And now Sharyn did fall. She sank to the floor and dropped her ball-point weapon. Susan stood over her, shouted at her: "Get up!"

Sharyn gave her a blank stare. Didn't Susan feel it? Didn't she know everything was going to hell, whirling down into the underworld, to Hades itself? It was then that Sharyn recognized the falling sensation for what it was.

When a god falls, it makes deep ripples in the world.

Sharyn felt those ripples acutely with her mania-sharpened senses, but Susan seemed oblivious to them, probably because she was in a blood-frenzy—because she was normally a *normal*, not a nutjob.

"Get up, they're coming!" Susan said as she kicked Sharyn's thigh with the ball of her bare foot.

Sharyn stammered: "Yu-you killed your hu-husband . . ." As she said this, she knew she couldn't absolve herself for her part in Dr. Knott's death, but she hadn't killed the man, she'd only imbibed his blood, tasted his sacrificial flesh.

Then Susan Knott did an astounding thing. She pointed a finger at Sharyn and said, "You're crazy. I didn't kill him. You did!"

It flashed through Sharyn's mind that perhaps Susan *did* feel the falling and that now she perhaps realized that no god was going to save her from the consequences of her murderous deed. And she was setting Sharyn up for a fall of her own.

Sharyn's outrage drove her to positive action. Her realization that she wasn't the one falling had recalled and restored her equilibrium.

She got to her feet and said, "You're not going anywhere, you crazy cunt."

* * *

Thorn's relief that he hadn't been killed by the girl with the ax was short-lived. His wounded shoulder knew no relief from the deep pain, but he could deal with that well enough, just as he now could accept the fact that he might have to shoot some of these crazed women if he wanted to survive. It was no longer an issue for moral debate. The thing that deeply troubled him now—confounded him, in fact—was the astounding thing that had come loping out of the woods and into Thorn's unsettled reality.

Pan. The goat-man. The mythical god of the woodlands was *there* before Thorn's eyes! Sharyn had been right about that too.

Thorn rolled onto his back and fumbled at the pistol in his belt. His hand was shaking so badly that he couldn't free the gun from its denim snag. Though the heavy rain blurred his vision, he kept his eyes on the goat-man as it advanced on Deputy Rourke. He saw Rourke shoot down another woman and then turn his pistol on the terrifying man-beast of antiquity. The bullets seemed to have little or no effect on the monster. The creature was wounded and bleeding—hit twice in its massive chest—but did not slow down.

It flung out an arm and knocked Rourke down.

"Per-fess-or!" cried Mrs. Leatherwood. "The stump!"

Thorn gazed dumbly at the tree stump.

"Grind it down!" the old lady yelled. "Hurry for God's sake!"

Thorn got to his feet and finally freed his .45 from his belt as the beast stalked closer to Mrs. Leatherwood. A skinny woman with long teats came at him with a baseball bat. He raised the gun and shot out her right kneecap and she went down screaming.

Thorn fired three shots into the beast's back, diverting its attention from the old woman. It turned and snarled at Thorn with its hideously wide mouth. He fired another shot into its muscle-rippled belly. The thing threw its head back and howled with such volume that Thorn feared his eardrums would burst.

And then it charged him.

Rourke was up now, firing at the goat-man. With two guns shooting slugs point-blank into the beast's belly and chest, finally the monster slowed and staggered a little.

A peregrine falcon swooped down out of the rain and would've sunk its talons into Thorn's face if he hadn't thrown up a forearm in time to block the attack. But now the bird was attached to his forearm and he tried to fling it off. On his third attempt, he did get free of the falcon but the pistol slipped from his grip and landed several feet away.

"Per-fess-or!" Mrs. Leatherwood shouted with a scolding inflection.

"Right," Thorn said, more to himself than to her. He ran to the rumbling stump grinder, took a moment to familiarize himself with the controls, and then he put the thing in gear and guided it right up to the stump of the felled tree. The grinder's spinning teeth began to chew up the stump, spitting out shreds of mulch.

The falcon attacked again, this time striking the back of Thorn's neck and shoulder and digging in its talons. He shrugged his shoulders and did his best to bear up under the painful assault. He couldn't have said when he'd begun to believe the old lady's assertion that the beast could be driven away by the vengeful spirits trapped in the ghost tree, but the fact was, he did believe it now. He believed it with all his heart. And it was going to take more than a fucking falcon to stop him from grinding the tree stump to smithereens.

When the goat-man saw what Thorn was about, the beast came at him in a desperate, jerky lurch.

* * *

Rourke had reloaded and was leveling his pistol at the rain-thing when the woman with the blown-out kneecap struck his wrist with a baseball bat and knocked the gun out of his hand. She swung again, this time without benefit of a windup, and he managed to thwart the blow by throwing up both arms. He took the bat away from her and used it to sweep her legs out from under her.

He looked up to see the unnatural thing closing on Thorn and knew he had no time to retrieve his pistol. He went after the beast with the baseball bat, hoping to buy Thorn and himself a little time. And after that? Who knew?

* * *

Liza pulled open the door and slid in behind the wheel of the police car. The engine was still running. Cops always left their squad cars running, didn't they? Made sense, sure, but it must cost the taxpayers a pretty penny, gas prices being what they were nowadays.

Concentrate, old girl. Think sharp. Was that Wilbur's voice in her head? More likely, it was the ghost of Liza's younger self offering frisky counsel.

She put the car in gear, gripped the steering wheel as firmly as she could with her gnarled fingers, and then put her foot on the gas pedal. The car eased forward over the grassy ground at five miles per hour.

Through the rain-smeared windshield she could see the deputy going at the tall beast with a bat. Professor Thorn—God bless him!—was grinding the stump even though a bird of prey appeared to be attached to his back, angrily flapping its wings.

Liza lined up the car so that there was a straight path to the goat-footed monster and then she put the gas pedal to the floor and the car shot forward, finding little traction on the wet ground, then fishtailing, the front-end swinging to the right and taking her in the wrong direction.

"Lord, Liza," she said, jerking her foot off the gas. "Be sharp!"

She turned the wheel until the beast was once again lined up in front of her, about nine yards away. She pressed down on the pedal with a gentler foot this time, and the car's aim stayed true.

She evenly increased the gas feed, gaining speed as she kept the vehicle going straight ahead, the goat-man growing bigger in the glass screen of the windshield.

Then she stomped the gas pedal and braced for impact.

* * *

Up close, the thing was repulsively grotesque. And it stank worse than a wet graveyard dog. It towered over Rourke and fixed him with molten eyes. It growled, then screamed like a panther as it reached for Rourke with big hairy hands.

Rourke swung the bat and thought he heard a knuckle crack, not that it mattered because the beast seized Rourke by the throat with one of its hands as it closed the other hand over his face, like a gigantic NBA player palming a basketball.

Blinded by the thing's stinking hand, Rourke swung the bat one-handedly, to no effect. The monster lifted him off the ground, held him up so that their faces were inches apart and Rourke could smell its carrion breath, and then the mad beast began to crush his skull between those massive hands.

* * *

Thorn glanced up from the diminishing stump and saw the creature pick up the deputy by the head. *Sweet Jesus, the thing's going to kill him and there's nothing I can do. Nothing but to keep on grinding this damned stump and hope for a fucking miracle before it kills me too.*

As he was about to avert his eyes from the killing of the cop, Thorn saw the police car barreling down on the beast. He couldn't see who was behind the wheel, not that he much cared, because he was suddenly preoccupied with working out a fast physics problem in his mind, calculating force, mass and trajectory. Yes! With any luck the goat-man monster would—

And then it happened just the way he foresaw it.

The beast looked up a fraction of a second before the police car rammed into him. The front bumper clipped him just below his oddly bent knees, sweeping his hooves off the ground, and the car carried him forward and dumped him right on top of what was left of the stump—and right into the heavy spinning teeth of the stump grinder. The deputy fell beside the stump, dead or unconscious.

Thorn kept the grinder going full guns. The teeth chewed into the goat-man's thick neck and shoulder, pinning him to the stump, grinding him *into* the vanishing wood.

The thing screamed and shook his head as if to deny what was happening to him. He thrashed his legs and kicked at the muddy ground with his hooves as the grinder ate into his torso and churned out a bloody mulch of flesh, wood and bone.

Thorn watched in sick horror as the goat-man's head finally rolled free of the pulped upper body and fell to the ground, coming to rest against the unmoving deputy. The falcon relinquished its grip on Thorn's back and fell dead at his feet.

An enormous death-throes erection sprouted from the monster's furred loins. Thorn winced as the grinder's spinning blade chewed up the hideous cock and spat out bloody threads of its remains.

And then the stump grinder's motor died and an eerie silence hung over the land, blotting out the sound of falling rain.

CHAPTER THIRTY-SIX

JULIE ARCHER HALTED WHEN SHE SAW what looked like a bunch of flaccid Halloween masks arrayed on a gory stump. She moved cautiously forward, sniffing the air and drinking in the musky scent of the dark one who had summoned her. No, these weren't masks. They were the human faces these crushed skulls had worn.

She understood that these heads had been offered to *him* in some dark ceremony she could only imagine.

She stuck a fingertip into the goo oozing from one of the shattered heads and then tasted it. Saliva flooded her tongue. She smacked her lips hungrily and wished she'd been here to see the sacred ceremony.

A piercing scream echoed through the woods. In apparent response to the shrill sound, urine ran down Julie's bare legs. All at once weak-kneed, she sat down on the wide stump. The screaming went on a few moments longer and then suddenly stopped.

The kitchen knife slipped from her fingers. An overwhelming emptiness opened a fathomless gulf inside her, and she began to sob. Then she was bawling like a small child whose mother won't be coming ever again. Tears streamed down her dirty cheeks. She shivered, naked and cold even though the canopy of trees kept much of the rain off her.

Something whispered in the trees.

"Michael? Is that you? Oh, Michael, please help me. I'm sorry, so sorry . . ."

But no, it wasn't her Heavenly guardian. He was done with her. It must have only been the wind.

Then she thought of Angela and of what she'd done to her. *Was that me? Did I really do that?*

The whispering came again, louder and insistent. More than one whisperer. A chorus of hissing voices. *Angry* voices.

She picked up the knife, stood up and fearfully looked around. She couldn't see them but she knew they were there. Knew they wished her ill.

She jumped onto the pedestal-like stump and danced madly about, slashing the air with her blade.

"Come on then!" she shouted with hollow bravado. "You want a piece of me? Come and get it! Don't you know who I am? I'm Julie Archer. I'm the queen of fucking horror!"

* * *

His head throbbing with a deep ache, Rourke leaned against the cruiser and surveyed the bloody battlefield. Of the fallen women, only two remained alive, dazed and in need of immediate medical attention. What was left of the monster wasn't easy to look at, never mind that it had nearly killed him.

Professor Thorn waved a hand at the beast's lower legs and head and said, "We'll want to make sure those don't get away from us."

"I don't expect they'll get up and run off," Rourke said.

"No, I mean they're too valuable to turn over to your forensic people and have them end up incinerated. This is an important scientific discovery and it must be treated accordingly."

"Aren't you gonna see to them women?" Mrs. Leatherwood asked the two men.

"Yes ma'am," said Rourke. "I've already called for an ambulance. I've got a First Aid kit in the car but I don't know if they'll let me get close enough to do anything for them."

"I don't think she can hear you," Thorn reminded Rourke.

"Well I reckon she can read. I'm going to write her an official letter of commendation. You'll get one too. If you two hadn't done what you did, I'd be dead. Now get your shirt off and let's have a look at your wounds. Those two crazies can wait."

Unbuttoning his shirt, Thorn said, "I think a couple of their cohorts ran off when I started grinding up that hairy son of a bitch."

"I doubt they'll be doing any more hell-raising."

While Rourke was getting the First Aid kit from the cruiser, the radio crackled with static and the dispatcher called for all available units to respond to a report of multiple homicides at the Trucking-A.

"Jesus," he said. "Now what?" Was there another band of wild women on a murderous rampage? No, he didn't think so. He didn't *want* to think so. More likely, these same women had hit the Trucking-A before coming here. The truck-stop wasn't that far from here. And the women had been wearing blood when they first came running out of the woods.

Rourke felt certain that it all ended with the killing of the goat-man. The monster's evil influence was no more. All that remained was the messy cleanup. He would probably have nightmares for the rest of his life, but the flesh-and-blood horrors were over and done.

But there *was* one thing that worried him now. In the cave he'd had that mind-warping vision of the strange world from which the beast had come.

Were there other monsters there, waiting for the way to open again so that they might come shrieking into this world?

* * *

Liza Leatherwood wiped her bifocals with the hem of her dress, put them on and looked down at the beast's severed head.

"Humph. All my life I was afraid of you. 'Fraid you'd come back. Well, you did. And now look at you. Humph. Once upon a time you had your way, but you weren't no match for *this* crop of mountain folk."

She hawked up a meager wad of phlegm and spat it on the goat-man's lifeless face. Then she turned to Thorn and said, "Professor? After you get yourself patched up, I'd be obliged if you was to take me home. I'm a mite behind on my beauty rest."

Thorn smiled and gave her a courtly bow.

"Humph," she said, grinning inwardly.

DIME DETECTIVE

April 2012

When barroom bouncer Joe Dall's ex-wife is murdered, he finds himself pressed into service as a novice private eye. Something very dark and deadly lurks in the lush shadows of the sleepy Florida town and if he can't unmask the killer soon, others close to Joe will die. Working on a powerful client's dime, Joe Dall's first case could be his last.

BAD JUJU: A NOVEL OF RAW TERROR

From Acid Grave Press

Dark forces are afoot in Vinewood, Georgia, a deceptively sleepy town where the dead don't stay dead and a sinkhole is as sinister as it is deadly. Violent events both natural and supernatural build to a chaotic crescendo of horrors that will threaten the entire town and everyone in it.

An odd handful of townsfolk put their lives on the line to save the town—but the darkness may swallow them up before they have a chance.

"Hot and thick, the atmosphere reeks of earth, blood, and decay. The astringent air carries with it a sense of malevolence and resentment. No matter where you look, no matter how shallow you breathe, this town will touch you."
—Kelly Tomblin, *Horror-Web*

DEADCORE
4 HARDCORE ZOMBIE NOVELLAS

By Randy Chandler, Ben Cheetham, Edward M. Erdelac, and David James Keaton.

"Randy Chandler's *Dead Juju* is a wild, graphic ride—a fast-paced array of elements including religion, politics, race relations, news media, socio-economic classism, contumacy—all handled with skillful precision as Chandler gives us deft glimpses of humanity in all its chaotic, whacked out splendor."—Walt Hicks, *Page Horrific*

"DEADCORE achieves all extremes. Violent, perverse, depraved and, as such, quite recommended." —*Fangoria*

THE DEATH PANEL
MURDER, MAYHEM, AND MADNESS

13 Hard boiled, violent tales of crime and horror from Randy Chandler, Tom Piccirilli, Scott Nicholson, Simon Wood, John Everson, and more.

"...be prepared to be blown away by some of the best genre short story fiction written in the last few years." —*Horror World*

"With sharp writing and a crisp design to match, the anthology makes a strong case for 2009's best. It's only Comet Press' third release, but already, the small-press label has distinguished itself as a reliable name brand. Pick it up, if you've got the balls." —Rod Lott, *Bookgasm*

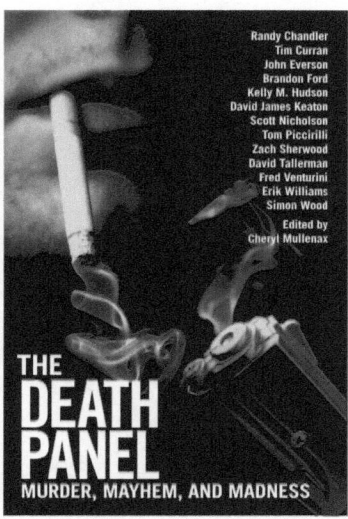

Comet Press is an independent publisher
of horror and dark crime.

Visit us on the web at:
www.cometpress.us

and follow us on twitter and facebook:

twitter.com/cometpress
facebook.com/cometpress